Butterfly Collector

Adam Dickson

Visit us online at www.authorsonline.co.uk

A Bright Pen Book

Copyright © Adam Dickson 2012

Cover design by Alex Dickson ©

All rights reserved. No part of this publication may be reproduced, stored in a retrieval system, or transmitted in any form or by any means, electronic, mechanical, photocopy, recording or otherwise, without prior written permission of the copyright owner. Nor can it be circulated in any form of binding or cover other than that in which it is published and without similar condition including this condition being imposed on a subsequent purchaser.

British Library Cataloguing in Publication Data.
A catalogue record for this book is available from the British Library.

ISBN 978-0-7552-1533-1

Authors OnLine Ltd
19 The Cinques
Gamlingay, Sandy
Bedfordshire SG19 3NU
England

This book is also available in e-book format, details of which are available at www.authorsonline.co.uk

Books are never written by one person alone. Therefore, I would like to thank the following for their valuable contributions:

Robin & Jean Dynes for their editing, critique advice and continuing support & encouragement.

Lynda Appleby, Julie Herring (Bournemouth University), Deano Pickering (Arts University College Bournemouth) and Suzanna Gonsalves for their help in researching Natalie's artistic background.

Steve Scott-Bowen and Neil Hayward for technical golfing advice.

Lisa Jones for background information on the role of a Medical Rep and Roger Colmer for management advice.

Annabel Sampson, Lisa Wright & Jamie Dickson for critique and belief in the book.

Alex Dickson for the sublime cover art.

And last, but not least, Liz Gordon for proofreading, editing, an unfailing eye for detail and for being with me on this incredible journey.

www.adamdickson.co.uk

One

The Ski instructor's girlfriend grabbed the last sandwich. She danced her way back to the noisiest corner, hips swaying, arms above her head. The Polish girl had found someone else. Her new friend hovered over her, nodding his head as though he were really listening, his lazy smile assured of an outcome. Like vultures, some people. You turned your back for five minutes and they went in for the kill. The Polish girl was too nice to see what was happening. One more victim of the night. She'd end up staked out in some low-life studio flat, while the predator lined up his favourite dance tracks and chopped out lines of powder on the mirror.

He watched casually from the doorway. Envious, disillusioned. Nothing left to do but drink yourself senseless and wish you were somewhere else. That's what happened when you lost the party spirit. You saw things as they really were. People looked ugly. The laughter came from another planet. The song playing took you back to a place you didn't want to be.

'Having fun?' Erica said, at his side.

'I was until someone jumped in my grave.'

She followed his gaze, to the predator leaning over his target. 'You must be losing your touch, Peter.'

'We were just talking, that's all.'

She stepped back in amazement. 'Is that what you call it?'

'What am I supposed to do – stand in the corner on my own all night?'

She gave him a mock frown. 'Oh, you poor thing. I knew I shouldn't have left you on your own so long. When's Claudia back?'

'Tomorrow.'

'I said I'd keep an eye on you. Make sure you were a good boy. Have you missed her?'

'No,' he said, honestly, and Erica laughed. But the truth nagged at his conscience, a mild discomfort when he least expected it. There was always someone to remind him about Claudia, his dubious behaviour, events in the past that could never be forgiven. The past was like a finger pointing, a mugger lurking in the shadows, waiting to jump out when you least expected it.

A balloon burst somewhere and a raucous cheer went up.

'Where's Marco?' he said.

'Gone to get more booze, you know what he's like.'

'I'm surprised you invited him after the last time.'

'Oh, he's a sweetheart, really. As long as I don't find him hanging off the balcony at three o'clock in the morning, we'll get along fine.'

Marco's stunts were legendary. Like the time he pushed Tony Banks' daughter in the swimming pool on her 21st. She hadn't found it all that amusing and had him forcibly ejected. Marco did what he did best and talked his way back in. The ex-public schoolboy, with a love of chaos and a blatant disregard for consequences.

He felt a wave of affection for Erica and gave her a hug. The two of them once an item, their friendship surviving the passage of time.

'Happy Birthday,' he said.

'Thank you, Peter.'

'You look great. For someone pushing forty.'

'Er – thirty-five thank you very much! And you're treading a very thin line. One more comment like that and I'll take you off my Christmas list.'

The Isley Brothers came on again, soulful harmonies from a bygone era. The man with thinning blonde hair grabbed the Ski instructor's girlfriend and they danced an unsteady tango in the middle of the room. Her breasts ebbed and flowed in a dance of their own, barely held by the rim of her top. Most of the guests had drifted off and missed the private floorshow. The hard-core drinkers were out on the balcony, entertaining each other around a wrought-iron table. A bottle of Glenfiddich stood in the centre, an object of worship.

'Well, at least everyone else is having fun,' Erica said.

'Is that what you call it?'

She shook her head in despair. 'Don't be so anti-social. If you want something to do, run along and refill the ice bucket for me.'

'And what do I get in return?'

'A good word from me when Claudia gets back.' She prodded him with a red lacquered finger nail. 'If you're lucky.'

He wandered along the hall with the ice bucket, the conversation and music fading behind like a memory. An Oriental figurine in the glass cabinet stared back, thousands of years of inscrutable wisdom in its carved wooden features. Further along, the portrait of a pretty girl in black gown and mortarboard, smiling down at him. One of Erica's many cousins or nieces, pampered and adored like the children she'd never had. He thought of Leanne with a misplaced sense of pride. One day her portrait might adorn his hallway, for visitors to gaze up at in silent admiration. He could tell them all how lucky she'd been, to inherit so much talent from the universal gene pool.

A shriek of laughter distracted him. The Ski instructor must have passed out in Erica's bedroom, freeing his girlfriend to land in someone else's lap. Or the Polish girl had ditched the predator and found a more suitable playmate. The rest of the evening was predictable. Marco would come back with more supplies, and they would all play last-man-standing. The options were limited. Try to win back the Polish girl, or refill the ice bucket and call a taxi home.

He went into the kitchen.

The woman in funeral black stood alone by the window. Some artist friend of Marco's who'd spent the evening avoiding everyone. She glanced blankly up at him, and went back to her silent vigil. He tried to recall her name but gave up. Her name meant nothing anyway. The look said it all. An instant barrier between them. Her way of avoiding conversation and deflecting unwanted attention.

He studied the contents of the fridge. Lean cuts of beef and strawberry yoghurt pots stared back. He found the last surviving beer, buried among the items on the top rack and closed the door. The cutlery drawer opened on smooth runners, his noisy search for the bottle-opener giving him a perverse pleasure.

'Is this what you're looking for?'

She held up a sophisticated-looking torture device.

'Thanks,' he said, taking it from her. Their fingers touched briefly. 'I'd use my teeth normally, but…'

She watched his failed attempts to open the bottle without comment.

'Jesus!' he said. 'These things should come with an instruction manual.'

'It's the serrated edge.'

'It's the what?'

'The inner ring with the serrated edge.'

He managed to prise off the bottle cap and thanked her again. She said nothing, the view from the window more meaningful. Again, he was struck by the impression of black, from her long hair to her calf-length leather boots. But for the Isley Brothers and the canned laughter along the hall, she could have been a widow in mourning.

He tried to think of something clever to say. 'Are you waiting for someone?' he said, instead.

'I'm waiting for a taxi,' she said tersely.

'Friend of Erica's?'

'No, I'm not. I've only just met her.'

He took a sip of beer and studied her side profile. She looked pale under the light, her flawless complexion contrasting with her long black hair.

'Enjoying the party?' he said.

'Not really.'

'At least you're honest.'

'It's not my scene.'

'That makes two of us. The cheesecake was pretty good though.'

She shifted from one foot to the other, no indication that she cared either way. Music drifted along the hall, a burst of laughter from people he didn't know or even like that much. In spite of her antagonism, her presence made him feel strangely secure. Her brooding silences matched his weary cynicism. She was tired of the world and its serial disappointments and this was her way of showing it. Alone out here in the kitchen they were somehow bound together, conspirators in the same rebellion.

'What do you do?' he said.

'Sorry?'

'Marco said you were an artist – is that right?'

'Look, I'm really not in the mood right now, OK?'

'Sure,' he said equably.

She glanced at her watch and swore under her breath. They took up their separate roles again; her silent vigil and his hidden fascination. The ice bucket sat untouched on the worktop. He badly wanted a reaction from her but couldn't work out why – this woman, whose name he couldn't recall, standing motionless by the window, dignified in her comforting funeral black.

He took another swig from the bottle and planned his next move, overcome by a warm glow. Intricate harmonies soared in the background, taking him to a place of intense sadness. The music touched on emotions buried for so long.

'This song has a special meaning for me,' he said.

'That's nice for you.'

'I lost a good friend of mine a few years ago.'

'I'm sorry about that.'

Her abruptness didn't matter. The fact that she was a stranger made it easier in some ways. Someone to hear his sordid confession while the band played on.

'Music's a powerful thing. Takes you back a long way. Do you ever get that?'

'Not really,' she said, distracted.

She took out her phone and stared at it.

He laughed privately.

'What's so funny?' she said, looking up.

'I was just thinking how technology killed the art of conversation.'

'Oh, and how's that?'

'Everyone tapping into mobile phones so they don't have to talk to each other. It's a sign of the times.'

She stared at him evenly. 'Did you come in here especially to annoy me?'

'No, I came in to fill the ice bucket.'

'Please don't let me stop you then.'

He settled back against the sideboard and assumed a nonchalant pose. The beer bottle felt clammy beneath his fingers, a useful prop in the absence of conversation. The challenge lay in provoking a reaction without going too far, using her sullen mood to gain an advantage.

'So what's the connection then?' he said.

'The what?'

'You said you didn't know Erica. I just wondered who – '

'Marco invited me,' she said, quickly. 'as a friend. We're not linked or anything.'

'That's a relief – for you I mean. How long have you known him?'

'Long enough.'

He smiled with empathy 'He can have that effect on people, can't he. I remember once, we were at this party in – '

'I'm really not all that interested.'

He shrugged, enjoying the flash of eye contact. 'Just being sociable. Stuck out here all on your own, I thought you might like the company.'

'Look – I didn't come here to socialise or swap business cards, OK? I'm just waiting for a taxi so I can go home and go to bed.'

'Are you coming down with something?'

'I will be if I stay here much longer.'

He put his hands up in a gesture of surrender, conceding the point to her. She withdrew and stared through the window, an overhead spotlight on her solitary figure. The song played a more upbeat theme. Sweet days of summer and jasmine in bloom. The magical bliss of lovers surrender. Love, the most beguiling thing of all. You gave in to the moment and it all went wrong from that point on. People got hurt. Lives were ruined. You tried to forget but the people you'd hurt wouldn't let you.

She made a phone call, an elbow propped on the arm that circled her waist. While she waited, she focused ahead, ignoring him. The call connected and her body-language changed. She stood upright, confident and precise, no sign of her previous tension. He listened to her conversation with an odd sense of privilege, a moment of intimacy forced upon them.

She put her phone away and took a deep breath, exhaling softly through pursed lips.

'Problems with the babysitter?' he said.

She looked up, remembering he was there. 'Sorry?'

'I couldn't help hearing – you've got a daughter as well?'

'Yes, I have.'

'Something else we've got in common. How old is she?'

'Five.'

'Good age. Make the most of it though. They get worse as they get older.'

'You're giving me advice on childcare now are you?'

A burst of manic laughter came from the front room, followed by a raucous cheer. Someone changed the music. The soulful harmonies of the Isley Brothers became a frantic drum and bass beat instead. He faced the tiled mosaic on the opposite wall and drank to the two of them. Now they were partners, he and the woman in black. Alone with the tribal drums until her taxi arrived or some other fate intervened.

He glanced over Erica's prize kitchen, looking for flaws in the finish. 'I can't understand why they left that vent up there.'

She followed the direction of his gaze and frowned. 'What's wrong with it?'

'It's an antique.'

'Is that a crime?'

'It is in a twenty grand kitchen.'

She sniffed disdainfully. 'I suppose if you look hard enough you can find fault with anything, can't you?'

'That's the price you pay for perfectionism.'

'You seem to be the expert.'

He held her gaze. 'Well, you know what they say, don't you? You can put a diamond choker on a dog but at the end of the day, it's still a dog.'

She looked away, refusing to play the game. Her resistance added to her appeal, her sense of self-containment, of being withdrawn from her surroundings but secure within it.

Erica appeared in the doorway.

'There you are! I thought I sent you out to fill the ice bucket about three hours ago?'

'I got sidetracked.'

'Men! It's a good job I'm used to doing everything myself around here.' Erica stopped and looked at them both. 'I take it you two have met before?'

'Only in a previous life,' he said.

Erica laughed heartily. 'She knows what you're like already then. I'll get the ice myself shall I?'

The insane drum and bass beat thumped along the hall. The hard core, left behind to keep up the party spirit. Erica filled the ice bucket, disturbing the uneasy truce.

The woman in black glanced over at him and a strange understanding passed between them. She went back to her vigil at the window. Seconds later, she snapped upright. 'At last! Taxi's here.' In one movement she was up and gone, deserting her post by the window and passing him without a glance. She mumbled a quick thank-you to Erica and went out along the hall.

Her departure left a void in the room, a sense of loss that he couldn't explain.

Erica turned to him with a coy smile. 'So what did you think?'

'About what?'

'Natalie.'

Now he had a name for her. He pondered the question and shrugged. 'Ignorant bitch with no sense of humour.'

'Charming, *you* are.'

'So was she. Some people are miserable for the sake of it. You try to make conversation but it's like raising the dead.'

Erica made a face and touched his cheek. 'Oh, honey. Didn't she respond to your cute little seduction lines?'

He pulled back in embarrassment, laughing along with her. 'Listen – I've got better things to do than waste time on women like that. Who is she anyway?'

'Friend of Marco's, apparently. She's just moved down from London. Very quiet, isn't she? Hardly said a word all night.'

'She probably racked up loads of debt and screwed some poor fucker out of everything he owned. That's why she's down here. You can see the type a mile off. Trouble written all over her.'

Erica stared at him in wonder. 'My God, Peter. She really did make an impression on you, didn't she?'

'I don't think so.'

'Never mind. She's not your type anyway. Far too intelligent for a start.' Erica laughed at his reaction and pinched his cheek. 'Only kidding, honey. Now come and help me deal with those drunken reprobates in there. I'm dreading the state of the carpet tomorrow morning, I really am.'

The party followed the standard formula. Marco returned with a case load of booze and took centre stage. The degenerate Master of Ceremonies, who had to have the last word. The Ski instructor's girlfriend had an argument with the blond man and threw a drink in his face. The Polish girl moved on to the next level of her education. Erica's crowd sat out on the balcony, helping her celebrate thirty-five years on the planet with the honorary Glenfiddich.

He stood alone by the kitchen window and called a taxi.

The woman in black would be home by now, or wherever else she was heading. Perhaps she had a boyfriend waiting. Some rich academic with a degree in astrophysics to provide the mental stimulation. Someone used to putting up with her sudden mood swings and acid put-downs.

He couldn't work out why he was drawn to her. Maybe she reminded him of someone else. She was alone and vulnerable among strangers. Her rudeness presented a challenge that he couldn't resist. Maybe there wasn't a reason. She just happened to be there.

He made a deal with himself to stay away from her. He had enough problems. Claudia would be back tomorrow and life would continue as normal. He would do his best to comply, bending to her plans without a will of his own. His life was set. Friday night out with the boys, a few hours on the golf course at weekends and devote the rest of the time to the serious business of making money.

But he couldn't stop thinking about her. All the way back in the taxi. Natalie – the sullen and unresponsive woman in black.

Two

Ring tones echoed along the hall. The phone lay buried somewhere in the chaos of the front room. He started the dishwasher and went through, noting the dust sheets and paint tins by the front entrance. Later, he would dump them all out in the drive for Jarvis's men to trip over the next day. The same organised clutter lay everywhere. Unpacked boxes and random electrical tools. Bags full of clothes and bin liners crammed with decorator's rubbish.

The phone turned up beneath a Homestyle magazine. Her name caused him an odd wave of anxiety as he hit the connect button. More unexpected problems to deal with.

'Why didn't you answer the first time I called?' she said.

'I couldn't find the phone. It's like a war zone in this place.'

'What are you up to?'

'Looking at bathroom suites.'

'Thrilling.'

'It is when you haven't had a bath for six weeks.'

She sighed. 'I said you could have stayed at mine while all this work was going on. What are you doing tonight?'

'Meeting the old man.'

'What for?'

'He wants me to look at the plans for Henley Park.'

'Can't it wait?'

'I'm trying to earn a living here, Claudia.'

She sighed heavily at the intrusion. 'I don't know. If it's not work it's golf. Anyway, how have you been, all on your lonesome?'

He ran through his current agenda. The unpacked boxes. The stack of invoices piling up in the bedroom. She ignored him and talked about her trip to Birmingham as though he shared her enthusiasm, that her job and the people she worked with mattered to them both. Soon they would be married and the finer details wouldn't matter. She would get what she wanted and he would have to put up with it. Her father, directing operations from the sidelines. His father, standing alongside, one eye on future business opportunities as they strolled up the aisle.

'How was the party?' she said.

'Predictable.'

'I spoke to Erica last night. Someone spilt red wine on the carpet, apparently. Can you believe that?'

'That's what you get for inviting assholes around your house.'

'You were there too!'

He ignored her attempt at humour and sank into his favourite armchair. One more item on her list of things to get rid of. Soft leather gave way beneath him, giving him an alternative view of the work in progress to add to his troubles.

She rambled on about the party, making bitchy comments about the guest list, hoping to draw him in. 'I hear Marco fell asleep in the bath, then woke Erica up at four in the morning looking for his shoes.'

'I told you it was predictable.'

'Anyone interesting there?'

'Some Polish girl who worked in a rest home or something. I think she got kidnapped by the neighbourhood coke-dealer.'

'Sounds like I didn't miss much.'

'You didn't.'

'Who's Natalie?'

The question caught him unawares.

'The girl you were talking to in Erica's kitchen?

'How should I know? I only went in to fill the icebox. She was there waiting for a taxi.'

'I'm just asking.'

'You've only been back five minutes and you're hassling me already.'

'OK. Forget it. It's not important.'

He said nothing, implicated in the silence.

'How about I bring a takeaway round later? I can help you unpack. Then we can, you know, get an early night or something.'

The subtle reference to the bedroom reawakened his interest. But he resented her tone of voice, her devious attempts to pacify him using the guilt angle. He played along out of habit, a kind of weary auto-pilot that kicked in just for her.

She droned on about the hotel she'd stayed at in Birmingham. The room was too hot and she'd slept with the fan on. The group of Japanese businessmen staying were too noisy when she came down the next morning. He tired of her tedious account and switched to a subject closer to home. 'Cooked breakfast?'

'Continental.'

'What did you have?'

'Croissants and honey with orange juice. Why?'

'Beats cornflakes, I suppose.'

She laughed, humouring him, saddened at the fact he'd been left behind. 'I'll take you with me next time if you like. Oh, and while I think of it, I spoke to the guy from McQueen's. The couple who pulled out of the original sale might be interested again. Don't you think that sounds hopeful?'

'Sure.'

'I thought you'd be more enthusiastic than that.'

'Claudia. I haven't got the time to –'

'I am *so* looking forward to it. Selling my place and moving in with you. Have you thought any more about Spain? I thought we could go out a couple of days earlier. Enjoy some quality time before your mum and dad join us. What do you think?'

He opened the Homestyle magazine and detached from her voice, the auto-pilot taking over. She rambled on as he turned the glossy pages, her voice like the whirring of the extractor fan, familiar but intrusive. The prospect of selling her house filled her with great anticipation. She could move in with him and they would live happily ever after, arguing over colour schemes and which set of friends to invite round for dinner.

'What time shall I come round?' she said.

'I'll call you when I've finished with the old man.'

'You don't sound too happy. Is everything alright?'

'It will be when the shower's fitted. And Jarvis starts clearing all the debris out of the front room.'

'As long as it's finished before I move in. Indian or Chinese?'

'Whatever.'

'If I get an Indian, you won't moan about the yoghurt sauce again, will you?'

He reminded her how much the last takeaway had cost him. How the driver had turned up an hour late and they still couldn't get the order right. Minor details that upset him far more than they did her. She could never understand the pressure he was under. The old man, hassling him about the plans for Henley Park. The burst water main at Priory Road that set the job back a week. On top of all that, he had her plans to contend with, demanding he finish his place so she could move in and change everything.

He rang off and stared at all the unpacked boxes. The disorder that came from living out of a suitcase and eating frozen meals in front of the television. His own personal cinema in the front room. 42 inches of plasma widescreen, fresh out of the packing and already gathering dust. One more thing for them to bicker about. The relentless diet of Coronation Street and EastEnders forcing him to make a stand or find an alternative distraction. There was always the bedroom. The best distraction of all. Then, when she lay back, drained after a long session under the duvet, she could look up and moan about the cobwebs around the light fitting.

He loved her in his own way. After two years you got used to someone being around, even if you didn't always relate to them. You knew all their bad habits and tried to make allowances for the odd difference of opinion. But sometimes it was hard work. Claudia had a way of changing his plans before he'd even made them. Along with all her other qualifications, she had an honours degree in manipulation. Something else she got from her father. He could live with that. But the past got in the way of everything. His past especially.

She tried to understand. All the things he'd buried and refused to talk about. She tried to understand but his silence baffled her. He'd told her once, shortly after they'd met and that was it, the subject finished with. He told her what he thought she needed to know. The rest she would pick up from other sources. Marco. Erica. Friends who'd stood by him when everyone else was walking away. He couldn't expect people not to talk. The whole town knew what had happened, a collective intake of breath to ensure that whatever else happened, he would never forget.

The phone rang again.

Provocation from a different source. Leanne's college trip to Barcelona. It wasn't fair that Roy should have to pay. Roy had his own problems, what with his hernia and his bad back. He paced the room, dogged by conspiracy, expected to put everyone else's needs before his own. The hollow rap of his footsteps on the bare boards added a touch of melodrama. The universal jester, listening-in, hoping he'd get the joke.

Sylvia's voice had an insistence that was hard to ignore. He couldn't switch off like he could with Claudia. Sylvia had an in-built radar for deception, and could tell the moment he stopped listening. But he did what he could. As ex-wife and mother of his only daughter she deserved at least a token consideration.

'I'll talk to her,' he said indignantly, following an old, familiar script. Sylvia came back at him right away, reminding him of several inescapable facts he'd clearly forgotten. Leanne was his daughter. He needed to take a more active role in her future development. He responded without thinking. The torrent of a flood. All the uprooted and damaged stock from the past, churned up in the undertow. As soon as he'd finished, he was sorry. 'Look Sylvia, you've caught me at a bad time, OK?'

'So when's a good time?'

'I'm surrounded by boxes and bin liners full of clothes.'

'I'll send her round to annoy you then, shall I? Really give you something to moan about.'

He took a deep breath and stared at the ceiling. The anger and frustration receded, put on hold for the time being. Sylvia said nothing, a malign force, waiting in the background. Her silence spoke of all the things he'd never been. The missed appointments. The numerous breaches of trust. The times he'd had turned up late or not bothered turning up at all.

'How's Claudia?'

He picked up on the change in tone, the sudden lighter note to lower his defences.

'Claudia's fine.'

'I hear she's selling her house.'

'Who told you that?'

'Never mind who told me. Is she planning on moving in with you?'

'Possibly.'

Sylvia gave a dry, humourless laugh. 'Well, I take my hat off to her anyway.'

'What for?'

'Putting up with you. Not the easiest job in the world, that's for sure.'

Sylvia left him feeling unsettled. No matter how many college trips he paid for, he could never quite lose the sense of accusation. The past that could never be undone and would always remain, a crime on record.

The view from the bay window distracted him. The grass needed cutting. His reluctance to get out there and do it depressed him almost as much as the phone call. With some women you had no choice. You had to respond whether you liked it or not. Mental tennis. You thought you'd pulled off the perfect backhand and the ball came straight back at you.

Leanne was an ongoing problem. One more puzzle he couldn't solve. In spite of the handouts he dished out on a regular basis, and the lifts he gave her when no-one else was around, she never said a single 'thank you' She only ever smiled when she wanted something. The rest of the time she treated him with a contempt reserved for inferior beings. Daddy's little girl – always expecting him to be there for her. Never quite able to forgive him for the years he'd been missing.

He settled back in the armchair and gazed at the wide bay. He saw her clearly, a perfect vision in his mind's eye. The woman in black, looking out of Erica's kitchen window. She had her arms folded and one shapely leg crossed in front of the other. He couldn't see her face but he knew what she was thinking. She was thinking about him and hoping they could be together. The fantasy amused him for a moment, at direct odds with reality.

Natalie.

He said her name out loud and the image vanished. He wished he knew more about her. Marco had mentioned her on a few occasions, but only in passing. Perhaps they had been an item at some point but it seemed unlikely. Marco's wide and varied circle included women he claimed never to have slept with. Most of the time he was too busy entertaining himself, with his clandestine antique deals and powerboat friends. Natalie herself had been quick to state that they were nothing more than friends.

She was an artist, he knew that much. She had a five year old daughter and she had just moved down from

London. He couldn't remember seeing a wedding ring and there had been no mention of any partner.

He tried to shut her out. She was trouble. The type of woman who would drain all your resources for no significant return. Then, when you were in too deep, she would leave you stranded to cope with the fallout. Other people would get hurt too. Just like they did before. With consequences so painful you couldn't bear to look at them. And all you could say in your defence was that you failed to see it coming. Like a car crash. You opened your eyes at the moment of impact and it was too late.

Three

Marco had his own way of looking at things. He barged in one evening, stepping over suitcases and power tools, to sink his bulk into the leather armchair. Other people's problems were of minor importance and would resolve themselves over time. Even one as baffling as Leanne.

'She's a teenager,' Marco said. 'They're a breed apart.'

'So what's the answer then?'

'The next time she wants a lift at two in the morning, tell her to jump in a taxi like every other fucker.'

He pondered the advice. You had to have kids to appreciate the dilemma. Marco had a nephew who'd been caught using heroin, but it wasn't the same thing. Your own children were special to you in ways you couldn't explain. You hurt when they hurt. You shared in their successes as if they were your own.

'I just wonder what I did to deserve it, that's all.'

Marco laughed. 'What – Leanne?'

'Women in general.'

Marco observed him carefully, drumming his fingers on the arm of the chair. 'You know what your trouble is. You take things too personally. Look at the way you reacted to Simon the other night.'

'Simon's a prick.'

'Oh come on. You jumped down his throat for no reason at all.'

'He should think before he opens his big mouth then, shouldn't he?'

People like Simon invited criticism. No-one cared how much he'd earned the previous year, or that his new Volkswagen Golf did 155 miles per hour in a snowstorm. Sometimes the barroom bragging got too much. All those frustrated amateurs, competing for a top spot that didn't exist.

Marco remained unconvinced. 'You need to chill out, darling. Not good for the heart, getting yourself all worked up like that. Claudia sold the house yet?'

'She's got someone interested.'

'Not long now then, eh? Then it's goodbye to the bachelor lifestyle forever. You'll need a weekend pass to come out once every six months and she'll still want you in by ten o'clock.'

He went through the motions, letting Marco believe he'd spent his adult life waiting to install a woman in the place. The thought of Claudia moving in depressed him further. His comfortable routine would be turned upside down. She would control everything, from the thermostat to the television channels.

Marco cast an eye over the general chaos. 'Er – wasn't it like this when I came round last week?'

'I've been busy.'

'What, playing golf with Tim?'

'Organising scaffold lifts and meeting Building Inspectors. Things you wouldn't understand.'

Marco ignored the slur and sank back, lounging in the armchair with his legs crossed. A strip of pale ankle showed above his black socks and patent leather shoes. Marco's way of ingratiating himself had a crude appeal. The ex-public schoolboy, who'd abused every opportunity he'd ever been given. Proud of his boast as the laziest man on the planet. No matter who he upset, Marco always seemed to land on his feet. He could afford to play the part, living in his cousin's house by the sea, even if it was awaiting demolition. Marco thrived on his ability to prosper in any situation. The jaded tenant on millionaire's row, upsetting the neighbours with the loud parties he held. Moaning about the sand blowing in from the beach when the winds picked up. Public school must have taught dissent as a part of the curriculum. But Marco had no real ambition. Perhaps that's what came of having everything when you were younger. You rebelled against the system and chose the alternative, ridiculing the values you were meant to uphold. Marco's lifelong dilemma – how to find something to relieve the boredom. His attitude was one of contemptuous resignation. You live, you die. Everything else is wallpaper.

'Looks like you *need* a woman's touch to me,' Marco said, sweeping the room again. 'At least with Claudia you'll get your washing done and your meals on the table. Speaking of which – are you going to buy some furniture for this place or what?'

He ignored the comment and went over to the bag in the corner, selecting the driver. Feet apart and facing the bay, he sighted along an imaginary fairway. His reflection in the window revealed his stance, the club pulled back behind his head in a slow-motion simulation.

Marco watched unimpressed. 'You start teeing-off in here and the neighbours are going to love you.'

He swung the club through and lofted an imaginary ball, holding the classic finish for a few seconds.

'Wonderful!' Marco said. 'Now all you need's a sand pit to practise bunker shots.'

'It's the only thing that keeps me sane.'

'My heart bleeds for you. I take it Claudia's back?'

'She got back yesterday.'

'Proper little jet-setter, isn't she. Where was it this time?'

'Birmingham.'

'Still dealing in pharmaceuticals?'

'Not the kind you're thinking of. Unless you can find a market for insulin meters on your travels.'

He flexed the club and mourned the lack of regular play. So much craftsmanship sitting around in the front room gathering dust. But you could forget about expensive equipment when it came to improvement. Seve Ballesteros taught himself every shot in the book with a three-iron.

Marco yawned and looked up at the ceiling. 'I do admire Claudia's work ethic you know. She makes me feel lazy sometimes.'

'Maybe that's because you are.'

'Matter of opinion, darling. I don't see much point in leaving a warm bed to make someone else a fortune, do you?'

'Most people have to. I think it's called a mortgage.'

'Well, I'm sure the two of you'll make a go of it. I like Claudia. She's got style. And if it doesn't work out, there's always the divorce court.'

'We're not married.'

'Yet,' Marco said with a sly grin.

He put the club back in the bag and went over to the window. The grass seemed to have grown several inches since he'd last looked. Claudia would take a firm stand regarding all household chores, her obsession with neatness driving him to new heights of despair. He wouldn't even be able to leave his shoes lying around, or his jacket draped over the back of a chair. Of course there were positives, but he couldn't think of any at that particular moment.

Marco swung his feet over the side of the armchair and put his hands behind his head. The same devious smirk creased his plump cheeks.

'I hear you made a big impression on a friend of mine the other night.'

'Who?'

'Try thinking laterally.'

He shrugged, guessing what was coming next.

'Oh come on! You can't have that short a memory. You spent long enough talking to the girl.'

'Remind me'

'Natalie!'

He feigned ignorance, as if the name had no particular ring.

Marco watched him carefully.

'She'll be so upset. Especially after she spent so long teaching you how to use a bottle opener.'

He smiled casually at the reminder. Marco honed in on him from the armchair.

'You must have made *some* impression. Erica said you could have cut the atmosphere with a knife.'

'Erica's a drama queen, she watches too much television.'

Marco laughed, relishing the unfolding of a far better entertainment. 'Never mind. Natalie doesn't know you like I do. I mean personally, I wouldn't have said you were arrogant, but there you go. Everyone's entitled to their own opinion.'

'She said I was arrogant?'

'Well – self-opinionated in a smug sort of way. Same thing really, I suppose.'

He tried to hide his outrage, the unexpected stab at his pride. 'I talked to her for five minutes.'

'She's very perceptive.'

Marco's attempts to lure him in succeeded. He gave up the pretence and tried the direct angle. 'So who is she then? Where do you know her from?'

'We go back a long way. Her father was a friend of my father. She sees me as the big brother she never had.'

'No wonder she's so fucked-up.'

Marco rolled his lower lip in mock outrage. 'I don't know where you get this jaundiced opinion of me from, I really don't.' Marco ran his fingers through his fringe and sighed. 'I really must stop crashing out in people's bathrooms, you know. I'm sure that's how I put my back out the last time.'

'I'd have turned the cold tap on if I'd have been there.'

Marco smiled, immune to his insults. 'The next time Erica has one of her little soirees, I'll tell her to leave you off the guest list, shall I?' Marco opened a bin liner next to the armchair and sifted through some curtains Claudia had donated. 'Can't say I like the colour scheme too much. How much have you spent on this place so far?'

'Too much, that's for sure. What's happening with the Ballroom?'

Marco dropped the curtains and sank back, staring off into space. The question made him pensive, a distinct change in his outward demeanour.

'The Ballroom's been sold ... I found out yesterday.'

'How long have you got?'

'A few weeks at the most.'

'Where will you go?'

Marco gave a vague shrug. 'Fuck knows. I haven't thought that much about it.'

He shared Marco's sadness at the prospect of losing the old house. Marco's reasons were more pragmatic: the sole remaining tenant, living rent free in his cousin's summer house, a mausoleum once owned by his late uncle, who'd been an advisor to Ted Heath. As soon as

Marco moved out, the wrecking ball would move in. All that faded grandeur, reduced to a pile of rubble overnight.

Marco gave a philosophical sigh and sat upright. 'Well I must say I'm disappointed in you as a host. I've been here over half an hour and you haven't offered me a drink.'

'There's no booze in the place.'

Marco rolled his eyes. 'Don't tell me you haven't got a kettle?'

'Course I've got a kettle.'

'Well put the fucker on then! Milk and two sugars, please.'

He admired the kitchen interior while the kettle boiled. The one room that he could say was finished. Claudia thought the oak units were too dark but he liked the way the sun picked out the polished grain of the wood, and the inset lights that cast the units in a warm evening glow.

Marco called out from the front room. 'So you don't remember her then?'

'Who?'

'Natalie.'

'Why would I remember her?'

'James's wedding.'

The name jarred him instantly. Dark memories, buried deep in his sub conscious. A grey stone church and an overcast spring day. Confetti trodden in to the wet tarmac. The photographer hustling them all together for the group shot. He failed to place Natalie.

Marco was standing at the bookcase reading the cover of a book. He put the coffees on the window sill and sat down, still lost in the past.

'Have you read this?' Marco said.

'What is it?'

Marco flipped the cover over and read the title in a solemn voice. 'The Tibetan Book of Living and Dying.'

'I read it ages ago. Borrow it if you like, you might learn something.'

Marco nodded sagely and put the book back. 'Looks heavy going to me. Sort of thing Natalie would read. She's into all that Far Eastern bollocks.'

He sipped his coffee and thought about Natalie. The subject would come up again, sooner or later. With Marco it was a case of waiting, his motives usually transparent, a way of amusing himself at someone else's expense. But James's wedding was different. There weren't too many fond memories for anyone to speak of. Only the knowledge of what had happened later on.

He forced himself to ask. 'What was Natalie doing there?'

Marco put down the brass candlestick he'd been examining and looked up. 'Where – Erica's party?'

'James's wedding.'

Marco gave a puzzled frown. 'She came with me.'

'So you and her were? …'

Marco laughed at the thought. 'She came as my guest. She'd just finished university and had nothing better to do.' Marco's amusement faded. 'She's a friend. I don't sleep with my friends as a rule.'

He ignored the comment, intrigued more and more by Natalie's role in his troubled past. 'Did she know James?'

'Not to my knowledge.'

'But she knows what happened to him?'

Marco shrugged, irritated by the questioning. 'I probably told her at some point. Like I said, she was bored. She came to the wedding because she had nothing better to do.'

He gazed through the window. The grey stone church and the people outside seemed so remote. Everyone had said what a wonderful couple the Bride and Groom were. He had the photographs to prove it, buried among the suitcases and the cardboard boxes in the bedroom. Hidden away so he didn't have to look at them and be reminded. But he couldn't recall Natalie.

Marco crossed the room, examining various items like a prospective buyer. He rooted through a box of CDs, making the odd critical remark out of habit. 'Talking of weddings, what's happening about yours?'

'It's on hold.'

'How long for?'

'Until I can talk my way out of it permanently.'

'Too late for that, darling. Claudia's got plans for you.'

His denial must have been a defence mechanism. In reality, the wedding was scheduled for the following July. He'd tried to claim work commitments as a mitigating factor, but no-one seemed to listen. Claudia had found a venue, courtesy of her father's Freemason connections, then decided the location was too remote and changed her mind. They settled on the Harbour Heights instead, a prime location, with a magnificent view overlooking the bay. Both families would be pleased. The old man would see it as a step in the right direction, business and pleasure forged with a secret handshake.

Marco finished his coffee and stood up, brushing the creases from his trousers.

'Next time I come round, you might have a table and chairs installed. It's like a fucking obstacle course round here.'

'That's right. It keeps out unwanted visitors like you.'

Marco stepped gingerly over an extension lead on his way to the door. 'I'll give you a call midweek. Maybe we can get a few frames of snooker in if you're not ripping up floorboards. Say hello to Claudia for me.'

Natalie still bothered him, long after Marco had gone. He went over the scene at the party, analysing the things he'd said and her reaction to them. The moment Erica had walked in on them, the parameters had changed. He'd picked up on this intuitively and filed it away. Her comments about him to Marco fuelled his interest. Women always had an agenda, but Natalie defied a category. She was all the things he would usually avoid. Highly strung. Prone to sudden mood swings that needed no provocation. Her presence at James's wedding increased his fascination. Then, meeting her at Erica's party, the two events unconnected but relevant in some strange way.

Life had a habit of turning full circle. You thought you'd moved on and a sharp reminder took you back. Maybe certain events you weren't supposed to forget. You only thought you'd dealt with the guilt and the shame, when all you'd done was bury it deeper beneath layers of self-justification. The soul searching made no difference. No matter how many times you went over the details, it came back to the same thing. You couldn't change a single aspect of the past.

James was gone. Nothing anyone said or did would bring him back.

Four

Trench collapse. The next unexpected disaster. Five hours of torrential rain in mid summer to set the job back days. Barry Jarvis was nowhere to be seen. The precision right-angles, cut the previous Friday afternoon, now a mass of sodden earth.

Sean stood at the foot of the trench, red-faced and sweating. Ordinary common or garden labourer. A lower life-form with a talent for avoiding responsibility and deflecting blame.

He stared at Sean's glowing face and wished he'd stayed in bed.

'When did this happen?'

'Dunno.'

'Fuck!'

Sean surveyed the disaster area without expression, one mud-encrusted boot resting on the shovel. The gravity of the collapse registered only in terms of hard work and even more digging.

'Where's Barry?' he said.

'Southampton.'

'What's he doing in Southampton?'

'Storm damage. I think.'

'When's he back?'

'Dunno.'

'Why didn't someone phone me?'

'Dunno.'

'You're a real hive of information aren't you, Sean?'

'What?'

'Forget it. Just keep digging.'

He made a call inside the house. Jarvis's answer machine cut-in – a rambling newsreader with a failed autocue. The mess in the front room incensed him further. A bag of plaster lay opened against the skirting, pink powder spilled out over the bare boards. Next to the plaster, a pair of fur-rimmed work boots, metal toe-caps poking through the torn leather. Empty crisp bags and old newspapers littered the floor. He picked up a copy of the *Sun* and admired the page three girl. Heidi, 23, from Reading, who claimed to enjoy windsurfing and sailing among her varied interests. He saw her arching her back against the wind, perfect in spray-soaked neoprene and, for one brief moment, the trenches were forgotten.

The upstairs rooms were more orderly. An upturned bucket sat in the back bedroom, a glossy magazine beside it. From the front bedroom window he looked down onto the skip. Someone had thrown in a child's bike, a rusted front wheel upright amongst the builders rubble. These people must have thought he paid to have the skip put there for their convenience. The bike – like Barry Jarvis and the trench collapse – set his nerves on edge. You spent your whole life trying to avoid such petty grievances but it never quite worked out. Frustrated anger always rose to the surface or found other outlets. The poor checkout girl, stuck with an endless queue. The erratic driver, who beat you to the last parking space. These things were sent to try you and that's what they did. Every day a struggle to keep the lid on.

He went back out into pale sunlight. Sean was working to loud, pumping music, heaving shovels of dirt up onto the bank beside him.

'Turn that thing down a minute!'

Sean stopped working and looked up. 'What?'

'The noise factory! Turn it down!' Sean adjusted the paint-streaked, alien spacecraft that topped a mound of earth. 'That's better. Any louder and we'll have the Noise Abatement Society round.'

'The what?'

'Forget it. Have you seen her next door?'

'Not today.'

He nodded vaguely, preoccupied with so many other concerns. The old woman next door wasn't the problem. Neither were Sean and the mounds of earth filling the trench. Marco's comments about Natalie kept coming back to him, an irritant he couldn't ignore.

'Can't you get the digger back?' Sean said.

He looked up, distracted. 'Too late for that. Just keep plugging away.'

'Til when?'

'Til you hit Australia.'

He looked out over the garden. The fencing had collapsed in mid-section, overgrown by the neighbouring bushes. The grass beyond the dirt banks obscured the path, a tangle of gorse bushes and weeds that would all need to be cleared. The fencing was a problem. How to rip it out without disturbing the old woman's precious rhododendrons. She hadn't said much lately but she was always there in the background, waiting for an excuse to find fault and cause trouble.

Sean's exertions were muffled in the trench, a kind of comic desperation behind every lunge. After several vocal efforts with the shovel, Sean paused to take off his baseball cap and wipe his brow. He took pity on the lad, and the monumental task ahead of him. 'How's your love-life, Sean?'

Sean looked up, squinting, glad of the chance to stop work.

'Still seeing the little blonde one, are you?'

'Which one's that?'

'The one with the spiky hair and the leather boots. She came on site looking for you a few weeks back.'

Sean blew his fringe away from his eyes and practised the vacant look he wore for Barry. Banks of sodden earth rose on either side. While he rested, a robin flew down and settled on the bank beside him. Pat Clements said that robins were reincarnated bricklayers, come back to inspect the job. The theory had a strange plausibility.

The sight of the trenches dulled his humour. Far too much work to be done to waste time talking. 'Get on with it then, Sean. I want this lot out by the end of the day.'

The robin flew off to find another disaster to inspect. Sean shook his head, chewing his lower lip with angst.

'What's the problem now?'

'Nothing.'

'Get on with it then.'

Sean put his cap back on and swore under his breath. He let the remark go unchallenged. Slave revolts were started with less provocation. A murmur of unrest that gathered momentum and exploded into violence over some trivial incident. Better to indulge a little harmless insubordination if it meant the job was finished quicker.

He called Raul from inside the house. The tones rang on. The curse of the answer-machine. The whole world incommunicado when you needed someone to talk to. Raul worked to an unorthodox time frame that didn't take anyone else's schedule into account. Long siestas and random cycling holidays, out on his state-of-the-art racing bike in all weathers. Raul seemed to have found the balance, running the bar with Helen and doing the odd removal job in his beloved Transit van. Solid and loyal as a friend. But when you needed him, he was always somewhere else.

He called the old man and explained the trench collapse. The old man was dismissive and brought up the subject of Henley Park instead. Twin blocks of luxury two bedroom flats and a penthouse in a choice location, courtesy of an insider in the planning department. Local residents had opposed the plans right from the start, but the deal went ahead regardless. Everything down to who you knew in the end, and the old man knew them all.

He said he needed more time to think.

The old man was insistent as always. 'You've seen the plans, Peter. What's stopping you?'

'I'm busy with my own stuff. I don't want to take too much on right now.'

The old man knew all about leverage and how to apply the right amount of pressure at the right time. Henley Park would be his swansong, the result of months of planning, sweeping aside the opposition like a warring General. 'Listen – I'll guarantee you at least twelve months work. Bonuses every lift. You want to carry on with the small stuff? Fine. Let Barry run that side of things for you. But this is a real opportunity, Peter. I want you in on it with me.'

He said he'd think about it over the next few days.

Sean's vocal efforts rose from the trench, the dirt bank growing ever higher. Sean stopped working and made a show of puffing and blowing, one hand on his hip, the other on the shovel. His reversed cap and open mouth gave him a dazed, moronic look, burdened with the injustice of it all.

He stood at the edge of the trench, looking down. 'Here, Sean?'

'What?

'How do I come across to you?'

Sean pursed his lips, unsure. 'What d'you mean?'

'Well, do I seem, arrogant?'

Sean gave the question some thought and sniffed self-consciously. 'Dunno what you mean, like.'

He felt a moments empathy and gave up. Sean had all the knocks and hardships to come. Nineteen years old and still living at home, his life experience reduced to the Champion's League and borrowing money from his mum. The chances of Sean helping him improve his social graces were slim.

'Forget about it. Just keep digging. I'll get Barry to send someone over to help you, OK?'

He made it to his car before the old woman next door had a chance to intercept him. The neighbours were an added burden. As if he didn't have enough to do, without having to worry about public relations. You had to treat them all with the same professional courtesy, even the difficult ones. He'd learned that much from his granddad, whose working rules had been set in stone.

Traffic slowed to a crawl approaching the lights. A motorcyclist overtook, passing close to the car on the outside. He envied the freedom, balanced on two wheels in all weathers. An escape from the daily grind of irksome people and work in progress.

He trawled through the radio stations and found a female voice – a crude mixture of dry humour and childish seduction in a broad northern twang. She stopped the chatter and introduced a song, strident piano chords and a haunting falsetto that took him back years. Memories of Clubland, gliding out on the dance floor with the beautiful people. Music that opened up horizons you never knew existed. Allison Limerick and Pacific State. Dance fusion in the K Bar and the Manor House.

Walking to the taxi rank in the cool night air with some dance track pulsing in your head and a chemical rush that bound you to total strangers.

The song left an imprint. The yearning for a past that no longer existed. A past found only in memories and … photographs.

Five

Ibiza 2000. A photo album filled with happy, smiling faces, buried in a suitcase in the spare bedroom. More emotive memories. Dancing with the blonde Thompson's rep in Amnesia. Arguing with the hotel manager over girls in the room. Marco being arrested and bundled into the back of a police car in the street of bars. Exodus from Clubland into the glazed early morning – the Island never sleeping – alive with every form of intoxication under the sun. And the best memory of all, being alone on the balcony with the girl from Prague, the two of them inseparable in the three days remaining. *'Welcome to the honeymoon suite,'* scrawled across the bathroom mirror in bright red lipstick. An ode to their passion, left by an unseen hand.

The photographs captured the mood well. The hotel bar in San Antonio. Northern Mike, with his arm around a girl he'd trapped the night before. The rest of them looking jaded and washed-out, survivors of a long endurance. The Thompson's rep had fallen in love with him. Not the ideal place to form a serious attachment, but she'd been persistent and he'd given in. In one shot they were seated, cheek to cheek at the bar, drinking exotic cocktails through a straw. Northern Mike had spoiled the tender illusion by calling out, 'Hey, love? Give the boy a break – he's done two of your lot already!'

He found the wedding pictures at the bottom of a sports bag. Time had given them a haunting quality. His face looked strained, an impostor in a borrowed suit. Even Tim looked uneasy. Photogenic Tim, glaring at the camera as if he'd just been told something he didn't want to hear. Everyone said they'd looked like brothers, smooching with the bridesmaids on a heaving dance floor.

He flipped through the pages, overcome with a painful nostalgia. Here they were in celebration. Tara, holding a glass of champagne in mock surprise. James seated next to her, eyeing his new bride with mild trepidation. Married five minutes and the two of them were arguing like old hands.

'Go easy on the Champagne, Tara.'

'Don't tell me what to do!'

'I'm not telling you what to do. I'm just saying, take it easy.'

'What, so I don't embarrass you in front of your precious friends?'

They'd always been like it – totally unsuited. Everyone had said the same thing. They should never have been left alone in the same room, never mind walk up the aisle together. But in the end, Tara was stronger. She was headstrong and knew what she wanted, refusing to stay in a marriage that threatened her health and her sanity. James fell apart because he couldn't live without her.

Tara's memory had lost its hold over him. For all its power, the experience might have belonged to someone else. Strong feelings diminish. You become an observer, able to look back over the details without the same turmoil. What happened had been a mistake. He should never have got so involved. Tim had warned him. Marco had predicted the outcome in chillingly accurate detail. But he hadn't listened to either of them. He'd got involved because it seemed like the right thing to do at the time.

He turned another page. The group shot outside the church. Bride and Groom in the centre, the Bride immaculate in virginal white. Two cherubic bridesmaids either side, each clutching a posy of flowers. The Groom, flashing his perfect white teeth, his Top hat worn at a jaunty angle. To an onlooker, their happiness seemed assured. They were young and in love. The bitter disputes over money were part of the process, a rite of passage for any young couple looking to settle down. But the magic wasn't to last. A few months later it was all over, ended by tragedy and a newspaper headline.

The Best Man stood beside the Groom, unsure of his role in the unfolding ceremony. The protocol had been the hardest part. Forced to greet strangers and shake hands before his nervous speech in the plush function room. He'd agreed to it for James's sake. They'd been friends as far back as he could remember and it was an honour to be asked. The honour meant nothing now.

He studied the group shot in more detail. A woman in a pink jacket stood at the end, set apart from the main group. The rim of her hat cast her face in shadow, a bob of dark hair tapered in at the neckline. She faced the camera with a fixed expression, unsmiling, her handbag clutched protectively at her front.

He slipped the photograph from its sleeve and stood it on the mantelpiece. Five years could alter a person's appearance to a degree, but the woman in pink looked too familiar to pass over. She might have grown her hair and lost the hat but the steady gaze was unmistakeable. She looked composed. Self-contained.

He left the photograph on the mantelpiece and stood back. A wave of excitement gripped him. Like staring at destiny waiting to happen. But for all its allure, the prospect was unthinkable. He couldn't risk his comfortable life for a sudden affair. He had too much to lose in terms of security and contentment. The messy drama of his old life had caused enough problems. The days of clubbing and partying were over. Even Tim had settled down to a degree. But the transition had been far from smooth. He'd deleted all the contentious numbers in his phone book to please Claudia. She responded by throwing herself into elaborate plans for the future. Their future. Marriage. Children. Claudia had it all worked out.

In many ways, Claudia was the ideal partner. She had the perfect temperament to deal with his complex nature. When they argued, she knew exactly when to back off. When he exploded over some minor irritation, she soothed him with carefully worded practical advice. Her bad habits rankled, but she had good qualities too. She was caring, loving and kind, all the things he tended to dismiss in the day to day running of their lives.

Sometimes it wasn't enough. The comfortable life with the lucrative business and the holidays in Spain left a void that couldn't be filled. Sometimes he yearned to escape the serial monotony of it all. One simple act of sabotage that would destroy everything. The kamikaze pilot, nose down in a screaming, vertical descent.

The photograph stayed on the mantelpiece as a reminder.

When he came into the room later, it had fallen onto the floor. He picked it up, gently brushed off the flecks of dust, and stood it back up again.

He had to admit. Natalie looked good in pink.

Six

He brought up the subject with Raul in the King Charles. Both its profound effect and the implications. Raul listened intently, and gave his standard shrug, elbows in, palms-up. These things were common enough. They happened all the time, to men who weren't prepared in advance to deal with them. 'Sounds like you make a big deal of it to me. Who is she anyway? Just some woman you meet one time.'

'That's right – but look at the grief it's causing me.'

Raul studied him with amusement, his gold tooth glinting in the light. 'And now you fall in love with a photograph.'

'Do I look that stupid?'

'Hey – I'm only trying to help. I can see this is serious for you.'

'I don't need help. I'm just telling you how it is.'

Raul opened a packet of salted peanuts and gave the matter some thought. 'Maybe you just need to get it out your system?'

'How?'

'You could meet up with her and discuss your differences.'

'I don't think so.'

'OK – forget about it.' Raul lay the packet on the table, picking off the overspill one by one. Coloured lights flashed on a fruit machine as a mini jackpot paid out. The issue with women could be dealt with like any other. You talked about it and gained a new perspective, an angle you hadn't seen before. But you had to be careful who you shared the details with.

'She said I was arrogant as well.'

Raul looked up, grinning. 'She say that to your face? Wow! I need to meet this woman.'

'She said it to Marco.'

'And you believe that fat fuck?'

He shrugged, hoping to change the subject. Raul waved a hand in dismissal.

'The way I see it – you got enough problems. Claudia's gonna move in soon and you need to be focused.'

'On what?'

'Everything. The whole nine yards.'

'Jesus. I meet some neurotic woman at Erica's and you're laying all this bullshit on me. Forget it. It's not that important.'

Raul crunched a peanut between his teeth, nodding slowly at some obscure train of thought. 'I'm just saying, look out. Don't let your dick rule your brain.'

He sipped his drink and said nothing. Raul formed a devious smile.

'Marry Claudia tomorrow and your troubles are over. Lots of little babies running round to keep you in line. Then you ain't got the time to think about this woman.'

'Thanks for the advice, Raul.'

'No problem. I like to help if I can. Here, have a peanut …'

Raul offered to get the drinks, leaving him to ponder the dilemma alone. The young couple at the corner table seemed contented enough. They even shared the same bag of crisps, a solemn ritual they might go through every evening. The lad looked around Sean's age, the girl as though she might still be at school. Perhaps the secret of their happiness could be applied to his own situation. Put in more effort to make it work with

Claudia. Cut back on the business meetings. Play less golf.

Raul came back with the drinks and continued the same theme. Women were a universal puzzle, entirely baffling to men, who made up for their ignorance by becoming experts and offering advice to their friends. Raul claimed to be an exception by virtue of his birthright, having received a far superior schooling in the arts of love. Spanish men, he claimed, had an innate understanding of a woman's needs. The English were boorish and unimaginative by comparison and generally didn't have a clue. But Raul was always willing to share his broad experience.

'Hey – you wanna hear about problems? I got problems. Helen says she wants to sell the bar.'

'Why?'

'Beats me, man. She gets tired, you know?'

'What about the re-fit? I thought it was all up and running?'

'She won't take a break. She's in the place twenty-four seven. We see each other maybe thirty minutes around the dinner table.'

He smiled to himself at the irony. They had the same problem in reverse. Raul and Helen needed more time together. Him and Claudia needed more time apart.

'Listen,' Raul said seriously. 'You gotta keep the woman happy, OK? Everyone knows this. But I can't be in that place listening to those bullshitters talking champagne and credit cards all day long.'

'You need to be more autonomous.'

'What the fuck is that?'

'Independent.'

Raul gave a solemn nod. 'Yeah. I need to be like that as well.'

The young couple in the corner were joined by friends. The crisp sharing ritual was forgotten in a flurry of back-slapping and overloud greeting. Their bonding took him back to his teenage years, sitting in the pub with half a lager, worrying what he looked like to the serious drinkers at the bar.

'So tell me about this woman?' Raul said.

'Which one?'

'The pain-in-the-ass woman in the photograph. Who d'you think?'

'There's nothing to tell.'

'So now you're keeping secrets from your friends, huh?'

'I told you what happened. We met at Erica's, had a brief conversation and she was gone.'

'Where did she go?'

'How the fuck do I know? I didn't follow her out in the street to ask her.'

Raul fingered his gold tooth and frowned intently. 'You know what I think?'

'No, but you're going to tell me anyway.'

'I think for you this is the mid-life crisis.'

'What, at thirty-four?'

'I'm serious. You need to get out more. When was the last time you had a holiday?'

'I don't need a holiday.'

'So take a break.'

'I take a break on the golf course every weekend.'

Raul sat back unimpressed. The young lovers at the corner table looked on in amusement, drawn by Raul's lyrical accent and coded hand gestures. He thought of Claudia and her plans for the future, the colossal burden of work to dampen any hope of a respite.

Raul drained his bottle and set it down hard on the table. 'Time to go my friend. I got a washing machine to move.'

He shook his head in disbelief. 'Don't look at me.'

'Hey! Did I mention your name?'

'You didn't need to. I can still remember the last time. Stuck up three flights of stairs with a leather sofa that weighed half a tonne. It ain't happening.'

Raul spread his arms, mortally offended. 'All the things I do for you, man, and you can't help me this one time?'

'OK, where's it going?'

'Uh?

'The washing machine. Where are you moving it to?'

'The utility room, for now. Then I gotta take it to the tip. I need some help, OK?'

He laughed at Raul's wounded expression, shaking his head at the sheer audacity. 'I spend my whole life avoiding people like you, you know that?'

Helen was out when they got back. Raul's deviousness paid off. They manhandled the washing machine from the kitchen to the stairs, water from the disconnected tubes leaving small puddles on the laminated flooring. Raul dismissed this as a minor detail. The real task was getting the dead weight downstairs without ending up in A&E.

The washing machine came to rest in the utility room. Bike frames and bike parts hung from fixings on one wall. Raul's multi-coloured cycling tops and high visibility jackets hung at intervals. The narrow, windowless room had a coarse, damp smell, like the changing rooms at the local park. He cursed Raul for the tight angle of the staircase and his total lack of humanity. Raul ignored his complaints, bemoaning the lack of space needed to carry out vital repairs to his odd collection.

Helen joined them later. She sat at the kitchen table and massaged her fine blonde scalp, immune to the politics of football around her. Raul's analysis of Wayne Rooney turned into an attack on the Premiership. For him, nothing could match the quality of La Liga, and the timeless magnificence of Barcelona.

Mia, Helen's tiny Shiatsu, wandered in, looked mournfully up at the table and wandered out again, the finer points of International football lost on her also.

Helen ignored the commentary from Raul and looked over. 'How's Claudia?'

'She's fine.'

'And the flat?'

'Pretty good.'

'Is it finished yet?

'The painters are in at the moment, but it's getting there.'

Wherever he went, people asked the same questions. How's Claudia? When's the Big Day? As if domestic bliss was a kind of religious ideal that everyone should strive for. Helen was only being polite. She'd met Claudia on a few occasions but they never looked destined to become great friends.

Raul hovered at the table, the over-attentive house husband, insisting Helen eat a sandwich or drink a glass of milk – if only for the calcium. Helen waved away his constant attention with a good natured smile. 'I've only just walked in the door, for goodness sake. Make a coffee.'

'You need to eat. I told you before.'

'I do eat!'

Raul looked over in a solemn appeal. 'She hides Maltesers in the fridge, man. Can you believe that? *In the fridge!*'

Helen rolled her eyes. 'See what I have to put up with, Peter? It's no wonder I rebel occasionally, isn't it?'

Raul filled the kettle and entertained them with a tirade against a couple he'd delivered a three-piece suite to earlier that day. After the unfortunate couple, came the subject of the bar. All the work that had gone into it. The hiring of staff who proved to be unreliable. A shadow crossed Helen's expression that she tried to hide.

'Are you really thinking of selling-up?' he said.

'Probably.'

'But you put so much into the place.'

'I'm just tired, Peter. I've been working twelve hour days for the past two years and all I seem to get is more bills to pay.'

Raul cupped her chin, holding her face up to the light.

'Look at this beautiful face, man. Too many late nights and shitty, shitty people. What happened to the gym and the running machine, huh?'

Helen pulled back, affronted. 'Er – excuse me! When do I ever get time for the gym?'

'You make time. Like I make time to walk that beast of yours every morning.'

'There's only one beast around here.''

'And that's the way you like it, Baby!' Raul kissed her cheek with a flourish and went back to the worktop to make the coffee, banging cupboard doors and humming to himself, content in his own space. Marco called him a freeloader, out for what he could get. Helen was a few years older and in a good position financially, with her own business and equity from her recent divorce. But Raul saw himself as her saviour, out to liberate her, body and spirit. They seemed to work well together. Raul helped run the bar, and kept her motivated with his quirky humour and relentless optimism. She took him on skiing holidays and indulged his love of sport, kitting him out in expensive cycling gear and buying racing wheels for his latest bike.

Raul served the coffee and left them, wandering off along the hall. Mia padded along behind, her tail stuck up in the air like a feather duster.

'Raul says Claudia's selling her place to move in with you.' Helen said.

'That's the general idea.'

'You don't sound too enthusiastic about it.' He smiled artfully. She leaned closer, sensing his reluctance. 'Talk to me, Peter.'

'Well, it's just …'

'Just what?'

'Claudia makes all the plans and I go along with them. She's even finished the guest list for when we get married. Shouldn't I have a say in all that?'

'Yes, I suppose you should, really.' Helen's playful smile faded and she stared at the table. After a long silence she looked up, pursing her lips with some hidden concern. 'Do you ever hear from Tara?'

'Not since she went to America.'

Helen nodded and studied her polished fingernails. 'Such a terrible thing to have to deal with. I suppose you never really get over it. How old was he again?'

A container of some sort crashed downstairs, its contents spilling audibly over the laminate flooring.

'Raul,' Helen said with a note of resignation. He laughed, glad of the interruption.

'Does he ever sit still?'

'Only when he's watching the football.' They listened out in the ensuing silence. A stream of profanities drifted back in coarse, broken English. Helen shook her head, with a rueful grin. 'The Tour de France starts soon. God help me.'

'Is he planning on going over again?'

'Of course. And guess who'll be there with him? Stuck halfway up a mountain, waiting for a bunch of lunatics to come cycling round the corner. I can't wait.'

He enjoyed the imagery, Raul's insistence that Helen go with him to appreciate the noble spectacle. The two of them up there with the goats and the Citroens and the thinning air.

Helen grew quiet again. 'I hope I didn't upset you, Peter.'

'About what – the Tour de France?'

She smiled sadly. 'You know what I mean. I don't see you all that often, but I know how hurt you were by the whole thing.'

He shrugged. 'Life goes on, doesn't it?'

'Yes, of course it does, but it doesn't make it any easier. I'm always here if you ever want to talk, OK?'

Raul strode noisily along the hallway to linger in the doorway.

'Helen – I can't find the G38.'

'The what?'

'The oil for my bike. I've looked everywhere.'

'I know – we heard! Try looking in the garage where it's supposed to be.'

'Jesus Christ. You put things down for five minutes in this place!' Raul turned and strode away, muttering in Spanish. Their domestic sparring had a certain charm, a mutual affection that showed, despite Raul's claims to the contrary. In a way he envied them both. His and

Claudia's relationship seemed strained by comparison. Raul said that it was all down to how much work you put in. Women needed to be pampered. You had to make them feel special or they lost interest and found someone else.

He thought about Natalie, propped up on his mantelpiece – seductive in pink. Helen might be able to offer advice from a woman's perspective. He took a sip of lukewarm coffee and looked for a suitable opening.

'Funny how a total stranger can have an effect on you, isn't it?' he said.

'In what way?'

'You know – wind you up the minute you walk in the room. Like they've been put there just for that purpose.'

Helen smiled coyly. 'Er – who are we talking about here?'

'I was just talking in general.'

She frowned and considered the question from a different angle. 'Well – you can take an instant dislike to someone without knowing why, I suppose. Like the traffic warden who gave me a ticket Tuesday afternoon. I won't tell you what I called *him*.'

'But that's different.'

'Why is it?'

'You reacted to the uniform, not the person in it. I'm talking about the gut feeling you get when you meet someone for the first time.'

'Go on.' She watched him with the same thoughtful frown. He felt himself on the verge of some profound insight.

'Can I ask you something, Helen?'

'Of course you can.'

'Do I ever come across as, arrogant?'

She put her head back and laughed with gusto.

'It's just a question, that's all.'

Her laughter faded. She drew a deep breath and laid both hands flat on the table. 'Peter. Listen to me now. I don't know who you've met, or what she's done to upset you, but you'd better find a way to get over it.' He said nothing, squirming under the spotlight. She patted his hand, gently. 'I'm only telling you because I'm your friend, OK?'

He smiled at the old joke, but the issue sat awkwardly between them.

Helen sat back and toyed with her hair, pleased with her detective work. 'Raul keeps talking about having another barbeque. What do you think?'

'Didn't he burn the sausages the last time?'

'God, yes, I remember now. Be nice though, wouldn't it? You can bring Claudia.' She flashed him a look of comic disdain. 'Unless you've met someone else by then.'

He drove home in a state of confusion. Like most men, he liked to think he was au fait with a broad range of social skills. But when it came to women, he was struck dumb with incomprehension. Perhaps Raul was right and it was all to do with geographics. The English as a race had never learned how to relate. All that male posturing down the pub was an anachronism, left over from the Viking age. Even the New Age man, with his hastily written Valentine's cards and bunches of red roses, couldn't quite cut it in the real world. The first signs of trouble and he was off down to Waterstone's, searching for answers in the self-help section.

Natalie baffled him. He couldn't understand his reaction to her, the extraordinary level of attention given to a complete stranger. He had to put her out of his mind. Concentrate on the things that mattered. Work. Better relations with Leanne. Building a future with Claudia. Natalie didn't mean a thing to him. Some overstressed prima donna with an attitude problem and the usual issues with men. Women like that were never worth the legwork.

He pulled into his driveway and turned off the ignition, wondering what she'd be wearing the next time they met.

Seven

Claudia pulled on her shoes and crossed to the mirror, her heels striking the bare boards. She coaxed her hair back into place with a grimace, the hairpin clamped between her teeth. He lay back and watched, preferring her now with her clothes on.

'Are you getting up?' she said.

'In a minute.'

She tugged at the hem of her top, squashing her breasts against the thin material. 'God! Look at the state I'm in because of you.'

'So you weren't an eager and willing participant yourself then?'

'Pardon?'

'Never mind. I'll get up.'

He made the drinks. Earl Grey for her, Douwe Egbert's for himself. She strutted around the kitchen behind him, complaining in her half-joking manner about the lack of service, his selfishness, the fact that he never left the tea bag in the cup long enough. Soon she would move in and take over completely, his precious independence gone forever.

They adjourned to the front room. He stretched out in the worn, leather armchair that she hated so much and surveyed the general chaos. Power tools and extension leads. Cardboard boxes filled with books and CDs. She perched on the window-sill and focused on him over the rim of the cup, planning the next six months of his life in her head.

'When are you going to finish the bathroom?' she said.

'When I stop getting sidetracked.'

'By me, I suppose?'

He ignored her and stared at the mantelpiece – the space where the photograph had been. The deception made him feel bad. Like hiding pornography and hoping you wouldn't get found out. He had to be careful. Claudia might get suspicious and start asking questions. Why the sudden interest in a woman he'd met five years ago and could barely even remember?

'What's happening with the shower unit?' she said.

'It's coming.'

'When?'

'Soon.'

'You said that two weeks ago. Why don't you get on to them and chase it up?'

'I have done.'

'And what did they say?'

'Same thing they said the last time – delays with the manufacturer.'

Claudia hadn't known him at the time of the wedding. By the time they met, that aspect of his life had been dealt with and was clearly not up for discussion. James and Tara were names he avoided in conversation, only referring to them when someone else brought the subject up. Claudia respected his wishes and didn't push for details. After all, his past life had nothing to do with their future happiness. Had she known about the photograph and the identity of the woman in the pink jacket and wide-brimmed hat, she might have been less understanding.

The neighbour's black cat jumped onto the window ledge and reared up on its hind legs, pressing its head against the glass. Claudia made an excessive fuss of it, cooing through the window in a silly, high-pitched voice.

'It's just a cat,' he said. 'out for what it can get.'

'That's one thing you've got in common then.'

'What are you trying to say, Claudia? That I'm some sort of animal?'

He watched their feline bonding session with amusement. Her shrill voice brought out the perverse streak in him and without warning he launched himself at the window. The cat froze for a moment, sprang from the ledge and disappeared beneath the hedge. Claudia's dismayed reaction amused him even more.

She sat down, resigned to his grossness. 'You're so horrible!'

'I aim to please.'

'I don't know what I see in you sometimes.'

'I can think of one thing,' he said amiably and pinched her cheek on his way past.

He sank bank in the armchair, pleased with his performance. The sun shone on the untidy garden and Claudia's outline at the window. Traffic droned-by out on the road. He might have been trapped in the room for days, avoiding issues that piled up like mail in a disused building. You had to have an outlet for frustration. Sex was the best thing, but you couldn't stay in the bedroom all day. Sooner or later you had to face the enemy, the warring factions inside your own head.

Claudia had moved on, having forgotten the incident with the cat. She gazed across the cluttered room, making a mental note of all the fittings and fixtures, work pending her first spring clean.

'Have you thought about your dad's birthday?' she said.

'Not really.'

'So what are you going to buy him?'

'Nothing, like the last time I suppose.'

'God, you're unbelievable.'

'What can I buy him he hasn't already got – a golf course?'

'Er – I think you'll find it's the thought that counts.'

He laughed at her pompous expression, the chance to aggravate her for the sake of it. 'Listen – men don't do birthdays. That's what I employ you for.'

She turned on him. 'No – *you* don't do birthdays. You even forgot mine last year. What kind of a man is that?'

'I made it up to you didn't I?'

'What, by taking me over the Avon Causeway and giving me cramp in the back of your car? I don't think so.'

She stood at the window sipping her tea. He admired her sun-kissed outline from the comfort of the armchair. Her classic, child-bearing hips that she claimed to detest, always soft and pliable beneath his grip. Perhaps they would go through the bickering phase and become a regular couple, strolling along the promenade in sedate middle age.

'Have you spoken to your mum?' she said.

'What about?'

'Spain.'

'How am I supposed to fit Spain in with this lot going on?'

'She just thought it would be nice if we could all go. You could play golf with your dad while we were on the beach.'

'I can play golf with him any time.'

'But it's not the same, is it?' She eased her weight onto one foot and sipped her tea noisily. He could almost hear the wheels turning. Her perpetual need to tidy all the loose ends. Now the plot to lure him to Spain, in spite of his increasing workload. Priory Road, left in the hands of Barry Jarvis to run as he saw fit. Scaffolders and plasterers to organise and no-one to contact in an emergency. Every tradesman in the area, busy with some unavoidable project of his own. A world of answerphones and tedious excuses. And the old woman next door, standing guard at her boundary line, waiting for the first signs of brick rubble to warrant a lawsuit.

He wished he had Claudia's outlook sometimes. Her optimism. Her ability to organise several projects at once. Selling medical products to senior nurses and planning dinner parties in her lunch break. She must have got it from her father. The talent for organisation and running other peoples lives.

'How's Raul?' she said.

'Still walking the dog every morning and complaining about it to anyone who'll listen.'

'What's new? Helen OK?'

'Worn out with it all. She's thinking of selling the bar.'

She gave a vague nod. He sensed her unease, the fact that she had never really got on with Helen. Raul got on with everyone.

'Did you tell them I'd had an offer on my place?' she said.

'No.'

'Why not?'

'Because you haven't sold it yet.'

She stared at him in dismay. 'It's just a formality. Once the offer's been accepted, the sale will go ahead. It's not as if I'm stuck in a chain or anything, is it?'

He pictured her in residence. Her glossy department store bags piling up in the bedroom. Her dress suits hanging in his wardrobe. The scent of her perfume lingering in the hallway.

She turned from the window and glanced around the room. Her eyes brightened visibly. 'You know what you could do with in here?'

'What?'

'A piano. Erica's cousin's got one in the front room. It would look great in here. Especially with the wooden floor.'

'I thought you didn't like the floor?'

'Well – I could get used to it, I suppose.'

He pictured a Grand piano in the middle of the room. Marco had some latent musical ability. Maybe he could come round and serenade the pair of them on the nights he wasn't out drinking.

'So I go out and buy a piano because it looks good?'

'You could learn to play it as well.'

He shook his head, speechless. The spartan theme was lost on her. Next it would be a revolving bed, a Jacuzzi in the utility room. She saw everything in terms of image. Polished wooden floors and bean bags were far too simplistic when it came to entertaining.

She went to the mirror and began glossing her lips. The process held a crude fascination for him, her mouth drawn back in a wide O as she guided the tip around the contours.

'Fancy a drive out to Linwood tomorrow?' she said, between strokes.

'I'm playing golf with Tim.'

'What, all day?'

'I've got a stack of invoices to sort out as well.'

She put the lip gloss away and studied her face in the mirror. 'I thought you were going to stop playing golf at the weekend?'

'When did I say that?'

'I wouldn't mind if it was just a couple of hours.'

'I'll sell the clubs on e-Bay, shall I?'

She flashed him a warning look. 'You don't have to get like that. It would just be nice to spend a bit more time together, that's all I'm saying.'

Raul's theory was valid. Busy lives, driving ordinary couples apart. The comfortable domestic routine upset by work schedules and looming mortgage repayments. Golf was a luxury, one more obsession he was finding harder to justify.

'Why do women hide chocolate in the fridge?'

She turned to stare at him. 'What?'

'Just something Raul said. I thought it might have been common. Like a dog burying a bone in the back garden.'

'Bury you in a minute.'

He glanced through the Advertiser. A proposal for more flats in Branksome caught his eye. A spokesman for local residents complained that far too many trees were being cut down to make way for new buildings. The old man hadn't had the same reservations at Somerford, sending the labourer in with a chainsaw under the cover of darkness to cull a brace of tall firs. Money always talked the loudest in the end. Even burning environmental issues took a back seat in the name of progress.

He turned to the back and scanned the personal columns. The adverts to prospective partners read like coded messages. Woman, 35, with GSOH seeks mature male for companionship. Likes music, walking and eating out. He began to compose his own. *'Virile male 34, seeks like-minded woman for cleaning duties. Must be up for debauchery in every conceivable position.'*

'What are you reading?' she said.

'The swingers column.'

'The what?'

'Nothing.'

He watched her distractedly for a moment, struck by the fundamental gulf between men and women.

'Claudia?'

'What?'

'Do I ever come across as arrogant to you?'

She frowned at him in bewilderment.

'I just wondered if that was the general impression I gave.'

'Who said that about you?'

'It doesn't matter who. I'm asking what you think?'

She gave the matter some thought. 'You're horrible sometimes, but I wouldn't have said you were arrogant.' She began searching along the bookcase. 'Where's the incense burner I bought you last Christmas?'

'Pass.'

'It's a wonder you can find anything in this place.' She turned from the bookcase and stared at him. 'So who called you arrogant then?'

'Some friend of Marco's I met in the pub.'

'Male or female?'

'What difference does it make?'

'I'm only asking.'

'Male, actually.'

She shrugged. 'Probably just someone jealous of your amazing charm. God, there's no air in this place.' She went to the window and snagged her skirt on the stepladders. Her unusually foul-mouthed reaction amused him, a rare display of anger witnessed from the comfort of the armchair. She glared at him. 'Now you know why I can't live here in this. It's a death trap with all these tools lying around.'

She did have a point. The painter should have been back the previous week to finish the architraves and second coat the ceiling in the utility room. Some geriatric who used to work for the old man, filling in time until his retirement. 'I'll have a word with Barry,' he said.

She crossed her arms and stared angrily into space. 'Barry. Now there's someone who really is arrogant. I pity his poor wife.'

The black cat reappeared at the window, stalking the ledge and rubbing its head against the glass. He admired its sinuous grace and wondered if the vet had curbed its natural instincts yet.

Claudia fixed her gaze on the far wall, with more than a hint of malice. 'I wish you'd take that stupid photograph down. I can't bear it.'

He glanced over at Reginald Brown Senior. Cue Master 1823-1904. Poised above a snooker table with long white beard and a discerning eye. Not much known about him in the family, other than his talent for potting the black and spending fortunes in the ale house. The picture had come from his mother as a memento. He'd hung it up as a kind of joke to baffle visitors. But like the worn old leather armchair, he'd become used to it being there.

'Sorry, love – but old Reg stays.'

'I don't know why.'

'Because he's a valuable part of my heritage, that's why. He's the closest thing we've got to royalty in the family.'

'Huh. He looks like Moses with that beard.'

He faked a sudden interest. 'Yeah, he does, doesn't he. That's amazing! I might grow one myself, what d'you reckon?'

'Just try it, you won't see me again.' She watched the cat stalking the window ledge and a dreamy smile began to form. 'I saw a beautiful wedding dress with Erica the other day, did I tell you?'

'Don't start that again.'

She turned sharply, imploring him with a long, mournful look. 'I know we said we wouldn't talk about it until all this work's been done, but …'

'But you couldn't resist it.'

She came over and sat on the armrest, running her fingers through his hair.

'You do love me, don't you?'

'Claudia – '

'I just want to make you happy that's all.'

'You do make me happy. You don't need a wedding dress to prove it.'

She withdrew her hand and sat in silence for a moment. 'I can't help it if I want to spend more time with you, can I?'

'We spend plenty of time together. Like every spare minute.'

'You know what I mean.' She gave him a forlorn smile and looked away. Her sadness made her vulnerable, open to manipulation. He laid a hand on her silky thigh and squeezed gently. In truth she was perfect for him. He felt safe in her warm embrace, calmed by the smell of Body Mist and fabric conditioner.

'Please think about Spain,' she said

'Claudia – '

'I know you're busy, but it would be so nice to get away. Especially before I have the hassle of selling the house.'

'I'll think about it.'

She gave him a hug and kissed his head. 'Thanks, honey.'

Morocco had been an experience. Two weeks of sun, sea and sex. Lying around in the stifling heat, worrying about catching dysentery from the local produce. He hadn't known her long, but the strains had started to show. Shopping and socialising were never high on his list of priorities but he did his best to reach a compromise. The golfing holidays and stag weekends with the boys were dropped in favour of romantic dinners and quiet nights in by the television. The bachelor lifestyle – such an ingrained habit for so long – was hard to give up. Whenever Claudia went away on conferences, he relished the sense of freedom, and celebrated with small, childish acts of rebellion. One night he filled the car up with petrol and drove to Southampton in a thunderstorm, with *Cream Anthems* playing at full volume. These random acts fulfilled a temporary longing to break out. Then Claudia came back and their cosy, structured life resumed as before.

She could always go to Spain without him. To compensate, she could go shopping with his mother along the Explanada, or spend the evenings listening to the old man and his expatriate mates, putting the world to rights in the bars along the waterfront.

Claudia left early.

He sorted his washing in the utility room. White cotton socks had a disappointing shelf life. After one or two washes they developed the limp tee-shirt look, a sad imitation of white. Claudia would move-in and take over the domestic rota, ensuring that he never went short of clean underwear again. The thought left him feeling uneasy. In the event of her taking over completely, he could always convert the garage into a hideaway. Install a mini bar and Sky TV, staying put until she begged him to come back in.

He found a pair of black and white stripy ankle socks he didn't recognise. Claudia's perhaps. He held one up and stared at it. The limp sock jogged his memory. Exhibit A. His guilt in the matter unquestionable. One moment of weakness that he had sworn would never happen again. He dropped the sock onto the basket of clothing and thought back.

They'd been caught in a downpour walking to her place along the promenade. She'd dried his jacket and trousers on a radiator and leant him a clean pair of socks to go home in. He should never have gone back with her in the first place. That had been weeks ago. He hadn't heard from her since.

Marco rang. Was he interested in a meal at Pascali's to celebrate some girl's birthday he'd never heard of?

'Who's going?' he said.

'The usual crowd. Erica. Simon. The insurance company posse.'

The guest list failed to inspire him.

'Oh, I did think of inviting Natalie,' Marco said glibly. 'She'll probably bring Brad though. Have you got a problem with that?'

'No. Why should I?'

'He's a web designer, apparently. Good looking bastard with sunglasses and a pony tail. You should get on well with him. You still there?'

'I'll ask Claudia. She's the one with the diary round here.'

'Be great if you can make it. And don't worry about your little disagreement with Natalie. I'll arrange the seating so you're at opposite ends of the table. Worse comes to the worse, I'll bail you out with the old soda siphon trick. Toodle-pip!'

He slipped the photograph from its hiding place and stood it back on the mantelpiece. The pink suited her. The hat made her look dignified, suiting her solemn expression. The scene in Pascali's began to form. Him at one end of the table, her at the other. The thought of meeting her again made his heart race. A telepathic communication between them. The briefest eye-contact between the raising and lowering of wine glasses.

Warning lights went off. Raul was right. Falling in love with a photograph wasn't the act of a sane man. Perhaps he was coming down with something. Early onset senility from overindulgence and not enough hard work. The name Brad struck some dissonant chord. Someone else to plot against.

Marco's little soiree might serve a purpose. Help him get Natalie out of his system once and for all. Teach her a lesson in table manners by ignoring her completely.

He had one last look at the black and white socks before consigning them to the bin.

Eight

Barry turned up thirty minutes late. They stood at the back of the house, Barry with clipboard in hand, the red hairs on his forearms proud in the sunlight. The polythene membrane that sealed the back entrance flapped in the wind, an overworked lung. The muddied trenches were gone. In their place, a neat rectangle of concrete and three courses of red brick above ground.

The sight pleased him – the twin evils of time and the elements defeated for the moment.

'Roof on soon, at this rate,' Barry said.

'Good. I want to be out of this place in six weeks.'

Barry looked over the foundations with a lazy smile. 'That work-shy little bastard gets his arse in gear and anything's possible.'

A pinched squealing noise came from the side of the house. Sean emerged from the alleyway pushing a wheelbarrow filled with bricks. The barrow hit a divot, lurched to one side and tipped over. Sean, aware of his audience, cursed under his breath and tried to look nonchalant.

Barry shook his head at the travesty. 'It's enough to make you weep. If I had a kid like that, I'd strangle him.' Barry lapsed into nostalgia, recalling a bygone era when building sites were the domain of real men. Bricks were off-loaded by hand from straw covered wagons and the tradesmen all wore flat caps. Barry might not have been born in this era, but the imagery seemed to captivate him. Sean carried on reloading the barrow, red-faced, without a word. Barry watched, unimpressed. 'Had him up in Southampton the other week, gutting some flats on the main drag. Disappeared he did. Looked everywhere for him. Turned up an hour later eating a bag of chips.'

Sean would always belong to the underclass in Barry's eyes, unfit to earn any special favours or dispensation. Shape up or ship out – the standard message to all employees. Barry came from the same ruthless mould as the old man. You started work at eight o'clock sharp and if you weren't good enough, you were back down the ladder ten minutes later.

He turned to Barry. 'Seen the old woman next door lately?'

'She had a moan at me about the state of the road last week. I pulled Sean up on it but he never listens.'

'I'll talk to him about it.'

Barry grinned slyly. 'He listens to you then does he, Peter?'

Sean finished reloading the wheelbarrow and attempted to lift it, straining at the handles and bending at the knee. Barry grunted in disapproval, viewing some strange alien life form. 'Shameful. That's what it is. No wonder he still lives at home.'

He felt a mixture of empathy for Sean and professional self-interest. He did after all pay Sean's wages, even if it was indirectly.

Barry ran through the list of priorities. Tradesmen due to start, and jobs rescheduled. Unforeseen snags like late deliveries and a burst water-main, snagged by the digger's bucket. The clipboard sat propped on Barry's stomach, a pencil tucked behind his ear for any sudden amendments. Problems were dismissed, nothing that couldn't be dealt with throughout the course of the working day. In this respect, Barry was like Claudia, as unstoppable as the wind that blew the polythene. A trait to be admired, even if at times it did irritate.

They went upstairs. The smooth plaster finish changed the contours of the rooms, creating a sense of space. Tiny beads of moisture clung to the pink surface. He stood at the front window looking out. Three red cones sealed the entrance to the driveway. A rectangle of fine white dust had formed around the skip. Barry appeared alongside him, looking down. They surveyed the area in silence.

He thought back to his teens, knocking-up concrete in the big old diesel mixer while his granddad stood by. The shovel barely making an indent into the huge pile of ballast at the roadside. 'Sean wouldn't have lasted five minutes with my granddad.' he said quietly.

Barry nodded solemnly. 'Old school, your granddad was. He'd have you cleaning down the road at nine o'clock at night. They don't make 'em like that no more.'

'They certainly don't.'

'Never saw eye to eye with your old man though, did he?'

Barry's comment roused a fierce indignation in him. His granddad had been a man of few words, highly principled but with a legendary temper. Perhaps that's where he got it from. The tendency to explode first and ask questions later.

He became aware of Barry, standing calmly beside him and snapped into business mode. 'What happened to the painter at my place?'

'Old Fred? I thought he'd finished.'

'He missed some of the architrave. And the ceiling in the utility room needs a second coat.'

Barry nodded vaguely and watched a woman pass by the window. 'I'll chase him up. I know he's had a few health problems lately.'

'That's no good to me. I just want the job finished.'

Barry stiffened and pulled back from the window. 'I'll get onto it, Peter.'

They went downstairs. He found a bottle of Lynx aftershave on the kitchen window sill and unscrewed the cap. The sharp scent took him from the halogen lamps and cement bags, to kebab houses and late night taxi-ranks.

'Give you one guess,' Barry said.

He stood the aftershave back on the window sill. 'Sean. He'll be moving his wardrobe in at this rate.'

'Trying to impress that young bird of his. Cracking young party. Have a go myself if he ever gets tired of her.'

He pictured Barry with Sean's girlfriend, copulating among the leads and the dust, Barry's bald dome glistening with sweat, his head bobbing up and down like a piston.

They went out into the sunlight.

Sean rounded the corner with another barrowful of bricks, his face rigid with effort. He set the barrow down by the slab and wiped his forehead, his gloved hands like huge deformities. Barry watched his efforts, slapping the clipboard rhythmically against his thigh. 'Never make a bricklayer long as he's got a hole in his arse.'

Sean looked up, sweating. 'What?'

'Don't you *what* me, you little prick. I want all those bricks in off the road by tonight. Got it?'

Sean grunted a morose affirmative and carried on working.

Barry left, taking his clipboard and assumed air of authority with him. Sean stopped working and sat down on a stack of bricks, staring at his feet.

He felt a grain of sympathy for the lad, having to endure Barry's relentless sarcasm and the oppressive noonday heat.

'You hungry, Sean?'

'Huh?'

'Food. Carbohydrates. Come on, I'll take you up the café.'

'What about Barry?'

'You're entitled to a lunch break aren't you?'

Sean's mouth dropped. 'I'm skint.'

'Tell me something I don't already know.'

The Crossroads café served as a makeshift office. Work schedules reviewed in a roomful of noisy men. The all-day mega-breakfast, served on a huge oval platter with an extra round of bread as a surety. The girl behind the counter had bleached blonde hair and a nose stud, an undernourished waif who didn't smile much. She took the orders quietly, unable to compete with the eggs, beans and fried bread, the constant clamour of male attention.

They sat at the corner table, a view of the main road through the net curtain. Sean lounged in his chair with a smug grin, enjoying his sudden change of fortune. The age difference and working relations limited the topics for conversation. They settled for mobile phones as a common interest.

'Where's the best deals now, Sean?'

'Contract or pay-as-you-go?'

'Contract.'

Sean reeled off the latest hardware like a salesman. The endless possibilities of blue tooth and internet downloads. Sean's enthusiasm failed to impress him. 'I want a mobile phone not a space-station.'

'Talk to Frenchie. He'll sort you out a good deal'

'Who's Frenchie?'

'Mate of mine – works for Carphone Warehouse.'

Sean belonged to the generation weaned on technology. Computer literate but woefully ignorant of current affairs. He could tell you the results of last weeks Champions League draw, but the name of the Prime Minister would probably elude him.

The waitress with a nose stud came over and set down two huge platters without a word. The smell of fried food caused him a minor rapture. He watched her departing backside weaving between the tables and turned to Sean. 'How's Julie?'

'We split up.'

'What again?'

'It's permanent this time.'

'You said that the last time. Where you gonna go for your Sunday dinner now?'

'Dunno.'

'Got another one lined up yet?'

'Nope.'

'Why not?'

'Too busy.'

'Doing what?'

Sean gave a diffident shrug. 'Playing football. Going out with me mates.'

Crisp fried bread flooded his taste buds. The unbeatable taste of cooking fat and early-onset heart disease. He wondered how something so good could be so bad for you. Sean's blasé attitude to romance was more food for thought.

'How old are you now, Sean?'

'Nineteen.'

'I was mortgaged up to the hilt with a wife and kid at your age.'

Sean curled his lower lip and considered the matter.

'It's alright for you though, innit?'

'Why's that?'

'You don't have to work for Barry.'

The girl from Palmer's rang. The shower unit had arrived and they could deliver it at his convenience – sorry for any delay. He kept her talking, her silky-smooth voice a welcome relief from the all male banter around them. Warren Beatty was said to have favoured seduction by telephone. He could relate to that approach, the medium creating a subtle intimacy. You could talk about anything as long as you remembered to be discreet. Women were far more sociable than men, willing to engage in harmless small talk, as long as you threw in the odd joke and a strategically placed compliment to keep them amused.

He hung up and examined the charred underside of a piece of sausage. The chime on the door rang incessantly, as another batch of hungry workers filed in off the street. Sean sat hunched over his platter, engrossed, mopping up the remains with a limp crust. At least the lad had an appetite for something.

'You've got a lot to learn, Sean.'

Sean looked up, frowning. 'About what?'

'Life. You need some sort of goal. Something to aim for.'

'I have got something to aim for. Barry's head with a shovel, next time he has a go at me.'

They shared the joke at Barry's expense, Sean's malicious smirk one small victory for the downtrodden.

Claudia sent him an outrageous text message. He laughed out loud, shocked at the content. Three days in Birmingham had obviously done wonders for her libido. But the message left him feeling uneasy. Beneath the familiarity lay the foundations of a clever trap. She'd talk him into going to Spain against his wishes. Buy his shirts, organise the flights and plan the itinerary while he stood back and let it all happen. When they came back, she would sell her house and move in with him. They would celebrate by throwing a party and inviting all their friends. The perfect couple – primed and ready for the social circuit.

The girl came back to clear the table. He admired her slender form through a mild attack of indigestion.

'How long you worked here, sweetheart?'

'Six months.'

'Can't be an easy job, dealing with all these reprobates.'

She shrugged. 'It's alright.'

'How old are you – if you don't mind me asking?'

'Eighteen.'

'Boyfriend?'

'Not at the moment.'

He glanced at Sean. 'There you go. Perfect opportunity for you, Sean. She can come and watch you play football on a Sunday morning, before you go to the pub. What d'you reckon?'

Sean sat in red-faced silence, his nose in his mug of tea. Perhaps they were all like it, lacking the confidence to make the first move. Still kids, not yet having made the transition into adults.

He called his mother. She reminded him of his many responsibilities, her insistent voice merging with the nausea of fried food. The old man's birthday was looming and he would forget. The selfishness inherent in all men. He listened until her voice became an irritant, lost in the general chatter around him. 'Sorry mum. Got to go, I'm parked on double yellows.' She ignored him and rambled on in the same vein. Of course, he would forget his father's birthday. If men were left to their own devices they would forget everything. Birthdays and anniversaries ditched in favour of Sky Sports Plus and nights out with the lads. The whole card manufacturing business would go bankrupt overnight.

She finished up with a curt reminder. 'Speak to Leanne, Peter. She's at that age where she needs guidance.'

'She needs something.'

'And bring Claudia over for lunch on Sunday. We'd love to see you both.'

'I will if I get time. I'm working a seventy-five hour week as it is!'

He sat back, flustered. His mother would expect them to come over and discuss the Spanish conspiracy. The old man would make derogatory comments about the ex-pat community, lounging in the sunshine, drinking gin and tonics all day. Claudia would sit with a contented smile on her face, radiating warmth and understanding throughout. She felt comfortable with the routine, coming from a close-knit family herself. But she only saw what they wanted her to see. As an outsider, you had to look hard to see the cracks in the surface. The façade had been worked on over the years, polished smooth as a dining room table. Certain subjects were out of bounds, buried quickly, before they had the chance to disturb the equilibrium. He liked to push the boundaries sometimes to get a reaction. That sharp, warning look in his mother's eyes that meant he'd gone too far.

'Don't get married too soon, Sean.'

'Why not?'

'Because you'll wake up one morning and wonder where the last ten years went.'

'Is that what happened to you?'

The question bothered him more than it should have done. He'd said too much already, allowing Sean to become over familiar. His marriage to Sylvia had been a mistake, a battleground for the pair of them, but the memory of it made him feel oddly protective towards her.

'Drink your tea, Sean, I'll run you back.'

Sean shrugged and sipped his tea. A Cabstar pulled up outside, building equipment loaded on the back, ladders strapped above the roof. Sean had all that to look forward to. Forty-odd years of cement dust and brick bats in medieval working conditions. Slave-drivers like Barry Jarvis to work him into an early grave, reminding him of his lowly status on a daily basis.

He dropped Sean back at Priory Road and considered the options. Go home and work on the stack of invoices in the bedroom, or spend an hour in the gym. The gym option won. Plenty of good-looking women around to offset the boredom of the treadmill.

Friday's schedule loomed. Meet the building inspector at Priory Road. Get hold of Martin Jarvis – the more reasonable half of the duo – to fit the shower unit at the flat. Then spend the evening at Pascali's.

With Natalie.

Nine

The second bottle of Chateauneuf du Pape was opened. Marco raised his glass and proposed a toast to the entire restaurant, including the waitress, who smiled graciously and walked away. Applause rang out on the far side and Marco stood to take a bow, arms wide like a jaded celebrity. Orders in Italian rose above the tables, calls from waiters to the bar area and the kitchen. Opera music played in the background, creating a warm atmosphere and weaving all the scenes together.

Erica leant against his shoulder. 'You're very quiet tonight, Peter?'

'I'm fine.'

'Something on your mind?'

'Only that I'll have to listen to Simon all night.'

Erica gave him a mocking frown. 'Oh you poor thing. Don't you think Claudia looks lovely tonight?'

'Like a peach.'

'Is that sarcasm or are you actually being serious for once?'

'I'm serious. The dress cost a week's wages, but yes, even I'm willing to admit she looks good in it.'

Claudia chatted to the red-haired occupational therapist seated next to her. The silver earrings he'd bought her flashed at her slender neck. She did look good, in her tiered dress with its plunging neckline. Her hair – piled on top of her head – enhanced the firm line of her jaw and her smooth shoulders. He could hardly criticise her for being too feminine, even if it did take two hours to create the effect.

He counted eight of them at the long table plus the two empty places at the end. Simon's new girlfriend looked downcast, seated between Marco and the loudmouthed girl from Barclays. Marco did his best to entertain everyone, including the floor staff, toning down his act for their benefit, saving his more outrageous behaviour for later.

Simon leaned across the table with his irritating, flashy smile. 'Seen much of Tim lately, Peter?'

'Not for a while.'

'What's he driving these days?'

'A Skoda, I think.'

Simon burst out laughing, and gestured to his girlfriend. 'Kate – this is Peter. We went to school together. Didn't learn much did we, Peter?'

Kate forced a smile behind her wine glass. He squeezed her proffered hand as if they were sealing a business deal and wondered if she might be mildly anorexic. Simon excluded her without a second thought, moving on to the subject of old forgotten schoolmates. 'What was the name of that kid who wore his underpants on top of his trousers for a bet? He was like the worst kid in the whole school. The teachers hated him.'

He recalled a noisy playground, full of uniformed urchins intent on tearing each other apart.

'Colin Cottrell.'

'That's it! Cottrell! He was unbelievable.' Simon relayed the saga to a bemused Kate, who was forced to listen to Marco and the raucous girl from Barclays at the same time. Wine flowed with the conversation. The two empty spaces at the end of the table awaited the late arrivals.

He nudged Marco's arm. 'How much longer are we going to wait?'

'For what?'

'Natalie.'

Marco glanced at his watch. 'She'll be here when she gets here. Woman's prerogative and all that.'

'She was supposed to be here half an hour ago.'

'So what's the problem?'

'I'm hungry, that's the problem.'

'Lighten up, for Christ's sake.' Marco said and turned away.

Warm, sociable conversation went on around him. Marco's stinging reproach niggled, the entire evening put on hold for someone who couldn't be bothered to make the effort. He sat with the frustration a moment longer.

'Call her.'

Marco paused in mid-conversation to stare at him. 'What?'

'I said call her. Tell her she's holding everything up.'

'I'm not calling her!'

'Why not?'

'What am I, the maitre d? It's not my job to chase people up.'

'Well you invited her.'

Marco rolled his eyes and sighed wearily. 'You're really starting to get on my tits now – you know that?'

He sat back in self-righteous silence.

Marco took out his phone and laid it on the table. 'There you go. You call her if it means that much to you.'

'Why should *I* call her?'

'You're the one making such a big deal out of it. Now shut the fuck up, you're starting to sound like Raul.'

Marco went back to his previous conversation, leaving his phone on the table. Claudia sat engrossed with the red-haired occupational therapist. Erica was busy admiring Simon's new watch, that cost more than a months wages and seemed to give him some warped sexual pleasure.

He picked up Marco's phone and stared at the screen. No-one would know. He could make the call and be back before anyone missed him. The thought gave him a perverse thrill, too tempting to resist. He slipped the phone in his pocket, excused himself from the table and went outside.

A taxi pulled up and a young couple spilled out, laughing, absorbed in the moment. They passed him and went into the restaurant. A waft of garlic drifted through the open window and merged with the evening warmth. He felt exposed and vulnerable, caught out on the street in an act of crass stupidity.

He found her name in Marco's contacts. Heart pounding, he pressed the call connect button and waited.

The call connected. 'Yeah, I know I'm late, Marco. I had to drop Charlotte at my mum's, OK?'

She sounded breathless, irritable. He held his nerve and plunged in. 'Where are you, Natalie? The starters are all going cold.'

Silence. He thought he heard a man's voice in the background.

'Who is this?' she said.

'I'm just passing on a message.'

'Where's Marco?'

'He's in the restaurant waiting for you – like the rest of us. If you hurry up, we'll save you some garlic bread.'

'Look – who is this? I'm starting to get a bit – '

'Nice talking to you, Natalie. See you soon.' He hung up and breathed in the warm air. A sense of nervous anticipation gripped him. An evening of mild antagonism to look forward to, exchanging acid glances between courses and seeing who could rise above the provocation. Flattery and coercion wouldn't work. Natalie wasn't the type to respond to either. But antagonism worked where other means failed. He'd seen her resistance weaken at Erica's, in spite of her special efforts to prove otherwise.

He took his seat back at the table. Nobody seemed to have missed him. Claudia was still locked in conversation with the occupational therapist. Marco signalled for more wine, unaware that his phone had gone missing.

Erica turned to him. 'Why did you go outside?'

'To get some fresh air.'

'So what's that smug look on your face for?'

'What look?'

She frowned. 'You know you're really beginning to worry me, Peter. Not coming down with something are you?'

He handed the phone back to Marco and relayed Natalie's excuse for being late. Marco listened without interest, and returned to his captive audience, an unruly child in a public place. The more Marco drank, the louder he became and the more outlandish his stories grew. Lost on a Miami freeway with a psychotic, Puerto Rican drug dealer who kept pulling a gun and threatening to shoot people through the open window. The girl from Barclays tried to upstage him with tales of her own, their boisterous exchanges and her manic laughter drawing attention from the other tables.

Natalie arrived.

Behind her, a tanned and good-looking man with streaked blonde hair swept back in a pony-tail.

Marco gave a cheer and raised his glass towards the entrance. The waiter led the couple along the aisle to the empty chairs at the end of the table. Natalie took her seat, clearly uncomfortable with all the attention. Her pony-tailed escort took the seat opposite, smiling and confident. The cool, unflappable type, used to being waited on and getting his own way.

Marco made the introductions and proposed a crude toast, 'To Natalie, and all who sail in her!' Simon and the girl from Barclays competed for the most annoying laugh. Glasses chinked and the wine flowed. Threads of previous conversations were picked up around the table.

Erica leaned over and whispered, 'What's the verdict?'

'On what?'

'Natalie and her fella?'

'He's not my type.'

Erica beamed with sadistic pleasure. 'He's quite good looking though, don't you think?'

'Whatever turns you on, I suppose.'

'Ooh! Do I sense a bit of animosity there, Peter?'

'No. As long as they stay at *that* end of the table, we'll all get along fine.'

Erica brought Claudia in on the debate. With discreet glances along the table, they compared notes in hushed voices. Claudia's interest added to his frustration. He snapped a breadstick and focused on the shining bald head at the next table. Simon's nasal voice droned on about security passwords in banking systems, how even modern technology couldn't prevent the spread of fraud.

The starters arrived.

He stared at his gazpacho soup without interest. The nervous Kate probed her avocado with the painstaking care of a bomb disposal expert, cautiously inspecting the underside of a lettuce leaf for any stray prawns. Two seats down, the girl from Barclays talked non-stop, her jarring laughter alerting the entire restaurant. Marco topped up the empty wine glasses, his witty observations keeping everyone amused. Natalie sat demurely at the end of the table, the unsuspecting star of the show, poised above her carefully folded napkin.

Marco turned to him during a lull. 'I'm having a little shindig later – interested?'

'Who's going?'

'Present company. Nice quiet little gathering. Be a kind of send-off for the old house before I move out.'

'I'll probably give it a miss.'

'Suit yourself.'

Marco took a slug of wine and cut in on Simon's conversation. Some well heeled contact of Simon's wanted a swimming pool built. Marco, of course, could furnish all the details and would be happy to get involved, for a fee. The debate stalled and Marco lost interest.

'Why do you do that?' he said.

Marco looked over, puzzled. 'Do what?'

'We're in the middle of a conversation and you start talking to someone else.'

'Remind me. What were we talking about?'

'The Ballroom. Your little shindig later.'

Marco nodded vaguely and inspected the level of his wine glass. 'You should really talk to Simon, you know. These people are worth cultivating. They're all minted and they move in the same circles.'

'I don't build swimming pools. I told you that before.'

Marco sat back, shaking his head. 'What sort of an attitude is that? I don't mind putting work your way as long as you can follow it up. I don't want people thinking I deal with wankers, do I?' Marco drank to his own success. An entrepreneur without any real, saleable commodity, his only major export being himself. Marco fingered his glass and flashed a devious, sidelong glance. 'Shame you're not coming back to mine later. I could have introduced you to Brad.'

'I'm not interested in Brad.'

'He designs websites.'

'So what?'

'If you ask him nicely he might upgrade your PC for you. Or design you a business site and get you on a decent search engine.'

'I'm not interested in anything he's got to offer, OK?'

'Now you're just being pedantic.'

He laughed. 'I'm what?'

'It's that small-town, I'm-so-much-more-clued-up-than-every-other-fucker attitude that won't get you anywhere.'

'Is that right?'

'Absolutely.' Marco drained his glass with a pleasurable sigh. 'You need to broaden your horizons. Start thinking outside the bubble.'

The main course came. An absurd idea took hold that Natalie had somehow betrayed him. Even the table arrangements said so. Every time he looked up she was there, on the outskirts of his vision, mocking him without even a glance. Part of him blamed Marco. To Marco the whole thing was a joke, to be used against him at some future date. The swimming pool fiasco served as one more example of their opposing interests – socially and in business. Marco hardly needed the money. He only had to mail his father for a cheque, or dip into his substantial inheritance to keep from going under. Everyone else had to work for a living.

He glanced along the table at Natalie and Brad. The two of them looked like any other couple, feet entwined under the table, eye contact in the soft lighting. Lust, waiting in some private corner to carry them both away.

'Peter!'

He looked up, startled. Claudia glared at him.

'I was telling Erica about my CD player. The one you said you'd fix about six months ago.' She turned to Erica with a scowl. 'And he forgot my birthday. I had to phone and remind him.'

Erica taunted him. 'Oh, Peter. That's unforgivable. I hope you made it up to Claudia.'

'Oh I did. I gave her five hundred quid to get a facelift. As you can see, she spent the money on something else.'

Claudia threw her napkin at him. 'Thanks!'

Erica reached across and patted her hand. 'Don't worry darling, you have to humour him. He's like all men. He'd be completely and utterly lost without you.'

He found an unlikely ally in the barman. The language barrier might have been a problem, but they shared the same instinct, faced the same common threat. A flustered looking waitress joined them and leaned over the bar to gabble at the barman in frantic Italian. She finished her speech and strode off in a breeze of attitude. The barman gave a subtle nod in her direction. All women were this way. Something to be admired from a distance but rarely understood.

'Whereabouts are you from,' he said.

'Calabria,' the barman said with understated pride.

'You like England?'

'Is good.'

'Even the rain?'

'The rain – not so good.'

'You like English women?'

The barman made a tremulous hand gesture and they both laughed.

He ordered a Kronenburg and leant on the bar to scan the seating area. Marco presided at the centre of the table. Erica, Claudia and the occupational therapist had formed their own sub-committee, with Simon and the girl from Barclays as the supporting act. Poor Kate sat back, alone and neglected, staring at a painting on the opposite wall.

Natalie and Brad sat in intimate conversation at the far end. Brad, with his raised cheekbones and surfer's smile, looked supremely pleased with himself, relaxed and expansive in the company of strangers.

'Celebration tonight, Sir?' the barman said.

'Yes – I suppose it is in a way.' He glanced across at Claudia. 'Freedom from purgatory. Can you recommend a good cigar?'

The barman presented him with a small box, lined with an assortment of slim cigars. He selected one, savouring the harsh but pleasant aroma, the cigar a symbol of his hard won independence away from the table. The untouched bottle of Kronenburg gave him an excuse to linger and indulge in a little harmless self pity at the same time.

Erica joined him. 'Had enough of the company already?'

'I got bored listening to Simon going on about his off-shore bank accounts.'

'Are you going back to Marco's after?'

'I doubt it.'

'Why not?'

'Because I'd have to put up with Simon for another five hours.'

'God, you really are anti-social tonight aren't you?' She narrowed her eyes, honing in on him. 'I know what's really getting at you.'

'Nothing's getting at me.'

'I saw the way you reacted when Natalie turned up.'

He laughed defensively, backing away. 'Do me a favour! I didn't even notice her.'

'Peter, this is me you're talking to. I know what you're like. Remember?'

Erica had an uncanny knack of sussing him out. Like a malicious older sister watching his every move. Hard to believe they had once been lovers. The fumbling and awkward teenage version, sharing tense bus journeys into town, wondering if anyone would notice his hand stuck up her jumper. Now they were friends. In some ways friendship was the better deal. When you got lust out of the way there had to be something else to take its place or you never bothered speaking again. Most marriages ended this way. You thought you were in love but it turned out to be an illusion. You opened your eyes one day to find a stranger, slumped in the corner of the room, gazing vacantly at the TV.

Erica was still intrigued. 'What did you do to upset her in such record time?'

'Gave her a lecture on childcare, apparently.'

'You did what?'

He looked over at the table and hoped Brad would have a choking fit. 'There doesn't have to be a reason. Some people just rub you up the wrong way.'

'Why, for God's sake? What's she ever done to you?'

'She said I was arrogant for one thing.'

Erica laughed. 'Well you are, darling – in an endearing sort of way, of course.' She gave him a reassuring hug. 'Come back to Marco's later. We'll have a dance together underneath the chandeliers. Say au revoir to the old house before they knock it down.'

'I'll think about it.'

'And try to be a bit nicer to Claudia.'

'I am nice to her.'

Erica's indulgent smile faded. She eyed him carefully. 'She thinks the world of you, Peter. Please don't do anything to hurt her.'

'Like what?'

'You know what I'm talking about.'

He stayed at the bar with his untouched beer. The volatile waitress came back to harangue the barman, who faced her with a blank expression. She turned and marched off in her flat shoes, long legs and dark stockings beneath a short skirt. He thought about Claudia. Erica's parting comment had the touch of premonition. He had no intention of hurting Claudia but sometimes the thought of it was appealing. Like running upstairs and slamming your bedroom door as a kid. You could sit and revel in the aftermath, knowing that the shock waves would upset the entire household.

He went into the men's room. The silence came as a relief. Solitude, welcome after a long time spent in anyone's company. He checked himself in the mirror – the face he presented to the world – and forced a smile. The smile didn't look right. Forced smiles had that desperate, certifiable look, worn by politicians and failed Insurance salesmen. Better to save the energy and not bother at all. 'Peter has that mean look women like,' Erica had once said of him. He took this as a backhanded compliment and took to scowling more often. 'Smile and you win people's confidence,' proclaimed a magazine headline. You couldn't win either way.

The unease went deeper. Some basic disharmony at the core of his existence, growing like a tumour and becoming unbearable. This unease was reflected in the behaviour of those closest to him. Claudia's perfectly made-up face at the table, making plans for both of them whether he liked it or not. Her long term wishes, carrying them both along on a tide of natural exuberance. Claudia the organiser. Ambitious in her job and in her personal life; booking restaurants, arranging holidays, and filling the calendar with important events. Making sure the kitchen work surfaces were spotless, and the downstairs loo never ran out of toilet-paper. Soon she would sell her house and move in with him and it would be too late. The tidal wave would come crashing in and leave him washed-up on the shore, wondering what had happened.

He found Natalie standing at the bar. Almost without thinking, he joined her, scanning the optics a few feet away as if he hadn't seen her. The barman counted change into her hand. She put her purse away and snapped her bag shut.

The barman turned to him. He ordered a Jack Daniel's with ice, to go with the beer, and kept up the pretence until it became unbearable.

'Enjoy the meal?'

She looked up, distracted. 'Sorry?'

'The food – did you like it?'

'Yes, it was fine thanks.'

The whisky burned his throat, making his eyes water. Natalie changed her stance, frowning, uncertain.

'Was that you I spoke to earlier?' she said.

'It might have been. Is that a problem?'

'I don't like being hassled, that's all.'

He felt his cheeks flush at the tone of her voice, the need to fire something back right away. 'I was hungry and you were late. I'm not good at waiting.'

Marco called out from the table.

She grabbed her bag from the bar. 'I'd better get back.'

'Nice meeting you again, Natalie.'

She hesitated and turned back. 'Are you going back to Marco's later?'

'Maybe. Are you?'

She hesitated. 'Possibly.'

He watched her take her seat. She left him with a faint smile, the vaguest hint of a challenge in her departing glance. He raised his glass in a silent toast. The barman gave a subtle nod of understanding. The ways of a woman were hard to understand. This they could be agreed upon. But resistance was futile. When you wanted someone that badly, sooner or later you had to give in and do something about it.

Ten

He found her alone, gazing out at the dark horizon. For a moment the view was enough. The lights along the peninsula. The stretch of white sand. The crash of surf a few hundred yards ahead. He chose a spot a few feet from hers and stood in silence. The setting replaced the need for conversation.

'It must be the loneliest sound in the world,' she said finally.

'The sea?'

'Someone said it was the sound of eternity.'

'Maybe it is. Can you swim?'

She stared at him.

'I'm only asking. Some people can't. It's one of life's tragedies.'

'Really,' she said dryly and turned back to the horizon. 'It's such a beautiful spot here.'

'Third most expensive location in the world.'

'Is that right?'

'More money here than anywhere else in the country.'

'Are you selling shares in it?'

'Just enjoying the scenery like you.'

He waited for her to smile. Instead, she took a deep breath and sighed peaceably. Surf boomed along the shoreline, the sound of eternity filling in the silence. To the right, a group of fishermen were seated, posted at intervals like sentries. Each sat motionless in the dark, watching the line and the pull of the tide.

'Marco said you'd just moved down here,' he said.

'That's right.'

'From where?'

'London.'

'Tired of the rat-race?'

'Not really. My job prospects changed.'

He nodded, watching her profile. 'What do you do?'

'I'm a teacher.'

He mused on this for a moment. She seemed more amenable, calmed perhaps by the surf and the sea air. 'What do you teach?'

'You ask a lot of questions, don't you?'

'You said you were a teacher, you should be used to it.'

She accepted the challenge with a steady gaze, gripping the wooden handrail that connected them. 'I teach art therapy.'

'What's that – massage with paint?'

'Not quite,' she said without a trace of humour.

'So how would you go about teaching art therapy to someone like me?'

'I wouldn't.'

'Why not?'

'Because you're obviously beyond help.'

'Thanks.'

'Don't mention it.' She looked out along the peninsula, neutral in her stance and her tone. 'Shouldn't you be getting back to your wife?'

'She's not my wife. We're just good friends.' The comment failed to amuse her. He felt slighted but tried not to show it. 'How about you? Married?'

'No, I'm not. And before you ask, I'm busy most of the time.'

He laughed. 'That's good! That's one of the best put downs I've heard for a long time.'

She allowed him a faint smile. 'Just so we don't get off on the wrong foot or anything.'

'How could we with honesty like that?'

One of the fishermen prepared to cast out, a sudden lunge forward that sent the line arcing out over the water. He wondered if fishermen suffered the same injuries as golfers. Natalie scanned the horizon, alongside him, the breeze lifting her hair, lost in the blackness of the night sky.

He turned and looked up at the house. 'Not long now and this place will be a memory.'

She studied the house with him and shook her head. 'I don't know how they get away with it. Knocking down a lovely old building like this. For what?'

'You can't halt progress, as they say.'

'I wonder what they'll put up in its place?'

'A block of flats and a penthouse suite, I expect.'

She mused on the fate of the house. 'Marco doesn't seem too bothered about it.'

'Why should he be? He's just the sitting tenant until the wrecking-ball moves in. Do you know his family?'

'You could say that.'

She gave no further clues. The house became the focal point, a moral issue that couldn't be ignored. He felt an odd anger at the prospect of its demise. 'Marco's cousin stayed here two weeks last year. Can you believe that? Two weeks in a place like this. It's just a glorified summer house to these people.'

'Are you envious?'

He weighed the question and her serious face in the half-light. 'No, I'm not envious at all. Money doesn't bring happiness does it? Look at the rest of Marco's family.'

She turned back to the dark horizon. 'So what do you do?'

'I'm in the same business.'

'As Marco?'

'Not quite. I'm in the property business.'

'Ah. You're a landlord,' she said flatly.

'Not in the traditional sense of the word.'

'What does that mean, exactly?'

'Well, I own property, but not strictly for business purposes. More of an investment for the future really. Something to leave my grandchildren. If they deserve it.'

She seemed about to answer, but checked herself. Beneath the surface tension, he sensed a deeper connection between them. The solitude reinforced that feeling. So close that he could reach out and touch her. The perfect moment, inspired by the boom of the surf and the taste of salt in the cool sea-air. And behind them, the shadow of the old house waiting to pass into history.

'God, I need a cigarette.' she said, appealing to the night sky.

'I didn't have you down as a smoker.'

'I gave up about six weeks ago. It's the hardest thing I've done in my life.'

'Think of the health benefits though.'

'Benefits? What are they? I screamed at a woman in Asda the other day, just for pushing her trolley in front of the car.' She laughed to herself at the memory, a ripple of amusement not meant to be shared.

'So I caught you at a bad time the other night then?' he said.

'When?'

'At Erica's party.'

'Oh that,' she said evenly. 'I'm not the most sociable person in the world sometimes.'

'I gathered that.'

She flashed him a warning look. 'Especially not with people hassling me like you did earlier.'

He pictured her standing against the grey stone church in the photograph, radiant in her pink jacket and wide brimmed hat. The image made him eager to know more. The turbulent past that bound them together, waiting to unveil its secrets.

'You don't remember me, do you?'

She stared at him, puzzled. 'From where?'

'Five years ago. I was Best Man at James's wedding.'

She nodded slowly, the revelation making no obvious impact. 'I hardly knew him. Marco invited me for some strange reason.' She turned back to the darkness. 'But you're right. I don't remember you. Sorry.'

He said nothing, relieved in a way.

The wind whipped her hair across her face. She brushed it back, leaving a long strand across her cheek. On impulse, he reached out and eased it back for her. She made no attempt to stop him.

'I'd better go inside,' she said softly.

Footsteps rang along the side of the house. Brad appeared and, on seeing them, gave an exclamation of surprise. He joined them, standing alongside Natalie in a gesture of ownership. 'I wondered where you were. What are you doing out here?'

'Wishing I had a cigarette,' she said, with a note of tension.

'Are you coming back inside?'

'I will in a minute.'

Brad glanced at them both, unable to make up his mind. He put an arm around Natalie's waist and looked up. 'You're a friend of Marco's aren't you?'

'For my sins.'

Brad's smile looked fixed and unnatural in the light from the house. 'Funny bloke isn't he, Marco? I thought he was batting for the other side when I first met him.'

'Probably the voice. People tend to get the wrong impression.'

'Oh don't get me wrong. I get on well with the guy. Still not quite sure what he does for a living though.'

Brad's slick smile faded. In place of the customary handshake to establish a baseline, they stood apart. Nothing in common except Natalie.

Brad looked up at the house. 'Nice place he's got here. Must be worth a few quid. I could see myself living here. What do you reckon Natalie?'

'I'll see you inside,' she said and, without waiting, made her way along the path to the side of the house.

Brad took her place, standing feet apart and arms folded, the trace of amusement on his tanned face. 'Nice area this. We came here once a few years ago.'

'You and Natalie?'

'No!' Brad said, enjoying the intrigue. 'Crowd of us on a stag night. Good it was too. What I can remember of it anyway. You from round here?'

'That's right.'

'Local boy, eh? What d'you do?'

'I'm in property.'

'Maintenance?'

'Renovation, mainly.'

'Oh yeah. I know a few people in that line. Never easy though is it? Make a fortune, lose a fortune.'

'I make enough to get by.'

'Sure you do. What's your name by the way?'

'Peter.'

'Nice to meet you, Peter. I'm Brad …'

They shook hands in the shadow of the house. Brad's grip was firm, his gaze steady. The ritual lessened the tension between them, implying the beginnings of a friendship that would never happen.

Brad stood back and glanced at the house. 'Oh well, suppose I'd better get back. See what the good woman's up to. Married are you, Peter?'

'Feels like it sometimes.'

'The blonde lady not your wife then?'

'Not yet.'

Brad nodded agreeably. 'Funny things women aren't they? It's all plain sailing, then one day they give you that look. *What d'you mean you're going out again tonight!'*

They both laughed, a moments empathy in spite of their rivalry.

'Time to pack your bags when you hear that one.'

'You and me both. Nice talking to you, Peter.'

Brad strolled back along the side path, hands in the pockets of his durable Chinos. The house loomed in its soon-to-be-obsolete grandeur. The wooden balcony that looked out onto the sea, with a view worth more the land itself. Soon the place would be levelled, replaced by a more modern structure. But nothing else would change. The gulls would still dive-bomb the sand for food scraps, and the tourists would stake their claims amongst the windbreakers.

He went upstairs, unnoticed, and sat on the edge of the bath. Outdated porcelain and hospital white tiling closed in. The smell of damp and old furniture tainted the entire house, an aura of decay and emptiness. The previous tenants must have abandoned their memories and departed in a hurry. If you listened, you could hear whispers from spirits trapped in the woodwork, unable to leave. The voices and the music downstairs seemed disconnected – Marco's voice an entertainment in itself – broadcast throughout the house like propaganda.

The sense of isolation grew, of being alone with no-one to share the sadness. The moment outside with Natalie was gone.

He sat with the decay of the fine old house for as long as he could stand, before going downstairs to rejoin the party.

'Where have you been?' Claudia said.

'Staring at the porcelain.'

'What?'

'Forget it. Let's make a move.'

'What, now?'

'Yes now. If I stay here much longer I'll turn into a ghost like all the others up there.'

Claudia drove with both hands on the wheel, focused on the road ahead. Even with the change of scenery, his sense of loss persisted. The lights along the bay, reflected in the water like fireflies, deepened the feeling. He saw his whole life as a series of senseless ripples in the mainstream. Like the house in all its grandeur, standing for no purpose other than to be knocked down and levelled over. Traces, to be swept away in time.

'What do you think of Natalie?' she said.

'What's that, a trick question?'

'No. I'm just asking.'

'She's damaged goods.'

She glanced over at him. 'In what way?'

'In the way that people with issues always put the onus on someone else.'

'That's a bit heavy isn't it?'

'You asked.'

They passed the golf course, its undulating terrain rising from the night shadows. One more reminder of lost opportunity. Too busy to do the things you really wanted to do because you were tied to something you resented. Work. People. Especially people. In an ideal world you could pull a handle and flush the ones you didn't like down a long tube.

He glanced at Claudia's leg, positioned against the clutch pedal. Maybe if her leg was attached to someone else he might not be so restless. Its soft definition lured him, impossible to ignore beneath the folds of her skirt. He reached over and cupped the underside of her thigh, squeezing smooth and pliable flesh. 'Not while I'm driving!' she said. He ignored her and carried on, her token resistance an encouragement. The sense of loss began to fade and he gave in to the moment, Claudia's leg as worthy a cause as any for the time being.

Eleven

He met the old man in the Porterhouse. The afternoon drinkers looked liked permanent fixtures, strung out along the bar in varying poses. Roger the landlord, stood at the helm, steering the ship with a firm hand while the regular punters clung on like limpets. To get rid of them, Roger would have to run out of beer or declare a National Emergency. Then only the die-hards would remain, like partisans fighting a rearguard action. The old man preferred a corner table, with its wider view of the bar. For all his accumulated wealth and love of extravagance, the old man was at home in the Porterhouse. As comfortable among the three-card brag players and the domino kings as he was playing golf with the Director of the Nat West bank.

He stood at the bar, waiting to be served. The old boy seated next to him raised his pint in greeting and drank to the timeless routine. Even the bland face of the ticking clock had its place in the ceremony. Roger loomed, pulling a shapely pump handle with his impressive bulk. Framed photographs of his rugby playing youth hung behind him, to remind customers that in times of trouble he would take no prisoners. Roger's imposing size and blunt manner were ideally suited to the environment. From his side of the counter he could keep an eye on his flock, making sure nothing happened to upset the equilibrium.

'Pint of Boddie's, Peter?'

'When you're ready, Roger.'

Roger poured his pint, whistling tunelessly. He turned and leant an elbow on the bar. The old boy caught his eye and gave a respectful nod. He nodded back, enjoying the odd sense of privilege that went with the gesture. The drinking culture produced a natural hierarchy. You earned your status over time, watched closely by the old guard who'd seen and heard it all before. You proved your worth by holding court at the bar and standing your round, able to pontificate on any number of subjects, including politics and religion if the occasion demanded. In less discerning company you switched to default mode and talked about football.

He joined the old man at the corner table.

'Been in long?' he said.

'Just got here.'

'No Walter?'

'He's taking Jean shopping in town He'll join us later.'

'Rather him than me.'

The old man guarded his half drained pint, his folded *Times* and steel rimmed glasses nearby. The ritual wasn't quite the same for the old man, who had no great desire to socialise at the bar, and could please himself as to whose company he chose to keep. Everyone knew 'Big Jack' and everyone had some third-hand story to tell. Either the stunts he'd pulled when he was younger or the total disregard for convention that had characterised his business dealings down through the years.

He took a seat and raised his glass. 'Good health.'

The old man made a token gesture in response.

Sometimes it was hard going. Being the son of Big Jack was like standing in the shadow of a mountain. Whatever he managed to achieve would always be tainted in some way by the old man's influence. The Friday afternoon sessions in the Porterhouse served a purpose. He almost looked forward to the banter, the relaxed atmosphere, as a welcome end to the working week. The old man's empire was always top of the agenda. He accepted that. As true son and heir, he was an integral part of the plan, expected to take over at some point in the future. The fringe benefits couldn't be ignored. He owned property, ate out in swanky restaurants and drove a flash car, partly because of the old man. Being affiliated to a brand name meant that certain doors opened of their own accord. For that he should be grateful. Most of the time, he wasn't.

'How's the job going?' the old man said.

'Fine. Should be wrapped up in six weeks.'

'The old curtain-twitcher next door still playing up?'

'Sean had a gardening lesson from her the other day. She moaned about her driveway being blocked. Apart from that, she's been pretty quiet.'

The old man nodded thoughtfully. They could have been discussing the racing form at Newmarket, picking the winners from a brace of possibilities. 'Barry spoken to you about that corner plot in Iford?'

'Not yet.'

'Might be worth a look.'

'I'll talk to him tomorrow.'

'Don't leave it too long. I've had the nod and it's a good one. Claudia back yet?'

He gave the standard reply. Easier to discuss the business aspect of his and Claudia's relationship. The sale of her house. The work being carried out at his place. Any personal misgivings about their future together he kept to himself.

The old man took a drink and reflected. 'I don't understand why she wants to sell. She'd clear a grand a week easy, renting the place out.'

'She doesn't want to rent it out.'

'Guaranteed income and she wouldn't have to lift a finger.'

He felt compelled to defend Claudia in her absence. 'She wants to free up the equity. Pay off some of her debts. Anyway, I'm staying out of it. I've got enough problems.'

The old man said nothing. That was the way it went. The subject would be forgotten until it came up in a different context. Whether it was Claudia, Priory Road, or buying a new set of golf clubs, the old man had to have an opinion.

'Thought any more about Henley Park?' the old man said.

'Not yet.'

The old man rocked the base of his glass on the table and gazed out over the bar. 'I don't understand your resistance sometimes.'

'It's not resistance. I told you before, I'm busy with my own stuff. I need time to think about it.'

The old man grunted his disapproval. 'Well don't think too long, the roof goes on next April. Seen much of Derek?'

'Not for a while. Every time I go round there he finds me some job to do. He'd have me mowing the lawn if he thought he could get away with it.'

The old man chuckled to himself. Claudia's father came from the same stock, another self-made man with a clear vision of the future. Freemasonry gave them a step up in the world, an introduction to prestige and influence they might never have known. He'd turned down the offer to join once and the old man had never mentioned it again. That was his personal stand, his refusal to toe the line and do what was expected. The same stand his granddad had taken, many years before.

Walter joined them at the round table.

He listened to the two of them swap stories, absently peeling the top layer from a beer mat. Sunlight warmed the corner seat. The glint of real ale and raised glasses flashed around the bar. The old man pretended to plan his retirement, as he had been for the last ten years. A tour of all the finest golf courses and the best hotels. No more run-ins with the planning department and the Inland Revenue. Except the old man wouldn't get that far. The sunset view from a recliner, with an iced long glass and the nearby lapping of the pool, was for someone else. Retirement was a dirty word, something to be avoided for as long as possible.

Walter listened, with a raised eyebrow, used to dealing with the old man's flights of fancy. 'Sell-up and move to Spain, Jack. Nothing keeping you here, is there?'

The old man launched into a tirade against the tax man and the punitive laws that bound all businesses. Inevitably, the talk turned to politics and the criminal negligence of those in power. The old man's eyes bulged, his face red with effort. 'What's that lot done for this country, apart from open the floodgates and ruin the economy? Eh? I was better off twenty years ago.' Next it would be the Rivers of Blood speech and a diatribe on immigration. He switched to a harmless fantasy. Natalie on the beach. Natalie in his car. Natalie admiring the layout of his prized new kitchen.

Leanne came up in the conversation. The old man used her teen angst to illustrate a point he was making, aiming his comments at Walter, as if the two of them were alone at the table. 'Wearing dark glasses in the house she was. I said, you can take them off, sweetheart. Enough drama queens in this family already'

'Can't tell 'em though can you, Jack?'

'Listen. I've got five grandkids and none of them play me up like she does. We took her to Jersey last year and all she did was complain about the ferry on the way over. Never would've happened in my day.'

Walter nodded gravely. The old boy at the bar, raised his empty glass and signalled for a refill. Roger obliged, chatting away in a voice of richest mahogany. The place had a timeless appeal, a seductive charm in the murmur of voices and the stale smell of alcohol.

The old man finished his attack on Leanne with a sarcastic reference to Sylvia. He tried not to respond. Sylvia was one of the old man's favourite subjects, a good reason men should think seriously before settling down. Leanne was an awkward teenager, almost as hard to figure out as her mother, and equally in need of a firm hand. The old man warmed to his theme, almost as heated about Sylvia as he had been about the tax man. 'Never right that girl. Even at fifteen she was a pain in the arse. Climbing through his bedroom window at two o'clock in the morning and waking the whole house up. Trouble right from the word go.'

Walter sensed the danger and changed tack. 'Time marches on, eh Jack? Our Gwen goes up the aisle in a few weeks.'

The old man scoffed. 'I hope you've taken insurance out. Bernice's wedding cost me the best part of ten grand.'

'I don't begrudge the money, Jack. I just want to see her happy.'

'She ought to be at that price!' The old man thought for a moment. 'Sarah did us a favour though, getting married in Tenerife without telling anyone. Saved me a fortune.'

'Margaret must have loved that.'

'Oh I didn't hear the end of it for months, Walt. Months.'

Bernice's short and ill-fated marriage had upset the old man more than Sarah's sudden impulse had. But he never mentioned the money he'd spent bailing Bernice out from one financial disaster to the next. Perhaps, as the youngest, he thought she might benefit from the safety net he provided, and would somehow learn to manage her own life by osmosis.

Walter found the family subject amusing, able to draw on his own extensive experience for the sake of entertainment. 'No getting away from it really. We all end up paying one way or the other. How old's Leanne now, Peter?'

'Sixteen.'

'Difficult age that.'

'Does it get any better then, Walt?'

Walter laughed. 'That's debatable looking at my lot. How's the new place coming on?'

He ran through the various stages of development with a sense of pride. All the old services replaced with new. New electrics, central heating, kitchen and bathroom, when it was finally finished. He'd gone over the original budget, but the end result was worth it. Walter smiled at the thought of so much upheaval, his fourteen grandchildren giving him a sound grasp of economics.

'How's Claudia these days?' Walter said.

'She's fine.'

'When's the Big Day?'

'Next July, so they tell me. Haven't thought much about it to be honest, Walt. Been busy, you know?' But he had thought about it. Claudia made sure that he wouldn't forget, her subtle hints and coded references intended to move him swiftly up the aisle. He went along with her plans without ever committing himself, always vague when it came to specific dates and arrangements. But Claudia was way ahead of him in the planning department. One more trick she'd learned from her father.

Walter drained his pint and stood up. 'What you drinking, Peter?'

'Blackcurrant and soda, thanks, Walt.'

'What's that, a woman's drink?'

'I'm driving.'

Walter grinned slyly and turned to the old man. 'What you reckon of that then, Jack?'

The old man shook his head and said nothing.

Walter went to the bar. When he came back they would talk about golf. The new club Captain at Knighton Heath. The next playing holiday in Alicante. The dark wood panelling of the Porterhouse suited their long debates, like an old hunting lodge, dotted with trophies and photographs. A real man's retreat. The sun warmed corner reserved for the real ale drinkers and not a woman in sight.

He looked at the old man, with his fine head of white hair and spreading paunch. Good living might have taken its toll over the years but his mind was as sharp as ever. Always looking for the next angle, the next big deal.

'How's your blood pressure?' he said.

The old man shot him a warning glance. 'Same as it was the last time.'

'What did the doctor say?'

'Fuck all. That's how much they know. Seven years at medical school and the prick couldn't diagnose a sore throat. And I'll tell you this much …'

The old man railed against modern medicine and all its offshoots, another of his pet hates. He ignored the lecture and switched to his earlier fantasy. Natalie, standing at his bay window in a dark skirt and jacket. He came up behind her and whispered something provocative in her ear. She turned to embrace him, then Roger's booming laugh erupted at the bar and ruined the outcome.

'Claudia says you're not happy about Spain,' the old man said.

'I told her I'm busy. How many more times have I got to tell her?'

The old man shrugged. 'Up to you. I'd have thought the break would have done you good. Couple of weeks in the sun before we start Henley Park.'

'Before *you* start it.'

The old man ignored the challenge and drained his pint. The subject would come up again later. Like Claudia, the old man believed in persistence. Once you'd formed an idea in your head, everyone else should fall in line with it. Objections weren't given any credence, minor obstacles along the way.

His workload loomed, a huge, immovable object that blocked out the sun.

'What's the name of that painter who works for Barry?' he said.

The old man frowned. 'Which one?'

'Barry said he worked for you years ago. Some old boy, been off work with health problems.'

'Fred.'

'That's the one.'

The old man nodded slowly, the glimmer of affection for a former employee. 'I had old Fred with me years ago. He took over the contract at Drake's when I went in with your granddad. Why?'

He passed the incident off. The unfinished architraves could wait, hardly justifying the importance he was attaching to them. The place would get finished whether Fred came back or not. But the thought still rankled.

Walter came back and set the drinks down. The absent painter was forgotten. The talk resumed as before – families, and the endless scenarios that went with them. Walter's hypnotic voice rose above the general chatter, slow and methodical like his character. The old man always said that if a fire broke out, Walter would be the last to leave the building. Their talk reminded him of afternoons along the Quay. Sat outside the Nelson as a kid, with a coke and a bag of crisps, listening to the old man swap stories with his cronies. He'd grown up with it. The gospel according to Jack Calliet. All the wheeling and dealing that went with the territory and God help anyone who stood in his way. Nothing fazed the old man. He suffered setbacks and came back stronger. Even the allegations of exploitation in the nineties had been dropped through lack of evidence. Contractors had been charging up to three times the day rate paid to workers building a new leisure complex. The old man denied any involvement and walked away. Then there were claims of a different nature. The old man's womanising. Scandalous incidents, hushed up around the dinner table that reverberated for years to come.

The bar filled up with more seasoned real ale drinkers. Sammy came over to pay his respects to the old man. Sammy's obvious deterioration saddened him, an aura of slow decay brought on by decades of heavy drinking. The old man always brought out the trouper in Sammy, the two of them more like mates than former business associates. The best bricklayer foreman Big Jack ever had, even if the licensing hours had cut down his output and robbed him of his true potential.

He finished his blackcurrant and soda and stood up. Sammy couldn't let him leave without a good-natured ribbing. 'Hey, Peter? That you I saw driving a Ferrari up the M27 the other day?'

'Must have been someone else, Sammy.'

'Your old man must be paying you some wages these days, my son.'

'Not me, Sammy, I'm on a retainer.'

Sammy's leathery face creased in laughter as he took the vacant seat next to Walter. The three wise monkeys, ready to put the world to rights for as long as the ale flowed.

He sat in the car and thought about Spain, the future. The sun had baked the interior, scorching the leather seats. A mean-looking traffic warden passed, and stopped to note his registration number. The local council must have run training schools to turn them out. Even the man's posture made him a target. The uniform. The deliberate turning of the pages of the notebook. Grown men, getting even for being bullied at school.

The traffic warden moved leisurely on down the High Street.

A woman in a dark trouser suit crossed in front of the car. He followed the perfect crease of her trousers as she strolled past the shop fronts to vanish in a doorway. He looked sharp left and a honey-blonde took on the same role, passing the car in a flurry of steps, her breasts jigging in a thin white blouse. The scornful look she gave him increased his desire tenfold, a feeling made worse in the heat. He watched her disappear among the shoppers and ached with a futile sense of loss.

He replayed the earlier fantasy, improvising a telephone conversation between them. This time they were lovers. *'Hi, Natalie – it's me. I was just wondering. Maybe we could meet up and spend a few hours between the sheets.'* The traffic warden moved further down the High Street. The honey-blonde had gone forever. Natalie, no more than a frustrated daydream for someone with nothing better to do. Life – a long series of disappointments and lost opportunities. Falsifying tax returns and hoarding cash in shoe boxes like a miser. Dreaming of earning more than you could ever spend in one lifetime, then finding out you had cancer, or your wife had left you for the bloke next door. What you thought you wanted all along turned out to be a burden. One more rock in the backpack as you trudged further uphill.

He turned on the ignition.

Vorsprung durch Technik at its reassuring best. 3.2 litres of finely tuned engine. 255 watts of sublime sound at concert pitch. Money couldn't bring happiness, but it sure beat sitting in the underpass, rattling a tin at the hard of hearing.

Twelve

He added the tomatoes, stirred in the mixed herbs and covered the pan. The extractor fan roared, one more design fault to complain about. He shouted above the television, 'You want garlic bread with this or not?'

No answer.

He stirred the sauce and called out again, burning his fingers on the saucepan handle.

She appeared in the doorway, arms folded. 'What's all the noise for?'

'I called you about three hours ago.'

'I was watching something on the telly, what's the matter?'

'I just burnt my hand on *that* fucking thing!' She tittered behind his back. He turned to face her, waving a large wooden spoon. 'I'm glad you think it's so funny.'

'Sorry!' she said, grinning inanely.

'Grate some Parmesan, if you want something useful to do.'

She slipped behind him, graceful in her bare feet, and began humming an irritating tune at the worktop.

'I suppose that's what comes of being a man,' she said airily.

'What's that got to do with anything?'

'Multi-tasking. It's a recognised fact. Men are hopeless at it.'

'Cook the dinner yourself in a minute.'

They ate in the front room, with trays balanced on laps and the television muted. Before he could sample his own cooking, she began to complain. The lack of furniture. The undercooked spaghetti. The glazed salt and pepper pots that blocked-up whenever she tried to use them. He ignored her ramblings and focused on the silent TV screen.

'Marco said he'd find us a table,' she said, between mouthfuls. 'He knows someone in the pine business, apparently. I told him we were looking for a six-seater with matching chairs. It would go perfectly in the alcove.'

'So would a Sherman tank.'

She put down her cutlery, imploring him with a long look. 'We can't go on like this, can we?'

'Like what?'

'Eating on trays. I don't mind the odd takeaway, but this is ridiculous.' She wound a coil of spaghetti onto her spoon and eyed him carefully, the kitchen roll tucked into her top like a cravat. He watched the screen and waited for her next instalment. She didn't keep him waiting long. 'I saw a lovely dinner set in Debenhams the other day. I thought it could be a kind of house-warming gift from me. Oh, and I saw this lovely rug in the arcade. It had a kind of mosaic pattern with a wine-coloured border. When we next go into town...'

The newsreader began a slow seduction for his benefit, her rouged mouth forming suggestive phrases without a sound. Her smile, set in her perfectly sculpted model's face, looked strained and unnatural. She had the stress of the lights to put up with. The heat of the cameras. The fact that she had to look good at 6 pm every night, no matter how she was feeling.

'Peter!

He looked up, the spell broken.

'I was talking to you.'

'What now?'

'I said wooden floors look nice, but they're cold in the winter. I know you like the wood and it's your place and everything, but a rug would finish the room off nicely. What do you think?'

'Can I eat this first before I choke on it?'

She slumped back in the chair, defeated for the moment.

The newsreader raised a pencilled eyebrow, silent witness to his ongoing dilemma. She shuffled the papers on her desk with a look of serene intelligence, her smile more natural now that the show was coming to an end. He imagined undoing the buttons on her stiff red jacket and whispering lewd suggestions in her perfectly formed ear.

'Why don't you get a job on the telly?' he said.

'Doing what?'

'Hosting a chat show. They could call it 'Claudia's Half-hour.' You could invite celebrities on to tell you all about their sex lives.' She made a sour face at him above her spaghetti. 'Then, when you got bored with that, you could find out whether they preferred shopping at Waitrose or Marks and Spencer. Could be a sort of filler between the news and Coronation Street.'

'Oh you're so funny.'

'They could even film it round here. Use this place as a backdrop.'

'Not in your bedroom they couldn't. If it wasn't for me, you wouldn't even have clean sheets on the bed!'

He admired the room from the comfort of a bean bag. An odd mixture of old and new. Church candles flickered on the coffee table, creating a warm and mellow ambience. Wood from a four-hundred year old mill framed the mirror. Wall-mounted Pioneer speakers looked down in carbon black. Odd pieces like the stereo unit and the pine bookcase might have always been there, like the polished floor boards that reflected the lamplight. With all the boxes unpacked and the paint tins stacked outside, the place looked more like home. His home – until the situation changed. Until then Claudia was still only an invited guest.

'Fancy a weekend in Rome in September?' she said, scanning a brochure.

'No I don't.'

'Just a thought. I'm looking forward to Spain though. At least we'll get to spend some quality time together.'

'Who said I was going to Spain?'

'Oh come on. You could at least think about it.'

'I'm up to my ears in work Claudia. Doesn't that mean anything to you?'

'But the break would do you good. Think about it. You could play as much golf as you like.'

He aimed the remote control at her and pressed the mute button repeatedly to shut her up. She missed the joke and carried on talking. The overspill from her working day. Her ongoing plans to rearrange his life and his schedule. Part of him thrived on the attention, her voice waylaying him in every room with some new concept or other. The one constant in his life that he might feel lost without. Her comment about the bed linen had been partly true. She changed everything. Now she was planning six-seater tables and dinner sets, rugs to cover the bare boards because *she* didn't like them.

They cleared the kitchen together. She managed to load the dishwasher without breaking anything, and hovered at the worktop wiping down the surface. She talked about Leanne, the possibility of inviting her round one night.

'What for?'

'Because you haven't seen her for a while.'

'The last time I saw Leanne, she told me to fuck off.'

'But she doesn't mean it though, does she?'

He laughed bitterly. 'No, of course not. Telling someone to fuck off is a term of endearment really.'

She carried on polishing the surface, oblivious. Her sudden interest in Leanne's well being intrigued him, arousing his suspicions. 'I know what all this is about,' he said. 'You've been talking to my mother again.'

She looked up, perplexed. 'No I haven't.'

'Don't lie to me. When was the last time you played peacemaker between me and Leanne?'

'I just thought it might be nice if we could all spend some time together, that's all.'

'You mean my mum decided. Like she decided we were all going to Spain together last year. She's another one. Can't keep her nose out of other people's business.'

She sighed heavily and turned back to the worktop. 'Don't bother then. She's your daughter. It's not down to me to patch things up between you.'

Her sad moon face had the desired effect. He put his arms around her and squeezed, hugging her close to him. He kissed the tip of her nose gently. 'You organise it if it means that much to you.'

She brightened, visibly. 'Really? When for?'

'Next Christmas, preferably.'

She pulled a face and shrugged him off. But he accepted the idea in theory. She might even achieve the impossible and reunite him with Leanne, playing mediator while he chose the music and made the drinks. The last and only time Leanne had called, the place had been swamped in dust sheets. One quick, morose look round and she was gone, conning ten pounds out of him on the way out, leaving him wondering why he gave in to her so easily.

He put on a dance compilation CD and sprawled out on the bean bag. Claudia sat dejected in the leather armchair, resentful at the music and the lack of furniture. He pulled faces at her from the floor, to amuse himself, mocking her sullen opposition.

'So how did the conference go?' he said.

'I told you how it went. You never listen.'

'So tell me again.'

'I made a few new contacts. Made use of the sauna and gym in the hotel.'

'And you call that working?'

'You don't have a clue. I have to be really focused. We have new marketing campaigns coming up all the time and if my selling skills aren't up to it, it shows.'

'Any good looking doctors there?'

'No! What would you care anyway? You couldn't even be bothered to call me the whole time I was up there.'

He wondered how much of what she told him was the truth. Whether her numerous trips away were the tedious business events she claimed them to be, or if there were other diversions to keep her occupied. He recalled an incident she'd told him about, featuring some nameless male rep from a different company. 'What about that guy who tried it on with you the last time? Was he there?'

'What guy?'

'The one who chatted you up at the bar. You told me about him.'

'No-one tried to chat me up,' she said sharply. 'A group of us went out for a meal on the first night. The second night I stayed in the hotel. I was so tired I was in bed by nine o'clock.'

'What, on your own?'

'Oh shut up!'

He felt only a marginal interest in the male rep and his failed attempt in some lonely hotel corridor. Claudia must have been telling him the truth. Her pretty face wasn't suited to dishonesty. The interrogation process amused him in an underhand way. He enjoyed her reactions, even if they were predictable, and the ease with which he wore down her defences.

She fixed him with a quizzical, but steady gaze. 'Anyway, it's not all about me. What were *you* doing the other night?'

'What night?'

'At Marco's. You spent all that time outside, talking to Natalie.'

'It wasn't that long.'

'What were you talking about?'

'She said she was dying for a cigarette. She gave up six weeks ago apparently, and now she's running people over in Asda car park because of the stress.'

'And that was it?'

'Yes, Claudia. That was it.'

She said nothing, the lines on her forehead deepening. Any doubts she might have had could always be offset by the investment she'd made in their future. The sale of her house and her decision to move in with him were proof of her ongoing commitment and not something to be taken lightly. But she seemed distracted, unconvinced. She buried herself in a magazine while he flipped aimlessly through the television channels. Dolphins swimming alongside a boat. A fat, bearded man wearing a baseball cap, chewing gum and glaring at the camera. Two dour looking pundits debating some obscure football match. Over five hundred channels to choose from and only a three second span of attention.

At least these people were more bearable with the sound off.

Sometimes he resented her for no real reason. Sometimes her genuine, home-spun niceness stretched his nerves and he wanted an argument. The things that sent him into a homicidal rage, barely registered with her. Finding his car clamped. Losing his wallet in the cinema. These things were beyond his control. The self-help books he read on the subject failed to make an impact. Meditation tapes were fine until you fell asleep in the armchair and woke up four hours later, wondering why all the lights were on. According to Claudia, there was no point in having a heart attack over trivialities. That was how different they both were. But the opposing forces that threatened to pull them apart, somehow kept them together. Much as he hated to admit it, he missed her when she was gone longer than a few days. Even her heels over the bare boards left a strange psychic imprint.

'Funny how certain people end up together, isn't it?' he said.

'Like who – us?'

'Simon and his anorexic girlfriend. She must have eaten three prawns and a lettuce leaf all night.'

'Don't be so horrible.'

'Just an observation, that's all.'

Simon and his malnourished girlfriend weren't all that important. He had better things to think about. Natalie's lonely vigil by the sea increasingly obsessed him. When Brad had turned up on the scene, she'd seemed awkward and defensive. The two of them didn't look comfortable together. Not like they had been in the restaurant earlier.

'Was Simon like that at school?' she said.

'What – so far up his own arse he couldn't see daylight?' He pictured Simon, with his shirt hanging out and a finger up his nose, being screamed at by Caldwell, the History teacher. Claudia only knew his more recent incarnation, as financial guru and resident know-it-all. Ask Simon a question on any subject and he had to come up with an answer. His classroom recollections amused him for a moment. Secondary school had been a shock to the system from the relative innocence of First school. His introduction to a new code of conduct. The first time he'd witnessed a teacher assaulted by a pupil. The place was like a mini penitentiary, turning out hardened criminals and future malcontents by the dozen.

'Was Simon a friend of James?' she said.

He looked up, his recollections disturbed. 'Sort of. Why?'

She nodded vaguely. 'I just wondered.'

James had a rare gift. He stood up one day and recited a poem he had written to a spellbound class. His talent had been obvious from an early age. But the teachers found him disruptive and hard to deal with. James's moods could affect the entire lesson. Some days he was a real live-wire, entertaining the class with brilliant impersonations of some luckless member of staff. When he was down, he sat in long, brooding silences, never smiling, haunted by some inner turmoil he could never speak of.

'Break out the strawberry pavlova,' he said, ending the conversation. 'We can work off the calories later.'

They ate in silence, spoons scraping bowls in unison. Food and sex, the two most effective cures for boredom known to man. The crushed meringue melted with the double cream, a temporary heaven that filled the senses and left a craving for more.

She ran her spoon around her bowl distractedly. 'What was James like at school?'

'Claudia – '

'I know. I know. You don't like talking about it.' She bit down on her lip. 'I just feel that we should sometimes. It would help me to understand more.'

'There's nothing to talk about.'

She sat forward eagerly. 'But there is though. How can you just forget about a thing like that? I know how much it eats you up inside. Don't you trust me?'

'It's got nothing to do with trust.'

'So what is it then? Why won't you talk to me?'

'We've been through this before. I've got nothing more to say on the subject, OK?'

He walked her out to her car. She was leaving early for work the next morning and needed her own bed. He decided that there was really nothing wrong with her hips, her backside, or any other feature she was so concerned about. Poor Claudia. She only wanted what any normal young woman wanted. To balance a career with her maternal instincts, and all to the ticking of the biological clock. Perhaps they were hopelessly incompatible, one more couple destined for the divorce courts. To make it work in the long run, you needed a shared vision, or you ended up living separate lives in the same room.

She put her arms around his shoulders and gazed up at him. 'I love you, baby.'

'I love you too.'

She forced a smile. 'I just feel like I'm losing you sometimes.'

'You're not losing me. There's just things I can't talk about. You know that.'

He felt bad about the offhand way he treated her. But the guilt was worse. Thinking about James brought back the same questions. How could he have changed what had happened and would it have made any difference to the final outcome?

He kissed Claudia goodbye through the open window, and watched her drive off. Maybe she was the answer to his ongoing problems. He could settle for a comfortable life in the slow lane, watching the grass grow outside the window. She could cook and clean and take care of his every need.

Except one.

Every time he looked in the mirror he saw someone he didn't particularly like. He couldn't talk about it. Not to Claudia or anyone else. It sat inside him, growing, day after day. When James had died, a part of him had died also. He couldn't change it. He couldn't go back and say he was sorry. Then there were those who wouldn't let him forget. He saw them in bars, in the street, in supermarket queues, when he least expected it. They reminded him of his part in the event. Their veiled looks said it all. James had been distraught, confused at all the rumours going round. 'Please tell me it's not true, Peter.' But it was true. By the time it all came out, it was too late. James couldn't live with the truth. He was left behind to live with the consequences.

Thirteen

'Hi, it's me!'

From the tone, he took it that they were back on friendly terms again.

'Listen, honey, I'm driving. Can I call you back?'

He pulled into the next lay-by and turned off the ignition. White heat reflected back from passing cars. 33 degrees and the hottest day of the year, according to the weatherman. He rang the number and waited.

She picked up the thread with ease, pleasant and upbeat, the conversation delaying the inevitable request that would come sooner or later. But the deception didn't bother him. She was safe and well and that was all that mattered.

'I hear you're going to Barcelona,' he said.

'That's not until September.'

'But you need the funding for it, right?'

'That's not why I called you.'

He laughed. 'Course not. You called to see how I was because you missed me so much.'

'Yeah right! Can you take me to Bristol on Friday afternoon?'

'What for?'

'I'm staying at Nan's for the weekend.'

He thought about the long drive. The inevitable arguments about the crowd she hung about with when she was up there. 'How are you getting back?'

'Mum's picking me up.'

'Why can't she take you as well?'

'She's working. Is that a problem?'

'Kind of, yeah.'

'Why?'

Her keen sense of outrage had an immediate effect on his morale. He fought against the impulse to give in too easily. 'Some of us have to earn a living, Leanne. It doesn't just drop into your lap while you're driving, you know?'

'Can you do it or not?'

'I'll think about it. How's college?'

'Fine. Look I've really gotta go. Call me later.'

'Leanne – '

'Sorry, gotta go!'

He sat with the lead blanket of heat. Blinding sun spots lit the stretch of dual-carriageway as traffic flashed by. Everyone racing to their next destination. As you got older, life sped by. All the old folk would tell you. In order to catch up you had to increase the pace or miss out altogether. To escape the sheer insanity of it all, you had to seek out mindless diversions to keep you entertained. Television in every room. Mobile phones never more than an arms length away. Even driving, you could choose to waive your privacy and take a call hands-free while you cruised the highways between destinations. Everyone suffering the same disease. The desperate attempt to connect yourself to something illusory while the clock ticked down the hours and minutes of your precious life.

Now Bristol. Three hours with Leanne, avoiding subjects neither of them felt comfortable enough to deal with. Her, staring through the window and toying with her hair while he focused on the road ahead, agonising over the next line. And there to greet them at the end of the journey – Sylvia's mother. Another grim reminder of the past. The old witch might even invite him in and they could ignore all the terrible things he'd said to her. Bitter exchanges that could never be forgotten. As responsible adults, they tried to get on for the sake of the child. But the past kept coming up, repeatedly.

Marco called, his rich baritone filling the car's interior like a public address system. He listened on hands free, cruising at ninety in three lanes of traffic. Marco never called to discuss the weather. There was always an ulterior motive.

'Where are you now?' Marco said.

'On the M27 just past Cadnam roundabout.'

'What's the name of that mechanic Tim knows?'

'Why?'

'Natalie's car's broken down.'

The rest of the day took on an entirely different meaning. Limitless possibilities opened up before him.

'Peter?'

'I heard you. What's she driving?'

'A Peugeot I think.'

'What year?'

'How the fuck do I know? She just needs a mechanic and I said you might know someone. Can you help or not?'

'Text me her number. I'll see what I can do.'

Marco changed his tone. 'She'll be eternally grateful, you know.'

'Yeah, well I'm not in the habit of doing favours for people I don't know. Just as long as she knows that.'

'What – helping defenceless women in their hour of need? Come on, Peter, you love it. Look upon it as your chance to redeem yourself in her eyes.'

'Text me her number and go wind someone else up.'

'Toodle-pip. Happy hunting, darling!'

He parked the car at the cricket pavilion and found the nearest vacant bench. Traffic droned by on the main road. A boy rode a bike across the middle of the green.

He stared at the number Marco had sent. All he had to do was make a simple phone call, but even the thought made him sick with nerves. By making the call he would cross the invisible line and commit himself further. There seemed no way back. Forces beyond his control compelled him to take action.

He wiped the sweat from his forehead and pressed the call button.

Her prompt answer quickened his heart rate.

'Natalie?'

'Who's that?'

'Peter.'

Silence. Traffic and voices merged in the background.

'You alright to talk?' he said.

'How did you get my number?'

'Marco gave it to me. He said you were looking for a mechanic.'

Silence. He thought he could hear her disapproval. She surprised him, sounding reasonable and upbeat. 'Listen, it's a bit awkward right now. Can I call you back?'

'Sure.'

She hung up.

He sat back in the sun and enjoyed the scenery. An elderly woman passed and remarked on the weather. Her silky black Labrador sauntered ahead, nose to the ground, pausing here and there to pick up some previous spoor. The kid with the bike came back, standing up out of the saddle and throwing the frame from side to side, grinding out each pedal stroke with excessive effort.

He weighed the phone in the palm of his hand, reflecting on the moment while the heat bore down. Too late to back out now. The line had been crossed. Like a declaration of war, where one side makes the initial challenge then sits back to await the response.

His first impressions of Natalie had changed. Her cold exterior was probably due to nervousness. Marco was right. She didn't know anyone locally and would be grateful for any help she could get. The knowledge increased his chances, made her vulnerable, more open to manipulation if he chose to take advantage. He knew he was fooling himself. Obsession was a chemical reaction that you had no control over. You met some woman, nearly always a stranger, and convinced yourself that she was the one. The obsession took over. You became a slave to the impulse, unable to eat, sleep, or think straight until the two of you were together. Then, when it was too late, you found out she was just like all the others. Someone to argue with about the gas bill when you came home from the pub.

Leanne gave him something else to think about. The chance to improve relations between them in a neutral setting. He could buy her lunch and they could talk about her college life in awkward snatches. Maybe if he'd been around more when she was younger things would be different. She would have changed her attitude towards him, her habit of bringing up past events that he could barely remember and using them as fuel for her latest resentment. The time he'd promised to take her to Disneyland for her tenth birthday. His refusal to buy her a laptop because she wouldn't get a part-time job. These lapses bothered her in ways that he couldn't understand. He did his best to repair the damage but it never seemed to work out. As a child she'd been tactile and affectionate, always looking forward to the days he'd taken her out. Now she treated him as a convenience, someone to finance her school trips and chauffeur her around when no-one else was available. He referred to himself as a cashpoint machine and she reacted with indignation. But the comparison served to highlight the huge gulf of understanding between them. Perhaps it was a phase she was going through. The usual teenage rebellion. One day she would look up and smile when he walked in the room, instead of the caustic silence he usually met with.

The phone rang as he came out of a newsagents.

Natalie's businesslike voice shocked him from his reverie. 'Sorry about this afternoon,' she said. 'You caught me at a bad time. I was about to get on a bus.'

'How're you finding public transport?'

'More reliable than my car is at the moment, that's for sure.'

'Marco said you were looking for a mechanic.'

'That's right. Do you know someone?'

'I might do,' he said evasively and waited for her response. She said nothing. Conscious of the previous tension between them, he changed his tone. 'What is it?'

'Sorry?'

'Your car. What make is it?'

She gave him a brief history of the car; the year, the model, the dealer she had bought it from in Greenwich and how much she had paid for it. From the details he worked out her average income, her tax bracket, and the type of accommodation she was likely to live in.

'Leave it with me and I'll sort something out,' he said.

'Is that a definite?'

'Absolutely.'

'You won't let me down will you? I need it for work and it's messed up my schedule already.

'I won't let you down, Natalie.'

'If I don't hear from you tomorrow I'll get someone out the Yellow Pages.'

He laughed.

'I'm serious,' she said.

'Have you always been so upfront?'

'Not always. But sometimes it's the only way to get things done. Call me tomorrow.'

He thought about the implications. All he had to do was say no. Instead he'd given in to the cool seduction of her educated voice. Finding a mechanic for her would turn into a personal quest. His intentions – perhaps not so obvious to her – were perfectly clear in his troubled mind. He ought to sit her down in some quiet corner and explain them in detail. *'Look Natalie – I'm not the person you think I am. I really don't care too much about your car or your job or how many spoonfuls of sugar you have on your breakfast cereal. I just like playing games I can't win.'*

He made a phone call.

'Hey, Tim – what was the name of that guy you knew who worked for Vauxhall?'

Fourteen

The need to win must have come from somewhere. His grandmother perhaps, an above average tennis player in her time. Even old Reg, his great, great grandfather, hanging on the wall in his front room, handy at shove-halfpenny and potting the black. Whispered commandments learned as a child, sowing the seeds for future discontent. *Always be the best that you can be. Give a hundred percent in all that you do. Never, never give in.* The need to win was a neurosis. No matter how many hours you put in on the practise ground, there would always be a challenger to the crown. Then you had to bow out, and sit out your retirement as a spectator. It was only a game, they told you. But the people who spouted this nonsense had never sunk the perfect putt on a tough par four after three and a half hours in the pouring rain.

Tim understood. Athletics trophies lined Tim's mantelpiece. Junior badminton star five years running. County long jump record holder for under-16s. Simon might have beaten Tim on the squash court, but only because of the recurring groin strain that hampered his game. Like all true competitors, Tim had a heightened concept of failure and did what he could to erase any doubts from his mind. Golf seemed a natural progression, a way of testing his abilities without breaking a sweat.

They lined up at the First.

He miss-hit the tee shot thinking about Claudia. Tim recognised his frustration and tried to be diplomatic, referring to an earlier conversation they'd had. 'So what're you looking for – a diversion? Something to break up the monotony?'

'Right now I don't know what I'm looking for.'

'How does Claudia see it?'

'She's halfway up the aisle already.'

'That's what I thought. I got the feeling you'd had enough the last time I last spoke to you.'

He felt a stab of remorse for the seeds of disloyalty. 'Claudia's not the problem really. I'm just not sure I want her moving in with me. Not yet anyway.'

Golf – the perfect diversion. A haven for the terminally restless, complete with great landscaping and a well-stocked bar. Nothing quite like the hours spent checking your body position to the ball and endlessly perfecting your swing. Put a golf course near an airport terminal and you could barely hear the big birds coming in to land. Even on a desolate headland, the sense of contentment is the same. The big hitters ignore the local gale-force warnings, shrug on warmer clothing and head stubbornly for the First tee.

Walter gave him his first lessons at the age of twelve, patiently taking the time to correct his faults, stressing the importance of correct stance and balance. The old man was too impatient, resenting the attention given a mere boy, even if it was his own son. Walter said he was a natural. With hard work and dedication, he could progress to a 28 handicap and play from the men's tee area. But the after school club and Jim Kershaw's weekend academy proved too intensive. He didn't respond well to the discipline and dropped out after six months. His passion remained undiminished. He could still recall the first time he broke 100 on the course. The sense of achievement stayed with him for weeks after.

Then he discovered women and his dedication to the game changed for good.

Tim was upbeat and positive, having secured a lucrative deal with a new company, advising and implementing strategies. The work suited Tim's competitive nature. 'It's all about marketing. You've got to be able to sell the product, right? Most businesses fold because they don't research the market. I see it all the time.' But Tim's domestic troubles were never far from the surface. Like most women, Dianne couldn't see the link between hard work and personal sacrifice. The home front had to come first. Tim saw it differently. 'I work a six day week and all I get is hassle. She wants me to spend more time with the kids. I can't do it, Peter.'

'What happened to that woman who phoned the house?'

'She's history.'

'Dianne didn't find out then?'

'Not exactly. She found a Travelodge receipt in the glove compartment, though. I didn't even know it was in there.'

He mused on the pitfalls of infidelity. 'They say women pick up on subtle signals.'

'Sure they do. Lipstick round the end of your cock, that's a dead giveaway.' Tim's amusement was short lived. His tone changed. 'Dianne's not stupid. She knows what goes on out there in the big bad world.'

Tim lined up his shot. The green lay out of sight some four hundred yards away, hidden by the bend in the fairway. The shot went wide.

'Truth is I got careless. I can't explain it. It was almost as if I wanted to get caught. Shake her up a bit, you know? We've been married ten years this

September. Ten years. Sometimes we can't find two words to say to each other.'

'You could try Relate.'

'Fuck that. Two weeks in Lanzarote will do the same job. Least I'll get a sun tan out of it.'

Two female golfers appeared from the spur and began strolling towards the Ninth, pulling their trolleys behind them. One wore tight breeches over wide, bulbous hips.

Tim sucked in his breath. 'Jesus! Imagine that on top of you. You'd have to stop and come up for air every five seconds.'

'Rather you than me.'

'Don't knock it. The big ones are usually grateful for the attention.'

'I've never gone for big women, personally.'

'Maybe you need to expand your horizons a bit then. Get up the K Club one night and pull a real monster. Beats surfing the porn channels on a Friday night, that's for sure.' The two women crossed the valley beyond the Ninth. Tim watched their slow progress and gave a low whistle. 'Instant gratification, whichever way you look at it. Talking of which – what's happening with that school teacher you were telling me about?'

'She's an art therapist.'

'Whatever. Had a result yet?'

'I helped get her car fixed, that's all. There's nothing going on between us.'

Tim frowned at him. 'Really? So what are you doing, working on commission, or what?'

He tried to be vague, ignoring the impact Natalie had made on him from their first meeting. The deepening of their intimacy at Marco's that couldn't be explained. He trotted out the standard denial, 'She's not my type. Too much like hard work,' leaving out the finer details, the fact that she'd been a guest at James's wedding.

'Is she married?' Tim said.

'She's with some web-designer guy, but it's not serious.'

'That's what they all say. Remember that dancer I was seeing from Harlequin's? Her boyfriend worked the door on a Saturday night and she forgot to tell me about it. Silly bitch. Could've got my head kicked-in.'

The club scene had its downside. You came home at three o'clock one morning to find your wife waiting in the dark with an ultimatum. Either you changed your ways or you packed your bags and left. Tim's marriage had survived, but not without scars. Dianne was willing to put up with Tim's behaviour for the sake of the children. Sylvia hadn't been so lenient and took *his* indiscretions to the divorce court.

He played a better drive on the Eighth, another four hundred yard par four. For one split-second, he stayed with the shot. The sublime moment where the outside world fades away and only the precision-wound ball exists, rising high, its flight obscured by the sun. The ball dropped far ahead on the fairway, and the sublime moment ended. Worldly concerns crowded back in. Tim's serial infidelity. His own ongoing restlessness. Claudia's heels across the polished floorboards, her loving arms around him like a strait jacket.

They strolled towards the pin, the smooth circle of green unveiled in the valley below. He had a sudden flashback. Her eager mouth on the dingy stairwell. Their frantic efforts to remove articles of clothing soaked in the rain. The images nagged at him, demanding a hearing.

'I found a pair of Zoe's socks in my washing the other day.'

'Yeah? Could have been a lot worse. When was the last time you saw her?'

'Weeks ago.'

'How did you manage to keep it quiet for so long with her big mouth?'

'I always made sure she had something in it.'

Tim laughed. 'Can't argue with that. Her mum can't have taken too kindly to it though. All those lifts you were giving her daughter.'

Zoe's mother had made all the advances. He met her in the K Club one night and she took him back to her three bed semi. Sex was athletic in spite of the amount they'd both drunk, but it was clear at the outset they had nothing else in common. He took her out a few times because she asked him and because he had nothing better to do. Then they started arguing. She accused him of looking at other women when they were out. She clearly thrived on the attention she got from other men but this he was supposed to ignore. He saw the liaison for what it was. She was a good looking, forty- something divorcee, out to make up for lost time. He was ten years younger and looking for a deeper connection. They would have drifted apart anyway. Then she introduced him to Zoe.

'Ever make a move on Helen?' Tim said.

'No!'

'I just wondered.'

'She's with Raul. I wouldn't go there.'

'Course not,' Tim said, grinning. 'I always wondered what the score was with those two. They're always so fucking happy together. Like they're about to do a centrespread for *Hello*.'

He saw Raul, grinning for the camera, the suave romantic with his gold tooth and neat goatee, a protective arm around Helen's shoulder. Some people could live like that without a qualm, devoted entirely to each other. The rest of the population got bored after six months and looked for a different pasture to graze in.

Tim lined himself up at the Ninth.

The moment before the strike produces a profound concentration – even from the sidelines. The impact shifts the point of focus to the flight of the ball. Tim's shot rose high and touched down on the fairway, left of the dog-leg.

'So will you do the decent thing?' Tim said.

'With who?'

'Claudia.'

'She'll have to catch me first.'

Tim sheathed his driver. 'You could always emigrate, like Simon's brother. You wouldn't last five minutes though. You'd miss the bacon and eggs and the country pubs on a Sunday afternoon.'

Play ended with Tim one-up. In the long walk from the green to the clubhouse, he went over the flaws in his performance. Tim was a reasonably good loser, given his sporting background, able to rise above any loss of form with dignity intact. He, on the other hand, took any defeat personally, a weakness of character that couldn't be tolerated. He began to dissect his game, a natural defence mechanism to pre-empt criticism from outside.

Tim waved away his complaints with a genial hand. 'You've obviously got a lot going on. Can't always be on form can you?'

'I'm just out of practice.'

'Get the clubs out more often then. Stop chasing destitute school teachers round in your spare time.'

The clubhouse always had the last word. You sat with your pint and debated the state of play, or simply chose another subject to avoid the reminder. The silverware shone in the glass cabinet above the bar, a mark of excellence, setting standards and dividing the field. The trophies reminded the amateurs of their shortcomings. With hard work and a certain amount of luck, you might aspire to a better handicap. But the gap would always be there. The definitive gap between winning and losing. Success and failure. The old man's gold coloured Bentley had been a symbol of success in the late 80s. An impressive reminder to his critics of his acquired status. The old man liked to drive it down the High Street on a Saturday afternoon and wave at people he knew. *'Just to wind-up all those miserable fuckers who said I'd never make it!'* The trick was to enjoy success when it happened. Most people were too wrapped up in what could have been to appreciate what they had. Success was always relative to your living conditions. According to the experts, having your basic needs met put you in the elite bracket. Three square meals a day, clothes on your back and a roof over your head. For most people this was never enough.

Tim sat with his pint and the winner's view of the quiet bar. They drank to success, past and present. As you got older, the past took on a special significance. You could look back and see where you went wrong and the huge neon signposts that you'd missed along the way.

The story of the girls from Harlequin's came up – a parade of faces across a blurred cinema screen. The Beautiful people had all moved on to play the game somewhere else. Even the hardcore got married and had kids. Easy to give up on the dream and fade away, lose yourself in a monotonous job and stifling commitments.

Tim recalled the petite cloakroom girl from The Zone with mixed feelings. 'She must have been seeing half the town behind my back. I was the last to know. Erica took me to one side and had a quiet word with me one night. I was gutted.'

He smiled to himself. 'Erica would have known, she's like the Oracle.'

'Christmas time it was. I even missed the office party to meet up with her. Little bitch never turned up.'

'Saved you buying her a present.'

'You're joking. I'd already bought the silver earrings from Samuel's. I had to give them to my sister in the end. Took me ages to get over it.'

The cloakroom girl had proved illusive. The first time he'd seen Tim cry. Men choose to break down at odd moments, their sudden loss of control catching them by surprise. Tim's breakdown showed his vulnerable side, at odds with his guarded masculinity. But there would always be a sense of embarrassment from the sidelines. When women cried it was expected. When men cried, they looked ridiculous and let the rest of the team down.

Tim recalled Harlequin's with nostalgia. 'Some beautiful looking women in that place. Sometimes I wish I'd gone through all of 'em.'

'You mean you didn't?'

'I must've got sidetracked halfway through. But what a place. Don't you wish you could go back and live it all again?'

'Not really.'

Tim gave him an odd look. 'Why not?'

He shrugged, lost in a fog of memories, good and bad.

Tim sat back, quiet for a moment. 'I wonder what happened to Tara.'

'God knows?'

'Remember the time she crashed her old man's car?'

'How could I forget? I was in it at the time.'

Tara's plight took on a morbid fascination, a memory shared uneasily between the two of them. Strange how he could feel nothing at all for her now. All the pain and heartache associated with that period had gone, leaving a stone in its place. Perhaps that was how you survived in the long run. You drained all the colour from the picture and reduced it to a grainy black and white. A faded negative. Something that should never have happened.

'Amazing,' Tim said quietly. 'Me you and James, out on the dance floor. We were the business, mate. Best days of my life, they were.'

He couldn't share Tim's nostalgia. The nights out and the partying would always be overshadowed by what happened next. Then the remorse and the soul searching, the devastating sense of loss you feel when someone that close bows out without an explanation.

Tim looked over, noting his silence. 'You can't keep blaming yourself, you know. It would have happened anyway, no matter what you did or didn't do.'

He took a drink and stayed quiet. Words were meaningless. You went over the same old ground in an endless debate, unable to come up with any satisfactory answers. But he did appreciate their loyalty. People like Tim and Erica, who stood by him when the lynch mob threatened to close in.

'I always thought they'd end up killing each other,' Tim said.

'So did a lot of other people.'

'She punched him in the face one night. We were about to get in a taxi. She just went ballistic.'

The memories left scars on the inside. He couldn't speak about it, no matter how many years went by. Instead, he threw himself into work, exercise and all round self-improvement but the burden never lifted. The downside of being human. You set yourself high standards then failed repeatedly to live up to them. You never set out to hurt anyone deliberately but that's what happened. People close to you got hurt. And that was the worse thing of all. Taking responsibility for someone else's pain and confusion.

He recalled an incident with the old man. They were driving on the Spur Road one afternoon, after a huge row had engulfed the whole house. He was in his teens and had witnessed countless altercations between them before. This one was different. He'd never seen his mother so angry. The old man had come away chastised, bowed almost under the weight of her attack. They drove in silence, the old man driving, him in the passenger seat. After what seemed like miles of this awful silence, the old man turned to him and said, 'Don't worry about all that. Your mother says things she doesn't mean.' For the rest of the drive, he felt a sense of relief. This terrible conflict between his parents had been explained as a kind of mishap. He shouldn't read too much into it. But he knew what the argument had been about and the knowledge made him fearful. When you betrayed someone's trust, the bond you once had was irretrievable.

They shook hands in the car park. For one brief moment, he envied Tim. The tanned and successful businessman with the wife and two kids who knew how to play the game and hold it all together. The moment passed. He saw Tim as he really was. Restless and dissatisfied. Always looking for the next challenge, the next opportunity to break out of the rut and find something worth striving for.

'Sure I can't interest you in the Breakfast Club?' Tim said.

'I'm too busy.'

'Could generate a lot of business for you. What's an hour out of your day once a month?'

'Try Marco. He's always harping on about the contacts he's made.'

Tim scowled. 'Marco's a fucking liability. He can't even get out of bed in the morning. And when you're out drinking with him it's like having the Virgin Express around. Someone ought to put a restraining order on him.'

Tim's easy grin creased his tanned face. Good bone structure, according to his mother. Sure to make a success of his life and reach his true potential.

'Do me one favour,' Tim said.

'What's that?'

'The teacher. Send me a text when you finally get to grips with her. Just so I know you haven't lost the plot completely.'

Tim drove off in his sleek BMW. If Simon had been there, they could have argued the merits of suspension systems and power ratios between models, or who had earned the most in the previous tax year. He didn't care much either way. Material goals brought only a passing comfort. He needed a more worthwhile challenge. Someone to snatch away the safety net as he stepped out on the high wire. Someone like Natalie.

Fifteen

He grabbed his jacket, ready to leave, and the phone went. Her name came up, like the jackpot on a fruit machine. He took a vital few seconds before answering.

'Sorry I missed your call,' she said. 'I was taking a class.'

'Any joy with your car?'

'Yes, it's fixed.'

'Great. Was he reasonable?'

'Kind of. I just wondered if he had a problem with women drivers. Like it was my fault the car broke down in the first place.'

He laughed. 'So what was it?'

'The starter motor, apparently. But he doesn't think it'll get through the next MOT. Just what I need right now.'

He tried to find some other pretext to keep her talking but she wasn't the type. She didn't make small talk and ended all her sentences with an audible full stop. All he could do was back off gradually and leave her with a favourable impression.

'Well, I'm glad I could be of assistance,' he said.

'Yes, thanks. I appreciate your help.'

'If there's anything else I can do let me know. Earthquakes, floods. I turn my hand to most things.'

She laughed with genuine warmth, the joyous sound of barriers coming down. 'How about dripping taps – can you fix them too?'

'Sure. Give me your address and I'll pop round.'

'Er – I'll pass on that thanks.'

'You don't have dripping taps then?'

'Actually I do, but the landlord can fix them. That's what he's paid to do. When he can be bothered to come out, that is.'

He sensed the clock ticking down. The inevitable goodbye that would close off all future avenues. With nothing to lose, he went for the direct approach. 'So, can I call you sometime?'

'What for?'

'Check your car's still working. It's my reputation at stake here, remember?'

She laughed. 'I'm sure the car will be fine.'

'How about coffee then?'

'I'm busy.'

'You must get a lunch break.'

'I get time to grab a sandwich, that's all.'

'That's criminal. What about your day off?'

She sighed. 'Don't you ever give up?'

'Depends on the opposition.'

She paused, searching for a suitable reply. 'Look – you're putting me in an awkward position here.'

'Why – because you don't get a lunch break?'

'No, because I don't like feeling obligated.'

'I asked you if you wanted a coffee, that's all. You could have said no.'

'And that would have shut you up would it?'

'Probably not. I'm just trying to be reasonable here, Natalie. Give you a few options to work from, you know?'

She laughed, mildly outraged. 'Listen – I'm standing out in a corridor, with what's left of my lunch break ticking away. I'd love to stand here talking to you all afternoon, but I can't.'

'Just as we were getting on so well.'

'If you say so.'

He enjoyed the banter, the relief of a drowning man thrown a lifeline. The moment gave him time to regain his composure, bow out gracefully without making a fool of himself. Someone called her name in the background. She said a formal 'Hi,' careful not to arouse suspicion, seen hovering in the corridor making furtive calls to strangers.

'Look, I've really got to go,' she said.
'Sure.'
'I really am grateful for your help, OK?'
'No problem.'
She said goodbye and hung-up.

He wandered into the kitchen and leant against the worktop. The even lines of the tiling and the polished oak units couldn't compensate for the intense disappointment. He should have expected it. She owed him nothing, least of all the gift of her precious time. At least now he could drop the idea and look for a more constructive pastime, something that would yield positive results without the same level of effort.

He cancelled the gym and read a fitness magazine instead. An article on the high incidence of prostrate cancer in middle-aged men began to blur after the first paragraph. He turned the page. An exposé of illegal stimulants in championship weightlifting had the same effect. The television offered a simpler alternative. A female presenter with elfin features and windswept hair, talked about an animal sanctuary in desperate and beseeching tones. Unable to summon the remotest sympathy for her or the animals in question, he switched channels. A programme on debt collectors looked more promising. The two men being filmed looked like middleweight boxers and talked like jaded police officers, reviewing the case history of a suspect debtor as they prepared to hammer down his front door.

He turned the television off and sat in silence.

His message alert rang. He crossed the room to his phone. Probably Claudia, reminding him to get a pepper sauce for the steak they were having later.

He stared at the handset in disbelief and opened the message.

Sorry about earlier. I didn't mean to be rude to
you. Lot going on at the moment. Take care
Natalie

He read the message several times, analysing every sentence and looking for the hidden meaning. The cloud lifted. Her choice of wording left a warm glow inside him, the first sign of any compromise on her part. And she used real grammar in place of the standard textspeak abbreviation. Either this was due to her superior education, or she was trying to impress him. No kiss to sign off, admittedly, but a glimmer of opportunity.

He pondered a suitable reply. Flashes of inspired poetry came to mind, a long and tender message, stating his purest intentions and the sincerest hope that she would resolve all her current problems and change her mind. He settled for economy instead.

No problem. Take care

No kisses. No frills. Nothing she might take as inappropriate or misleading. The perfect way to respond without compromising his integrity. She had quite clearly left the door open. If she wasn't interested she wouldn't have bothered getting back to him in the first place.

He pressed the send button.

To celebrate the occasion, he took her photograph from the Adidas bag. She stood out from the line of wedding guests – pretty in pink. The wide-rimmed hat suited her solemn face and the dark bob of her hair. Alone in the crowd, detached from the bridal veil and the smiling faces.

He put the photograph back in the bag.

Getting involved would mean great upheaval. His comfortable life would be torn from its axis and left spinning out of control. The routine up until now had been fairly predictable but somehow reassuring at the same time. Bolognese on a Tuesday. Shopping every Thursday. An endless round of dinner parties and foreign holidays to add seasoning.

Claudia offered security, a warm and soothing embrace no matter what the occasion. Natalie was a risk. The lure of the unknown and all the danger that went with it. But the course was set. The lines of communication were open. No matter how much he tried, he couldn't stop the momentum.

Sixteen

Women were an alien life form, a species so baffling at times that you could only sit back in stunned silence at the things they said and did. Some men claimed to be experts and wrote books to help the unenlightened, but all this did was create more confusion. The struggle wasn't for the armchair or the remote control. Problems started long before they reached the punitive stage. The real breakdown was in communication and the lack of understanding on either side.

Claudia had her own way of settling disputes. She went off and sulked for a few hours. The cause then became a minor issue, referred to only in passing. But the subject would come up again and again over the next few days, weeks and months, bearing down on his subconscious like a juggernaut. Her persistence left him with little choice, either give in or make a stand. The easiest option was to accept defeat, the alternative being a long siege under constant attack, with Claudia doing her best to wear down his resistance.

Certain situations tested his powers of endurance to the limit. Shopping was one of them. Strange things happen to women inside a supermarket. Claudia was no exception, pre-programmed to go down every aisle, inspecting the labels of products she had no intention of buying. Always some excuse to linger. The lamb for next Sunday's dinner. The special offer on toiletries that she simply couldn't resist. Men might have felt a similar lure walking into a car showroom but the fascination ended there. Claudia saw in Marks and Spencer a glittering shrine filled with endless promise. He saw an hour or so of utter boredom, trailing behind her like a baggage handler, hoping to find some small consolation in the lingerie department.

She stopped in the tinned vegetables aisle, selecting a four-pack of baked beans for his inspection. 'Yes or no?'

'Whatever.'

'Well do you need them or not?'

'How do I know?'

'I told you to look before we came out.'

'So I'm supposed to remember every single can I've got in the cupboard, am I?'

She put the baked beans back and strode away in disgust. The young couple passing tried to hide their amusement.

He followed her along the next aisle, stopping at intervals to give his opinion on processed peas or tinned spaghetti. One more tedious item crossed off the list. He resented his subordinate role. Shopping trolleys were designed to humiliate men. You trailed behind, without a say in where you were going, then had to pay for the privilege on the way out.

He checked his phone. No missed calls and no new messages.

Claudia stopped at the meat section and examined a pack of frozen chicken breasts. After a mind numbing period of indecision, she dropped the pack into the trolley and looked up. 'Do you fancy a curry Saturday night?'

'Whatever.'

Her mouth dropped. 'I wish you'd stop saying that all the time. I'm just trying to be organised.' She paused, watching him, closely. 'Why do you keep doing that?'

'What?'

'Looking at your phone every five minutes?'

'Boredom.'

Her mouth tightened visibly. 'Not expecting a phone call then?'

They completed the ordeal without speaking. He amused himself with the checkout girl, a plump and amiable school leaver called Hayley. Hayley passed the items into the bagging area where Claudia stood waiting.

'Do you like working here, Hayley?' he said amiably.

'It's OK.'

'At least you're at the business end of production. Beats stacking shelves like Jim Bob over there, eh?'

'Leave the poor girl alone,' Claudia said, harassed beyond belief.

Hayley beamed an easy smile, an advert for good customer relations. The woman behind him glared at the hold-up, a real female bulldog, standing guard at the head of the queue. Hayley's natural optimism shone through, winning his admiration.

'I've got a daughter about your age. She doesn't smile like you though. Maybe it's a teenage thing. Were you like that with your parents, Hayley?'

Claudia gave a huge sigh from the end of the checkout. 'For goodness sake! I thought you wanted to get home tonight.'

He said goodbye to Hayley and pushed the trolley past the crowded checkouts. Claudia left him at the entrance, to scan the magazine stand for the latest *Grazia.* The security guard looked over with a thin smile of empathy. Women always kept you waiting. The taxi turned up and they were still putting on their make-up. You booked a table for eight o'clock and they decided to change their whole outfit ten minutes before you were due to go out.

As they were leaving, a couple in their thirties entered, hand in hand and engrossed in conversation.

The woman looked up, saw him and stopped talking. The man, alerted by the sudden change in mood, followed her gaze. The couple passed by with the same shocked look, warned off by something dangerous or predatory.

'Who was that?' Claudia said, outside.

'No idea.'

'Why did that woman stare at you like that?'

He turned on her, enraged. 'How the fuck do I know? Go and ask her.'

She looked at him in disbelief.

He relented, as surprised by the outburst as she was. 'Can we just put this stuff away and go. Please?'

The car park offered temporary relief. He helped load the boot of Claudia's car, finding space among the rainproof jackets and pharmaceutical boxes she seemed to accumulate.

Claudia shut the lid with a sigh, and faced him. 'Do you want me to drive?'

'I'm not bothered.'

She stood, hands on hips, and glared at him. 'What's the matter now?'

'Nothing.'

'Yes there is. You've been like it all evening.'

'I'm fine. Traipsing round a supermarket with you is the highlight of my week.'

She stared at him. 'Why are you being like this?'

'Like what?'

'A complete asshole. I don't see why I should put up with it.'

Her ripple of anger amused him, an insult that carried no weight. Her quivering lower lip had the desired effect and he gave in. 'Give me the keys,' he said softly. 'I'll drive.'

Women had more freedom than ever before. They could match men in nearly every department; playing International football, joining the armed forces and sailing single-handed around the world. But they still had trouble reversing in and out of parking spaces. Claudia's company car was too big, a solid and functional Mondeo, kept in pristine condition. What she really wanted was a Volkswagen Beetle, sunburst yellow like Erica's. He'd promised to buy her one when he made his first million, but the offer had slipped further down his list of priorities.

Driving back, he saw a spate of women who looked like Natalie. He tried not to think about her. Claudia might pick up on a subliminal impulse and accuse him of cheating. The images were far more powerful than his defence against them and in the end he gave in. One in particular kept coming back. The two of them alone in the shadow of the old house. He reached out to brush away the hair from her cheek and she turned to look up at him. The memory stirred a deep yearning within him, but the conclusion of these hopelessly romantic scenes was always pornographic.

The woman in the supermarket bothered him. He couldn't think who she was but he knew instinctively that it had something to do with James. He should have told Claudia. She could have been an ally. Instead he chose to keep her in the dark, preferring to deal with the issue on his own.

Home was a relief. He dumped the shopping bags in the hall. Claudia took over at this point, taking the bags to the kitchen to restock his shelves. He stood the last bag in the hall and went outside. The gothic arch over the entrance looked impressive from the drive. One of the features that had attracted him to the place initially.

The old weather-beaten door with its outline of thick black studs gave the interior an air of mystery. The entrance to a crypt or some ivy-covered stately home. Sherlock Holmes might have convened in an attic room at one time, before the place was turned into flats.

Empty paint tins were stacked inside the porch. Fred should have come back mid-week to finish off and clear his things away. The tins were an eyesore, spoiling the visual impression from the drive and cluttering the entranceway.

'What's the matter?' Claudia said, joining him. He ignored her. She stared at the stack of tins in the porch 'How much longer are they going to stay there?'

'Forget it.'

'Why don't you phone Barry?'

'I said forget it, Claudia. I'll deal with it later.'

He spent the best part of his working life chasing people who continually let him down and she couldn't see it. Her attitude made it worse. She had no idea of the stress involved in organising labour and materials to meet deadlines. Her job was different. Any problems with her schedule and she contacted her manager. The only person he had to call on was himself.

He went into the utility room and looked at the ceiling. The base coat had dried in patches, unfinished like the architraves to the front room and the bedroom. All the interior work marred by this one oversight. Even the step ladders and dust sheets were still there, taking up space when they should have been removed weeks ago.

He phoned Barry's land line. June answered. Barry was out, pricing some job, and wouldn't be back until later. He chatted with June for a while and hung up. The anger became a nausea, eating away at him. No-one listened until you raised your voice, or did something spectacular to shake them up. His grandfather, normally a man of restraint, reduced to bellowing from his bedroom window at the shirkers idling in the yard below. People drove you to it. Slovenly and unreliable people.

He jumped up and went outside.

Paint tins struck the edge of the drive and careened into the bushes on the other side. One after the other, hurled across the tarmac to land at various points in the undergrowth. The last item to go was a paint-roller on a long handle, flung like a javelin and narrowly missing the front of Claudia's car.

'What the hell are you doing?' Claudia said, bug-eyed in the doorway.

'Having a clearout, what does it look like?'

'You can't just throw it all across the drive like that! What about the neighbours?'

'Fuck the neighbours!' He swept past her and strode into the kitchen. She came after him, her heels striking the bare boards, and stood watching him from the doorway. He poured himself a glass of filtered water and turned to face her.

'Have you finished?' she said.

'What?'

'Your little temper tantrum. Is that it?'

'Drop it, Claudia.'

'Me? You're the one who needs to calm down. I can't believe what you just did.'

'I lobbed a few paint tins in the bushes, that's all. Don't make a big deal out of it.'

She shook her head in disgust and went out along the hall.

The aftermath left a strange serenity. He wished he'd launched the step ladders and the dust sheets out as well. Fred's unused tools, hurtling across the drive to join the rest of the junk in the undergrowth. He must have got it from the old man, this tendency to overreact. He did his best to control it but it never worked out. It just happened – like an earthquake.

Claudia left him to brood. She packed all his shopping away as an act of goodwill and made him a coffee, retiring to the front room to read her magazine. His mood by then had changed. The childish satisfaction he'd felt earlier turned to remorse. Not for the outburst itself, but for the loss of control that went with it.

He sat on the window ledge and looked at the garden. The grass still needed cutting. Perhaps if he apologised for his earlier behaviour, Claudia would go out and do it for him. The anger had gone, but the sense of frustration remained. A few empty paint tins and an unfinished ceiling shouldn't have bothered him that much. He wished he was more like the old man, able to throw his weight around regardless of who he upset. The old man's rages were frequent, but usually brief; he said what he needed to say and moved on. His own rages were seismic by comparison and always personal, whatever the reason. When he lost control, he said things that couldn't be retracted later. No-one was immune. Not even Claudia.

He went outside, retrieved all the paint tins and the roller from the undergrowth and stacked them by the garage. None of the neighbours seemed to have witnessed his earlier outburst. He went back inside feeling slightly better.

'Have you calmed down now?' she said.

He gave a sheepish nod.

'Good. Your phone went while you were outside.'

The one missed call from Leanne left him oddly deflated. He called her back from the front room. Claudia watched him from the bean-bag, her smooth, bare legs adorning the polished floor. He admired her figure as the tones rang. The perfect model for a home improvement magazine, laid out in her print dress and white cardigan, her shoes kicked-off beside her.

The call connected.

Leanne went straight to the nature of business. What time was he picking her up? What time were they likely to get there? She had things to do, a schedule planned. He tried to interact with her, but she gave only vague answers, leaving him to struggle with the awkward gaps in between. Perhaps she was like it with her friends. The entire generation reliant on text messages and e-mails to spare themselves the burden of conversation.

He finished the call in a state of frustration.

Claudia gave him a knowing look. 'How is she?'

'Same as ever. It's like pulling teeth trying to get anything out of her.'

'At least you're there for her.'

'I'm the chauffeur, that's all. I'll be lucky to get two words out of her all day.'

She curled her lower lip, mocking him gently. 'Poor baby. Come and sit with me and tell me all about it.'

Claudia's soft bosom was a welcome alternative. He settled beside her and laid his arm across her waist. She kissed his cheek and put her head on his shoulder. Soon it would feel like ownership. She would move in and lay claim to the rest of his territory and he would forfeit his rights as a free man. Claudia's silken web offered security and commitment. The prospect of marriage and children if things went smoothly between them. He even imagined what their children would look like and pictured them running across the lawn or sitting on his shoulders, like Leanne used to do. These odd moments drew him closer to Claudia, but he chose not to reveal them to her for his own reasons.

'Please tell me who that woman was?'

He stiffened, aware of her breath on his neck, the softness of her hair against his shoulder. 'I don't know who she was.'

'But why did she look at you like that?'

'I told you. I've never seen her before. Maybe she mistook me for someone else.'

'Like who?'

'Dale Winton. How should I know?'

Claudia forgot about the woman in the supermarket and focused on his forthcoming parental duties. The drive to Bristol would be an interesting diversion. Help him clear his head from the mounting stresses of the week. And whatever else he had to put up with – at least he didn't have to live with Leanne.

Seventeen

Spectacular countryside opened up around the next bend. Panoramic views of deep valleys and rolling green hills, a timeless England to admire from a distance. An arc of sunshine touched a crop of houses far below, lighting up the entire area. He drew her attention to the beauty of the scenery but she gave only a glance, lost in her thoughts and the stupid song playing on the radio. He tried to get her to open up, picking subjects acceptable to talk about. College. Her friends. Sylvia. Even the long-suffering Roy and his bad back. The mindless radio filled in the awkward gaps, the road signs flashing up the distance remaining.

The services at Warminster came as a welcome relief. He pulled into the forecourt and turned off the ignition.

She stared at him open mouthed. 'What are you doing?'

'I'm hungry. Come on, I'll buy you breakfast.'

'I don't want breakfast.'

'Coffee then.'

'I don't want anything! I just want to get to Bristol, OK?'

'Start walking then, I'll pick you up when I've had something to eat.'

She slammed the door and strode towards the entrance. Sylvia's slim waist and narrow hips. Defiance inherited from either one of them. He called out after her. 'Such a difficult child!' She stuck two fingers up and carried on walking.

He joined her at the window seat. Between them, the polished Formica table top, with its cluster of shiny plastic menus. She sat with arms folded, staring out at the car park. He tried to recall the last time he'd seen her smile.

The young waitress came over and stood by, pen in hand. He compared her pleasant, freckled face to Leanne's sullen pout and thought of taking the waitress to Bristol instead. At least the breakfast looked appetising in its full-colour spread.

He ordered coffee and a full English breakfast. The waitress made an entry into her pad and looked up.

'Leanne?' he said.

'I told you – I don't want anything.'

'You've got to eat something, you haven't eaten all morning.'

She shrugged her shoulders and sighed. 'A portion of chips then.'

'Please.'

'*Please!*'

'Anything to drink?' the waitress said.

Leanne shot the girl a narrow glance. 'A glass of semi-skimmed milk. *Please!*'

When the waitress had gone, she glared at him. 'Why do you always have to embarrass me in front of people? I saw the way you looked at her.'

'I was just making conversation, for God's sake.'

'Yeah. Like you were with that girl on the Quay that time.'

He sat back, stunned by the venom in her voice.

She crossed her arms and stared at him evenly. 'Don't tell me you find it embarrassing all of a sudden?'

'Leanne. The deal was that I drive you to Bristol, right? I don't have to put up with a cross-examination over something that happened ages ago.'

'It wasn't that long ago. How do you think I felt? All my friends coming up to me saying, "Guess who I saw your dad with the other night?" '

'That's enough.'

She slumped against the window and watched a car pull into the forecourt. Her shoulders rose and fell with each shallow breath. The thermostat for all her inner rage turned up especially for him. Being with her always turned into an act of contrition. The past dug up and heaped in front of him for everyone else's benefit. He didn't feel regret for what had happened, only that Leanne had found out. Zoe had been eighteen at the time anyway. Old enough to chose who she slept with.

His breakfast came first. She watched him eating with a look of disbelief, clutching her glass of milk, forced to sit through an autopsy. To entertain himself, he trailed a piece of bacon in the juice on the plate and lowered it, inch-by-inch, into his mouth.

She grimaced and drew back. 'God, that's so disgusting!'

'You want some, honey? I'll cut you off a nice bit of fat if you like.'

When her chips came she kept them at arms length, selecting each one with a hesitant thumb and forefinger and guiding it towards her mouth with a look of disdain.

He pushed his finished plate towards the centre of the table. She eased it back towards him with a grimace.

'Tell me about this play you're in.' he said.

'Who told you about that?'

'The old man mentioned it. He said you were walking round the house wearing sunglasses like Jackie Onassis, is that right?'

She shrugged. 'It's just a college play. It's no big deal.'

'Sure it's a big deal, if you're in it. What part are you playing?'

'Mistress Quickly.' She noted his blank look and rolled her eyes. 'It's Shakespeare.'

'Sounds good. Do we get to see you in it?'

She hesitated. 'If you want to, I suppose.'

Vague memories came back. Leanne as a sheep in a preschool production. Himself and Sylvia seated side by side, the doting parents, an electric fence and razor wire to keep them apart.

'What's so funny?' she said.

'I was just remembering you as a kid. How cute you were.'

'I wasn't cute. I had horrible teeth and straight hair.'

'That's not how I remember you. My little angel, you were. Now look at you, all grown up and destined for the big stage.'

She grew quiet, tweaking the edge of the menu. 'Claudia rang me yesterday.'

'What about?'

'Coming round yours for a meal one night.'

'How do you feel about that?'

She shrugged, the snap of the menu becoming louder.

'Leanne, can you stop doing that please?'

'Why?'

'Because it's fucking annoying, that's why.'

She stopped, and glanced at the few customers on the far side, a devious smile forming. 'I thought you didn't like me swearing?'

'I don't.'

'But it's alright for you to do it, though?'

'In a word – yes.'

'That's hypocritical.'

'It's called parental guidance, actually.

'That's ridiculous. Granddad swears all the time as well. What sort of guidance is that?'

He sat back, enjoying the debate at her expense. She smoothed the edges of the menu, eyeing him with an artful smile. 'Claudia said she's sold her house. Is she moving in with you?'

'She hasn't sold the house at all.'

'And Nan says you're getting married next year, is that true?'

'She says a lot of things, Leanne.'

She brooded over this for a moment. 'So why don't you then?'

'Why don't I what?'

'Marry Claudia. She's a nice person *and* she doesn't swear much.' She ignored him and sat deep in thought. All his previous girlfriends had upset her for one reason or another. Except Claudia. He'd learned to be discreet, keeping his private life away from her. She looked beautiful to him, whatever mood she was in. Braids in her hair and coils of jewellery around her wrists. The thinker. All the intricacies of her life unfolding in ways she had no control over. Her part in a play, that he might never get to see her in, dismissed out of hand as if it were of no consequence. He wondered what she'd make of Natalie.

He sipped his coffee, distracted. Natalie might be on a break right now, scanning her phone to see if he'd left a message. He could drop in and see her on the way back, take her for a spin in his car. The thought of their next meeting consumed him. All it needed was a well-timed text message, even a phone call. The thought of calling her made his heart beat faster.

'Roy said he might buy me a laptop.'

He looked up, his daydreaming interrupted. 'Is that supposed to make me feel guilty?'

'No. I'm just saying.'

'Why didn't you ask me first?'

'I did! You said no, remember?'

'I said I'd think about it if you got a part-time job.'

'I need a laptop not a job! How else am I supposed to finish all my course work?'

He found it impossible to be angry with her. His one major failing according to Sylvia. All the years of kowtowing to her and treading gently around her precocious mood swings had done nothing but produce a tyrant.

He tried a different approach. 'How are you getting on with the toxic twins these days?'

She laughed in spite of herself, a glint of genuine mirth in place of the usual daggers. 'I'll tell Mum you called them that.'

'Has Roy finally put his foot down and stopped giving them handouts?'

'How do I know? I hardly ever see them. They're always out playing tennis or netball or something.'

Her amusement helped clear the air. At least she still had a keen sense of the ridiculous. The complex family scenario she'd inherited didn't seem to bother her that much. Roy did his best, coping with Sylvia's foul mouth and his bad back. Taking on someone else's child can't have been easy, especially when he had two of his own to fleece him of his hard-earned wages.

He finished his coffee. 'Come on then. Let's go meet the old witch.'

The car's air-conditioning affected her within minutes. Like an ice-box, she said. He turned it down and opened his window to compensate. The incoming draft messed up her hair and caused her so much distress that he gave in and closed it. The temperature rose steadily, like the heat shimmer beyond the windscreen. He put the air-conditioning back on and glanced across at her. She sat, stony faced, staring ahead.

'You're a real treat to be with Leanne, you know that?'

'Yeah. Yeah. Put another log on the fire, Granddad!'

Her wicked laughter enhanced his view of the world. He joined in, in spite of the fact that he was the intended victim. The patchwork fields and the sun-kissed valleys came alive, as if for the first time. Perhaps this was his reward for being patient, a moment of levity bringing them closer together.

They drove through Norton St Philip. The George Inn stood out at the end of the High Street, monument to a bygone era. All blackened beams and leaning walls, the original building having survived Cromwell and centuries of termites. She ignored his commentary and pulled down the visor to examine her face in the mirror.

'I thought you liked history,' he said, offended.

'It's just another old building. I *have* seen it before.'

'What? This is our heritage, you know. They're tearing down national monuments to build shopping centres and no-one gives a shit. Don't you care?'

'Huh. Listen to Mr Environment. What about the houses you and Granddad pulled down?'

'That's different.'

'Why is it?' she said, with scornful laughter.

'That was an act of charity. New buildings benefit the community.'

'And shopping centres don't?'

'There is a difference between consumerism and earning a living, you know.'

'What about that house in the *Echo* then? The one you pulled down and built flats on. The one all the residents complained about.'

He glanced at her. 'You remember that?'

'Of course I remember it. Jody Stark brought the *Echo* in to school and showed everyone. So embarrassing!'

He thought about the newspaper spread and how many other lies he'd told her for the sake of convenience.

Marco's house came to mind. Another monument due for demolition, but one that even he would miss. The wide ballroom with its clusters of chandeliers. The flagstone path leading to the rear of the house. The eternal boom of the surf along the shoreline. Natalie, so close he could reach out and touch her.

'Know anything about Art Therapy,' he said.

'No, why?'

'Just a thought.'

'Why would I be interested in Art Therapy? I'm doing Drama.'

'Yes, I know. It was just … Forget it, Leanne.'

She lapsed into smug silence, bemused at his total ignorance of college affairs.

They rounded a long bend. More patchwork fields appeared in the valley below. He pointed out a bird hovering motionless in the clear blue sky. She showed limited interest and suggested he slow down. Moments later she sat up, adopting a more cautious, exploratory tone. 'How would you feel about me going abroad?'

'Barcelona?'

'Just on holiday.'

'Who with?'

'It's just a question. Would you let me, or not?'

He sensed a trap. 'It's not as simple as that. I'd need to know the details first.'

'Why?'

He laughed at her blank expression. 'Did you take evasion tactics at school, or what?' Her silence confirmed his suspicions. 'So who's funding it, then, this pie-in-the-sky holiday of yours?'

'Forget I even asked.' She sank down and put her knees up on the dashboard. His instinct to tell her off gave way to diplomacy. At least they were talking. If they reached Bristol without falling out again, he would see it as a major victory.

Bathampton Mill came into view around the next bend. The stone bridge and river looked idyllic, a still, pastoral scene far removed from the hustle of modern life. Sadness weighed him down, the beauty of the countryside glimpsed from a passing car. Leanne, next to him, silent and morose, blind to the scenic route he'd taken especially for her.

She circled the coil of bangles at her wrist and tried another angle, upbeat and more confident this time. 'Anyway, I need a break from all the studying I've been doing. A few of us are thinking of going to Reading this summer.'

'What for?'

She stared at him in disbelief. 'It's a festival. God, didn't you even know that?'

'Who are you going with?'

'Gemma and a few others.'

'What did your mother say about it?'

'I haven't told her yet.'

'So you thought you'd run it by me first and swing the deal that way.'

She stayed silent. He pictured a sea of multi-coloured tents and malnourished faces, a vast crowd grinding their hips to mindless electronic music.

'I don't like it.'

'Why not?'

'Because I don't that's all.'

'Oh, so you never did anything like that when you were my age?'

'It was different then.'

'Why was it?'

'You didn't have so many lunatics running round on crack cocaine.'

'I don't even take drugs.'

'Leanne.'

She observed the ritual silence for as long as she could bear it. 'So I can't go then?'

'No, you can't.'

'Great!' She slumped back in the seat and hugged her knees, staring through the windscreen. 'What if I go anyway?'

'Don't even think about it.'

'Why not?'

Because I'll come and find you in whatever muddy field you happen to be in and drag you all the way back home again.'

He tried to focus on the road. She returned his occasional glances with a fierce glint, part mischief, part rebellion. He loved her more than ever. The child now a young woman, growing steadily away from his influence with each passing minute.

The City centre helped raise his blood pressure. The maze of one-way systems and contra flows seemed to alter each time he came. Landmarks from previous visits must have been removed deliberately to confuse him further. He cursed the planners, the traffic, even the old woman herself for opting to live there in the first place. Leanne added to the stress by criticising his driving. He should have known the route by now and it was his fault they were lost.

The sign for Horfield came up and he breathed easier. Two wrong turns later, he found his bearings, a familiar street of drab red council houses, cars double parked and glinting in the sun. The area brought back vivid memories. Early visits to see Sylvia when she was still sixteen and he'd just passed his driving test. His cautious introductions to her maladjusted family.

He pulled in a few doors down from the house and turned off the ignition. Leanne reached out for the radio, 'Hey, I was listening to that song!'

'Forget the song and listen to me for a minute. Make sure you've got everything. I'm not coming all the way back because you left your phone in the glove compartment.'

She stared ahead in mute protest. He wanted to make a speech, a gesture that would bond them in some way, remind her that he would always there for her, no matter what the circumstances. Instead, he wished she would show a little more respect and take her frayed knees off the dashboard.

'Have you got enough money?' he said.

'Yes. Well, not really.'

He took out his wallet, peeled off two ten pound notes and gave them to her. She stared at the notes in her hand.

'Aren't you coming in?' she said.

'Not with the old witch about. She might try to lynch me.'

'Don't be so horrible,' she said, grinning behind her fingertips.

'And you take it easy. Stay away from the assholes drinking rocket fuel and climbing in other people's windows.'

She released her seatbelt and turned for the door.

'Leanne?' Before she could pull away he leaned over and kissed her cheek. 'Say hello to her indoors for me.'

She took her bag from the back and shut the door. He sat alone inside with the void left by her absence.

The old woman appeared at the front door, a stern face on a squat, enduring body. Like some rural peasant worker who tended the land. Solid and dependable as an old armchair. He studied her through the passenger window, relieved that he no longer had to deal with her. If she had noticed him, she chose not to reveal it, so much bad blood between them that would never be resolved.

Leanne opened the gate and walked up the path, her bag slung over her shoulder. He felt uncomfortable watching her. Council estates were breeding grounds for crime and unemployment. But he couldn't stop her from visiting. The truth was that she felt more at home on the estate than she did anywhere else. Living there for a short period as a child had forged a bond with Sylvia's family that even he couldn't break.

The old woman shifted on the doorstep. The deep-set frown reserved for the rest of the world became a warm and tender smile. Alone in the privacy of his car, he found a distant part of himself warming to her. At least, concerning Leanne, they were united in one thing.

The front door closed.

He took out his phone and stared at the handset.

The voice of reason had lost. The insistent voice inside his head had taken over. He gave in and called Natalie.

Eighteen

'Sorry I'm late, I got held up in traffic.' She raised her sunglasses, her smile firm but uncertain. The smile meant more to him than the apology. She might have rehearsed the moment as he had, the awkwardness of meeting in public for the first time. Her unease made it easier for him, revealed a side to her he hadn't seen before.

She took the chair opposite and put her bag down, taking in the crowded table area. 'Is it always this busy here?'

'Would you rather go somewhere else?'

'No. It's fine.'

'We could sit inside if you like.'

'No, honestly. This is fine.'

She ordered a Cappuccino. When the waiter had gone she settled back to enjoy the sun on her face. Her sunglasses were raised above her forehead, a knot of her lustrous, dark hair piled on top, fixed with a silver slide. With her eyes closed she looked almost serene.

'When do you have to be back?' he said.

'In about an hour.'

'Taking a class?'

'It's a part-time mentoring job I've started. Two of us take young children out to local places of interest. It's not a paying job but I enjoy doing it.'

'You don't get paid?'

She smiled at his reaction. 'It's voluntary.'

'Not even expenses?'

'Well, I could claim petrol I suppose, but it's hardly worth it.' He gave a vague nod of understanding and a shadow crossed her face. 'The voluntary work leads to opportunities in other areas that I'm interested in. The work I do with children for instance. It makes a big difference to an employer when you've had previous experience.'

He drained his coffee, aware that she was watching him. He wanted to be tactful and say all the right things, but the desire to antagonise was stronger.

'You don't seem all that convinced,' she said.

'I just don't agree with it, that's all.'

'With what?'

'Voluntary work.'

'Why not?'

'It's an abuse of manpower.'

She stared at him. 'Are you being serious?'

'Well, if I could get people to work for nothing, I'd put an ad in the paper tomorrow, wouldn't I?'

She frowned, clearly undecided. 'So you've never done anything without being paid for it?'

'No I haven't.'

'What, never?'

'Well, I moved a washing-machine down three flights of stairs the other day, but that was a favour for a friend.'

'So you wouldn't consider giving up your time to help a worthwhile cause? A charity or something?'

'I don't agree with charities either.'

'Why not?'

'It's a cynical misdirection of public funding.'

She laughed with him, delighted at the absurdity of his argument. He wished he was seated closer to her, without the table to cut them off. The babble of foreign voices around them prevented any real intimacy. But she had agreed to meet him. He'd passed the first test already.

'Does that answer your question?' he said.

She shook her head. 'You're just, unbelievable.'

'So we can agree to disagree?'

'Oh I don't think there's much chance we'll agree on anything, do you?'

Her Cappuccino arrived. She dissolved a sachet of brown sugar with the thin wooden stirrer. Her fingers fascinated him. Long and elegant with blunt, bitten-down nails. Her attitude to work intrigued him too. He tried to imagine giving up his time and not being paid for it; convincing Barry to build a double garage out of the kindness of his heart.

While she sipped her coffee, he kept a look out for danger. Faces among the crowd, ready to leap out and betray him to Claudia at some future date. He glanced at Natalie and decided the risk was worth taking.

'Such a beautiful day,' he said. 'Who wants to be working?'

'Some of us have to.'

'Wouldn't you rather be sat here in the sunshine, surrounded by all these wonderful people?' She smiled, humouring him. 'I'm serious. I feel alive. Connected to the whole human race. Don't you ever feel like that?'

'Usually after the third vodka and tonic.'

'That's another of your bad habits is it?'

'I wish I had the time.'

'What about your social life? You must go out now and then?'

'Oh sure. I take Charlotte to school. Then I bring her home again. In between that, I work. If there's any time left after that I sink into an armchair and fall asleep in front of the TV.'

'Sounds like you need some excitement in your life.'

'No. I just need more hours in the day.'

The sun glanced on the aluminium chair backs and glass tabletops. The faceless crowd passed by, a continual flow of students and tourists, converging in the Square, swept away to remote parts of the town. The likelihood of being seen by someone he knew raised the stakes. Erica might appear and come waltzing over to join them. He could explain how they'd met by accident, that she shouldn't read anything untoward into two people having coffee together.

'How does all this compare to living in London?' he said.

'I'm still trying to work it out.'

'Were you born there?'

'In London? God, no. I was born in Scotland.'

'Really?'

'Don't look so surprised. I was born in Scotland. I didn't grow up there.'

Her teasing smile faded and she looked away. Other than the few details she had given him, he knew nothing about her. Each new fact was a glimpse, peeling back the layers to reveal more of the truth.

'What do you miss most about London?' he said.

She fingered the rim of her cup and shrugged. 'Nothing much. I was glad to get away in the end. Stuck on the Tube with no room to breathe. Rush hour was an absolute nightmare.'

'There must have been other things.'

'Well yes, there were. Sitting in the Tate Modern looking out over the Thames. Walking along the South Bank with Charlotte.' She smiled to herself with a touch of sadness. 'Charlotte loved the human statues. She used to stand in front of them for ages, waiting for them to move.'

'I've got a few people like that working for me.'

She missed the joke, lost in her memories. Aware of his gaze, she shifted in the seat. 'So where were you born?'

'A few miles east as the crow flies. Bit of everything in my family. French, German. There's even an American connection.'

'Really?'

'Nothing exciting. No big-time gangsters. Distant relatives went over in 1861, apparently. Some died of tuberculosis and never made it. There's a whole side of the family I've never seen.'

'How come you know so much about them?'

'My sister did an archive search. Probably to see if we had any super-rich uncles anywhere.'

'Any charity fundraisers among them?'

'Not in my family. I come from a long line of self-made men.'

She watched him carefully, gauging his reactions. He smiled, enjoying the tension. The two of them alone in a swarm of people, knocking the ball back and forth across the glass-topped table.

She talked about her job, the stresses of working for the local council and putting up with all their petty regulations. He listened in part, more concerned with the openness of their location, the constant threat of being caught out by someone he knew.

'... I suppose I'm not used to it, being under observation like that. For me it's a challenge. The one aspect of the job I dread most of all.' She frowned at him intently. 'Have you been listening to me at all?

'Of course.'

'No you weren't, you were miles away.'

'You were talking about the school you work at.'

'It's not a school, it's an Adult Learning Centre.' She put an emphasis on each word for his benefit. 'I was saying that I just don't deal with pressure all that well. That's why I'm not looking forward to the assessors coming in.'

'And what do they do?'

'They come in as observers. Make sure you're doing your job properly. We're all rehearsed beforehand, but I still find the whole thing nerve-racking.'

'I thought working for the council was a job for life?'

'Not the department I'm in. We're contracted for five classes a year, but two of those might get cancelled due to lack of funding. Nothing's guaranteed.'

'You could always come and work for me.'

She arched her eyebrows. 'Doing what?'

'I'll find you a nice little desk job, sorting out my invoices. I've always wanted a secretary.'

'I don't think so.'

'Just a thought. Fancy an ice-cream?'

They left the café and strolled down into the Lower Gardens. Clusters of people lay out on the grass, enjoying the sun. The resident hot-air balloon loomed above them, suspended from its moorings by a network of ropes and pulleys.

'Have you ever been up in that?' she said.

'I like to keep my feet on the ground, thanks. If you want real excitement, try white-water rafting in the Pyrenees.'

'That doesn't appeal to me.'

'Why not?'

'I can't swim.'

He laughed unintentionally.

She stared hard at him. 'I'm glad you think it's so funny.'

'I don't. It's just – '

'I nearly drowned in a swimming pool as a child. Since then I've been pretty nervous around water.'

'Jesus. That's terrible.'

'My mum found me face down, apparently. I was too young to remember, but I think she must have passed on her phobia to me as I was growing up.'

He walked beside her in silence and thought of Leanne. The shock you feel when a child goes missing that stays with you long after. To find a child face down in the water must have been unbearable.

Natalie burst out laughing.

'What's so funny?' he said.

'Your face. It's an absolute picture.'

He stared at her in bewilderment. 'You made all that up?'

'Well yes, actually I did. I just didn't expect you to swallow it so easily.'

He shook his head, unnerved by her deception.

'And before you ask – yes, I can swim. I wasn't good at many things at school, but that was one of them.' His reaction seemed to give her a great deal of pleasure, an easy victory she could claim without having worked too hard. He wondered how many other games she intended to play, expecting him to go along with them without a word of complaint.

They joined a small queue at the kiosk. The pressure of staying hidden in the crowd, gave way to the thrill of being with her. Her slim waist beside him. The strip of pale flesh beneath the hem of her tee-shirt. As the queue moved forward, her leather handbag nudged his elbow, connecting them in some small way. He tried not to think of the consequences of his actions. *'It was nothing,*

Claudia. We just went for a quick stroll through the Gardens, that's all.'

They found a space among the sun-worshippers and made camp. She spread her denim jacket on the grass and sat down, drawing her knees up to study her ice-cream. He sat a respectful distance away, careful not to invade her personal space.

Her nose touched the tip of the ice-cream and a sliver of chocolate dropped onto her knuckle.

'There is an art to it you know' he said.

'What – eating an ice-cream?'

'Sure. You have to get your mouth around it quick and stop it dripping all over you.'

She flashed him a warning look.

'By the way,' he said. 'You've got a spot on the tip of your nose.'

She wiped her nose with the back of her hand and carried on eating. He settled back and finished his strawberry Cornetto. Crushed wafer and melted ice-cream eclipsed even her presence for a moment, a sensual pleasure shared between them in the heat. He gazed at her with a mixture of desire and amusement at the way things had turned out.

'Something you'd like to share with me?' she said.

'I was just thinking about the night we met.'

'What about it?'

'Well – we didn't exactly click, did we?'

'Like I said before, I was having a bad day.'

'It wasn't just me then?'

'You were partly the reason, but there were other factors involved.'

He watched her lips mould to the ice cream. Choosing his words with caution, he asked, 'What about Brad?'

'What about him?'

'Are you? ...'

'Serious?' she said, nipping at shards of chocolate with her teeth. She answered her own question, catching droplets with her tongue. 'We go out sometimes. He knows I'm busy with my work. With Charlotte. Anything else you want to know?'

'Not really.'

'Good,' she said, with the trace of a smile. 'Because I don't like people prying into my business.' Her smile faded. She put her head back and closed her eyes. 'It's no big deal, anyway.'

'Sorry?'

'Me and Brad. It's not serious.'

'If you say so.'

'Don't you believe me?'

'Sure. Why wouldn't I believe you?'

'He works away in the week. I hardly see him at all, OK?'

She clearly felt the need to explain, but she couldn't look at him. She kept her eyes closed, her voice coy and seductive in the heat. He listened with a measure of disbelief, wanting to believe her but aware of the distant past, clouding the issue. She could tell him anything and he would have to accept it. She told him she nearly drowned in a swimming pool. How many other lies would she tell him?

She talked about London, how she'd been let down repeatedly, without saying why. Her tone grew weary. 'I'm not interested in making a commitment to anyone right now. I was in a long-term relationship before and that didn't work out. I just need my own space for a while.'

He gazed up at cloudless blue sky. The long-term lover bothered him. The man must have left an indelible mark, whoever he was. A nameless threat to spoil the present moment, the progress he'd made so far.

The spirit of competition stirred within him. With the lover gone, and Brad no more than a passing impulse, the signs were positive. All he needed to do was follow the cardinal rules. Never try too hard and in moments of doubt, act as if you don't care anyway.

'How did it end?' he said.

'Pardon?'

'The long-term relationship you were in.'

She stared at him dubiously. 'You'd probably get on with my mother. She likes to know the ins and outs of everything as well.'

'When can I meet her?'

She laughed abruptly. 'You wouldn't want to, believe me. She'd probably make some comment on your upbringing. Your learned responses to things you couldn't deal with as a child.'

'What is she – a social worker?'

'Close.'

'What does she do?'

'She's a child psychologist. She analyses everyone she comes into contact with. A sort of ongoing research for the book she's writing at the moment.'

'I take it you don't get on?'

She looked up sharply. 'You could say that.'

The relationship between her and her mother intrigued him. He built a composite picture with the few details she'd given; a tough Joan Crawford character, domineering and neurotic, ruling over every area of her daughter's life. He felt no great urge to be introduced.

'So where do we go from here?' he said.

'What do you mean?'

'You know what I mean, Natalie.'

'I told you before that I didn't want to get involved.'

'Sure. It's nice meeting you, blowing the breeze and all that, but …'

'But what?'

'I'm just saying.'

'What do you want me to do – sign a contract?'

He laughed, conceding the point to her for now. 'OK. Let's just enjoy the sunshine. I'd hate you to think I was putting pressure on you.'

She put her head back, quiet for a moment. 'What about you? I thought you were already involved with someone.'

He said nothing.

'What's the matter? Don't you want to talk about it?'

'It's a loose arrangement, that's all.'

She laughed scornfully. 'What does that mean? You meet up once a fortnight and sleep with whoever you like in between?'

'No. It just means …'

She watched him closely, nodding with grave understanding. 'I know what it means. It means you want what you can't have. You're completely fucking selfish like all the other men I've ever known.'

He stared at her in shock. She flashed him a bitter smile, revealing more of herself than she'd intended. The outburst seemed to drain her and she sighed heavily. 'Please don't look at me like that. I'm just saying how it is, that's all.'

The warmth of the sun purified all conscious thought. Around him the hum of voices, the raucous cries of a gull in flight; external influences that were absorbed and became a part of him for as long as he remained aware. His cheeks burned with her rejection.

He let his mind wander; along the stream and across the bank, to the stone-grey buildings rising above the trees. Himself and James, caught up in a human stampede. The threat of violence from an unknown quantity.

'We were chased through here once,' he said.

'Who by?'

'Spurs supporters.'

'I didn't know you were a football hooligan as well.'

'I wasn't. We just got caught up in it one Bank holiday. Me and a friend from school.'

'How old were you?'

'About fourteen. Great adrenalin rush though. Riot vans everywhere. Windows being put through. You can see why people get addicted to that sort of thing.'

He told her for effect, but she gave no outward reaction. The details had some obscure meaning for him. His past severed from hers, perhaps. His memory of James that he didn't want to talk about. The undeniable fact that they were still complete strangers, playing mind games in the sun.

'I had a run in with football supporters, once,' she said.

'You did?'

'In a pub in Camden. I did bar work part-time while I was at Uni. They all came in one Saturday lunch time, singing and chanting.'

'And you stood up to them?'

'I had no choice. The landlord was hiding out the back and I was the only one behind the bar. It wasn't too bad though. A few glasses got smashed and they all left.'

Her past was off-limits, full of events and milestones he couldn't share. The only link between them the sound of broken glass in some rowdy barroom. Soon she would make her apologies and move on to her next job. He would go through the motions, resenting her inwardly for spurning his advances and wounding his pride.

'How long have you known Marco?' he said.

'Long enough.'

'But you and him weren't ever? …'

She stared at him in horror. 'Marco? Please! I've got enough problems.' She grew thoughtful. 'He was like a family friend. I suppose you could say we grew up together by accident.'

'How does that work out?'

'My dad had this habit of dropping me at friends' houses and leaving me while he went off to meet all these important people he knew.'

'What did he do?'

'He was a salesman.'

'Insurance?'

'Not quite. He went round the world for a big electronics firm. He was very good too. A real charmer. My mum always said he should have gone into politics.'

He sensed her discomfort. The subject obviously stirred up emotions she preferred to keep hidden. Her father. Her childhood. Secrets in a locked room. Now was the time to tactfully steer the conversation away and talk about something else. But he couldn't leave so many angles unexplored.

'Is he still around?'

'My dad? God, no!' She gave a sad smile and picked at tufts of grass. 'He went to Singapore on business one year and never came back. Well, he did eventually but I didn't see him. Then I found out he'd got remarried. Sort of confusing really.'

'How old were you when he left?'

'Seven.'

He said nothing, picturing her as a child.

'I didn't see him for years. Then he contacted me one day while I was still at Uni. We met for lunch in this typically English tea room in Finsbury.' She paused, alone with the memory. 'It wasn't the same, though. He spent the whole time trying to blame his job for the way things turned out. He didn't even ask how it had affected me. The whole thing was, disappointing.'

'Do you still see him?'

'Now and then.' She gave him a puzzled frown. 'I don't know why I'm telling you all this, really.'

The shadows lifted. He glanced over the groups of mainly young people dotted around the gardens, as if noticing them for the first time. All of them looking for variations of the same thing. Warmth. Security. Happiness. The balloon hovered above them, motionless in the clear blue sky, and with the scene a warm connectedness. Natalie sat close by, hugging her knees, comfortable in her own space, no longer such a stranger.

She stood up, brushing flecks of grass from her jeans. 'Oh well. Better make a move or I'll be late. Thanks for the ice-cream.'

He picked up her jacket and held it out for her. The two of them like any other couple, at ease in each others company. All around them, the enemy eyes. The chance he could be caught out and shamed publicly.

She shrugged on her jacket and clamped her bag to her waist. 'If I wake up with sunburn, I'll know who to blame.'

'I'll bring the suntan lotion, next time.'

'Next time?'

'Joke, Natalie.'

He walked her to her car, through crowds of holidaymakers and foreign students. His elation turned to realism. The rules had changed. From now on he would have to play a dual role. Tell lies about his whereabouts. Keep track of the lies he'd told in order to invent new ones. The whole process mentally and emotionally draining.

He had Claudia to think about. He'd made her out to be nothing, a passing interest that could be dropped as soon as a better option came along. But his future course was set. He knew this without any doubt.

Natalie eclipsed everything.

She walked beside him, alluring in her worn-down heels and dark glasses, shoulder bag swinging casually against her hip. He would have to give up so much to be with her. Disrupt his whole life. Her cautious smile made it all look so inviting, the barriers between them tumbling down.

'I'll give you a call,' he said.

'Sure.'

'Maybe we could do this again. Bring the windbreaker and the cool-box like proper tourists.'

She turned and smiled. 'Why not? Give me a call.'

He watched her go, his heart filled with an absurd and childish happiness.

Nineteen

Friday night at the Blue Bar, centre of decadence for the local in-crowd. The place had a Mediterranean feel, an illusion fed by the potted palm trees and the warm evening sunshine. Clubbers spilled from taxi cabs in a warm-up for the main event. Girls on high heels, ringed with fake jewellery, wild and raucous like children in a playground. Gangs of lads, hurling good-natured abuse across the street, led by the pack instinct and the eternal promise of the night.

Raul went inside to get the drinks.

His phone rang. Sometimes people caught you at the wrong time. Modern technology gave you the means to vet your calls, but you couldn't escape indefinitely. Persistent callers left rambling messages on your answerphone. Sooner or later you had to reply. The name on the screen flashed an instant warning, a wave of anxiety felt deep inside.

'Yeah?' he said tersely.

'What you up to?'

'I'm sat on the terrace waiting for Raul.'

'I'm glad I'm not,'

'What do you want, Zoe?'

He hadn't seen her for weeks but she talked as if it were yesterday. She didn't like his attitude, the way he spoke to her. The fact that he was with Raul implied a conspiracy that would exclude her somehow. But she kept her tone deliberately light and playful, ensuring his attention. Behind every word, a seriousness of purpose that couldn't be denied.

'I thought you might have called me to see how I was.'

'I've been busy.'

'What – too busy to make a phone call?'

He laughed at her sudden change in tone as a girl strolled by his table, rolling her hips.. One more glimpse of bare flesh to divide his loyalties. 'Listen, Zoe. It's a bit difficult right now. I'll call you later.'

'You said that the last time, remember?'

Raul came out with the drinks and squeezed between the ornate metal chairs along the gangway. His pink shirt stood out like a neon sign.

'Zoe – something's come up. I'll call you later.'

He hung up and breathed easier.

Raul set the drinks down and stood back, spreading his arms in apparent outrage. 'Can you believe this? Some asshole spilt beer on my shoes! Then he gives me a VIP pass to some new club in Brighton.' The outrage became a devious grin. 'Think I should go?'

'Not in that shirt I wouldn't.'

The terrace filled up. A real treat for the in-house voyeurs. The girl at the next table wore a shimmering green dress held up with micro-thin shoulder straps. She drank a cocktail through a straw, a mass of untidy black hair piled above her head. But she looked good. Bare shoulders and a slender neck. Pert breasts that barely made an impression. Her buxom friend had the advantage in this department, her twin assets spilling out of her halter-neck top. The genetic lottery. The same draw for both sexes. Women had it worse in many ways, forced to compete with some air-brushed model in a magazine. Men went to seed without the same trauma, grey hair and a few lines being socially acceptable. Even a beer-belly added status in some quarters.

He thought about Spain. Hand in hand with Claudia along the tapas bars and the noisy tavernas, the slick, tourist-driven industry that Raul despised so much. Claudia would have chosen his wardrobe by now, right down to the style of his shirts and the colour of his swimming shorts. He saw it clearly. He'd be lying in the sun for two weeks, thinking about Natalie, wishing he was back home.

Raul glanced at his watch and shook his head. 'The fat man is late.'

'He's always late.'

'He'd move quicker with my foot up his ass, that's for sure.'

Marco set his own schedule. Daylight hours were viewed with suspicion, to be avoided whenever possible. Without a good reason to get up he often stayed in his pit until late in the afternoon. He envied Marco's attitude at times, his utter contempt for the common herd and their tedious work-driven lives.

The girl in the green dress strolled classily towards the entrance. Several male heads turned in her direction.

Raul whistled softly. 'Look at that ass, man. Beautiful.'

'She knows it too.'

'Like a dream, huh?' Raul fixed him with a broad grin. 'How about I bring her over? Put a smile back on your miserable face.'

Zoe's call distracted him from the beauty parade. Perhaps he should call her back and remind her that it was over between them. Their last meeting had been a mistake and he needed her to know that it could never happen again. The idea sounded absurd. Delusional, even by his standards. But the call made him nervous, a future conflict waiting to happen.

'These assholes don't have a clue,' Raul said, looking out at the terrace. 'All these beautiful women and no-one's making a move. It's a disgrace. I'm ashamed to be here, you know?'

He viewed the scene from Raul's perspective. The men stood in groups of threes and fours, engrossed in conversation. The women stood by in small clusters of their own, clearly unaffected by the separation. 'Maybe you should show them how it's done. Give them the benefit of all that profound wisdom.'

Raul gave a solemn nod. 'Yeah. Maybe I will too.'

The girl in the green dress came back and sat down. Soon the place would be overrun. The drinkers faces would change as the night wore on, a subtle transformation brought on by alcohol and fatigue. The long endurance of staying on your feet and talking nonsense to people you hardly knew . Sometimes it was easier to sit back and watch from a distance. The observer, cut off from the mainland, nothing to do but drink excessively and criticise the natives.

Marco made a sudden entrance, nonchalant, strolling through the crowd clutching his pint. Raul shook his head and swore. 'Unbelievable! Two hours late and that fat fuck comes in through the back door.'

'He's probably just woken up.'

'Lazy bastard. He ever does a real days work, it will kill him for sure.'

The mood around the table changed. Marco sat down and took over without a word, planting his keys and mobile phone centre of table and one foot on a vacant chair. Raul made an immediate reference to his weight. Marco smiled indulgently and patted his stomach with fondness, claiming that it was all paid for.

Raul raised his sunglasses to stare at Marco, incredulous. 'Come on then. Tell us how you do it.'

'How I do what?'

'How you manage to be so fucking late with nothing to do all day?'

'It's called time management, actually. Not that you'd have learnt much about that where you come from. What was the name of that village again?'

Raul jabbed a warning finger in Marco's direction. 'Hey! I don't come from no village, OK?'

Marco smiled lazily, aware of his wider audience, his genuine affection for Raul undiminished. The banter between them ran like a double act, a harmless sparring between two diametrically opposed forces. Marco tried to use his superior breeding to outwit Raul, who soaked up the insults and came back with more of his own.

He soon tired of their game. The volleys fired back and forth across the ornate table had a jaded quality, a repetition of countless previous nights. Marco's voice began to needle him. Marco should have been an entertainer, a stand-up comic whose vicious put-downs ensured he never played the same place twice. Some of his lines were good, but he always needed a victim. And he drank too much. When he was drunk, the humour turned to ridicule, and no-one evaded his poison radar.

Raul talked about Helen's bar and the likelihood of it's being sold. The prospect gave him a range of options, each one leaving him more bewildered than the last. Raul had no ambition. A serious career move was beyond his capability. The comfort zone of Helen's bar and the routine of his daily existence was enough; changing beer barrels and walking the dog; doing the odd removals job in his beloved Transit van. Keeping-fit was Raul's real obsession. The fifty mile rides with the Sunday morning cycling club fulfilled a bizarre need in him that no-one else could understand. Helen loved him unconditionally, even if he did eat all her Ferrero Rocher to replace carbohydrates lost out on the road.

Marco took the opportunity to bait Raul with a series of pointless questions. 'What was the name of that guy with the nightclub? I thought he was interested in buying the bar.'

'What guy?'

'The one with the Sunseeker and the jewellery shops in Tenerife.' Raul looked baffled. Marco kept a straight face. 'I thought the idea was that you'd sell the bar and go in with him as an advisor. You know, based on your extensive experience as chief shelf-stacker and men's room attendant.'

Raul took the insult with a dignified silence. To Marco, the bar belonged to Helen and would remain that way until she sold it. Raul was the glorified errand boy, without a say in the decision making.

The buzz around the terrace picked up. The party crowd, alive and living in the moment. The girl in the green dress had gone. In her place, a slim and good looking black guy with a polished-bullet head, chatting amiably to her buxom friend.

Raul decided the time was right to delete the hundred and six messages clogging-up his in box, one by one. Marco took this as a cue, and leant over conspiratorially. 'I hear you sorted Natalie's car.'

'I passed on the number of a mechanic, that's all.'

Marco nodded vaguely, tracing lines on his pint glass. 'I was going to have a word with you about it at some point.'

'About what?'

'Natalie.'

He took a long drink and tuned in to the party people. Marco sat silently by, plotting his next move, his long standing friendship with Natalie giving him some imagined influence over her private life.

'I know you've been seeing her, of course. It doesn't take a genius to figure it out.'

'I had a coffee with her one lunchtime. What's wrong with that?'

Marco inspected his fingernails and said nothing.

'What do I need – your approval?'

'No, of course not. I was just – '

'Forget it. I don't want to hear it, OK?'

Marco gave a passive shrug and spread his hands, suddenly the most reasonable man in the world. 'Look – all I'm saying is be careful. Don't get too involved. For your own good.'

'What am I, a five-year old? I need you to tell me who I can and can't see?'

Marco shook his head wearily and took a drink.

The debate began to incense him. He turned his chair a few degrees to face Marco and folded his arms. 'Come on then. Give me the rundown. I'm waiting.'

'You don't know Natalie like I do.'

'What are you, her councillor all of a sudden?'

'She's got a lot of issues.'

'What the fuck does that mean?'

'Look – just take it from me. I can't go into all the details. She's just…' Marco slumped back in the chair and stared out at the terrace.

'She's just what?' He waited for a response. 'Come on, you started this shit.'

Marco sighed heavily. 'Do what you like. But don't say I didn't warn you.'

Raul finished editing his phone and the conversation changed direction.

Marco's comments left a bitter aftertaste. He tried to focus on the scenery; the flow of bodies by the entrance, dance music trapped in the cellar bar, pounding on the walls to get out. The evening's entertainment was mapped out. Raul would make his excuses and go home early. Marco would get steadily drunk and complain about the music or the people, insisting they go somewhere else – the Litten Tree or the Brass House – where Marco would hold court at the bar, amusing the punters and charming lines of cocaine from his power boat friends.

Raul commented on a passing cyclist. The man's lean face was oily with sweat, his black shorts and blue singlet clinging like a second skin. Marco sneered at the sight. 'He should try taking a taxi like any normal person.'

Raul whipped round, inspired. 'Hey! I know what you need, my friend. Fifteen minutes on the cross-trainer three times a week. Work off that greasy kebab round your belly, you fat fuck.'

Marco rolled his eyes. 'Listen – the only reason Helen bought you that bike is so you'd get run over by an artic. Then, she can claim on the insurance she took out on you and fuck off abroad with the bloke she's been shagging. That right, Peter?'

'If you say so.'

Marco hovered, puzzled at his lack of response, before turning back to Raul in disgust. 'He used to be quite sociable at one time, you know. Then Claudia came along and turned him into a lemon. Funny that, isn't it?'

The terrace filled with more party people, eager for the nightlife. The buxom girl leaned seductively towards the good looking black guy at the next table. Their subtle body language caused him a weary envy, his thinking off-key like the music inside. The backdrop never changed. The potted plants swayed in the breeze. The doormen eyed the new arrivals with detached menace. The toxic hint of fast food drifted along on the warm current.

Marco told of an antiques dealer he knew who'd been burgled by his next door neighbour. The details had changed since the last time he'd told the story, but Marco was too engrossed to care. He had the voice, the rich baritone, weaving bizarre scenes together to amuse himself and anyone listening. The subject of the Ballroom was brushed aside, the imminent demolition of the old house a minor detail that didn't worry Marco unduly. He claimed to have had several offers of accommodation from friends, although he didn't say exactly who they were. Raul saw this as his chance to get even. 'So what will you do now, my fat friend? No more wild parties by the sea, huh?'

'Everyone moves on,' Marco said curtly.

'Sure. But you gotta settle down sometime. You can't spend the rest of your life falling asleep in other peoples' bathrooms. Looks bad on your CV, man.'

Marco looked away, unable to find a suitable reply.

Raul left soon after, claiming he needed his beauty sleep. With Raul gone, the mood changed again. The smooth vultures with their neat black suits and Colgate smiles, closed in. The girls looked stunning, but somehow mean and avaricious, strategically placed to maximise their potential. He felt even less connected.

'Fancy the K club?' Marco said.

'Not tonight.'

'You OK?'

'Fine.'

'Not still brooding about what I said earlier? I'd hate to think I'd sabotaged the romance of the decade.'

Marco's cynicism washed over him. He studied the group on the terrace instead. A woman with a cascade of dirty-blonde ringlets and a lean, tanned face joined the group. She paused to light a cigarette before entering the general conversation. He tried to place her, sure that he'd seen her before.

Marco spoke of a friend of his who'd sold his house and bought a yacht. The idea intrigued Marco in an odd way, like contemplating lunar flight or living in a cave, when the closest he'd get to real discomfort was the hangover he woke up with on a Sunday morning. The woman on the terrace drew on her cigarette and blew a haze of smoke upward. A lazy saxophone played somewhere inside.

'... I never could see the fascination with it, personally. Too much like hard work, if you ask me. All that swabbing down the decks and eating tins of tuna. Then you get washed overboard and eaten by a shark. I mean, come on ...'

Marco's voice receded. He watched the woman on the terrace with detached interest, certain now who she was.

'... And what happens when the wind drops? You're completely fucked. Stuck out in the blue beyond, waiting to get rolled over by the channel ferry. You don't get that problem with a pair of twin Johnson's strapped to the back.'

'What was the name of that bridesmaid at James's wedding?'

Marco stared at him, bemused.

'Tara's cousin. Tim spent most of the night dancing with her.'

Marco gave a curt shrug. 'How the fuck should I know? What sort of a wedding was it anyway? They closed the bar at twelve. I ended up with Erica's brother, cruising the streets trying to get a proper drink.'

The woman on the terrace looked over, sweeping the table area with a glance. She came back to his table and lingered. Recognition dawned. Her entire demeanour changed.

Marco glanced at his watch. 'I might take a leisurely stroll towards the Rock Café. This place bores the tits off me. Coming?'

The woman continued to stare at him. A man in the group joined her in conversation and she looked away. Marco drained his pint, oblivious, and looked over. 'What is it with you? You've been staring into space all night.'

The dance floor of the hotel had been packed with writhing bodies. The bridesmaids looked like royalty in their long crimson dresses and matching shoes. Tara was the real star, baring a stockinged leg to the flash of cameras on the sidelines. He'd danced with her once, one hand resting on her white laced hip. Neither of them had an inkling of what was to follow. 'Like a bad dream,' he said thinking aloud.

Marco glanced towards the group on the terrace, unable to get the connection. Perhaps they all knew. The woman had told them the details and they were standing round discussing his guilt like barristers in a long running trial.

'What you need is a good blow out,' Marco said, standing up. 'It's like being with a fucking morgue attendant sometimes. You coming with me or staying here?'

'Staying.'

Marco left to seek out the serious drinkers, unburdened by tired concepts of loyalty and friendship. He stayed behind, alone at the ornate table, with its perfect view of the busy terrace. The woman and the group she was with had moved on. He couldn't get the look she'd given him out of his head. The same look the couple had given him outside the supermarket. These people weren't satisfied with tragedy, they needed a scapegoat. He was supposed to suffer for the rest of his life for one moment of weakness, blown out of all proportion.

He walked the streets in the warm, evening sunshine, passing the café in the Square, where he'd sat with Natalie. Two days had passed without any contact. No messages or calls. All he had was the enigmatic smile she'd left him with in the gardens that day. Lurid images of her expert tongue catching droplets from a melting ice-cream. If he waited any longer to contact her, she might forget him completely. But the timing had to be right. You had to play the game according to the rules if you wanted to progress to the next level.

Claudia called to remind him about the old man's birthday. She described the gift she'd bought for him, a small brass golfer captured in mid-swing. The gift was from both of them, all he had to do was sign the card. He mumbled his thanks, disconnected, wishing he was somewhere else. 'What's the matter?' she said, her optimism deflated by his tone. He couldn't tell her. He barely knew the reason himself. His whole world was balanced on a precipice, about to come crashing down and all she could think about was balloons and party hats.

'I'll call you tomorrow,' he said and ended the call.

The old man turned sixty-five at the weekend. Sixty-five was a good age. After that, the inevitable slide into illness and infirmity that everyone has to go through. At least the old man had enjoyed a good innings. Out on his boat with the good old boys, thinking up ways to cheat the tax man. He'd got off lightly. Claudia had done all the work. All he had to do was sign a birthday card.

On impulse he made a phone call.

'Are you in?'

'Yeah.'

'On your own?'

'Lenka's here. You coming round?'

'I might do.' He waited for the formal invitation but none came. 'Give me ten minutes. Anything you want?'

'I'm out of milk.'

'Gimme a list and I'll do the rest of your shopping, shall I?'

She laughed in her quirky, offbeat way, immune to his myriad troubles.

Ten minutes later, he stood outside her block and rang the bell. No movement in the grimy second floor kitchen window. A few cooking utensils stood in a pot on the sill. He waited – milk carton in hand – gazing up at the window like a spurned Romeo. A girl in combat trousers came out with her tattooed boyfriend, the two of them eyeing him with suspicion on their way to the car park. He shuffled his feet and glanced at his watch. Tinny music came from inside the building, filtered out through an open window. The entire block needed a fresh coat of paint to ward off the decay, a target for drug dealers and shyster landlords. He felt stupid, loitering outside in his handmade Italian shoes and button-down shirt. At least he understood his motives. The alcohol had worn off.

The milk carton swung heavily against his thigh, a ridiculous prop, fooling no-one.

The window opened above.

Zoe leant out. 'I'll throw the keys down.'

He caught the bunch in his left hand as she closed the screeching window.

The dank hallway was lit by a bare bulb. The smell of old carpets and stale air closed like a fist. He climbed the worn staircase, thinking of all the things he would say to her. A mixture of lies and half-truths to keep her pacified. But all his good intentions meant nothing. As soon as he saw her his instincts would take over, a blind pulled down to shut out the light.

Twenty

He found her in the kitchen, preoccupied with the aftermath. Empty glasses and dirty plates. Serviettes and plastic food cartons. The catering never less than first class, even if it was only for the old man. And always the personal touch. Home-made pastries and decorative fairy cakes on the silver cake stand handed down from some great aunt or other. She never seemed to tire – at least not in company. By the time the guests had all gone home, the kitchen would be immaculate.

'What happened to Bernie?' he said.

She half-turned from the sink, glancing over her shoulder. '*Bernice* couldn't make it.'

'Why not?'

'She had to take the kids to a football tournament in Southampton.'

'She could have dropped a card in for him at least.'

'Don't start on about Bernice right now, Peter. I'm really not in the mood for it.'

He lingered along the worktop. The remains of the old man's birthday cake sat on a plate, melted chocolate and air-filled sponge to satisfy the addict in anyone. He dipped in a finger on his way over to the mini pork-pies. 'There's enough left over here to feed the five-thousand.'

'Take some home then.'

'Why not? Stick some in a doggy-bag and I'll drop it round to Bernie's on the way back.'

She spun round. 'Peter? If you want something useful to do, grab a tea towel and give me a hand over here. If not, go and annoy someone else.'

Samantha wandered in, shining like a Christmas decoration in her sequinned red dress. She ran a podgy little hand along the edge of the pine table, and with one eye on the cakes and the food cartons, spoke up in a plaintive voice 'Auntie Margaret?'

'Yes, darling?'

'Can I have some more trifle, please?'

'Yes of course you can. Peter, would you give Samantha a bowl of trifle, please?'

Samantha waited, fat fingers on the pine surface, two beady eyes watching him intently. He dished out the trifle with a table spoon, doling out the jelly first, holding back on the custard and cream to further the suspense. Veiled eyes flashed with resentment. Mean eyes like her mother's. Auntie Pat – scourge of all able-bodied men under the age of sixty, fortified by expensive brandy and always on the lookout for trouble.

Samantha said a gracious 'Thank you, Auntie Margaret,' and wandered out into the hall, cupping the bowl in both hands.

'Pat needs to put that kid on a diet,' he said when she'd gone.

'What?'

'Samantha – she eats more than me and the old man put together.'

She stared at him in dismay. 'What the hell's the matter with you tonight?'

'It was a joke.'

'Well it wasn't funny. If you can't think of anything *nice* to say, don't bother opening your mouth at all. Has Claudia had enough to eat?'

'She's watching her weight.'

'Don't be ridiculous. There's nothing wrong with Claudia's figure.'

He moved along the sideboard and lifted a piece of silver foil. Roast chicken carcass beneath, the skin charred and wrinkled. She continued to berate him from the sink.

'You should be more supportive. She gets tired, poor girl. All those long hours up and down the motorway. No wonder she needs a holiday.'

He picked at the chicken carcass, tearing off a strip of white breast. She talked about Leanne and how sorry she was that Leanne couldn't make the party. He mumbled an agreement with a mouthful of moist and tender chicken. Sixteen year olds had their own agenda. Beloved grandparents were relegated when it came to meeting friends and socialising.

'How was the trip to Bristol?' she said.

'Wonderful.'

'Did you speak to Sylvia's mother?'

'You're joking. She can just about tolerate me from a distance these days.'

'Well at least Leanne has regular contact with that side of her family.'

'Some family. Leave your car too long and they prise the hub-caps off and use them as Frisbees.'

'I'm sure they're not that bad.'

'You don't know the half of it.'

He sat at the table and licked the grease from his fingers. The only trouble with parties was the leftover food. You couldn't help but get a guilt complex at so much wastage. The noise from the front room confirmed the guests enjoyment. Kids and adults thrown together in a volatile mix.

'Has your father talked to you yet?' she said.

'What about?'

'Henley Park.'

He tensed at the reference without knowing why.

'He said you were thinking of taking it on yourself and running it for him.'

'That's right – thinking about it.'

She turned to face him, one foam covered hand poised above the drainer. 'So what are you saying – that you've changed your mind?'

'I don't know yet.'

She sighed heavily and turned back to the sink. 'I really can't be doing with all this, you know. Worrying about your dad's health when he's supposed to be taking it easy. He should never have taken it on in the first place.'

'Sorry – not my problem.'

She glanced over her shoulder, tight-lipped, her face flushed. 'Why do you have to take that tone with me every time we have a conversation?'

'Sorry.'

'No you're not. You're not sorry at all.'

'I'm just saying, I've got enough problems of my own without worrying about the old man. Priory Road's set me back two weeks at least. Plus I've got Claudia harping on about the work that needs doing at my place. It's all pressure. Constant pressure.'

She made no comment, stacking plates noisily on the drainer. She could have used the dishwasher like any normal person, but that would have been too easy. He couldn't resist a final dig, push her to the limits of her patience to get a reaction. 'Anyway, if I don't take it on, he can always farm it out to the secret handshake club can't he?'

'I'm not even going to answer that.'

'It's true enough.'

'Peter.' She turned slowly, eyeing him with scorn. 'Please go and find someone else to irritate, will you? I'm really not in the mood for your *stupid* comments.'

He made the rounds of the visiting aunts and uncles. Big Jack's successful son, poised to take over when he retired. The old man as head of an empire. His philosophy simple; to get ahead in the game you had to grab every opportunity and make the most of it. Develop an attitude to success that doesn't accept failure as an option. Failure – the cancer that people allowed to eat away at their lives, stopping them from getting what they wanted. The old man's relentless power drive made unsettling waves for those left in its wake. No room for negotiation. No prisoners taken. Even as a kid, he recalled listening in awe as the cyclone raged through the house, unleashed over some minor setback. Cupboard doors ripped off hinges. Holes punched in stud walling. The Bentley reversed into the garage wall one night. And always his mother in the background, waiting until the worst was over. No raised voices. No recriminations. Only her quiet disapproval, honed to perfection over thirty-eight years of putting up with the same thing.

He found the old man staring through the leaded window in the dining room. He looked like Rod Steiger in *Waterloo,* hands clasped behind his back, facing his demons on the eve of battle.

He stood alongside the old man and they watched the boys outside. Harry and the kid with the hearing aid ran in circles on the immaculate lawn, chased by the two yapping terriers. The old man's disapproval could almost be heard, even above Pat's abrasive voice at the table.

'It's the additives they put in the cake, you know.'

The old man grunted and shook his head. 'Be the back of my hand in a minute, they don't come in off that fucking lawn. Where's Sarah?'

'Upstairs with Claudia.'

The old man resumed his stance, watching the spectacle through the window and shaking his head. 'Thought any more about Henley Park?'

'Not yet.'

'Why not? You've had enough time to think about it.'

'I've been busy.'

The old man tutted, shaking his head again. The view from the window took precedence. 'Fucking kids. I told Sarah I didn't want them running all over the house. Where's your mother?'

The old man left his post and excused himself from the room. As he passed, Auntie Pat raised her brandy glass and called out a mocking 'Happy birthday, Big Boy!' The adults at the table sniggered like children, none of them willing to risk offending the old man to his face.

He stood watching the scene unfold on the lawn.

Sarah came and stood alongside him. They watched the proceedings together, with shared amusement. Harry and the deaf kid weaved a figure of eight on the sacred lawn, the terriers yapping at their heels like homing missiles. The old man strode out onto the driveway and yelled for them to come inside.

'Cantankerous old sod, isn't he?' Sarah said.

'I suppose he's earned the right to be.'

'Not good for his health though, is it? He needs to watch his blood pressure these days. Where's Claudia?'

'I thought she was upstairs with you.'

'That was ages ago. Typical, you didn't even notice. What did you say to upset Mum?'

'Nothing. I just mentioned Bernie not turning up.'

'Bernie's got a lot going on at the moment what with Jasmine being ill.'

'So we're all supposed to rush round after her are we?'

Sarah fixed him with a big sisterly look of reproach. 'God, you're all heart today, Peter. You get more like Dad every time I see you.'

He felt justified in his anger. Bernice always played the victim. The youngest and most wayward child even at twenty-nine, always expecting someone to come running and clean up the latest mess she'd made. With her model looks and baby-doll eyes, she reeled in the suckers from a distance. The suckers never lasted when they found out what she was really like.

His phone rang.

He stared at the handset in horror, caught in an immediate dilemma. 'Sorry, Sis, gotta take a call.'

She watched him go, open-mouthed. 'Hey? – when are we going to have that lunch you keep promising?'

'Soon,' he said, heading for the door.

The Green room proved a welcome sanctuary. His favourite room in the house. Off limits to people like Auntie Pat and her noisy troupe of kids. He shut the door and pressed the call connect button. 'What d'you want?'

'That's nice. What happened to hello, how are you?'

'Zoe, I haven't got time for all this.'

'Neither have I really. At least I made the effort.'

He lowered his voice. 'What did I say about ringing me?'

'*Sorry.* I forgot you had such a busy schedule.'

He sank into the Ercol rocking chair and breathed in the lemon-scented air. Part of him wanted to give in to her blackmail. The privacy added a degree of tension, making him careless. Claudia could walk in at any minute and catch him in the act. 'Look, Zoe. You know how it is. I explained all that to you on Friday night.'

'Amongst other things.'

Laughter filtered through from the dining room. He tried to suppress a rising irritation, the impulse to scream his frustration down the line at her. 'Look, I've gotta go. I'll call you tomorrow.'

'Yeah Yeah!'

'Zoe – I said – '

She was gone.

He breathed easier in the quiet of the room. The absurdity of the conversation cancelled out the danger. He admired her persistence, her self-righteous anger disguised as small talk. In another life they might have been good together. In this one they were distinctly off key.

He rocked himself back and forth in the chair, comfortable in the silence. The evening light cast the room in sombre shadow. Through the leaded window – the misshapen trunk of the old beech tree, various enticements for the birds, hanging from it's branches. He couldn't imagine the house belonging to anyone else. Someday it might even belong to him, unless the old man weakened and left it to Bernie.

Children's voices rang along the hallway. Footsteps rapped along the driveway, Harry's goading voice calling out a challenge. Zoe's parting shot still rang in his head. She didn't contact him for weeks, then expected a sudden commitment from him. Like all women, relying on a combination of feminine charm and subtle manipulation. Then, when she couldn't get her own way, the gloves came off. He had to keep away from her for his own sake.

The door opened. Claudia peered in at him. 'What are you doing in here on your own?'

'Thinking.'

'Can I join you?'

'Do what you like.'

She closed the door and padded over in her flat shoes, breaking the unwritten house rule. She stood before him, hand on hip, blocking out the sombre light from the side window. 'Who were you on the phone to earlier?'

'No-one.'

'Sarah said you went out to take a call.'

'Can't I move without someone breathing down my neck every five minutes?'

She shifted uneasily. 'You don't have to get like that.'

'Look – I came in here to get away from that lot. Pat telling everyone what I was like when I was fourteen. Someone ought to take the car keys off her, the amount she's been drinking.'

She frowned at him. 'What's the matter with you tonight?'

'Nothing.'

'Yes there is. Please tell me what it is?'

He stared back at her, rocking gently in the chair, an old homesteader on the front porch. The outline of her hips intrigued him, adding to her soft, maternal appeal. He reached out a hand. 'Come over here.'

'Peter, I don't think – '

He put a finger to his lips to and took hold of her wrist. She stood meekly between his legs, unsure. He tightened his grip on her wrist.

'Peter!'

'Ssh.'

'You're hurting me!'

He relaxed his grip on her wrist and let his fingers stray to the hem of her dress.

'What're you doing?' she said.

'What d'you think I'm doing?'

'You can't.'

He ignored her, tracing the softness of her thigh beneath her thin dress. She stood over him, clamped between his knees, her hands resting on his shoulders. He gazed up at her anxious face, seeing how far he could go.

She pulled back. 'Peter, please! Someone might come in.'

'So?'

She laughed nervously. 'I'm not doing anything in here.'

'Why not? I thought you liked the danger?'

'For God's sake!'

He released her. All the anger came flooding back. Sullen, brooding anger with no outlet. Now she was the enemy, sent to test him in all manner of ways. The shadows in the room lengthened, a perfect backdrop to his darkening mood.

She took a step back, staring at him with a haunted, vacant look. 'There is something the matter with you, isn't there?'

'I don't know – is there?'

'Is it Spain?'

He said nothing.

'I mean, if you really don't want to go just say so.'

'It isn't Spain.'

'So what is it then? Is it me? Have I done something to upset you?'

'You haven't done anything, Claudia.'

She watched him in agonised silence, clearly undecided.

'Please come back in with me.' she said finally.

'I will in a minute.'

'Please. I can't bear it when you're like this.'

'I just said, didn't I?'

She closed the door quietly behind her, leaving him alone with the shadows.

He thought of all her good qualities. How much he would lose if they split up. Her warm and fleshy embrace, always there for him. Marriage on the near horizon. The two of them settled in to some pleasant, domestic routine where nothing much changed other than the bed sheets in the master bedroom.

He sat alone in the Green room, his favourite room in the house. Sooner or later he would have to sort his life out. Put an end to all the neat little diversions that came along. Grow up and take some responsibility. He could change his phone and get a new number. No more unexpected calls from Zoe. No more unwanted intrusions.

He thought about Natalie

The compulsion to call her had grown in the last few days. He could try to talk himself out of it, but the thought was always there in the background, a warning sign to be ignored. Like swimming in shallow water and heading out to sea. You put your feet down to touch the bottom and nothing was there.

He took out a coin. Heads he would call her. Tails he wouldn't.

It landed heads-up.

Twenty-one

It happened before he could think. They were standing in her hallway and he made a joke about the lack of time, the fact that wherever they were, she was always planning to be somewhere else. She reacted with her usual indignation. Some people had to go to work. He should be glad that she had invited him round in the first place. He took a tentative step towards her. She took a step back.

'I have to get ready,' she said.

He put his hands on her hips, his face inches from hers. Her shoulders rose with her quickened breathing, her thin black bra strap visible beneath her white t-shirt. He leaned in to kiss her and she teetered. Then, as if a spell had been broken, she pulled back in alarm. 'Please!'

'Relax, Natalie.'

'I can't. I've got to get ready.'

But the lure was too strong. She gave a deep sigh and allowed him closer. He kissed her neck, her mouth and this time she responded eagerly, her tongue probing his, flecked with saliva. Now he had the element of surprise. All he had to do was steer her towards the bedroom before she could change her mind.

After, he lay beside her, listening to her breathing. Now they were lovers. The moment he'd been waiting for, here and gone. Neither of them able to change the timing, the way it had happened. He hoped she wouldn't blame him exclusively, for the ruination of her satin bedspread, her clothes strewn across the bedroom floor, the disruption to her work schedule. Perhaps they needed to talk and get it all out in the open, a kind of debriefing session to work out the best way to proceed from here on.

'You OK?' he said.

She laughed softly. 'I was before you came round.'

'Thanks.'

'Don't mention it ... Will you do something for me?'

'Sure.'

'Get me a glass of water from the fridge before I dehydrate.'

He wandered out into the kitchen and opened the fridge. One Greek yoghurt and a carton of double cream. Half a quiche next to a near empty vegetable tray. Nothing much to fill the emptiness. The afterglow left a strange hollow, a kind of delayed shock, like being removed from reality then plunged back in.

He filled a glass from the large bottle of Evian and called out. 'You want ice?'

'Whatever!'

He found a blister-pack of ice in the sparse freezer compartment. Not much in the way of sustenance here either. One pack of frozen vegetables, a box of fish fingers and a bag of chicken nuggets. A few stray frozen peas lined the bottom. She obviously didn't have Claudia's penchant for hoarding.

He went back into the bedroom.

Now they were lovers the rules had changed. Every remark she made, every shadow that crossed her face had to be analysed and interpreted a different way. Already she seemed remote, lying still on the crumpled white sheet, her breathing smooth and rhythmic. Even in the same room, you were somehow apart

'What time do you have to be back?' he said.

'Two o'clock.'

He glanced at his watch. 'That gives you about ten minutes to get ready.'

'I'll ring in.'

'Sorry.'

'No you're not.'

He rolled onto his side to look at her. Strange that after so much intense physical contact between them he felt reluctant to reach out and touch her. She seemed resigned to the outcome. Her lateness. His being there. Content to lay back in private reflection while he worked out the ramifications.

He soaked up the ambience of the room. Perfume and body-oil heavy on the air. The pine dresser lined with cosmetics and jewellery. Her black bra draped across the full length mirror stand. Even with the window open and the sounds of traffic drifting in, they were stranded in a world of their own. Strangers, without the aid of easy conversation.

He felt he should say something, as a token, to reconnect them.

'Who's the greatest artist of all?'

She looked up at him, puzzled. 'What?'

'Van Gogh. Was he any good?'

'Are you being serious?'

'Sure.'

She stared at the ceiling. 'I can't answer that.'

'Why not?'

'Because it's subjective. It's like music. Who's the greatest composer? Everyone's got their own opinion.'

'Why did he cut his ear off?'

'I don't know, I never asked him.'

He lay back and reviewed his earlier performance. Memories to play back over and over. Her jeans unbuttoned revealing her smooth navel. The enticing line of her black knickers as he undid her zip. Her nakedness, paraded before him without embarrassment. She'd given in much easier than he'd expected, but he didn't feel any sense of victory. The tension between them was still there. Strangers in the same room, trying to understand why they were together and how it had happened so quickly.

'How come you don't have any of your work on the wall?' he said.

'Because I can't bear looking at it.'

'Why not?'

'It makes me feel uncomfortable.'

'Can I see some of it?'

'Not right now.'

'Some other time then.'

'Maybe. Some other time.'

He left her to get dressed and went out to the kitchen. To distract himself, he picked fault in the décor; the cheap melamine units and the uneven tiling, the old gas cooker with its chipped enamel surface. Her personal effects added a poignant touch and made up for the poor furnishings. Humorous magnets and handwritten notes were stuck to the fridge door. Blotches of garish colour, signed 'Charlotte' in the bottom corner. Pot plants lined the window sill. Cookery books were stacked against the microwave. The window looked out over the bay, four floors up and a vision of clear blue, not even a lone seagull on the horizon.

She walked in, flustered, tying back her hair.

'Is that Charlotte?' he said.

She glanced at the photograph on the fridge door. 'Two years ago. She doesn't look like that now.'

'She looks cute.'

'Don't be fooled by appearances. She's a monster, take it from me.'

She rifled the contents of her purse, pulling out receipts and business cards and dropping them on the table. He sensed her restlessness, her change of mood since she'd dressed and left the bedroom.

'What have you lost?' he said.

'My hairdresser's appointment for tomorrow. I had the time written down somewhere.'

'Do you save all your receipts?'

'Not all of them, why?'

'I suppose it's a woman's thing.'

'Really,' she said dryly.

'It goes back to Neolithic times when we were all cave-dwellers. Women are hoarders. It's all about providing in times of famine.'

'If you say so.' She looked up, distracted. 'Are you coming with me?'

'To the hairdressers?'

'I meant out! Now! Some of us were supposed to be at work half an hour ago!'

She found her appointment card and stuffed all the receipts back into her purse. With her bag over her shoulder, she flashed him a strained smile. 'Ready?'

'Do I get a kiss before we go?'

'No, you don't. I'm late enough as it is.'

'Some other time then.'

'Why not? You've thrown the rest of my life into confusion.'

She stopped to examine an eyelash in the hall mirror, the gymnastics in the bedroom now forgotten. She focused on the way she looked, intent on keeping him at a safe distance.

He caught her arm at the door and pulled her to him.

'What now?' she said.

'I don't like unfinished business.'

'What? You must have a pretty short memory with what we did earlier.'

He circled her waist and kissed her before she could react. The fear of losing her gave way to a sense of urgency. The same need in them both that even she couldn't deny.

They parted without a word. Lovers again, alone in her hallway. The shock still registered in her eyes, a kind of disbelief that she could give in without the slightest resistance.

'Where do we go from here?' he said softly.

She looked up, eying him carefully. 'I don't know. You're the one who's got it all worked out. But right now, I really have to go to work.'

The red digits in the lift flashed on the way down. He stood beside her and focused on the whir of movement, the vacuum of stale air. She stared ahead, saying nothing. He wished he knew what she was thinking. If he knew what she was thinking he might know how to respond. Her silence acted as a snub and left him feeling uneasy.

The lift doors opened and she stepped outside.

Bright sunshine and fresh air changed the mood again. She made a phone call, switching to her business voice without a trace of her previous awkwardness. After, she seemed more amenable, even if he had been the direct cause of the delay.

He walked her to her car, anxious at the next step, the moment they would say their goodbyes and part company.

'Are you busy this week?' he said.

'I'm always busy.'

'How about the weekend?'

She laughed abruptly. 'I pick Charlotte up from school on Friday afternoon and that's it. Not a moments peace from there on.'

She unlocked her car and paused, indecisive. The tower block loomed behind her. Her place of seduction, a stifling room on the fourth floor.

'Look – this is really difficult for me,' she said.

'What is?'

'The whole thing. You coming round. Me getting involved. It wasn't meant to happen.' She looked away, unable to voice her concerns. The outcome seemed to hang in the balance.

'So what do you want to do?' he said.

'I don't know.'

'Can I call you?'

'After the trouble you've got me into already?' She smiled coyly, leaving him to work out the nuances.

Now they were lovers he could afford to take chances. Test her commitment without leaving himself too exposed. But whatever doubts she may have had, her smile said it all. An open invitation. All he had to do was take advantage.

'I'll call you tomorrow,' he said.

'OK.'

'Is that alright?'

'Yes, it's alright. Now if you'll excuse me, I've really got to go.'

He watched her drive off in her bright red Peugeot, sunlight reflected from the roof. Images of her stayed in his mind. Her body, naked on the crumpled white sheet. The two of them together, unable to speak. Already he ached for her again. Tomorrow, too far off. Too distant.

He turned to go and thought of Claudia. All he needed to do was keep cool and act as if nothing had happened. But somewhere up ahead was the fallout. The inevitable price you paid for being found out.

Twenty-two

Claudia clipped her pink laced bra over her full bosom, her prize assets paraded in front of him. He lay back and reflected on lust's passing. Her naked body usually demanded his full attention, now it was an attachment, packed away after use like the sugar or the coffee jar. The prospect of being denied this pleasure filled him with a hollow regret.

'I thought we might drop in to Erica's later,' she said, adjusting a shoulder strap. 'Is that okay with you?'

'Fine.'

'What's up? You've been really quiet all morning.'

'I'm just thinking.'

'What about?'

'Nothing.'

'It's impossible to think about nothing.'

'No it isn't. You just blank your mind. That's the purpose of meditation.'

'Frances meditates,' she said, rooting through her wardrobe. 'I don't know how she finds the time really.'

'It's easy to empty your mind when there's nothing in it to start with.'

'I'll tell her you said that.'

'Tell her what you like.'

She held up a cream coloured V-neck. 'What d'you think – this one or the yellow one?'

'Whatever.'

He pictured her sister, legs crossed in the lotus position, trying to block out last month's credit card statement or carnal images of her latest boyfriend. It was all about sex whichever manual you read. The one basic instinct that bound all human relations together. More compelling than good job prospects and a shared taste in music. Glimpses of flesh in supermarket queues. High heels on a deserted stretch of pavement. Sordid fantasies conjured up in the cesspool of your own mind.

Claudia's assets disappeared beneath her thin yellow jumper. Like most women, her obsessions ran along similar lines. The classification of body-shapes gave her a category whether she liked it or not. Not much scope for change beyond the superficial. You were born with your body and couldn't do much to alter it beyond repressive exercise and plastic surgery. Claudia didn't like exercise and couldn't afford the surgery, so her pear-shaped physiology hung around, chipping away at her self-image and annoying him in the process. Personally, he couldn't see what all the fuss was about. There was always liposuction if she won the Lottery. Failing that, it was back to the treadmill like everyone else.

Claudia had the body most women could only dream of. Men gawped at her in the street and in bars. But as a regular service user, he'd become used to it.

She lingered in the doorway, frowning at him. 'What are you thinking about now?'

'The riddle of existence.'

'Well when you've found the answer to that, help me get some clothes out of the loft, will you?'

He lay back on her soft bed and heard her rooting around in the spare bedroom. Lying next to him, the worn teddy with the shiny red waistcoat, longest surviving companion from her childhood. The guilt trip continued. He'd failed already according to his conscience, although the judgement seemed harsh in reality. All he'd done was follow his instincts and satisfy the primal call. No great crime in the scheme of things.

Notions like fidelity and loyalty were millstones, rocks in the backpack you were forced to carry in the search for freedom. But the situation saddened him. He didn't want to hurt Claudia any more than was necessary.

Green bin liners dropped from above, their ends tied in neat bats ears. He caught the first three and stacked them against the wall. 'How many more?'

'That's it.'

He listened to her, rummaging in the dark corners of the loft.

'What're you doing up there now?'

'Looking for net curtains.'

'What for?'

'Because the bedroom ones need changing.'

'They looked alright to me.'

Her red face loomed in the loft hatch. 'And that from a man who only hoovers once every six months!'

Her pear-shaped backside swung through the loft hatch. Rubber-soled flat shoes testing out the metal rungs of the ladder on her way down. He mused on the way a woman's mind works. The assigning of random tasks in no apparent order. For the moment she was happy, content to be with him and all his bad habits. But he was somewhere else. Lost in a sweet-scented room on the fourth floor of a tower block, with only one thing on his mind.

Claudia stood on the landing, breathing heavily, hands on hips. 'I can't find them.'

'You can't find what?'

'The nets.'

'What does that mean – three hours trawling the shops looking for new ones?'

'What with you? You must be joking.' She looked at the bin liners and sighed. 'I'll sort them out downstairs. Most of it will end up in a charity shop, anyway.'

Natalie had a thing about charity shops. He pictured her holding up a silky number, hunting out the bargains along the high street. The thought of her wearing second hand clothes was strangely off-putting.

'Why do people buy clothes from charity shops?' he said.

'Because it's cheap, why d'you think?'

He thought this over. 'Erica wouldn't though, would she?'

'How do you know?'

'Because she wouldn't. It's degrading. Wearing someone else's cast-offs.'

'Don't be ridiculous. No-one knows where they come from. You're just a snob.' She gave him a devious smile. 'I'll buy you a pair of Levi's from Marie Curie one day, you'll never know the difference.'

She went through each bin liner with her exacting eye. Navy blue dress suits and white blouses covered the carpet. She held up a crumpled pair of jeans and looked them over before consigning them to the junk pile. 'I don't want to leave it all until the last minute. Things could move quickly. Especially if that couple make an offer on the house.'

'What couple?'

'The guy from Chase Manhattan and his girlfriend. I think she's a hairdresser or something. I told you about them.' She noted his blank expression. 'You never listen, that's your trouble. Anyway, John said he'd ring and let me know.'

'John who?'

'The Estate Agent from Connelly's.'

The name registered vaguely. Someone he'd met once before and didn't like.

She rummaged in the next bin liner and discarded a pink blouse. 'Something might come of it. And they weren't stuck in a chain either.' She looked up mournfully. 'You do want me to sell the place, don't you?'

'Of course I do.'

'It makes me wonder sometimes, you're so negative about the whole thing.'

She found another wrinkled pair of jeans and held them up for inspection. He pictured the prospective couple – two more hopefuls to influence the roll of the dice. Guilt found its way into the process once more. The sale of her house would leave her without a home, without security. With guidance from him, she could have rented it out and kept one foot on the property ladder. But he was too busy running his own life to worry too much about hers. Now he had other things to consider. The impact of sleeping with someone else and keeping it hidden.

They took a break from the bagging area. He took a seat on one of her rigid aluminium stools while she put the kettle on. He would miss her house. Lying in her warm double bed and watching late night films on her portable television. Private barbecues in her poky back garden. All these things would go, replaced by the gnawing uncertainty of life without her.

'Toast?' she said.

'No thanks.'

'What's up – you haven't eaten anything all morning?'

'I'm not hungry.'

'Not coming down with something, are you?'

'Touch of full moon syndrome maybe.'

She put the kettle on and put two pieces of wholemeal bread in the toaster.

The property section of a newspaper lay open on the worktop. Boxes of neat semis and spacious bungalows to gaze upon. Work issues came to mind. Priory Road, one more lost item on the agenda. Apart from the odd phone call with Barry and a pint with Sean in the Hog's Head, the job had been neatly sidelined. Strange how a woman could take precedence over the need to make a living. The roof was due to go on during the following week and all he could picture was Natalie.

'I've made a decision about Henley Park' he said.

She looked up, puzzled. 'What d'you mean?'

'I'm not taking it on.'

She froze, the future she had planned for them both under immediate threat. 'But I thought – '

'I'm not doing it and that's that.'

'But your Mum said – '

'Forget what she said. I've been living in the old man's shadow too long. It's time to move on, do something else.'

'But Henley Park was such an opportunity.' She slumped visibly. 'Oh, Peter. I wish you'd talk it over with your dad first.'

'There's nothing more to say. I've made up my mind and that's it.'

He pitied her for a moment, her dreams so far out of sync with his own. Beneath all the warmth and loyalty, her natural instinct for security dominated all other concerns. Perhaps she saw him as a means to an end. The cheque book for the joint account. The villa in Spain. She swore that she loved him, regardless of his material status, and he believed her. He must have also trusted her. You had to trust someone to let them make plans for the rest of your life while you were busy strolling round a golf course.

She took a phone call in the front room. He ate the wholemeal crust on her plate, obliterating her teeth marks in a single swoop. Her pompous phone voice alerted him, an annoying tendency she got from her mother. She sounded upbeat, a note of pleasant surprise to warn him as he looked around for something else to eat.

She came back with a broad grin. 'See – I told you!'

'You told me what?'

'The couple that looked at the house – they've made an offer.'

'Great.'

Her face clouded. 'I thought you'd be happy for me.'

'I am.'

'You don't look it.'

'Just don't get your hopes up too much, that's all I'm saying. Look what happened the last time.'

She came over and stood quietly beside him. 'You're not having second thoughts, are you? About us, I mean?'

'No, of course I'm not.'

She put a hand on his shoulder and squeezed gently, a ripple of childlike happiness lighting her face. 'I'm so excited about the future. So excited.'

He loaded the charity bags into the back of her car. The odd-job man, making amends for his derelictions by clearing out the old and making way for the new. In this case, the anonymous banker from Chase Manhattan and his hairdresser girlfriend. Two more candidates for the endless waltz.

Erica welcomed them with her usual exuberance. She hugged Claudia, enthusing over the new prospective buyers like an old aunt. When she hugged him it wasn't quite the same. He wasn't part of the inner circle – the Cauldron, as he called it. One day someone would invent a pill that made men think like women. Until then, you were stuck on the sidelines, a visitor in a foreign country minus the guidebook.

He watched the kettle boil through its blue neon port hole. The spot where Natalie had stood several weeks before looked forlorn, part of a dismantled film set. He ached at the thought of her and stood at the window, looking out. Gossip flowed. Some woman Erica knew who had slept with someone's else's boyfriend. Between them they took the nameless girl apart, blackening her reputation for ever after.

He wandered into Erica's sun warmed lounge and thought about vanishing. The headline – *'Local entrepreneur disappears without trace.'* Running away was always an option. He'd thought about it after James's death, when the rumour mill started up. Whispered insinuations that reached him third-hand. He learned what it was like to feel ostracised, labelled a betrayer, a thief of the worse kind.

The girls joined him, sinking down onto Erica's pristine cream sofa with plump, matching cushions. They sat facing each other with their knees drawn-up and ignored him completely. Erica flipped through a John Lewis catalogue, the two of them debating the price of various kitchen accessories. The woman who'd slept with someone else's boyfriend was relegated for the time being. He compared the two of them, huddled together on the sofa, their knees touching. Sex got in the way of everything. Even friendship. At least he didn't feel that way about Erica any more. Claudia accepted that whatever had happened between them had all been so long ago, and rarely questioned him about it. She had no need to. He recalled Erica's supple, school-leavers body with fondness. Like going over holiday snaps and rediscovering places you'd forgotten you'd been. Seated next to her on the back seat of the bus with his hand up her jumper. The two of them, wedged-up against his bedroom door, listening out for footsteps on the stairs as he unhooked the clasp of her bra.

Erica snapped the catalogue shut and looked up. 'I ran into Tim the other day. He looked a bit down to me. Everything alright with him?'

'Far as I know.'

Claudia smirked. 'He's thinning a bit on top, lately. That might have something to do with it.'

Erica reacted with mock surprise. 'God! Imagine that. Definitely not good for his image. Mind you, Tim was never as bad as Peter. Checking his hair in the mirror every five minutes, weren't you, darling?'

Claudia's comment about Tim made him feel better, a lifelong character weakness, thriving on someone else's misfortune. Tim had a thick skin and could take the flak. But he felt uneasy, vulnerable and open to suspicion. Erica's good natured probing might expose more than he wished to reveal. She'd witnessed his reaction before, the night at Pascali's, when Natalie had turned up late and spoiled his appetite.

Claudia talked about work. The strain of monthly sales targets and the prospect of promotion. She was good at her job, proud of the cash bonuses she earned for hitting the targets and achieving the highest call rate. No reason why she couldn't make hospital rep in a few months, then senior hospital specialist, before moving into marketing. But her confident tone betrayed a lack of conviction, an underlying sense that she was somehow going through the motions.

'All those good looking doctors,' Erica said, for his benefit. 'It's no wonder you enjoy your work so much.'

Claudia fingered a cushion and shook her head sadly. 'I don't enjoy it though. Sometimes I feel I'm in the wrong job. All I've done since I left school is study and pass exams, and I did that mainly to please my dad.'

Erica waved a hand dismissively. 'My dad didn't care what I did when I left school. I think he just wanted me out of the house because I was such a bloody nuisance. But you work so hard, honey. You deserve to be successful.'

Claudia nodded thoughtfully, embarrassed by the attention.

'Look on the bright side. You're getting married next year. You'll be so busy planning that, you won't have time to think about anything else.'

Erica saw them to the door, diminutive in her bare feet, her silver toe ring almost buried in the plush carpet. She embraced him while Claudia looked on, their friendship more enduring than a quick fumble behind the bedroom door. He loved Erica, but more in the familial sense. She would have made a good mother, fussing about him getting enough vitamins, and making sure he wasn't working too hard. The theory that all men were looking for a mother figure didn't ring true. The age old question of lust had yet to be resolved. The same dilemma for men the world over. Sleep with a thousand women or find that special *one* to share the rest of your days with.

Claudia waited until they were outside to tug at his arm. 'You were a bit off in there, weren't you? Moody all the time. Snapping at me for no reason.'

'I've got a lot on my mind at the moment, that's all.'

'Because I'm selling the house?'

'No, I'm just preoccupied.' He gave a token explanation of his troubles. Conflict with the old man over business deals. Unfinished work at home. The pressures of modern living.

She linked arms with him, and looked up with a sad smile. 'I know it's stressful for you at the moment. But it won't always be like that. We've got each other, haven't we?'

'Sure we have.'

'That's enough, isn't it?'

He gave her a reassuring hug and felt worse than ever. 'It's just me. I've got to get a few things out of my system.'

She drove back through the centre of town. He criticised her driving out of habit, but his heart wasn't in it. According to Erica, women had a different spatial awareness, and this tied-in with his cave dwellers theory. He thought it also likely that women were too busy thinking about acrylic nails and hairdressers appointments to concentrate on boring road-signs. He tried not to snap at Claudia. At least the intention not to snap at her made him feel more noble. He contented himself with watching girls on the high street, a habit she found equally off-putting. Something unappealing about a man in the passenger seat of his girlfriend's car, leaning on the window sill and leering at the local talent. But he'd gone past caring. The talent passed by like window dressing. Only the dark haired ones held his attention for longer than a millisecond. The ones who reminded him of Natalie.

Twenty-three

Artists have extreme mood swings. Van Gogh cut off one of his ears and gave it to a prostitute. A deviant artist by the name of Egon Schiele seduced an underage girl and made pornographic sketches to relieve his tortured mind. He read this in one of her books – *The Creative Mindset.* Clearly, these people were unbalanced and in need of treatment. Reading about them gave him a new insight. But it wasn't some penniless foreign artist whose light had burned out too soon that he cared about. He wanted to know more about Natalie.

She came out of the shower, a faded orange towel wrapped around her like a sari. He pretended not to notice, absorbed in the exotic world of Art. She stepped past the bed and glanced at him. 'What's that you're reading?' He showed her the cover. She perched on the end of the bed and shook her hair loose, inspecting the wet ends with her fingertips. The heat of the shower had reddened her pale skin in places.

'Ever been to Paris?' he said.

'No. Why?'

'I took this girl years ago. Romantic interlude to celebrate my divorce coming through.'

'Did you propose to her while you were there?'

'Not quite. We had an argument at the top of the Eiffel Tower and didn't speak for three days.'

'Remind me never to go anywhere with you in future.'

Paris – an opportunity missed the first time he'd been in Europe. Chasing French women in café bars and upsetting the locals. Jealous youths riding scooters onto the pavements in an unconvincing show of strength. The girl he'd met in Rouen had made an engaging travelling companion, the two of them hugging and kissing on the back seat of a beat-up old Citroen all the way down to Toulouse. Always a woman in it somewhere. The inevitable pain of separation and a sense of loss that would cling for days. Coming home to dull grey skies after blinding sunshine.

She began to towel dry her hair with a look of fierce concentration. Strange how you got used to someone so quickly. The habits and quirks so alien at first, now barely noticeable. Even her dry humour, once abrasive and cutting, seemed natural, almost proof of her real affection for him. He began to recognise her moods and understood that they weren't always influenced by him. Other factors played a part. Her job. Charlotte. Her past that she chose not to talk about. The tough exterior was an act, of course. Underneath this, a deep sensitivity that she revealed only at odd moments. He saw the same tendency in himself. The need to protect the inner core and ward off danger.

He put the book down and watched her instead.

'I wish you wouldn't do that,' she said.

'What?'

'Lie there staring at me all the time.'

'I can't help it, you're mesmerising.'

'Yeah right.'

She brushed her hair with long, measured downstrokes, tilting her head and gazing trance-like at the opposite wall. Now and then she hit a snag and stopped, sighing with irritation. He pictured himself alone in the Green room, taking the call from Zoe. Elements beyond his control, threatening his future security.

He plumped the pillow and wedged it behind his back. 'My old man turned sixty-five at the weekend.'

'That was nice for him.'

'The doctors told him to slow down a couple of years ago, so he took a week off and built a fish pond instead.'

'Built one?'

'For my sister. Dug it out himself. Lined it, landscaped it and filled it with koi carp.'

'Maybe he found it therapeutic.'

The thought amused him. 'You don't know the old man. He treats everything like a military campaign. Taxi's two minutes late and he wants to shoot the driver.'

She brushed out the snags on the other side. The sound and motion of the brush lulled him. The two of them alone together. No world to intrude beyond the humid, perfumed bedroom. He slipped further down her satin cover and thought about carp. The fish pond had been a success, the whole family seated around it one summer evening, admiring the lighting and the tiered rockery. The old man might have built million pound houses for a living, but the sight of a few bloated fish swimming in Sarah's back garden was his finest hour.

'Funny how people react to stress, isn't it?' he said.

'In what way?'

'Some people seem to get a real pleasure out of making their lives harder. Take on things they can't finish.'

'Like fish ponds, you mean?'

'I'm serious. My old man could retire and spend the rest of his days on the golf course. What drives him to keep chasing the pound note, even when he knows it might kill him?'

She hitched up her jeans and buttoned up over her flat belly. Her hair fell in damp rats-tails across her face. 'My dad was the same. He didn't play golf as far as I know, but he went halfway round the world chasing something that wasn't there.' She went to the dresser, speaking with her back to him. 'Probably some woman, if his past track record was anything to go by.'

'Like that, was he?'

She peeked at him severely through the rats-tails. 'He was a man. That's what men do, isn't it?'

'Not all men.'

'So what are you doing then, lying around here for the good of your health?' He laughed at her without meaning to. She sniffed disdainfully and crossed over to the mirror. 'I don't expect you to understand. You probably had a nice cosy upbringing with everything done for you. Waited on hand and foot like my brother.'

He watched her naked back, not sure how to respond. 'Something you want to share with me, Natalie?'

'Forget it. It doesn't matter.' She sat on the end of the bed and clipped her bra. On impulse, he knelt behind her and kissed her neck, aware of her faltering breath, the small murmurs of pleasure she gave in response. The moment his hand touched her thigh, she stood up and went to the dresser. He sat back in frustration. Her subtle resistance made her even more desirable, the unspoken threat that she could withdraw her affections at any moment.

Her family intrigued him. 'What does your brother do?''

'He's some sort of financial genius in New York, apparently. He probably earns more in a month than I do in a year.'

'I take it you don't get on with him?'

'We don't speak much. He phoned me once last year, to ask when Mum's birthday was. I thought that was quite rich, considering how wonderful she thinks he is.'

She selected a top from the dresser. 'He hasn't fathered any children yet, though. I suppose that could be classed as a black mark against him.'

'Perhaps that's what we've got in common.'

She looked at him quizzically. 'Who?'

'You and me. We're both children of high achievers. Too many expectations to live up to.'

She shrugged, unconvinced.

'Did your dad push you to succeed?'

'He didn't push me to do anything. He was hardly ever there.' She pulled on her top. 'I grew up in a dysfunctional household. My parents pretended to get on for the sake of the children.'

'Everyone's dysfunctional in this day and age. You have to be to survive the madness of it all.'

She ignored him, preferring her own analysis. He enjoyed the debate, this perverse streak of hers that she tried to keep hidden. They were alike in many ways. Her heightened sense of injustice matched his own. The feeling that life had somehow dealt him a poor hand, in spite of so much privilege.

He thought about Tara, driven from her home by a witch-hunt. Even her own family conspiring against her in an attempt to deepen her guilt.

'Sometimes it's better to make a stand,' he said.

She frowned. 'Against who? Members of your own family?'

'I'm just saying, you can't spend your life running away. Sooner or later you have to face up to what's bothering you.'

'Nothing's bothering me.'

'I'm not saying there is. I'm talking in general.' He saw the look on her face and laughed. 'Forget it, Natalie. Really. It's not that important.'

She tugged at the hemline of her top, glancing at her bare shoulders. Her breasts made a modest impression under the thin material. Claudia's expansive cleavage came to mind. Poor Claudia. He hadn't given her much thought. The whole devious process had carried him away, denying him the usual caution. Now it was too late. He'd made his move and crossed the invisible line.

Natalie's bed gave a different perspective. He felt relaxed, comfortable. In spite of her occasional lapse in mood, she too seemed comfortable. The tension between them was acceptable, creating a warm undertow of desire. He picked up the paperback on her bedside cabinet, *Star Signs for Lovers.*

'Do you believe all this stuff?'

She glanced at the cover. 'Someone lent it to me at work. I haven't looked at it yet. I'm too busy to even read these days.'

He found the section on his sign. The opening paragraph described a mix of traits, best suited to a mercenary or a cold war spy. Astrology might hold the answers to their future happiness. He shut the book and looked up. 'When's your birthday?'

'July. But you won't find any hidden secrets about me in there.'

'That's a shame, I'd have gone out and bought a copy myself.'

She put her hair in a ponytail, eyeing him with scorn. 'Don't be getting too cosy in here, either. I want you dressed and out of the bedroom before Charlotte gets back.'

'Have you told her about me?'

'I said you were a friend of Marco's. She thinks you fixed the car.'

'Great. Now I'm the greasy mechanic round here.'

'I shouldn't worry about it. She'll either take to you or she won't. But if she doesn't – look out. You'll soon know about it.'

Charlotte's solemn face stared down from a portrait in the front room. A pretty little urchin with war-like tendencies. Dark and baleful eyes without a hint of self-consciousness for the camera. With her paintings decorating the fridge door and her shoes lined up in the hallway, he felt he knew her already. Whether she would accept a strange man in her home was another matter.

Natalie opened the bedside cabinet drawer and tossed a large manila envelope on the bed.

'What's that?' he said.

'You said you wanted to see some of my work.'

She left him with the envelope and went out along the hall.

The label read *Natalie Parker, Unit Four,* with an address in London W1. He pulled out a sheath of papers and photographs all bundled together in no apparent order. The photographs were of paintings hanging in an exhibition. Swirls of vivid colour without any form. Shocking reds and yellows in violent sunbursts. In one, Natalie stood with a bearded, middle aged man. They were both smiling, each with a glass of white wine. Behind them, a stark Vesuvius on a stretched canvas. The man looked flushed with benevolence. Natalie looked uncomfortable.

He thumbed through the sheath of papers. Sketches in pencil. Faces that had a profound lifelike quality. A skeletal woman, her mouth hanging open in anguish. An old man with a wrinkled face and missing teeth. The sketches reminded him of death and suffering. Not the kind of thing you would want hanging on your wall. But the meticulous lines and the dark shading had obviously been drawn by an expert hand.

She walked in and glanced at the contents of the envelope, scattered over the bed.

'I'm impressed,' he said.

'Thanks.'

He studied the gallery of haunted faces, overcome with admiration. 'They're brilliant. When did you do them?'

'Second and third year at Uni, mostly. It's a jumble of things. Life drawings and a couple of exhibitions. Most of my earlier work is at my mother's.'

He found the photograph with her and the bearded man. 'Who's that, your dad?'

She burst out laughing.

'I just thought …'

The comment continued to amuse her, the punch line to a particularly good joke. She grew serious. 'That was one of my tutors. My dad was too busy jetting off round the world to take that much interest in my work.'

He gathered up the loose papers and photographs and put them back in the envelope. The gesture touched him in a strange way. The first time she had made any attempt at a connection beyond the physical. A glimpse into her private world that might leave her vulnerable, expose her to ridicule even. He could have been critical, made clever comments to undermine her ability. Instead he felt privileged. Closer to her now than before.

She made coffee while he sat in the front room. The sense of comfort that he'd felt earlier faded. A more critical voice demanded his attention. Now he had succeeded in breaking down her resistance, he had to justify his reasons for disrupting her life any further. Soon he would have to leave. The warm and tender embrace he had planned as a parting gift would never be enough to convince her. Her limited expectations of him were already tainted by his commitment to another woman. He had no choice. Leave and come back. Come back when the pain of separation was too much to bear.

She put his coffee down on the table beside him. The child's face on the wall looked down with an adult disdain.

'How long before Charlotte gets back?' he said.

'Ten minutes.'

He said nothing.

'Are you nervous?' she said.

'A bit.'

She laughed. 'Well don't worry too much. She'll probably take one look at you and ignore you completely.'

He stared up at the portrait. 'She looks angry.'

'That's one of her more agreeable poses. You wouldn't want to see her when she's really upset, believe me.'

He drank his murky coffee and waited, unsure if he should be there at all.

The doorbell rang as he was thinking of leaving. He sat upright and listened to Natalie's steps along the hall. A burst of excited conversation followed, a child's voice clamouring for attention.

Small footsteps beat along the hall towards him.

He looked up. A small figure stood in the doorway, staring at him intently. He smiled warmly in greeting, unable to hide his amusement. Now he had real competition in the form of a mini Boadicea.

'Hello, Charlotte.'

Natalie appeared behind her. 'Say hello to Peter, Charlotte.'

The child stared back in mute defiance.

'Charlotte! Don't be so rude! Say hello to Peter.'

'Hello!' Charlotte said, and turned smartly, marching out of the room.

Natalie saw him to the door.

'Thanks,' he said.

'For what?'

'Letting me take advantage of your good nature.'

'Is that what you call it? Next time I'll be better prepared. You won't catch me by surprise like you did earlier.'

They kissed, standing in the hallway. Behind them the boom of the television, and Charlotte's omniscient presence to keep them in order. He hated the thought of leaving. In her own awkward way, Natalie had made it clear that she felt the same. They were good together. An island, cut-off from the mainland, needing no help from the outside. But the past always intruded, an ugly insinuation to spoil the progress they were making. So much he wanted to ask her. So much of his own life that he couldn't reveal. Guilt and remorse. Regret for something that couldn't be undone.

Natalie closed the door. He headed for the lift, burdened with thoughts of Claudia.

Twenty-four

Sean called in the afternoon. 'We've got a problem.'
'What's up?'
'Dust.'
'What d'you mean, dust?'
'You better come down and have a look yourself.'
'Her next door?'
'Who else? She said she wants a word with you.'
He tried not to overreact. He could almost see the old woman's face, bird-like and on the offensive, hovering at the end of the drive in her wine-coloured carpet slippers.
'Give me about an hour, OK?'
'Sure, Boss.'
On the way over, he picked up a kitchens brochure from Balmer's. The older woman with the seductive phone voice had been replaced. The new girl behind the counter lacked the personal touch, and deflected his attempts at humour with a fixed smile. He asked after her colleague.
'She's off sick until Monday.'
'That's a shame. Could be a lot worse though. They could have put Ronnie in charge.'
'Ronnie works in the yard.'
'Yeah, I know he does. It was a joke, love.'
She stared blankly at him. 'Is there anything else?'
'No. You've been wonderful. Say hello to Ronnie for me, won't you.'
He left Balmer's pondering humourless women. An attractive woman had a distinct advantage when it came to customer service. She could sit behind a counter all day, filing her nails and staring at the ceiling. Men came

in and gawped at her, making senseless remarks without a clue why. But she could fend them all off the same way. She knew what she had and the knowledge bored her. The girl's older colleague had at least bothered to learn the language of the natives.

Priory Road loomed.

He parked a short distance from the house and turned off the ignition. The new skip sat outside, two planks resting against its buckled rim. Scaffolding framed the front and side elevations of the house. White dust scarred the red brickwork along the side, proof of Sean's efforts with the grinder. Next to the house, the old woman's neat bungalow, the two properties divided by thick hedgerow. He understood the opposition. People paid taxes and expected to live in harmony with their environment. Constant noise and brick rubble were not always good for public relations.

He found Sean upstairs, seated on his favourite upturned bucket. Empty crisp bags lay nearby, spots of strawberry yoghurt from a spilt container. Next to him, legs crossed on the bare boards and biting into a huge pasty, sat Con, the bluff northern bricklayer Barry used for snagging.

He shook his head in disgust, 'This place is a tip, Sean.'

Sean looked up, mouth agape. 'Why is it always me?'

'Who else eats Bovril flavoured crisps round here?'

'Don't look at me, pal,' Con shot back.

'OK, forget the health and hygiene for a minute. What's the problem next door?'

'Dust in the conservatory,' Sean said.

'Have you been round and had a look?'

'Nope.'

'Why not?'

'Cause she ain't right in the head. She had a go at me for having me top off in the sun the other day, silly cow.'

Con laughed. 'Probably frightened her to fucking death, the sight of you, lad!'

He focused on Sean. 'Been using the grinder, have you?'

'Yeah.'

'Made sure all her windows were shut first, did you?'

'Yeah.'

'I hope you did, Sean. If I get a cleaning bill for five hundred quid, it's coming out of your wages.'

He went downstairs, noting the halogen lamps in the back room. Everything a drain on resources; the scaffold tower from U-hire Raul had borrowed, stuck in Helen's back yard for weeks on end while Raul worked up the enthusiasm to replace her rotting fascias. The minor details added up, chipping away at profit margins and creating new overheads. But the newly plastered walls stood for progress. The dampness had gone, replaced by the distinct smell of Carlite finish and the circulation of fresh air.

His phone bleeped.

One new message from Zoe. He opened the text and read a sick joke about Muslims. She must have thought he needed cheering up. An afternoon of frantic sex would have been better, acted out in her front room, her bedroom, and anywhere else they could find. The joke was a tactic, a reminder she was still there in the background. He pressed the delete button.

He went next door and rang the bell.

The old woman answered, peering at him through a gap in the doorway. He slipped into business mode and flashed an easy smile. 'Morning, love. I'm Peter Calliet. We're working on the house next door.'

The door opened a fraction wider.

'The young lad said there was a problem. Was there something you wanted to speak to me about?'

She hovered, indecisive. 'You'd better come in.'

He stepped over the threshold and into a time warp. Mothballs and heavy dark wood furniture.

'Wipe your feet first, won't you.'

He shuffled his feet dutifully on her coconut matting. She led him along a cream carpeted hallway, lined with old family portraits, and into a small but pristine kitchen. She chatted away as though they were already well-acquainted, her list of grievances unspoken so far. Her main concern seemed to be dangerous drivers. Council plans to install traffic-calming in the road had been postponed, furthering the hazards to local school children. But children weren't entirely blameless. Some older kids had broken into her shed and smashed all her pot plants, leaving a trail of havoc across her lawn that took her days to clear up.

'I'm sorry to hear about that,' he said.

'Yes, well nothing ever seems to get done about it. I've even written to the local MP, but he didn't reply.'

She moved on to her dear departed husband, who had passed away two weeks short of his eighty-second birthday. He listened until his patience ran out. 'I'm sorry, but was there something you wanted to see me about?'

She folded her arms and gave him a long, quizzical look. 'Do you like flowers – Mr?'

'Calliet.'

She repeated the name as if it was pleasantly familiar. 'That's rather an unusual name, is it French?'

'Yes it is, but I'm not.'

She missed the sarcasm and gave a distant sigh. 'We went to Provence once. I did love the scenery, but I've never been too good with foreign food. We went to this little restaurant and – '

'Sorry, but what was it you wanted to see me about?'

She led him through into a stifling conservatory cluttered with plants. Beyond the conservatory, her immaculate garden, basking in the sun. She picked up a plant from the sill and stroked the leaves as though it were a pet. 'Do you know what this is?' she said.

'I've absolutely no idea.'

'It's an African violet.'

'Well – you learn something new every day. Now, can we – '

'They like the warmth you see. The sun comes round about midday in here. Normally I'd leave the door open but I've not been able to because of all the dust.' She put the plant back and ran a finger along the plastic window sill. 'See for yourself. It really is quite dreadful. It gets everywhere.'

He ran a finger along the surface. She stood beside him, two experts debating the strain of a deadly new virus.

'It looks like ordinary household dust to me.' he said.

She stood back, frowning severely. 'You're not implying that I leave it like this, are you?'

'I'm not implying anything. I'm just saying that whatever it is, it's not brick dust.'

She took a step back and considered him for a moment. 'Come outside and I'll show you something.'

She led him out into the garden and along the border to point out a lush green bush. The leaves were coated in a fine and unmistakable layer of red dust. Surely, even he could see the evidence now? The fallout had covered the soil, a fact that she was also keen to point out. She described the condition of her garden as if a violation had taken place, pausing at intervals to ensure that he was listening.

At the end of the garden, she stopped. Before them stood a cluster of tall sunflowers, their broad faces bent towards him in deference. A butterfly landed on one, close enough to touch, the russet colouring on its wings like the finest artwork.

'You do see the extent of the problem, then?' she said.

'Well, I do. But unfortunately I can't change the way the wind blows.'

'I was hoping you'd be more understanding than that.'

'I could send the lad over to hose down the flowerbeds, if you like.'

'I don't want *him* tramping through my garden thank-you very much.' She crossed her arms and looked towards the offending property. 'You don't understand what I've had to put up with. The mess they left out in the road. The lorry that blocked my driveway for hours on end. The way that awful man spoke to me when I complained.'

'I'm sorry for any inconvenience, but it's the nature of the beast, I'm afraid.'

'What do you mean?'

'Well – when you take walls down and knock doorways through, a certain amount of dust is unavoidable. We do what we can to keep it to a minimum, but …'

She seemed not to hear. He looked out over her picture-book garden and felt a moments regret. Barry would have said that you couldn't halt progress. But that didn't stop you questioning your motives. As soon as the roof went on, the For Sale sign would go up. He would cash the cheque and lay siege to another run-down building, destroying the neighbourhood peace with jackhammers, assorted power tools and more layers of unavoidable, fine red dust.

Zoe's stupid joke played on his mind. The fact that she'd even bothered sending it in the first place. Consequences. Every wrong move you made in life paid for in some way. Tara went to America to escape the things people were saying about her. James took the easy way out. Strange how these clichés came about. What was easy about jumping over one hundred feet onto stone cold concrete? There had to be easier ways. James would never see the sunshine, the colours of the flowers in the old woman's garden. All because of consequences.

'Quite beautiful,' she said, leaning towards the sunflower. The butterfly settled, spreading its wings. She looked up at him with the trace of a smile. 'You know what they say, don't you? Try to hold one in your fist and you'll crush its wings. Open your hand and let it fly and one day it might come back to you.'

The words made sense in some obscure way, a poetic interlude to their ongoing dispute. Perhaps now she'd forgiven him for the plague of dust in her garden. The plaintive ring of steel on brick drifted over from next door. He made a note to speak to Barry about the next scaffold-lift.

The butterfly flickered on the surface of the sunflower and took off, an illusion in the lazy summer heat.

'Well, if that's it, I'd better make a move,' he said.

She looked up, and gave him a weary smile. 'I just wanted you to see for yourself, that's all.'

She saw him to the front door. He bent to pick up a letter addressed to 'Mrs Thelma Burton.' The name added a personal touch, gave the old woman an identity to go with the mothballs and the heavy furniture. Now they were connected. He could no longer dismiss her as the nameless enemy.

She stood on the doorstep and watched him walk to the gate.

'When will you be finished?' she said.

'End of July, hopefully.'

'As late as that? My goodness.'

He flashed his businesslike smile. 'Don't worry, love. Once the roof goes on the scaffold can come down. You won't even know we've been here. Have a nice day, Mrs Burton.'

He went back next door. Sean was filling a bucket from the makeshift tap on the outside wall, staring fixedly into the churning surface.

'Sean?'

Sean turned off the tap and stood waiting.

'I've just seen the old woman next door. The next time you use that grinder, make sure her windows are shut first. And sweep that fucking road down, before you go. I don't want to be darting back in there every five minutes apologising for the mess you've left behind.'

He left Sean and went through into the front room. The painter was knelt at the skirting boards, making long, even strokes with a small brush, his flat cap mottled with paint. Music played from a paint-flecked radio, balanced on a pair of step-ladders. The man stopped working and looked up.

'Where's Fred?' he said.

'Touch of the flu, I think.'

'Why didn't he phone and let me know?'

The painter shrugged, uncomfortable in his kneeling position.

'I've been waiting two weeks for my place to be finished. He was supposed to come back last weekend and he never turned up.'

'I'll pass the message on when I see him.'

'It's too late for that, I'm trying to run a business here. Tell him not to bother coming back, I'll get someone else.'

He turned and walked out, leaving the painter in a state of shock.

The skip sat out on the road, a blight on the neighbourhood. Loose gravel lay scattered around its base. His Grandfather's words echoed back, *'You'll never leave a good job if you leave a mess.'* He felt like a fraud, a conman preying on the weakness of others. Mrs Burton was a lonely old woman who really wanted someone to talk to. No-one cared either way as long as the roof went on and the cheques kept coming in. He was the middle-man. He got the work and settled any disputes. But no-one told you how to cope with the self-doubt and disillusion that came as an unavoidable part of the job. You learned a cynical take on the true value of friendship and focused instead on how to cultivate the right people. Success breeds more success. Lunch at the golf club, the yacht club, or any other club worth the subscription fee. The old man's utter ruthlessness in business had prepared him well. Then there was always the Freemasons, a comfortable and well-earned niche as you headed toward retirement, filled with the chink of whiskey glasses, and the spirit of free enterprise.

His Grandfather would have frowned upon the silk shirts and handmade Italian shoes that lined his wardrobe. The old boy had preferred the simple pleasures in life. Long walks along country lanes with his black Labrador. Shooting pheasant with one of his cronies from the gun club. His Grandfather rarely raised his voice to make a point, but on the occasions he did lose his temper you could hear the windows rattle. His philosophy had been simple, based on a few basic, working principles. *'Always take pride in your work. Always pay your way in life. Don't take handouts from anyone.'*

He unlocked the car with a vague feeling of unease. Sacking Fred had been impulsive, lacking any prior thought. Repercussions were inevitable. Barry would find out soon enough. Then the old man would get involved and demand an explanation. Fred was in his mid-sixties, part of the old firm, who'd been with the old man since the early days. But in the end, it was his decision. He might have acted on impulse, but the grounds were justifiable. If you weren't up to the mark, you had to go. His grandfather would have agreed with him on that score.

The incident touched a nerve within him. Trivial enough to be dismissed, but having implications he couldn't ignore. The old man's influence in everything. His future guaranteed because the old man said so. All he had to do was comply. And that was the hardest thing of all. Complying. Sometimes it felt better to bring the whole thing crashing down around you, no matter how much trouble you caused.

Twenty-five

They parked in a lay-by overlooking a wide valley. Copper tinted heath land stretched below. Several distant figures made their way along a winding dirt track, a bright red jacket stark against the wild and open scenery. A small black dog went ahead of the group, nose to the track, the faithful pathfinder.

Natalie stood watching the group in the valley below. Charlotte came bounding past and headed off down the track in her white hooded top and sandals. He watched her go, the bogus family man, trying to earn prestige through false pretences.

'Fancy a hike through the wilderness?' he said.

'Looks like I don't have much choice.'

Charlotte's dark bob of hair weaved ahead of them. Natalie's shouts for her to wait went ignored, answered by the small dust cloud kicked up by her feet. He thought of Claudia and her yearning for children, how he went along with her plans out of a sense of duty. This way it was easier. He could participate in the role playing without getting too involved.

At the bottom of the track, the valley levelled out. Natalie began to complain, swearing under her breath.

'What's up?' he said.

'My feet are aching in these shoes.'

'You should have thought of that before you put them on. Want me to carry you?'

'Er – I don't think so.'

The track ahead narrowed. He fell in behind, content to admire the scenery. Natalie's backside swayed from side to side in a unique rhythm of its own. She stopped to adjust a shoe, standing on one leg and fiddling with the heel. The fading dust cloud rose up ahead. Charlotte seemed a reasonable enough kid, a credit to her single parent upbringing, even if she did take-off without warning. Natalie's misgivings about introducing him had proved unfounded. Perhaps she saw it as a test. The three of them out together for the first time. A lowering of her unassailable defences, allowing him a step closer.

He waited while she emptied her other shoe. 'Better get a move on. We're holding up the chain-of-command.'

She stood upright and scanned the horizon.

'Charlotte!'

The dark bob froze up ahead. A small face turned slowly to stare back at them. He sensed the child's rebellion, the natural urge to disobey. Charlotte took off again, arms outstretched like a mini glider.

'Selective hearing.' he said with amusement. 'Reminds me of Leanne when she was a kid.'

She shot him a steely glance. 'She'll hear me when I catch up with her, don't you worry about that.'

The path narrowed. Dense firs enclosed them, their tips forming a canopy against the sky. She called out for Charlotte repeatedly, cursing the child's disobedience and blaming him for the choice of terrain. Alone in such an intimate setting, his thoughts turned to other things. He slipped an arm around her waist and drew her towards him. 'She'll be fine. We'll catch up with her in a minute.'

She pulled away. 'You don't know Charlotte. I've only got to turn my back for five minutes and she's gone.'

'Don't worry about it. If she gets too far ahead I'll call out the rescue services on my phone.'

'Thanks,' she said tartly. 'You're so understanding.'

Charlotte slowed enough for them to catch up. He stood back as an observer and watched the drama unfold. Mother and child face to face. Natalie overcome with anger. Charlotte detached, almost serene, having endured countless similar episodes in the past. She reminded him of Leanne. The same look of martyrdom. No matter how unjust the punishment, she would somehow manage to rise above it.

Natalie bent to deliver the classic reprimand.

'What's the hell's the matter with you?'

'Nothing.'

'Do you want to go home now?'

'No.'

'So why didn't you stop when I called you?'

Charlotte shrugged a lame apology. Natalie stood up and glared down at her.

'Don't push me today, Charlotte. I'm really not in the mood, OK?'

Charlotte came away chastised, but wearing the unmistakeable smirk of victory. Once more they advanced – together this time.

The scenery lost its appeal the further they walked. Nature lovers must have been gifted with a strange vision, finding so much pleasure in varying shades of green. But with Charlotte in their sights, and the promise of an invigorating walk in the fresh air, they at least had a semblance of unity.

He caught up with Charlotte, who was swinging her arms in a robotic, marching fashion. 'Enjoying yourself, Charlotte?'

'Yes, thanks.'

'Look out for Henry the Eighth. I saw him a while ago, out on a deer-hunting expedition with Anne Boleyn.'

Charlotte looked up, bemused. 'Really?'

Natalie gave him a light shove from behind. 'Just ignore him, Charlotte, he's being stupid, as usual.'

Charlotte narrowed her eyes, seeing him in a challenging new light. *'I've* been to Lawrence of Arabia's house.'

'Have you? Was he in?'

Charlotte's raucous laughter infected them all for a moment. Even Natalie with her blistered heels and parental nightmares. The laughter tailed off. They advanced through the foliage – single file like a jungle reconnaissance.

Claudia loved walking. She could go for miles and he would be the one complaining. The walk would be abandoned in favour of a pub lunch, for him to eye-up the bar staff, while she worked out the calories in the chef's special. Today he didn't mind. The sensual roll of Natalie's hips made the struggle worthwhile. Charlotte up front, picking the heads off tall ferns as she passed along the track. Natalie, striding after her, muttering about the distance they'd come and bemoaning her poor choice of footwear. Henry the Eighth would never have put up with it. The party would have been over long ago. The woman en-route to his private bed chamber. The child banished to the kitchens to scrub floors and ponder the grave nature of disobedience.

Natalie paused atop a sedate rise. He stood beside her and breathed in the fragrant, summer air. Beneath them lay the soft valley in varying shades of green. Charlotte stopped a few paces ahead, mindful of the new rule changes.

'Smell that invigorating country air,' he said.

'Wonderful.'

'I thought you would have loved it out here.'

'What, chasing *her* all afternoon?' She glared at him for daring to laugh. 'What's so funny now?'

'You are.'

'Why – just because I don't like wandering aimlessly round the countryside?'

'This is the New Forest, Natalie, not the Himalayas.'

'Well I'm not going much further in these shoes, that's for sure.'

'Whatever you say.'

She put a hand on her hip, observing him carefully. 'You love this, don't you? Taking advantage of the fact that I'm stuck out here in the middle of nowhere. Do you even have a clue where we're supposed to be going?'

'Of course I do.'

'Where?'

He made a dramatic gesture up ahead. 'What I thought we'd do was head for those woods and make camp for the night. I read this book on survival once, so we'll be fine. Make a few traps. Catch a few wild animals. Are you up for that?'

She mouthed a cheerful profanity in his direction and walked off to join Charlotte.

They came across the group with the black dog, a friendly, wire-haired terrier that took an instant liking to Charlotte. The usual pleasantries were exchanged, the woman's jolly red face reminding him that happiness was an achievable goal, even in late middle age. When the group had gone, he remarked on how sociable they had been, and how in tune with nature, particularly the woman with the jolly red face. Natalie rolled her eyes and sighed indignantly. 'How the hell do you know what she's like?'

'She was smiling. That's usually a giveaway.'

'So you think outward appearances mean that much, do you? Some woman smiles at you and all of a sudden she's some sort of countrified role model.'

'I only said hello to her.'

She ignored him, scanning the near horizon with a look of distaste. 'Can we head back now, please? My feet are killing me.'

Charlotte waited for them by the car, sentry-like, impeccable in her hooded white top and dust blown sandals. She watched their approach with an adult cool, silently working out the pecking order and whose resolve might weaken quickest under pressure. Natalie passed her with a scornful glance.

'Where are we going now?' Charlotte said.

'Home.'

'I don't want to go home.'

'You should have thought of that before you went running off.'

Charlotte flashed him a telepathic appeal.

He laughed. 'Don't look at me sweetheart – I'm just the driver.'

Charlotte had an endearing quality he found hard to resist, an ally to help overthrow the current regime. Between them they might hatch a plot to convince Natalie to reconsider. 'Let's take a drive over to the Red Shoot,' he said. 'It's only up the road. Charlotte can have a coke, and you can put your feet up.'

Natalie shot him a warning look. 'Charlotte doesn't drink coke.'

'She can have an orange juice and a packet of crisps then.'

Natalie sighed, bowing under pressure. She opened the passenger door and beckoned Charlotte inside.

Charlotte stamped her foot. 'I want to go to the Red Shoe, with Peter!'

'Shut up and get in the car.'

'No!'

'Charlotte. Get in the car – NOW!'

Charlotte climbed into the back of the car. Natalie glared at him, the cause of all the trouble. 'You're enjoying this, aren't you?'

'Nothing to do with me. Like I said – I'm just the driver.'

'Don't you think I have a hard enough job with her as it is?'

'She's a kid. Buy her an ice-cream.'

'That would solve everything, would it?'

He stepped closer to her and took hold of her wrist. 'What you need is an incentive scheme. Kids respond to promises like adults do. You have to give them a glimpse of the cake even if they can't eat it.'

'Really,' she said dryly. 'If you're such an expert, you have her for a few days. You'd soon change your tune, I can assure you.'

He held her hand, close enough to feel her breath, the silky texture of her hair. She squeezed his fingers in response, a harmless flirtation while she worked out what to do in the interim.

'So where is this place?' she said.

'Not far. Do you want to go?'

'Looks like I'll have to now.'

He bent to kiss her. She pulled back in alarm, aware of Charlotte, seated upright in the back like a visiting dignitary. He resented the child briefly for spoiling their one tender moment together. The forest scenery would have been the perfect backdrop for his continuing romance with her mother. Now all he could look forward to was their constant bickering, and his new role as unofficial referee.

The Red Shoot faced the forest road, set back in more tranquil scenery. His praise for such fine English heritage was ignored. Charlotte requested an ice-cream. Natalie demanded a table out of the sun.

They found a bench seat in the garden, and sat beneath the umbrella, with all the other happy families. A huge St Bernard lay against the pub wall, its nose flattened on the path, one soulful eye trained on the entrance to the bar. Charlotte sat absorbed in her own world, lemonade and crisps untouched in front of her. Natalie's thigh pressed against his, a current of desire that passed through him and heightened his senses. He was in control again. The trek across the countryside had served its purpose. Natalie's resistance had faltered and given way. Her veiled glances confirmed his intuition, the tension between them creating a real sense of anticipation, the promise of what might happen when they were alone together later.

The rustling of Charlotte's crisp packet opened the ceremony. The hum of voices closed in around them. He felt a warm connectedness to the scene, to the noisy family at the next table, whose accents were far north of the border. Even the obese woman in the floral dress and the wide-brimmed hat, tucking in to a basket of chips with her lean male companion.

Two boys loitered at the foot of an impressive oak on the far side of the road, busy in the plotting and carrying out of mischief.

'Can I climb up that tree?' Charlotte said.

Natalie looked up. 'No you can't.'

'Why not?'

'Because it's too big and you'll end up hurting yourself.'

'But I want to!'

'Drink your lemonade please, Charlotte.'

Charlotte's dissent ended. She lapsed into silence, watching the boys beneath the tree with quiet envy. Natalie reached over and picked out a leaf stuck in her hair, pausing to tidy her fringe. He watched, privileged to glimpse this brief moment of truce between them.

'Perfect day,' he said.

'Just as long as you don't get me walking any further in these shoes.'

'You'll be thanking me tomorrow.'

'Really.'

'What else would you have done? Stayed in and watched TV?'

'Er – I did have a life before you came along, you know.'

The warmth of her thigh reassured him, the genuine affection beneath her playful sarcasm. They could have been a real family, resting under the shade of the umbrella. The pleasant image was spoiled only by the constant danger, the real possibility of being seen by people he knew. He tried to relax and focus on the surroundings. The St Bernard had the right idea, propped up against the pub wall, its melancholy eye fixed on the doorway. An elderly man came out clutching a pint of Guinness and leaning on a walking stick. He thought of old Fred the painter, recuperating from some unnamed illness – minus a job.

'I fired someone yesterday,' he said.

She looked at him, intrigued. 'What for?'

'He let me down.'

'How did you feel about it?'

He shrugged. 'Not good really. He was an old guy who used to work for my dad.'

She nodded slowly, gauging his reaction. 'Oh well. These things happen, don't they. I got sacked from a waitress job once for being late three times in a row.'

'Did you appeal?'

She laughed. 'I don't think that would have made any difference. I hated it there anyway.'

He told her about the old man, his humble beginnings as a labourer after a period serving in the merchant navy. His move into construction and a partnership that ended in acrimony. The feuding and rivalry throughout his illustrious career. Battles with the tax-man, the planning department, even his own father-in-law. Finally, the old man's reputation as a dictator, hiring and firing at will, without a thought for the countless workers he'd sent down the road.

She listened to his summing-up with a thoughtful frown. 'Well, you know what they say, don't you? Like father, like son.'

He stared at her in bewilderment.

She reacted with amused indignation. 'Don't look at me like that I'm just making an observation.'

'I'm nothing like him, though. I treat people with respect. He just walks over everyone he comes in contact with.'

She put her hands up, suppressing her laughter. 'OK. OK. Sorry I mentioned it. I've got enough family issues of my own without listening to yours as well. Can we change the subject?'

He wanted to challenge her further, but Charlotte knocked over her lemonade and spoiled the moment.

Natalie stood up sharply. 'That's it! We're going!'

'It's just a drink. I'll get her another one.'

'She's not having another one. We're going. Now!'

Lemonade seeped between the slats in the table. Charlotte sat impassive on the other side, silent witness to a terrible injustice. The sentence had been passed and nothing she could do would change it.

He finished his blackcurrant and soda and they left, a family in disarray to the bemused onlookers at the other tables. Natalie marched off ahead, hands stuffed in the pockets of her jacket. He stayed back with Charlotte, embarrassed that the day had ended on such a sour note. The two of them were now accomplices, in league against her mother. Charlotte seemed unaffected by what had happened and bore no outward malice, skipping alongside him, humming to herself.

'Never mind, Charlotte. It was an accident.'

She stopped humming and looked up. 'Are you coming back to my house?'

'We'll have to see what mood your mother's in, sweetheart. Would you like me to come back?'

She gave this some thought. 'Only if you buy me an ice-cream!'

Natalie waited for them, leaning sullenly against the sleek contours of the car. Charlotte opened the passenger door and, without a word, climbed into the back. Natalie watched him approach, one source of her frustration now safely inside.

'OK?' he said cautiously.

'Not really.' She shuffled her feet in the gravel, the picturesque setting no longer enough to keep up the façade. 'We should have gone home when I said.'

He touched her arm. She bit down on her lower lip, tears filling her eyes.

'What's the matter?' he said.

'What do you think's the matter?'

'Charlotte knocked over a drink, that's all. That's what kids do, isn't it?'

'It's not the drink.'

'What is it then?'

She gave him a long and searching look, her sad smile fading. 'I just find all this really difficult. I can't relax, knowing I've got to watch Charlotte all the time. Can you understand that?'

'Sure I can.'

She dropped her head. 'I just don't want to put myself in a position to get hurt again.'

He thought of Brad, a succession of her previous lovers making it harder to respond. 'Who says you're going to get hurt?'

She shook her head, eyeing him carefully. 'You're very persuasive, aren't you?'

'Am I?'

'Yes, you are. You just like to keep up this easy-going front to fool people.'

The door opened and a small, weary voice called out, 'What on earth are you two doing out there? I've been waiting ages in here!'

Home. The tower block loomed before them, neat balconies rising, one above the other. A towel fluttered in the breeze, draped over a washing line like a makeshift pennant. He pictured himself as resident, taking the lift up to the fourth floor every evening and slipping his key in the lock. The noisy television in the front room. Spicy cooking smells drifting along the hall. Cool white sheets on the bed as he waited for Natalie to finish in the bathroom.

'Is Peter coming back to my house?' Charlotte said.

'I don't know – you'll have to ask him.'

'Are you, Peter?'

He laughed, exhilarated at the invitation. The doubts that surfaced could be sidelined and dealt with later. He felt good where he was. The transition had been easy. Like stepping from one room into another.

Twenty-six

Barry's nasal drawl drifted over from the bar. Most people kept their opinions to themselves in public. Barry preferred an open forum, where everyone's input, especially his own, was given a reasonable hearing. But you couldn't give him advice. His views were black and white, drawn from a lifetime's exposure to Medieval working conditions and the men who had to put up with them.

Barry cocked an empty glass and called out to Sean along the bar. 'Get 'em in, my son – it's your round!'

Sean looked up, bewildered. 'I haven't finished this one yet.'

'That's no good to me, son. You wanna mix with the big boys, you'd better learn to drink like one!'

Sean stood perplexed, not yet having earned the right to his own opinion. He had the gangly, dishevelled look, the type despairing mothers run around after, fussing over their hair and tucking-in shirttails. Even his boots were outlandish – bulbous steel toe-caps and dried-on cement, rooting him to the spot. His reversed Baseball cap further refined the image, a walking advert for mindless computer games and a failed education.

He envied Sean in some ways. Just starting out in life with fewer needs. Earn enough to feed the fruit machines and clear the previous weeks debts. Leave enough to take his girlfriend out at the weekend. Then one day, Barry Jarvis might meet with a terrible accident and his immediate problems would be over.

He took a break from the World Cup qualifier on the screen and turned to Sean. 'Back with Julie yet?'

Sean grimaced. 'No!'

'Who you shagging now then?'

'No-one.'

'Why not?'

'Because I'm not.'

He looked at Sean's sullen face, one so young, burdened with life's complexities. 'I'm getting seriously worried about you, Sean. You need to come out with me one night. Sort your priorities out.'

Sean said nothing. Barry and his drinking partners roared at some private joke, further along the bar.

'What's up? Barry giving you a hard time?'

Sean gave a dismissive shrug and stared at the dregs of his pint. He seemed unusually quiet and introspective.

'Gordon's offered me a job.'

'Doing what?'

'Roofing.'

The thought of losing Sean saddened him. He'd talked of leaving before but never with any real conviction. At least he would earn more with Gordon, cladding industrial units and travelling further afield. Barry's hold over him would also be severed.

'Have you told Barry?' he said.

'Not yet.'

'Well, I wish you luck, Sean, I really do. And if you ever need a reference, don't come to me.'

Sean managed a rueful smile, amiable enough in his cement-encrusted boots and torn jeans. Yet to be waylaid by a scheming woman and a high-interest mortgage.

'What happened to Fred?' Sean said.

The comment surprised him. He pondered a suitable answer.

'I got rid of him, why?'

Sean shrugged and drained his pint, too absorbed in his own problems to care much either way.

'Is that a problem?'

'No.'

'You don't seem all that sure.'

Sean gave a tentative frown. 'Barry said he had breathing problems from inhaling paint fumes years ago.'

'So?'

'I felt sorry for him. He was due to retire soon anyway.'

'Not my problem, Sean. I'm running a business not a rest home.'

The issue with Fred took on a new angle. People were hired and fired all the time, especially in an industry known for its mercenary tactics. But as an employer, it was always possible to underestimate the backlash you'd created with a snap decision. The general opinion had obviously swung in the old boy's favour. He could sense it. Barry hadn't broached the subject yet, but it was only a matter of time.

Marco joined them at the bar.

The restoration of Barry's four bed farmhouse became the next topic. One of Barry's ongoing projects that had taken the better part of three years to finalise. Barry described the complex business of thatching a roof, and how the reed had to be fixed to the rafters, starting at the eaves. Even the landlord appeared to take an interest, torn between Barry's impromptu master class and the World Cup action on the screen. To Marco, such a task was unthinkable, physical toil being the most worthless proposition of all. Eighteenth century furniture would have been more his line, good solid earning potential without a ladder in sight.

Marco grew bored of the roofing conversation and turned, leaning an elbow on the bar. 'So, how's tricks with you?'

'Still overworked and underpaid but I'll get over it.'

'Sure you will. You need a new investment portfolio. Talking of which, I ran into Claudia the other day.' He sensed an angle even before Marco could add the next sentence. Football continued on the screen. The Swedish referee kept interrupting play to flash the dreaded yellow card. His latest victim gave the standard response, stamping his feet and throwing a tantrum in front of fifteen million viewers worldwide. 'She thinks there's something wrong with you.'

He feigned disinterest. 'In what way?'

'Stress at work. That stuff you had going on with your Dad. Who knows?'

'And what did you say?'

'Nothing.' Marco took a long drink and set his pint down on the bar with a pleasurable sigh. 'Fuck all to do with me anyway. It's bad enough listening to Tim's domestic problems without getting involved in yours.'

Claudia hadn't mentioned seeing Marco. Apart from the odd comment, she'd kept any real concerns about their relationship to herself. His attempts at appearing normal obviously hadn't worked. The golden rule in being unfaithful. Keep up a front of normality and do nothing to arouse suspicion.

Marco spread his hands on the counter and faced the optic range, working himself up for the next round. 'Personally, I have to say, as a friend of course, that I think you're being a bit of a cunt.'

He waited, speechless.

Marco stared ahead. 'I can see exactly what's going on. You're chasing something that isn't there.'

The referee held up another yellow card, resulting in a mini pitch invasion. The job was fraught with danger. You made a decision based on a few simple rules and thousands of frenzied spectators wanted to tear you limb from limb.

'I'm not chasing anything. I know what I'm doing.'

Marco glanced over, way ahead of him in the tactical process. 'Really? So what're you going to do when it all goes tits-up?'

'When what goes tits-up?'

'Everything. The whole shebang.'

'I take it you mean Natalie?'

'Well, yes. Who else would I be talking about?'

'Haven't we had this conversation before? The old pals act you gave me the last time?'

Marco shook his head wearily. 'Listen – I gave you a bit of friendly advice before. I knew you wouldn't take it on board, so what's the point?'

He looked out over the crowded bar. The longer he stayed, the more chance he would fall out with someone. Especially Marco. Perhaps it was the season for falling out. You didn't have to do anything in particular to cause it, it just happened. He empathised with the Swedish referee, facing the wrath of the crowd, armed with a pair of black shorts and a shiny yellow card.

'Are you going to Spain?' Marco said.

'I doubt it.'

'Maybe you should. It'll give you time to think. Clear your mind.'

He stared at Marco's blotchy face and wanted to smash his fist into it. 'Why don't you go instead? I'll tell Claudia I've given you my ticket. You can go along as chief baggage handler when she goes shopping. You'll probably get on well together.'

Marco said nothing, staring fixedly at the optics.

The football commentary droned on. He thought about priorities. Your basic nature as a human being was selfish. You did what you could to improve your conditions without hurting anyone else, but that wasn't enough. People made demands upon your time, expecting you to make personal sacrifices that went against the grain. You filled your life with pointless commitments until they drained all your energy. If Claudia wanted to go to Spain, she could do so without him. He would stay behind and guard what was left of his beleaguered independence.

He decided to forgive Marco his interfering ways for the moment. Their friendship had always been volatile, built on heated debate and a shared cynicism. They saw the same hypocrisy in the world, the same basic absurdity of striving for success when your personal life was a disaster area.

He recalled a previous conversation they'd had, more evidence of Marco's withholding information for his own ends.

'How much does Natalie know about James?'

Marco turned slowly, frowning. 'Where did that come from?'

'I just wondered how much you'd told her.'

Marco faced the optics, impassive. 'She knows what happened.'

'What, all of it?'

'Nothing that would implicate you.' Marco's smirk faded. He gave a weary sigh, forced to be more explicit. 'Look, I put Natalie on a need-to-know basis, OK? We meet up occasionally for lunch and we talk. We talk about everything under the sun. We even talk about you, sometimes. But I can honestly say, knowing her like I do, that she's probably too busy worrying about her job to concern herself with something that happened years ago.'

The spectre of James's death lingered, an event so profound in its effect on everyone around him, that he still found it hard to contemplate.

'Does that answer your question?' Marco said.

'Sure.'

'Good. It's your round.'

He drifted away from the bar and went outside. Cars flashed by in the afternoon sun. A few drinkers sat at the bench tables, driven out by the World Cup takeover inside. He found a vacant seat and sat down. Now seemed as good a time as any. If he waited any longer he might change his mind, or she would pre-empt his decision and turn up unannounced to embarrass him in front of his friends.

He made the call.

They went through the usual evasive patter that passed as a greeting. He asked how she was. She said she was fine. He asked what she'd been up to. She gave a few sketchy details about being on the beach with Lenka and eating chips in Harry Ramsden's. She never volunteered information. He had to prise things from her instead. Now he had to override his own reluctance and tell her something he should have told her weeks, even months ago.

'Listen, Zoe – '

'Guess what?' she said, cutting in.

'What?'

'I'm moving.'

'Where to?'

'Southampton.'

He laughed, caught out by her bluntness. 'Couldn't you have found somewhere further than that?'

'I'm serious. Don't you believe me?'

'Why Southampton?'

She had friends up there, she said. She'd been offered a job cleaning in a hotel. No more run-ins with her despised landlord. No more homeless refugees on her worn leather sofa, smoking her last cigarettes. The finer details were irrelevant. Southampton might as well be South America in terms of convenience. The amusement he'd felt initially turned to a dull resentment. The ending he'd been trying to bring about for so long was now obsolete. Zoe had unintentionally beaten him to it.

'So when are you going?'

'Couple of weeks, hopefully.'

'What about all your stuff?'

'Ray reckons it'll go in his van.'

She'd dropped the name in casually and waited for his response. He fought against a rising irritation, guarding his voice. 'Are you back with him?'

'He's just helping me move. Is that alright?'

'Whatever.'

The dregs of his lager had gone warm in the sun. He rocked the bottle against the slats in the table and replayed some of their scenes together. Apart from the obvious, they had nothing much to offer each other in the long term. She wasn't much of a conversationalist. She couldn't even cook. She spent most of her time thinking up ways to get back at the people who had hurt her when she was younger – social workers, old boyfriends, Ray the jailbird, cashing stolen cheques and defrauding the benefits system, writing her long, impassioned letters from a prison cell.

'I'll miss you,' he said truthfully.

'I haven't gone anywhere yet.'
'Taking the lizard king with you?'
'Of course. He's my friend.'
'You always feed live crickets to your friends, do you?'

She laughed. Billy the leopard gecko would have to settle into his new home as well, placated by handfuls of insects and a fresh bed of sand.

'You can always come up and visit me when I'm settled in.'
'I doubt it, Zoe.'
'Why not?'

He couldn't answer. Instead he made a joke about her habit of changing address, her constant moves driving him to distraction. Her openness allowed him to be more honest with her. He hinted at the inevitable demise of their relationship in a frivolous manner, hoping she'd get the message. This time she would vanish for good. She'd meet someone else and he would never see her again. He told her this as a simple fact, something they should both get used to.

'Are you pissed off with me?' she said.
'No.'
'Yes you are. I can tell.'
''Zoe. You go off and do what you've gotta do. Send me a postcard when you get there, OK?'

He rang off and went back inside.

Barry noticed him at the bar and came over. They discussed the details of the corner plot that had come up in Iford. He listened without interest. Zoe and her pet gecko were still on his mind, cruising up the motorway in Ray's van.

Barry grew quiet and gave him a long, quizzical look. 'What happened with Fred then, Peter?'

'I sacked him.'

'Yeah, but why?'

'He was unreliable.'

Barry frowned. 'He's been off sick for two weeks. I took his wages round last week and the poor fucker was still in bed.'

The news failed to move him. If Barry expected him to reinstate the old boy, he was mistaken. The whole episode had drained him, left him exposed to an unexpected criticism from different sources. Rising anger stopped him from thinking clearly. Now was the time to walk away, let Barry form his own conclusions.

'I don't want to talk about it right now,' he said.

Barry put up a hand in deference. 'Just thinking about your old man, Peter. Him and Fred went back a long way.'

'I don't care how far back they went. It's my decision. I'm not going back on it.'

The football finished. Marco taxied into town to meet Simon. Barry went back to his renovated farmhouse in his mud splattered Land Rover. The new barmaid, an attractive woman in her forties, with an easy going smile, served a couple at the end of the bar. She sauntered over and he ordered a double Jack Daniel's with ice.

She put the drink on the bar and smiled sadly. 'Left you all on your own, have they, darling?'

'That's right. I'm drowning my sorrows with no-one to talk to.'

'Oh, did your team lose?'

'I wasn't watching.'

'Neither was I, darling. I've been a football widow for so long I'm past caring.'

Her mock sympathy cheered him. Perhaps that's what he needed, a neutral third party to give an unbiased opinion on his tale of woes. He didn't feel much like conversation but the occasion seemed to call for it.

'Ever thought about disappearing?' he said.

'Oh, all the time.' She cleared an empty glass from the bar and gave him a woeful look. 'And if you met my husband you'd know why.'

Failed human relations. If he stayed long enough she might tell him her life story. Women loved a listener, someone to hear about all their troubles without making light of them. That was how you worked your way in. Then when you'd put in enough groundwork, you could make a serious move and take it to the next level. Some men made a habit out of this approach. He couldn't be bothered. Without a spark there in the first place it hardly seemed worth the deception.

She left him and sauntered off, patrolling the borders with her hands clasped behind her back.

He sank the Jack Daniels and thought of calling a taxi. A part of him had surrendered to the inevitable. The dark clouds gathered up ahead. People were going to get hurt and nothing he could do now would change the outcome. Those closest to him would suffer the most. Claudia, with all her plans for the future. The old man, afraid to let go of his business empire, in spite of his health. He should have cared more but he didn't. All he could think about was Natalie, waiting at home for his troubled call.

Twenty-seven

Claudia's job took her away for two days. The process of selling her house was still ongoing, the holiday in Spain uncertain. Sensing that things weren't right between them and unable to effect a change, she broke down and cried in front of him before leaving. Her tears just distanced him further. He tried to be understanding but the willingness was missing.

He spent the first night with Natalie, a brief change of scenery to relieve the tension. Alone and less confident of the outcome, the shadows returned. The past that you could never run far enough away from. The universal truth that every action has a consequence. Throw a pebble in a lake and somewhere on the other side of the world a tidal wave wipes out the population of a small island.

Alone at the table, he sat waiting.

The couple by the window seemed to radiate pure happiness. The woman snapped a breadstick and gazed lovingly across at her man. The man stared back, entranced, and touched her hand unaware of the spectacle they made. He found their display off-putting, an unnatural act in a public place. Overt displays of affection should be banned, or at least made subject to strict by-laws. But he recognised the same weakness in himself. The pathological need to be bonded at all costs. The awful emptiness that follows separation.

Sarah turned up late. Her apologies came in a wave of Chanel and an awkward kiss to spoil his daydreaming. She sat opposite him and plonked her bag down, taking over the conversation as she'd always done. Well dressed and perfectly made up, tortoiseshell glasses perched on the bridge of her nose, she gave him the look. The same look she gave the children when she wanted their attention. How they came from the same gene pool, he had no idea. She had the summer baby's outlook, that inborn ability to look on the bright side, no matter what the situation. Winter babies had a darker perception. Storm clouds gathered for a reason and you had better be prepared when the rains came.

'Have you ordered?' she said.

'I was waiting for you.'

'Hungry?'

'Not really.'

'My God. Running a temperature?'

The waiter came over, cool and efficient in his black shirt and gold waistcoat. The winning team, all in the same strip and working to the same formula, taking orders to and from the kitchen in a seamless relay. Sarah ordered a white wine and fettuccine alla crema. He sat, subdued, with his half drunk diet-coke and opted for the carbonara.

The waiter bowed and swept away with the order.

Sarah sat back and sighed with pleasure. Her inner contentment shone through, all her movements light and effortless. Even the weight gain that had crept up over the last few years sat easily with her. She adjusted her glasses and peered at him. 'So – how's my baby brother then? Plenty of fun in your life at the moment?'

'Ask me another one.'

'Oh dear. That bad is it?'

'Let's just say, it's complicated.'

Life gave you options. Problems were made to be solved, but you couldn't always solve them on your own. Sometimes you needed a third party to put things in perspective. Someone to listen.

Sarah ran through a summary of her busy week. The kids at school and college. Brendan off work with a bad back. Her comfortable domestic life seemed at odds with his own. She paused mid-sentence and frowned at him. 'What's the matter, am I boring you already?'

He gave a vague smile, unable to answer.

'Leanne giving you a hard time?'

'I'm used to that.'

'How's the job going?'

'Fine.'

She cupped her chin in her hands and stared at him. 'So what is it then?'

'That obvious, is it?'

'You've just got that look about you. I could tell when I first came in.'

He sipped his diet-coke, the glass clammy in his hand. Ice and a slice, floating in the chemical stream. He thought about Claudia and wished he'd ordered a Jack Daniel's instead.

The waiter appeared with a plate of pasta, bound for the couple in love, on his dark face a sublime harmony with the present moment. He watched the pasta and the gold waistcoat pass by and wondered how he was going to break the news to Sarah.

'How's Claudia?' she said.

'Fine.'

'You didn't fancy going away with her then?'

'Not this time.'

'When's she back?'

'Thursday.'

She nodded slowly, watching him behind her tortoiseshell glasses. 'Mum says you're not going to Spain.'

'That's right.'

'Claudia'll be disappointed.'

'Nothing I can do about that, is there?'

The statement came out the wrong way. She picked up on the undercurrent and honed in on him. 'Why are you being so defensive?'

'I'm not.'

She hovered stubbornly, her persistence wearing him down. Further denial was pointless. He waited for the waiter to return, en route to the kitchen, before facing her.

'There's something I need to tell you.'

'What's that?'

He sat quietly and mulled over the options, all the convoluted ways there were of saying the same thing.

'Peter?'

He looked up and held her gaze. 'I've met someone else.'

'You've what?'

'I didn't plan it. It just happened.'

She slumped back in the seat, stricken by a sudden death in the family.

'Like I said – it just happened.'

She digested the sad news quietly. In Claudia, she would lose a valued friend, a prospective family member, loved by all. No more shopping trips to Bristol and Southampton. No more lunches in Debenhams and extended coffee breaks along the Quay. All these pleasures withdrawn because he'd met someone else.

She composed herself and sat forward. 'So who is she then?'

'She's a teacher.'

'Really? What does she teach?'

'Art Therapy to children with learning disabilities.'

She nodded, vaguely impressed. 'Where did you meet her?'

'Erica's birthday bash.'

'And that was it?'

'I didn't sleep with her if that's what you mean.'

'But you have now.' She let the accusation sink in. 'Is she a friend of Erica's?'

'Marco. They go back a long way, apparently.'

She thought this over. 'So it's serious?'

'Pretty much, I suppose.'

The waiter brought her white wine. She thanked him and sat back, mulling over her next line of questioning.

'Can I ask you one more thing?'

'Sure.'

'How long have you been seeing her?'

'A few weeks.'

She pondered the details, trying to hide her disappointment. The sense of relief he felt at unburdening himself made him careless. He told her about the meeting at Erica's. How Natalie's initial rudeness had somehow attracted him to her. The problem of being drawn to someone like that and being unable to stop the process. The verdict seemed inevitable. He'd been callous and unthinking, abandoning Claudia at such a critical time, with the sale of her house and the holiday in Spain looming.

'Have you told anyone else?' she said.

'Apart from Marco?' He shrugged distractedly. 'Tim knows.'

'And what pearls of wisdom did he have for you?'

'He just said do what you've gotta do.'

She laughed out loud. 'My God. What it is to be a man. No wonder the world's in such a mess.' She saw his reaction and sighed. 'Look, I'm sorry, but I just can't get my head round it. And to think – I was really looking forward to meeting you today.'

'Now I've ruined your afternoon.'

She softened visibly. 'Never mind that. What happens when you tell Claudia?'

The prospect depressed him further.

'She'll be devastated. All her hopes and dreams. Selling the house and moving in with you. She was so looking forward to it.'

'What about my hopes and dreams? Don't they come in to it?'

'Yes of course they do.'

'You wouldn't think so sometimes.'

She watched him steadily.

He focused on the couple by the window, consumed by the complexity of his life. 'I'm like the hired help around here. Waiting in the background 'til the next big job comes along.'

'What d'you mean?'

'The old man takes on Henley Park when he should be thinking about retiring. Right away I'm expected to run it for him. Claudia decides we're going to Spain for two weeks, so she books the flights on the internet without even asking me. How am I supposed to react when they're all pulling stunts like that behind my back?'

'Not by sleeping with someone else you don't.'

'That's got nothing to do with it.'

'Er – I think you'll find it has quite a lot to do with it.'

'Great. Now you're taking sides against me as well.'

'I'm not taking anyone's side. I'm just trying to help.'

He rattled the ice in his glass, tired of all the intrigue. 'I just need a break, Sarah. I feel like a rat on a wheel.

Spinning. Going nowhere. If I don't get off soon, I'm going to murder someone.'

'I didn't know you felt like that.'

'I never told anyone before.'

She leaned over and took his hand in hers, soothing him without words. The confession had wrenched a huge part from him and left a hole. Even Sarah, usually so intuitive to his moods, had no idea how he really felt. The few people in the restaurant looked like props, put there to remind him how detached he'd become from reality.

The waiter brought the food. Fettuccine alla crema for madam. Spaghetti Carbonara for sir. His appetite returned, stirred by the richness of the sauce, the network of creamy pasta. Guilt came with it, a poisonous side-dish, edged towards him by an unseen hand. The guilt was no worse than the confession when you looked at it. Like climbing a steep hill. The hardest part was the final push to the crest. You could catch your breath on the way down.

Sarah talked about Brendan and the kids. Her whole life revolving around her family, the washing machine on a permanent spin cycle. Trips to the school to discuss Harry's latest run-in with the head teacher. Brendan staying at home, coward that he was, to dream up his next work project at the bottom of the garden. He envied her dedication to the job. Years of sacrifice without any pay-off. The kids would grow up and let her down in one way or another. Smoke pot and mix with the wrong people. Stay out all night when they should have been revising for exams.

She sipped her wine, observing him quietly. 'So what's her name – this woman?'

'Natalie.'

'Kids?'

'Five year old girl.'

She nodded, slowly. 'You'd be taking on quite a workload then?'

'I wouldn't be taking anything on. She's got her life. I've got mine.'

'That's how it starts.'

'Whatever.'

She gave a knowing smile, quiet for a moment.

'Mum will be disappointed.'

'Tough.'

'Oh come on, Peter. Mum thinks Claudia's the best thing that ever happened to you. You can't hold that against her.'

'She'll get over it.'

She stared into her wine glass and sighed. 'I'm just sorry, that's all. For everyone.'

The waiter bent at a table on the far side. Some contented middle aged couple enjoying the Latin charm, the cool respite from the heat outside. A hand reached out from the past and choked off all the air.

'Remember Fred the painter?' he said.

'No. Should I?'

'He used to work for the old man. He painted the house a few years ago.'

'Can't say I do offhand, why?'

'I had him working at Priory Road and my place for a while.'

'And?'

'I sacked him a few days ago.'

She frowned, unsure of the implications. 'Does this have something to do with the woman you've been seeing?'

He laughed bitterly. 'Not quite. It might have a few repercussions though. I'm already taking a lot of flak for it. Ironic really, when you think how many men the old man fired in his time.'

'Why did you sack him?'

He shrugged. 'Different reasons.'

'And you think Dad will have something to say about it?'

'That's a foregone conclusion. I'm surprised he hasn't called me already.'

'Well, I'm sure it'll be resolved. It won't be the first time you've fallen out with him, will it?'

She picked at the remains of her fettuccini, uncertain as to which topic should take precedence. Years of witnessing the old man's violent outbursts had given her a better insight than most. He knew that he could rely on her support, whatever her doubts about his motives.

She looked at him intently. 'Do you ever think about James?'

The question caught him off guard. She noted his reaction and shifted in the seat.

'I just wondered that's all. You don't have to talk about it if you don't want to.'

'I think about him a lot. Every time certain songs come on the radio. Then I'm back there, re-living it all again in my mind.'

She nodded solemnly. 'It must be difficult for you.'

'What – dealing with what happened or knowing I caused it in the first place?'

She gave a small sigh and sat back. 'I wasn't referring to that at all.'

'But that's what comes up every time his name's mentioned. How I drove him to it. How it was all my fault.'

She stared at the table.

'Why should I spend the rest of my life with that hanging over me?'

'No-one's saying you have to.'

'Really? You didn't hear the whispering campaign behind my back. Why d'you think Tara went to America? Even her own family wouldn't speak to her.'

'Alright. I'm sorry I mentioned it.'

He finished his coke. The tight fist released its grip, allowing him to breathe easier. The dark place remained for him to revisit whenever he felt the need. Shock waves from news that had left them all reeling. That was the hardest part. To be so close to someone and then find out they were gone forever. The person you thought you knew so well had simply got up and left the party.

'Are you going to tell Claudia?' she said.

He barely heard the question, still lost in the past. 'I don't know what I'm going to do.'

She forced a smile. 'Oh well. I'm sure it'll all work out for the best.'

'Or maybe it won't.'

'Well you have to decide what you want. Claudia or this woman. You can't have both, can you?'

They argued over the bill as always, Sarah insisting that she pay as a matter of principle. He threw in a generous tip for the faultless floor service and bid a silent farewell to the young couple by the window, sipping their drinks, immune to the rest of the world.

They stood outside in the sunshine. Sarah gave him her benevolent, big sister's smile. 'Give me a call. Let me know how things go.'

'If I haven't left the country by then.'

'Oh you poor thing. Come and give me a big hug.'

They embraced in a waft of Chanel and fabric conditioner. The only member of his family he could truly relate to and he still managed to forget her birthday.

She stepped back, with the same maternal smile. 'Whatever happens, you know I'll support you.'

'Thanks. I might need it.'

'You know where I am if you need to talk.'

'I'll be OK.'

'I know you will. It's everyone else I'm worried about.'

He wandered back alone past the old stone church. Students sat out on the grass in select huddles, animated conversations warmed by the afternoon sun. He thought how good it would be to have no worries. Nothing to think about but the next in-breath.

He crossed the road and began composing a requiem. For Claudia.

Twenty-eight

He met her in Starbucks at lunchtime. Right away he knew something was wrong. Her nervous smile alerted him as she came through the door. Some inner conflict she was trying to hide. Pressures at work. Deadlines to meet. She'd only been back from Reading two days and already she needed a break. He watched her walk over to the seating area with a sense of foreboding. When you'd been with someone long enough you could read the signs. The accusatory silences. The long pauses boiling with resentment. Years of familiarity that peeled away the layers and exposed all the nerve endings.

She sank into the soft leather chair and undid her jacket. Claudia's most impressive feature, that guaranteed a male audience wherever she went.

'Busy?' he said.

'I got held up in a meeting.'

'I'll get you a coffee.'

'Don't bother. I had one earlier.'

He watched her closely. 'What's up?'

'Nothing. I'm just … I've had a hectic morning that's all.'

The low table kept them apart, his empty coffee cup on the smoked glass a statement of his independence. She fussed with her handbag and gave brief, stilted answers to his questions. Yes, her mum was fine. No, she hadn't slept all that well. Work was an effort but she could put up with it until something better came along. Her voice carried a note of tension, her usual optimism missing.

'Pharma-plus have offered me a job,' she said.

'Doing what?'

'The same thing. It would probably mean a wider catchment area, but the money would be better.'

'Go for it.'

She shrugged, unimpressed with him or the job offer. He watched the young girls serving at the drinks machine, distracted by the general chatter. Claudia's tension flashed up a clear warning. Her moods wouldn't normally have bothered him. This time he felt uncomfortable, that she was keeping something from him.

She sat upright and brushed a fleck from her skirt. 'Anyway, I've told them I'll think about it.'

'What's stopping you taking it now?'

'I don't want the pressure of a new job while I'm still in the process of selling the house.'

'Any news on that front?'

'I'm still waiting for the survey.'

The rich aroma of ground coffee filled the place, a modern lounge effect, with broad leather armchairs and low, chrome-edged tables. Most of the customers were students, their chatter competing with the gurgling coffee machine. He noted the female potential in an offhand way. Always a woman somewhere to take your mind off your troubles.

Claudia tapped her polished nails on the armrest and stared at the table between them. She seemed unable to look at him, or even to speak to him directly. 'You didn't tell me Raul was having a barbeque,' she said.

'I forgot.'

'What were you going to do – take someone else?'

'I said I forgot, didn't I?'

She put her hands in her lap, silent. The neck of her blouse lay open, the tiny silver chain she wore lost in her cleavage. She looked up and held his gaze with an effort of will. 'Where did you go on Sunday?'

'What?'

'Sunday afternoon. Your phone was off. I called you twice.'

He looked at her blankly.

'So you can't remember?'

'What is this – twenty questions?'

'If you don't want to answer just say so.'

'I was playing golf with Tim.'

'What all day?'

'No.'

'So where were you then?'

She watched him intently. He slipped further down in the soft leather and stalled for time. Two teenage girls sat in the next vacant seats along, the petite blonde reminding him vaguely of Zoe.

'I'm waiting,' she said.

'Look, Claudia – I can't remember what I was doing Sunday afternoon. I have trouble remembering what I did yesterday, for fuck's sake. Can't we just – '

'Are you seeing someone else?'

The question stunned him. He sat upright and hoped his shocked expression would answer for him.

'Don't play games with me. Are you or not?'

'Claudia – '

'Don't lie to me. Just, don't lie to me, OK?'

'OK.'

'So are you or not?'

'Do we have to do this right now, in here?

'Yes, we do.'

The teenage girls missed the drama, too wrapped up in their own lives to care about his. He felt mildly let down. Such a tense moment ought to have come with a fanfare, a drum roll to announce it to the rest of the world. Instead, the punters filed in off the street and the serving girls hovered endlessly around the coffee machine.

Claudia started to cry, soundlessly, her shoulders heaving. He sat back, detached, as if her reaction had nothing to do with him at all. As the direct source of her grief, he could offer no real comfort. And in a strange way she didn't deserve any. Troops were dying in far flung trouble spots. Kids were living in ghettos and running around with no shoes on their feet. He resented her for forcing him to defend himself. He tried to pity her instead, but the effort was too great. Where he should have felt love or compassion or some other noble human emotion, he felt only a void.

She stopped crying and looked up. Her pretty face was etched with tears, drained by the misery he'd caused her. 'I can't believe you've done this to me.'

'I haven't done anything to you.'

'You let me believe everything was fine between us. Why did you do that?'

'Listen, Claudia – '

'I thought you were happy with me. I thought that all the plans we made for the future was something you wanted too. Obviously I was wrong about that.'

'You weren't wrong. I was just – '

'Are you seeing someone else?'

The question stopped him again, as if he'd misheard her the first time.

'Just tell me – please.'

He sat forward and trailed a spoon in the empty cup. The heat was stifling, even with the door open. To lie to her now would be pointless. He needed to buy himself more time, ease her down gently.

'Listen, I've been under a lot of pressure lately. Work. The old man …'

'Is that a yes or a no?'

'I've been meaning to talk to you, but – '

She lurched forward. 'Will you just answer the fucking question.'

Nothing changed but the music. The teenage girls chatted at the next table. The steam blew from the coffee machine. Claudia sat with her legs crossed, hands folded on her knee, a look of devout suffering worn for his benefit. He might have prepared a better speech, a long and emotional appeal for clemency. She would have seen the unfairness of it all and granted him a pardon. But words failed him. Only the standard apology remained.

'I'm sorry it had to happen like this.'

'So you are seeing someone then?'

'I didn't plan it.'

Laughter burst from the next table, the teenage girls enjoying some private joke. The girls behind the counter flashed their fixed smiles, waiting on an endless queue. He looked at Claudia's stricken face and wished he was somewhere else.

'So who is she then?'

'Does it matter who it is?'

'Yes it does.''

'It won't change anything, will it?'

'Don't you think I have a right to know? Don't you think I'll find out anyway?'

He said nothing.

She faced him across the divide, rigid, breathing heavily. 'Come on. I'm waiting. Who is it?'

The name would give him away, betray a long kept secret. But she would find out anyway. Any deliberate withholding on his part would only cause more trouble.

'Natalie,' he said quietly.

She sat composed, hands resting on her knees. The name made no outward impression. He sensed a conspiracy.

'You knew didn't you?'

'No.'

'Yes you did. I can tell. Who told you?'

'Nobody told me.'

'Erica?'

'No.'

'Marco?'

She gave an exasperated sigh. 'Who cares how I found out? You've admitted it now. That's all I need to know.'

'So what happens now?'

'What do you mean?'

'I just thought that, as we were doing this the civilised way, there was some sort of correct procedure to follow.'

'Are you being funny?' She gave an indignant shrug and looked to the window. After a long pause she brought her gaze back to rest on him, the instigator. 'I'm not making a scene in here. You've done what you wanted to do. But then you've always done that, haven't you?'

'It's not all down to me.'

She stared at him, incredulous. 'I'm not the one who slept with someone else, remember?'

'Maybe you should open your eyes more often.'

'What's that supposed to mean?'

'All your forward planning and holidays in Spain. You never stopped to think about my needs, did you?'

'What're you talking about?'

'I get up and go to work. I come home to invoices and phone calls. Once a week, I get a progress report from Barry in the lounge bar of the Night Jar to justify my existence. Every day it's the same thing over and over.'

'What's that got to do with me?'

'Everything. I can't fucking breathe, Claudia. My life's been sold off, put up for auction. Not one single part of it that doesn't belong to someone else.'

'So now you're saying it's my fault you slept with Natalie?'

'I'm not saying it's anyone's fault.'

'Well it obviously wasn't me you wanted, was it?' She shook her head in disbelief, her eyes bright with fresh tears. 'I hope she gives you everything you want. Whatever that is.'

'Claudia – '

'Don't bother. Just don't bother.' She grabbed her bag and stood up, passing him without a glance.

He followed her out into the afternoon sun. The illusion that they were still a couple persisted, the scene in the coffee shop no more than a blip that they would soon get over. The only allusion to her mood, her angry heels ringing out along the pavement.

'Where's your car?' he said.

'In the car park.'

'I'll drop you round there.'

'No you won't. I can walk.'

'Claudia, you don't have to get – '

She turned on him. 'I've got nothing else to say to you. Leave me alone!'

He walked alongside her, trying to keep up with her absurd route march. In spite of his provocation, it seemed unlikely she would leave him. All he had to do was keep her talking and do his best to repair some of the damage.

'So that's it then?' he said. 'You're going to walk away without even talking about it?'

'I've told you, I've got nothing more to say to you.'

'I'll walk you to your car.'

'I don't want you to walk me anywhere. I want you to leave me alone.'

They walked in silence to the car park. She opened up her car. Without waiting for an invitation he climbed into the passenger side.

'What d'you think you're doing?' she said.

'We need to talk.'

'About what?'

'Please, Claudia.'

She sank onto one heel with a violent out-breath. 'You've just admitted you're seeing someone else! What am I supposed to do, spend the rest of the afternoon consoling you for it?'

She eased into the driver's side and put the keys in the ignition. Her well groomed company car with its hint of lemon air freshener, her favourite CD cases lodged in the handbrake well. One more aspect of her soon to be taken away.

He began an improvised speech, unsure of the outcome he was looking for. 'Look, Claudia, there's lots of reasons things happen.'

'Yeah. Like you can't keep your hands off other women.'

'I'm not trying to excuse it. I'm just saying that nothing's straightforward.'

She reached for the keys in the ignition. He grabbed her arm.

'It wasn't just you, OK? You weren't the only reason.'

She sat back and stared through the windscreen. 'What was it then – boredom?'

'Claudia – '

'I don't want to hear it. Whatever the excuse is, I'm not interested.'

'But you haven't given me a chance to explain.'

'I gave you plenty of chances and you lied to me. You've destroyed everything we had. All my trust in you. All my love for you. You've thrown all that away.'

An attractive woman and two small children spilled from a people carrier. The woman called the children to her side, checking her bag, the keys, the car, managing all the facets of her busy life with a consummate skill. Claudia sat beside him, her life in ruins, her mouth clamped shut to stop her from crying.

'Look, I'm sorry,' he said.

She gripped the steering wheel with both hands and turned to face him, her lower lip trembling. 'Remember all those things you said to me? How you never wanted to turn out like your dad? Well look at you now. You're just like him.'

She turned on the ignition.

With a final look at her tear-stained face, he stepped out of the car and out of her life altogether.

She pulled away quickly, leaving him stranded. Claudia gone. The end of an era. The future tainted without her.

He went out onto the High Street. The attractive woman and her two children were standing at the level crossing. He stood with them. The little blonde girl set off, swinging her arms in step beside him. He thought of Leanne, the constant worry that she would disappear or be knocked down, spoiling their weekly outings. The little blonde girl stepped safely onto the pavement. In a few years she would have grown beyond even her mother's control, looking to some man to bring her happiness.

Claudia was gone.

Already his memories were tinged with remorse and sadness. The law of karma. What you put into the vast melting pot you got back with interest. The unwritten law that forbade you to keep anything longer than its allotted time. Leanne's childhood. Claudia's devotion. All gone. Snatched away by the unseen hand. Perhaps he'd got what he deserved. The gaping hole in his life waiting to be filled by someone else. And the only candidate left was Natalie.

Twenty-nine

The house sat atop the rolling lawn, baking in the afternoon heat. Outside – the silver Mercedes, facing east, a star of sunlight reflected from its bonnet. The view from the front gates always struck him as imposing, a touch of the Colonial to impress visitors. Two dark shapes shot through the open doorway to greet him, barking in a shrill stereo. He parked and got out, the dogs fussing round him on the drive, miniature faces vying for his attention.

She stood in the doorway, watching him. 'I was expecting you earlier.'

'I had a few things to sort out.'

The dogs took off across the lawn, leaving him without a prop.

'Have you eaten?' she said.

'Sort of.'

'What does that mean?'

'I had a packet of cheese and onion crisps earlier.'

She snapped a command in her special dog voice. The dogs ignored her, running in manic circles around the water fountain. She clapped her hands twice. 'Suli! Simba!' The dogs turned and darted back across the lawn, racing over the threshold to nose at her feet.

'Where's the old man?' he said.

'Out on the boat with Walter.'

Scaffold tubes lay along the side of the new double garage. Always some job for the old man when he wasn't on the golf course or drifting around the Solent with the good old boys. She guessed what he was thinking and shook her head. 'I've given up telling him,

Peter. He does whatever he wants to do, you should know that. Come inside, I'll make you a drink.'

He sat at the scarred and pitted kitchen table, part of the rustic look that went with the Aga and the flagstones. She stood at the worktop, the dogs gazing up either side of her, programmed for food at all times. Glaring sunlight flooded the back garden through the open door – a quick escape should he need one. In the background, the ghost of Claudia, demanding an explanation for the shameful way he'd treated her.

She talked about Leanne and how well she was doing at college. Leanne's Shakespearian debut was especially poignant for her, a reminder of her own brief foray into the world of amateur dramatics. 'Have you spoken to her lately?' she said.

'I left a message on her answerphone last week. She never rings back.'

'She's at that age. Sandwich?'

'What've you got?'

'Ham or chicken.'

'Free range or battery?'

She turned, with an indulgent sigh. 'Peter – do you want a sandwich or not?'

'Ham'll do nicely, thanks.'

She sliced an uncut brown loaf, and talked more about Leanne. He listened with only marginal interest, aware of his poor track record over the past sixteen years and the battleground the whole issue had turned into. As she talked, she peeled off a piece of smoked ham from the pack and the dogs jumped eagerly up at her knees.

The topic changed. From Leanne to Bernice. His sense of outrage surprised even him, that he could feel so harshly about a member of his own family. 'It's no wonder she's like she is. You need to stop bailing her out all the time.'

She spun round, gesturing with the bread knife. 'Bernice is my daughter, thank you. What am I supposed to do – turn my back on her and see her go without?'

'Has she paid back that two grand yet?'

'That was a gift. Something from me and your father to help her get settled in when she moved. I told you that before.'

He nodded, unimpressed. 'I don't remember anyone ever giving me two grand for being a pain in the ass.'

'That's enough.'

'You might as well have given it to charity for all the good it's done. Look at her now. Living on a council estate, bringing up someone else's kid.'

'I said that's enough!'

He ate the sandwich against a blurred backdrop of the cardinal virtues. Morality learned at home, instilled in him by adults who changed the rules to suit their own agendas. Bernice, always beyond reproach, had learnt the age old truism. Play the victim long enough and there would always be someone willing to fish you out of the water.

'How's the sandwich?' she said.

'Fine.'

'I do worry you're not eating properly sometimes.'

'I do eat properly.' He peeled off a strip of fat and dropped it on the flagstones. Suli made an opportunist dash from beneath the table and wolfed it down. He sat back, impressed with the dog's quick reactions. 'Anyway, I've got the health angle well covered. I drink a glass of orange juice every morning and I only eat wholemeal bread. That OK?'

She cleared the worktop in silence, a force in her own right, able to apply herself to any task with a singleness of purpose. Even school teachers shrank from her, sensing her natural authority before she'd even opened her mouth. He'd learned much from watching her over the years. The best lesson of all – that silence would often win an argument where words failed.

She made coffee and joined him at the table. The dogs lay out on the flagstones in an arc of sunlight. Inside, the ticking of the clock and the lazy summer heat through the open doorway. He sensed that this was the moment. His trial, rehearsed by her at length in the days preceding.

She flipped vaguely through a magazine before looking up.

'I know about Claudia.'

'That figures.'

'You don't have to be like that.'

'Like what?'

'Look, I'm not having a go at you. I just feel, I just feel so sad for you both.'

He shrugged and picked at the crumbs on the plate.

'I thought you were both so happy together.'

'People fall out all the time. It's a fact of life.'

'But you both had so much going for you.'

'Like what – a winner in the Grand National?'

She sighed heavily. 'If you're going to be sarcastic I won't bother talking to you at all.' She sat in silence, staring at the table. 'So what will you do now?'

'About what?'

'Spain, for a start. I thought we were all going together.'

'Talk to Claudia. She booked the tickets without even asking me.'

She folded her arms, refusing to look at him. The stalemate changed her entire demeanour. The part she played best, refraining from direct criticism but expert in her show of disapproval.

'I'm thinking of going away myself,' he said.

She looked up, puzzled. 'Where to?'

'Anywhere. Jump on a plane and disappear. A million miles away from this place.'

She sat in quiet reflection, the issue with Claudia unresolved.

'How long have you known this, woman?'

'Not long.'

'She's a teacher – is that right?'

'That's just a front. She's actually a drug dealer in her spare time.'

She glared at him. 'You don't have to be clever with me every time I ask you a question.'

He accepted her reproach for the moment. Talking about Natalie made him uneasy, exposing him to more criticism. This was the backlash. The price you paid for spoiling peoples plans.

'Who told you she was a teacher?' he said.

'Claudia.'

'You've spoken to her then?'

'Only briefly. She was too upset to talk for long.'

'She'll get over it.'

'Don't you care what happens to her?'

'Of course I care.'

She frowned at him, perplexed at his cavalier attitude. He sat his side of the impasse and kept quiet. She recovered her brief loss of control and fixed him with a strained but determined smile. 'Oh well. Perhaps a break will do you good.'

'A what?'

'You've obviously been under a lot of stress lately, what with the sale of Claudia's house and everything else. Maybe some time apart will do you good.'

She already had the marquee planned. The invitations sent out. He laid both hands flat on the table. 'Let's get one thing straight here. I am *not* getting back with Claudia. OK?'

'We'll see.'

He pushed back the chair and stood up, incredulous. 'What is it with this family? No-one listens to a single fucking word I say.'

He crossed to the sink and ran the cold water. Suli raised an ear from the cool flagstones, her radar tuned to the slightest blip. The ordeal began to drain him. In the background her pious silence, worse than any criticism. He drank a glass of cold water and sat back down at the table.

She smoothed the tips of her fingers absently, while the clock beat time above them. The planned escape route began to look more and more appealing.

'Sorry,' he said finally.

She looked up. 'I won't have you speaking to me like that, Peter.'

'I said I was sorry, didn't I?'

She accepted his apology without further comment, her precious dignity intact. Now they could continue with some degree of understanding. That had always been her forte. The ability to rise above all forms of provocation without conceding defeat. The issue over Claudia would eat away at her until she could find a way of dealing with it. In the meantime, he would have to put up with her poorly veiled looks of disapproval.

'How's the old man?' he said.

'The same as ever.'

'Has he been back to the doctor?'

'What do you think?'

The old man's pride was also ingrained, any illness seen as a weakness. They were both the same, neither one of them willing to compromise. The old man refused to take the statin tablets the doctor had prescribed. Recent cholesterol tests seemed to prove the old man's theory. Staying active kept him fit. Doctors surgeries were a waste of time. He felt a degree of sympathy for her though, for putting up with it all.

She shook her head at the dilemma. 'He can't sit down for five minutes without the phone going. Either Walter or Frank. Someone from the committee expecting him to drop everything and rush out the door for them.'

He laughed ruefully. 'I shouldn't worry about it. He'll probably outlive all of us.'

'Not at this rate he won't.'

He couldn't resist a taunt at her. 'Been to any handshake functions lately?'

'I wish you wouldn't call them that.'

'What should I call them then – the benevolent society dinner and dance?'

'I am not getting drawn into a conversation with you about all that.'

'Why not?'

'You know why not.'

She refused to be drawn on the subject. The old man's membership gave her a certain prestige. The ladies nights were a regular fixture on her social calendar. She could dress up and mix with likeminded people in an atmosphere of camaraderie. She liked the secrecy, the sense of belonging, even when the whole business had caused a feud within her own family.

'How far up the ladder did Uncle Alf go?'

'Peter, I'm not going into – '

'He had plenty of money, didn't he? One thing this family's always excelled at, making money.' He sat back, enjoying himself at her expense. 'They don't let paupers in, do they? They wouldn't have old Ron the window cleaner off the estate up for membership. Lower the tone of the whole thing.'

'I'm not even going to answer that.'

'Granddad hated it all, didn't he? He used to call it the back-slappers club. Must have really hacked him off when the old man got put up for membership'

She fixed him with a clear, warning gaze.

He sat with his grandfather's memory. A robust and highly principled man, Storehouse of knowledge and insight, struck down by cancer at the age of sixty-eight. She never said much about him, her memories tainted by some vague and undisclosed fear. His grandfather had been the master of the house. The strict disciplinarian calling for silence at the dining table, barely needing to raise his voice to make his irritation known. His contempt for freemasonry had caused frequent rows throughout the years. Rows with the old man. With her.

He recalled the rows when he was a boy. How his grandfather would grip the edge of the table, the broken veins in his cheeks standing out, breathing heavily through his nose until the old man had left the room.

'They should never have worked together, should they?' he said.

'Probably not.'

'The old man tried to cut too many corners. Had to do things his way. Even Barry called him a maverick.'

She tensed, visibly. 'Barry said that?'

'Well, he wasn't far wrong, was he?'

She folded her arms and sat back, morose. 'Your grandfather wasn't exactly blameless.'

He recalled an incident in his teens and smiled to himself. 'He got me to paint a door for him once. Fifteen glass panels in it. When I'd finished he pointed out every single speck of paint I'd got on the glass. Then he made me go over it with a Stanley knife and white spirit until every speck was gone.'

The heartening chirp of birdsong came from the garden. Bright sunlight lit up the flagstones by the back door. His grandfather's memory stood like a monument, unblemished.

She stood up, taking his plate. 'Would you like a cold drink?'

'What've you got?'

'Blackcurrant or orange squash.'

'No strawberry milk-shake, then?'

She paused to look him over, immune to his foibles. 'Peter. Wouldn't it be nice if you could be reasonable, just once for a change.'

He sipped his Robinsons blackcurrant, rolling the ice in the tall glass. Brand names only in the Calliet household, a snobbery he'd inherited from her and been unable to shake off. Inferior products made a statement about your self-worth. You risked being labelled a cheapskate, or at worse a fully paid-up member of the common herd. Even the ice had to be vetted before it made the shopping trolley.

She began to clean around him, her favourite pastime. While she cleaned, she talked about the future with a note of optimism; the prospect of six weeks in South Africa at the end of the summer if the old man was well enough to travel.

'Why don't you retire out there?' he said.

'What with your father? I don't think so somehow. I can't see him retiring anywhere, can you?'

'Go without him then. You only get one life, don't you?'

She laughed softly. 'I've thought about it a few times, believe me.'

'Anyway, he'll probably croak on the golf course and you won't have to worry. His last moment on this planet, wondering whether he should have used a seven or a five-iron.'

'Yes, thank you, Peter.'

He went through to the dining room and stood at the leaded window. The two cars sat out on the driveway, a few feet apart. The old man's gold Mercedes, solid and functional, old-fashioned by modern standards. The phantom black TT, streamlined by comparison, built with a different clientele in mind. Beyond the driveway, the rolling lawn, smooth as the fairway at Knighton Heath.

He ran a hand over the polished mahogany tabletop and heard her proud voice informing visitors. '*This is my favourite piece. Cuban you see. It came from my father's house. We had it restored when we moved here.*'

The photographs on the dresser caught his eye. Family portraits. Sarah's wedding shots. Not one of Claudia among them. The thought caught him off-guard. He pictured her standing at the window in her flimsy summer dress, his hands on her hips, his mouth on her neck, her vain attempts to stop him, spurring him on to more advantage.

He paid his respects to Claudia's memory and left the room.

He found her outside on the garden bench, her eyes closed in meditation. Suli raised a sad eye from the shaded spot beneath her. Simba barely stirred, laid out beneath the silver birch, dreaming of chicken leftovers and pigeons that couldn't fly.

He perched on the low brick wall and admired the flowerbeds. 'Funny – I never knew what an African Violet was until the other day.'

She opened one eye, drowsy in the heat. 'Sorry?'

'The old woman next door at Priory Road gave me a tour of her garden. I was quite impressed at all the effort that goes into it. Takes me six months to mow the lawn.'

She smiled and let her gaze wander. 'Barry came round at the weekend.'

'What for?'

'Your father's asked him to take on Henley Park.'

The news came as a snub, a personal insult dreamed up by the old man over his lingering indecision.

She opened both eyes and stared at him. 'Well you weren't interested, were you?'

'Why didn't the old man talk to me first?'

'Because you made it quite clear that you didn't want the responsibility.'

'So he goes behind my back and offers it to Barry instead.'

She gave a weary sigh. 'Oh, for goodness sake, Peter. It wasn't like that at all. Please don't go causing trouble over this. I couldn't bear it. I really couldn't.'

He sat with the frustration, a sense of betrayal that wouldn't leave him. Something wasn't right. Her initial reaction hadn't been all that convincing. He went over recent events and guessed the real reason behind the old man's decision.

'I know what all this is about,' he said evenly. 'This is about me sacking the old boy, Fred.'

'I don't know what you're talking about, Peter.'

Her denial incensed him further, proving her complicity without a doubt. The three of them in it together. Herself, Barry and the old man, scheming behind his back. He looked away, disgusted at their treatment of him. Especially her – guardian of the moral code – always careful to avoid a scandal to protect her precious reputation.

He shook his head in disdain. 'Funny how things work out, isn't it?'

'What do you mean?'

'Something Claudia said.' He paused, making sure he had her full attention. 'She said I swore I'd never turn out like the old man. Now look at me.'

She shifted uneasily. He ignored her discomfort, needing her to understand.

'Remember the flats in Christchurch? He came down one Saturday morning and sacked the ground workers. Ordered the whole gang off his land because he had a row with the head honcho the day before. By the time we put the roof on that place, it was me that needed a holiday.' She closed her eyes to shut him out. 'I learned a lot from him though. About how to treat people. Especially people who rub you up the wrong way. But then you'd know all about that, wouldn't you?'

'What do you mean by that?' She lurched forward. 'What's the hell's wrong with you? Did you come round especially to upset me?'

He said nothing, gloating at her reaction.

She eased her shoulders back against the bench. Birdsong played in the sun trap, the heat oppressive like the mood between them. The immediate future bothered him. The expectation that he would take a lead role if the old man's health failed him was now under question. The onus had always been on him, the only son, to take over. Henley Park was too lucrative a prospect to lose outright. Barry's possible tenure had come as a shock. He'd never considered the possibility that the old man might ease him out without telling him.

The faint drone of traffic from the main road made him eager to move on. Escape from all her woes and bitter disappointments. Complex family issues that drained all his energy. He had to make a stand, remind her that he could think for himself and run his own show.

A bird landed on the wooden perch and stabbed insanely at stray breadcrumbs. She fed them every day, taking great pains to ensure their safety, chasing prowling cats away with handclaps and clashing saucepan lids. He felt a wave of empathy for her, sitting in the sun with her eyes closed. They were alike in many ways. They both hid behind well constructed defences, careful not to reveal too much of their inner feelings. She didn't have his temper. Hers would simmer and percolate beneath the surface, until she'd found a suitable outlet, a sensible, practical way of dealing with whatever it was that was bothering her. She could have left years ago. She had enough reasons. Losing the house in Branksome after Sarah was born. Having to live at his grandparents, paying off one more draining tax bill after the other. Then the best reason of all. The old man's philandering ways, hushed up to spare everyone's feelings, including her own.

He looked up at the house. The leaded windows. The steep pitch of the slate roof. The place had character, a real picture book charm that caused visitors to fall in love with it the moment they set eyes on it. If it wasn't for the faint drone of traffic, you could have been deep in the countryside, breathing pure air.

'Marco's place is coming down soon,' he said absently.

'Where will he go?'

'No idea. Long as he doesn't come knocking on my door.'

'What about his family?'

He laughed. 'He could always go and stay with his sister in London. She put up with him for a few weeks once before. Then she got up one morning to find some Rastafarian crashed out on her living room floor. That was it. Marco had to go.'

She made no comment. Marco's feckless lifestyle appalled her. To come from such a privileged background and end up homeless, relying on handouts. The shame was unimaginable.

The sun disappeared behind a small cloud. The picture book garden lost its veneer. The thought struck him that you could lose everything and still be happy. People spent their lives acquiring objects that had no intrinsic value, only to lose them at some later stage of the game. The Buddhists were right. You might as well give it away for all the good it did you.

The sun came out again. The house gleamed, resplendent under a clear blue sky. He shifted in the heat, sedated almost. No matter how spiritual you tried to be, the material plane would always have its merits. Comfort zones, as Tim liked to call them. Everyone out there seeking some form of security. Even Marco.

'James used to love this house,' he said, and the past engulfed him. She looked up with a glimmer of concern. They'd never discussed what had happened. He'd told Sarah all the details but never her. She of all people might have understood. The thought ignited his anger. Anger at being denied the right to voice his feelings.

'Remember when you caught us in the drinks cabinet at two in the morning?' he said, detached from the memory. 'And the night we came back from Fantasia and you locked us out?'

She gave a hesitant smile, caught in strange territory. The urge to confess came over him, to share the burden.

'I never even went to the funeral.'

'Yes, I know,' she said softly. 'That was an awful time for you.'

'I was advised not to go under the circumstances.' He looked away, aware of the intense heat, the bead of sweat along his spine. She sat silently by, drawn into a blind alley. He slapped his thighs in a gesture of finality and stood up. 'Oh well. Time to make a move, I suppose. Places to go, people to see …'

She saw him to the front door.

Before he left, she touched his arm and smiled sadly. Her look reassured him in an odd way. She was there for him, even if she couldn't always show it. But the sense of foreboding stayed with him. You pushed something to the back of your mind and it pushed its way to the forefront. James was gone, but his legacy remained, a shadow hanging over so many lives. Perhaps that was the real tragedy. You never really learned from your mistakes, you just went on repeating them, blaming other people for the fallout.

Thirty

6 am Saturday morning. Natalie tired and irritable. Woman's trouble, she told him – not that he would understand, of course. He did what he could to help, but after several failed attempts to seduce her, gave up and read a book instead. She wanted only to sleep. Her strained and weary voice set the boundaries as surely as a line down the centre of the bed.

He listened to the dawn chorus, lying back on her satin quilt. Charlotte had her own schedule, independent of the rest of the household. He heard her tramp through to the kitchen in bare feet and pour herself a bowl of cereal. The same routine every morning. Coco Pops in a wide-rimmed soup bowl, carried through to the front room and eaten in front of the television. Natalie's concerns about his sleepovers had proved unfounded. Charlotte paid no more attention to his visits than she would a new set of cutlery.

Natalie lay beside him, breathing in starts as if she was dreaming. Charlotte marched back along the hall and past the bedroom door. Cartoon voices rang out – the volume turned down as an afterthought. Charlotte had spirit, despite the tantrums and the constant demands for attention. Nothing much seemed to faze her. Power struggles between adults only gave her more options, new ways of working things to her advantage. Charlotte was amusing, endearing even, but Children's TV at six-o'clock in the morning would put a strain on any friendship.

He rolled over and hugged the curve of Natalie's warm body. She moaned pitifully and drew up her knees

'You awake honey?' he said.

'Mmm?'

He ran a hand across her thigh. She reacted instantly, drawing herself into the foetal position, moaning in the same tired voice. 'Leave me alone, I don't feel well.'

'I'm bored.'

'Go home then.'

'Charming.'

'Tough. You kept me awake half the night as it is.'

He lay back in defeat while insane cartoon characters fought to the death in the front room. At least Charlotte had her priorities worked out. No petty disputes to spoil the Coco Pops. He raised himself on an elbow, sensing Natalie was still awake. 'How does a man get breakfast round here?'

'Make it yourself.'

'Where's the fun in that?'

She lay with her back to him, a spiteful lump under the satin cover. He rolled over against her, their bodies interlocking. She gave the cover a vicious yank and decamped to the farthest side of the bed. He sank back with a deep sigh.

'What's the matter now?' she said.

'Nothing.'

She raised her head from the pillow, straining to make out his face in the gloom. 'I told you I don't feel well.'

He resisted the urge to laugh at her pinched expression, her wild tangle of black hair. 'Shall I call a doctor?'

'I don't need a fucking doctor! Just stop hassling me and let me go back to sleep.'

He put his shirt on and went through to the front room.

Charlotte looked up without interest, the special blank look children wore for gullible adults. The same response as her mother, but without the threat of violence. He sat in the armchair by the window. Charlotte went back to gazing at the television, sat upright on her knees, her face inches from the screen. The wide-rimmed soup bowl sat beside her, stained with chocolate flavoured milk.

'Did you sleep well, Charlotte?'

'Mmmm.'

'Enjoy the Coco Pops?'

'Mmmm.'

'And would you say you're a morning person like your mother?'

She looked up with a puzzled frown. 'What?'

'Never mind. I'll go make a coffee.'

He took the drink back into the bedroom. Natalie stirred and lay staring at the ceiling, her pink pyjama top twisted, exposing her smooth belly. The soft rise and fall of her breathing and her pale, mournful expression gave her a strange vulnerability. He sat on the edge of the bed and feigned sympathy, a doctor or a bona fide care worker without the uniform.

'Feel any better?' he said softly.

'No.'

'Why don't you take a shower?'

'The shower's broken. I told you that ages ago.'

'Have a bath then.'

'I don't want a bath.'

He studied the outline of her legs beneath the cover, her bare torso stark beneath her pyjama top. He never had the same problem with Claudia. She was always up first, planning the rest of the day with military precision.

'Charlotte's got good posture hasn't she?' he said.

'What?'

'She sits upright with her back straight. Some kids slouch. Not good for the spine when they get older.'

'Did you come in here just to wind me up?'

'I came in to get away from the telly, actually. Does she always sit that close to the screen?'

'Please leave me alone.'

He stood up and walked over to the door.

'Peter?'

He looked back. 'What?'

'I'm sorry. Please don't be angry with me.'

'I'm not angry with you.'

'I just feel, I'm just not …'

He put a finger to his lips, soothing her fears as if he knew what they were, before closing the door quietly behind him.

Charlotte loitered in the hallway, a small militant figure with suspicious eyes. She glanced at his bare feet, his shirttails barely hiding his Calvin Klein's. He made a dramatic plea for silence, pointing to the bedroom behind him as if it harboured a dangerous animal.

'When can I go to Nanny's?' Charlotte said.

'I don't know, sweetheart.'

She reached for the bedroom door. He blocked her path.

'You can't go in there.'

'Why not?'

'Because your mum's not well.'

'What's the matter with her?'

'I'm not sure but it might be contagious.' He ushered her into the kitchen and sat down at the table. She stood in front of him, defiant in her teddy bear pyjamas and pink furry slippers. They discussed the issue of her going to her grandmother's in hushed tones. The diplomacy angle failed.

'I want to go now,' she said.

'Sorry, but you can't.'

'Why not?'

'Because …' Her fixed expression stumped him. He gave up. 'Look, get dressed, Charlotte and I'll see what I can do, OK?'

Charlotte turned and strode along the hall with an assumed dignity. The cartoon voices went up a notch in protest.

He sat with the pleasant hum of the fridge and a clear view across the bay, the awkward guest in a strange environment. Doubts began to form. Thoughts of Claudia. The simple and uncomplicated life he'd left behind. Their break-up had left a void, something he couldn't talk about. Natalie's reaction to the news had been disturbing. He'd expected more of an emotional response from her. Instead she'd been vague and withdrawn, hiding what he felt was a sense of disappointment, consumed with the drama of her own life. The last thing he needed, freed from one relationship to become a burden in another.

He went back into the bedroom and closed the door. Natalie's sleeping form lay hunched beneath the satin quilt cover. She looked up drowsily. 'What's going on?'

'Charlotte wants to go to your mum's.'

'She'll have to wait.'

'I don't think she does waiting.'

She laid an arm on her forehead and stared blankly at the ceiling. 'I feel like shit.'

'Can't you take something?'

'Like what?'

'You've got half of Boots in your bathroom cabinet. You must have something.'

'Ibuprofen,' she said, resentfully.

'Anything else?'

'You could run me a bath.'

'You didn't want one earlier.'

'I've changed my mind.' She lay still, gazing at the ceiling, way beyond his stupid jokes and lame compassion.

He ran a bath for her. Herbal salts and aromatic Sandalwood swirled beneath the waterline. Charlotte hummed a forceful tune outside, marching up and down the hallway in a show of strength. He felt like the home-help, a glorified nursemaid playing nervous fetch-and-carry. He left the bath running and went outside.

'Everything all right, Charlotte?'

'No, it isn't. I want to go to my Nanny's.'

'Better start walking then, honey.'

She tramped along the hall in her pink furry slippers and turned sharp right into the front room. He crept back in to the bedroom and shut the door, the torrent of bath water receding behind him.

'Your bath's running, madam.'

'What's Charlotte doing now?'

'Sulking, I think.'

She ignored him and stretched her legs, a glimpse of soft inner thigh setting off the same yearning. The ghost of Claudia to spoil the present moment.

'Do you want the bath?'

'Yes. I do want the bath. Please don't leave the water running.'

'What did your last servant die of?'

'Look – if you can't be nice to me, fuck off and leave me alone!'

She lay immersed beneath a layer of foam, only her head and shoulders visible. The steady drip, drip of the tap was surreal, the gentle lapping of the water at odds with her sullen expression. He sat on the edge of the bath, watching her. To amuse himself he listed some of the factors that might have caused her distress. Not taking enough vitamins. Not getting enough sleep. Going to bed with damp hair. She dismissed all of these in a tone of belligerence. 'That's got nothing to do with it. You don't know what you're talking about.'

'Because it's a woman's thing?'

'No. You wouldn't understand.'

'Try me.'

She looked up and focused on him with a luminous sadness, anaesthetised by the heat of the water. 'Have you ever felt so bad you wanted to die?'

The question brought up so many issues, buried under layers of guilt and resentment. She lay motionless, waiting for his answer.

'I've felt like disappearing off the face of the planet a few times, is that the same?'

'Not quite. 'She swirled the water with her fingers, deep in thought. 'I went to a faith healer once.'

'What for?'

'Looking for answers, I suppose.'

'To what?'

She slipped further down the bath and lay still. The bathwater lapped in reply.

'My life was a mess. I was going nowhere. This woman told me more about myself than anyone I've ever known.'

'What did she tell you?'

'She called me a reluctant incarnate.'

'What's that?'

'Someone who doesn't want to be born on the earth plane.'

'And you believe all that stuff?'

'Some of it.'

She spoke with a quiet conviction, repeating a fact she had accepted long ago. He could have made a joke and dismissed her theory out of hand. Faith healers were the worst kind of charlatans, preying on weakness and superstition. But her words invoked a strange fear in him. Ominous links with the past. James's numerous breakdowns and desperate bids to pull himself back from the brink. His own battles to face life after James's death, knowing he'd played a part in the tragic outcome. Natalie's words sounded too much like a premonition. He looked down at her, lying still in the bath and felt a colossal burden of responsibility.

'I had a friend like that,' he said. 'Believed in curses and fate. That your whole life was mapped out for you.'

'But you don't.'

'I just think it's a dangerous way of thinking. Everything you do ends up as a self-fulfilling prophecy.'

She stared at him, her mouth open in disbelief. 'Thanks a lot.'

'What for?'

'You've just dismissed everything I said in one sentence.'

'I don't believe in faith healers, that's all.'

She shook her head and looked away in disgust.

'Can I get you a drink?' he said.

'Just close the door and leave me alone.'

He read a magazine article on sexually transmitted diseases while the kettle boiled. Young girls, it seemed, no longer valued their chastity. Multiple partners led to an increase in the problem with no immediate solution. The article went on to name peer pressure and the erosion of family values as the primary causes. The kettle boiled and he snapped the magazine shut. The model on the front cover appeared in a less glamorous light.

He put her drink down and settled back on the rim of the bath. Hot water with honey and lemon, his grandmother's cure for colds. She reached up, peering at him over the glass. 'Did you put sugar in this?'

'Yes – I did put sugar in it.' He watched the foam swirl around her hips and thought about Brad. 'Did you ever use condoms?'

'What?'

'I've just been reading about the future generation – drifting like a rudderless ship. They don't use precautions, apparently.'

'And that worries you, does it?'

'Of course. Every time Leanne goes out I worry about her. Who she's with, how she's getting home.'

'You can't stop her doing what she wants to do.'

'Wait 'til Charlotte starts bringing home the local delinquents. Then you'll know what it's all about.'

He leaned over the edge of the bath and trailed a finger above her navel, a small ripple breaking the surface. Her dark pubic strip faded, in and out of focus like a mirage. When he came to the soft rise of her breasts, she said a firm 'Don't!'

He withdrew his finger and stood up.

'What's the matter?' she said.

'Nothing.'

'Yes there is. You've got that look on your face.'

'I can't sit here staring at your naked body all morning, can I? You look like Cleopatra, lying there.'

'I think you'll find she bathed in milk.'

'She had slaves waiting on her, too. Maybe I should throw in a barrelful of rose petals to make you really feel at home.'

She stared at her feet, ignoring him. 'Does Leanne have a boyfriend?'

'Several. She seems to pick the geeks. The one's who don't answer back.'

'So you don't approve then?'

He thought this over. 'I did have a problem with one of them. He threatened her one night, so I had to straighten him out on a few things.'

'What did you do?'

'I grabbed him round the neck and rammed him against a wall. I think he got the message after that.'

She gazed up at him with her dark and soulful eyes. He felt mildly embarrassed, admitting to something shameful that was hard to justify. If she thought he was bad, he could tell her stories about the old man, threatening to have peoples legs broken, punching one of Bernie's boyfriends in the face on his own doorstep.

'You've got it all to come, Natalie.'

'Yes. That's what I'm worried about.'

He held the towel as she stepped out of the bath. While she dried herself, he recalled his past experiences of the genital kind. An old prefab behind a sprawling red-brick hospital. Waiting room with stiff-backed chairs and worn magazines. Subdued, male faces, waiting for their number to be called over a battered looking intercom. Your own personalised number. You stood up and your shame stood with you, as obvious as a withered limb. Then – second door on the left – you were greeted by a smiling Pakistani doctor, white-coated and with nimble latex fingers. There beneath the strip light, the good doctor invited you to drop your trousers– the root cause of your problem soon to be revealed.

Charlotte stood waiting for him in the hallway, dressed as if for school, with her back pack on and sandals buckled neatly over pristine white socks. She fixed him with a scathing look she might have learned from her mother.

'Going somewhere, Charlotte?'

'I want to go to Nanny's.'

He smiled at her persistence. 'Can we reach some sort of compromise here, or is that asking too much?'

'I'm fed-up waiting!'

'Join the club, sweetheart. Waiting's what we have to do. It's a fundamental part of the human condition.'

Charlotte glared at him and stamped her foot, dancing an angry jig along the hallway. Her bedroom door slammed shut behind her.

He went into the bedroom. Natalie was wearing her silky blue dressing gown, knotted at the waist. She looked up as he entered, the captive to the jailer. 'What's the matter with Charlotte now?'

'She wants to go to your mum's and she won't take no for an answer.'

'You'll have to take her then.'

'Me?'

'Well I can't do it can I?'

'Your mum's never even met me before. What's she going to say when some stranger turns up on the doorstep with her Granddaughter in tow?'

'I'll call her and tell her you're coming over.'

He opened the top window and a scant breeze lifted the net curtain, relieving the humidity in the room. She shivered, pulling the dressing gown around her. He stood over her and laid a hand on her shoulder, barred from making any sudden moves. The hem of her gown lay open revealing her soft and milky inner thigh.

Charlotte came in and dived on the bed. She lay with her chin cupped in her hands staring up at her mother.

Natalie raised a weary arm and called out for her. Charlotte wriggled up the bed and settled in beneath the waiting arm, mother and child reunited.

Natalie kissed the dark crown of the child's head. 'What's the matter, Princess?'

'Peter won't take me to Nanny's.'

'He will soon, honey.'

'Er – do I get a say in this?'

Natalie looked up. 'Please will you take her for me?'

Charlotte joined in, imploring him. 'Yes. Please will you, Peter?'

He laughed at the two of them, huddled together like refugees. 'I don't have much choice, do I?'

Charlotte lurched off the bed and ran out along the hall, certain this time of a more favourable result.

Natalie made the call. Her voice changed on connection – an edge of tension that she tried to hide. She mentioned his name with an easy familiarity, as if they discussed him regularly. The thought reassured him, made him feel better about his new role.

She put the phone on the cabinet and lay back to stare at the ceiling.

'What did she say?'

'Nothing much.'

'Is she OK with it, or not?'

'Of course she's OK with it. Will you close that window, please.'

He closed the window, muting the sounds of the traffic along the bay.

'So what's the protocol?' he said.

'The what?'

'With your mother. What subjects do I avoid to stay on her good side?'

'Say what you like. Just don't mention condoms. And make sure Charlotte takes a coat.

'In this heat?'

'Just do it, please.'

Charlotte stood beside him in the lift, her sandaled feet tucked neatly together, her backpack strapped high on her shoulders. The mechanical whir of the lift replaced conversation. Now they were moving, a journey into the unknown, with him as the responsible adult. He thought of Natalie, alone in her big double bed. The reluctant incarnate, full of doubts and fears that he might never understand.

The lift doors opened, and Charlotte ran blissfully out into brilliant sun light. All he had to do now was meet the grandmother. One more test to pass before the next level.

Thirty-one

She opened the door with a smile rehearsed for salesmen. Charlotte ran over the threshold and down the hallway, backpack lurching on her shoulders. He stood on the gravel drive, the outsider, unsure of his welcome

'Would you like to come in?' she said.

'Er – I wasn't going to stay, but …' Her smile convinced him. With a quick change of plan, he accepted the invitation and followed Charlotte inside. Mrs Parker led him along the hall and into an imposing, book-lined living room. Wide patio doors opened onto a neat and well tended garden. Charlotte was visible outside, balanced in the lower branches of a gnarled old apple tree. A large black Labrador sat watching nervously below.

'I thought it was only boys who climbed trees,' he said.

'You don't know Charlotte.'

Mrs Parker went to the open patio door and called out a sharp command. Charlotte leapt down from the tree and danced across the lawn, followed by the faithful, tail-wagging dog. The pair disappeared around the back of the house, rapid footsteps ringing on gravel. Mrs Parker closed the patio door and stood looking out. 'I don't mind so much when she's with Bobby, but she does have a habit of wandering off.'

'I can imagine.'

'She went missing in Greenwich Park once – at the start of the London Marathon.'

He laughed. 'I didn't know they took them that young.'

She turned and fixed him with a look of mild disapproval. 'Charlotte doesn't like to think she's missing out on anything, believe me. Can I get you a drink?'

She left him alone with the view of the garden and the neat rows of books. He wondered if she'd read them all – enough volumes on display to fill a small library. A sleek racing yacht with tall, billowing sails, hung central between the shelves, captured in grainy black and white. On the far side of the room was a piano, it's lid raised, sheet music open above the keys. The mahogany furnishings gave the room an austere quality, the ideal setting for her to interview prospective clients and relieve them of their childhood insecurities.

Several small portraits lined a glass-fronted dresser. In one, a familiar face, proud and unsmiling, dark eyes bright with an inner rebellion. He bent to take a closer look and heard footsteps behind him.

'Natalie at Grammar School,' Mrs Parker said. He stood back, caught out. She set a tray down on an ornate circular table and glanced at the dresser. 'She hated having her photo taken, right from a child. I was forever telling her to put a smile on her face. Do you take sugar?'

He sank into a shiny, green leather armchair and tried to relax. Mrs Parker put the table between them and drew up a chair, gripping the armrests and easing herself down with some effort. She poured the coffee from a silver pot. Elegant china cups and a silver sugar bowl covered with a lace doily. She might have brought the set out to impress visitors but she didn't seem the type. Too assured and outwardly confidant to bother with niceties.

'I drink far too much coffee,' she said with a note of humour. 'But I'm sure there are worse things in life. I did try to cut down but I found it impossible. I can't seem to work without it.'

'What do you do?'

'I'm a writer.' She gave a curious frown. 'At least that's what I seem to spend most of my time doing at the moment.'

'What sort of things do you write?'

'Text book manuals for psychiatry mainly, and a column for a magazine that seems to get harder every month.' She gave a short, ironic laugh. 'I might take a holiday one day if I can find the time.'

He glanced over at the far wall and thought of the old man. 'Lots of books. Have you read them all?'

'No, I haven't, unfortunately. Perhaps that's something to look forward to when I retire. Do you read?'

'I do, yes. I'm reading a good book at the moment.'

'And what's that?'

'Cosa Nostra – a history of the Sicilian Mafia. I was hoping to pick up a few business tips.'

She smiled dubiously. 'Yes, I imagine you'd learn quite a lot from a book like that.'

Footsteps pounded the gravel. Charlotte ran past the patio doors with the dog in tow, for one more lap of the house. The location seemed ideal for Charlotte's inherent restlessness.

Mrs Parker sighed. 'I do feel for her. Stuck in that flat with nothing to do all day.'

'She does seem to have pretty high energy levels.'

'Yes, she does. Do you have children?'

'Only the one. She turned sixteen this year. Costs me an arm and a leg but I'm sort of getting used to it.'

She raised her eyebrows but made no comment. The chair she was in seemed unsuited to her needs. She crossed her legs stiffly, expecting sudden pain. She suffered with her back, according to Natalie. An ongoing problem resistant to painkillers and numerous trips to the chiropractor. He compared the two of them, mother and daughter. No immediate likeness other than a similarity in build. The lean, athletic type who eat what they like and never put weight on. She could have been a smoker, the lines in her face deep-set, her voice resonant. The conflict between them intrigued him most of all. Complex issues going back decades that had never been fully resolved.

'Natalie says you're in the property business,' she said.

'For my sins.'

'Are we heading for another recession?'

'The experts say we are but it hasn't happened yet.'

She gave a solemn nod and gazed out at the garden. He heard the dog bark. Charlotte's laughter.

'She does far too much, that's her trouble.'

'Sorry?'

'Natalie. She takes on too many commitments and wonders why she can't cope.'

'I thought she needed the money.'

'We all need money. But your health has to come first, doesn't it?'

She trailed her spoon in the cup leaving the thought unfinished. He recognised the theme. Children the world over, failing to live up to expectations. She didn't look like the type to put up with excuses. A touch of the schoolmistress about her. Educated. In control.

Charlotte burst in with Bobby behind her. The dog padded over and put its head in his lap. 'He's called

Bobby,' Charlotte said. He stroked the bony ridges of the broad head, and said a token 'Hi Bobby.' Two doleful eyes looked up at him, seeking approval, the tail twitching like a metronome. Bobby soon lost interest and turned to the tray beside him, drawn by the promise of illicit food. Charlotte bounced up and down on the piano stool, humming to herself and striking her heel against the bowed wooden leg.

'Take your shoes off, please, Charlotte,' Mrs Parker said.

'Can I have a biscuit?'

'Take your shoes off first, please.'

Charlotte took off her shoes and placed them neatly by the stool before leaving the room. The rules of the house accepted without question. Bobby waddled after her, tail raised. Mrs Parker watched them go and arched her back with a grimace.

'Natalie said you had some sort of accident,' he said.

'I broke my hip in Greece, three years ago. I've had nothing but trouble ever since.'

'Isn't there anything you can do for it?'

'The doctor recommended walking but I'm not convinced. I have to watch my posture. Apparently they don't make furniture with people in mind these days.' She patted the armrests of her chair. 'This is about the only thing I can sit in for any length of time.'

'Who plays the piano?'

She glanced across the room. 'That's another thing that's suffered because of my back. I have tried to interest Charlotte, but she won't sit still long enough to learn. Are you musical?'

'I sing along to the radio while I'm driving, but that's about as far as if goes.'

'I see,' she said dourly. 'Help yourself to a biscuit, won't you.'

He took a plain digestive and ate in silence. The rows of books and dark wood units indicated a bygone era. Charlotte's feet on the gravel outside could have been Natalie's as a child, echoing down through the years. The fixtures all had a worn and personal feel, the effects of a previous generation handed down. He felt comfortable, a privileged guest, plied with digestives and coffee from a china cup.

'That's a nice looking boat,' he said.

She followed his gaze. 'You mean the yacht? That was taken in 1952. If you look closely you can actually see my Father on it. He skippered the race series that year.'

'You come from a sailing background?'

'Yes I do, but I much prefer my feet on dry land. Having your head in a bucket for hours on end loses its attraction after a while.'

He pictured the old man, pottering around the bay fishing for mackerel. The nauseating smell of fish blood and engine fumes to turn the stomach over.

'Are your family local?' she said.

'My dad's a Londoner. He left home at fifteen and never went back.'

'What does he do?'

'He's a developer. Started with nothing, now he owns the company, that sort of thing.'

'And you work for him?'

'Not if I can help it.' She smiled politely at the slur. In spite of her apparent graciousness she seemed to analyse every word he said. He felt the need to explain in more detail. 'We tend to clash. He has his way of doing things and I have mine. I'm expected to take over when he retires, but I'm not too sure that's going to happen.'

'And I hear you play golf.'

'Not as much as I used to. I've been pretty sidetracked lately, running round after other people.'

She missed his sarcasm and sipped her coffee thoughtfully. 'Do you know much about Natalie?'

The question caught him off guard. He sensed a trap and answered cautiously. 'Only what she's told me. How she misses London sometimes. Pressures at work, that sort of thing.'

She appeared not to hear him and gazed out at the garden. 'Natalie's been through an awful lot over the last few years. I had hoped that moving down here would have been good for her. She would have been more settled. But she doesn't like to be told. She thinks I'm interfering.'

'She's headstrong.'

'You had noticed then,' she said with an ironic smile. The brief flicker of humour passed and she grew serious again. 'She takes on far too much work. Far too much. Then there's Charlotte to think about. You can't have children and expect them to bring themselves up. It just doesn't work like that.'

She stopped, aware that she might have said too much. He could think of nothing to add in Natalie's defence, the entire catalogue of her past misdemeanours yet to be revealed. Beneath Mrs Parker's apparent bitterness, he sensed a genuine concern, hints at some past trauma that she wasn't prepared to discuss. The generation unwilling to disclose secrets. His mother's generation. Better to keep children in the dark than have them stumble over the truth with their eyes wide open.

'Natalie showed me some of her work,' he said.

She looked up, distracted. 'Yes. She's very talented. I've got a room upstairs filled with drawings and paintings she did as a child. Would you like to see?'

She led him up the stairs and along a hallway, framed in the same dark wood. The room at the end had a single bed with a tartan cover, a chest of drawers, and inbuilt wooden wardrobes. A faint mustiness hung around. No outward signs of any permanent resident. He wondered how such an empty room could house talent of any kind.

Mrs Parker opened the top drawer in the chest and took out a large portfolio covered in worn blue material. 'These are things Natalie did before she went to university. If I hadn't saved them they would have ended up in bin liners and taken to the tip. She always said she couldn't bear to look at them, but I think she's secretly pleased that I kept them here.'

She laid the portfolio on the bed and opened the cover. Tucked in the inner sleeve was a wedge of large, poster size papers. She began to ease them out one by one, giving a brief summary of each like the owner of a private gallery. He stood beside her, a little in awe at the quality of the work. Sketches of strange, tormented faces. Violent sunbursts like the ones in the photographs Natalie had shown him. Unfinished pencil drawings that ended as if the artist had simply got up and walked away.

Mrs Parker pulled out a smaller pencil drawing, the rough outline of a young girl's face, partially shaded in. The face looked familiar. 'Is that a self portrait?' he said.

'She did that from a photograph. She used to spend hours drawing faces at the dining table. Fascinated with faces, right from a child. And this one ...' Her voice faltered as she pulled out a painting, a blotch of thick, childlike colours with a bright yellow sun in one corner. 'So much talent,' she said softly. 'So much talent.'

The remark puzzled him, almost a lament for someone no longer around.

'Does she still do her own work?'

She let the painting fall to the bed, and gave a weary sigh. The odd collection lay before them, a testament to something fragile and unfathomable. 'Natalie thinks that I pushed her too hard when she was younger. I only wanted her to make the most of what she'd been given. People don't understand. You make sacrifices for your children but sometimes it just isn't enough.'

He remembered Natalie's faith healer story. 'Was there some sort of illness she had?'

Mrs Parker looked up. 'Hasn't she told you?'

'Not in any detail.'

She looked at the paintings scattered over the bed as if they might have the answer.

'Natalie had a breakdown when she was in London. She got involved with someone she shouldn't have. Charlotte was very young. It was an awful time.'

The mention of another man made it hard for him to be objective. 'Is that why she left London?'

She looked at him, puzzled. 'She left because she couldn't cope on her own. That's always been Natalie's problem. She has to have someone to pick up the pieces when things aren't going her way.'

She gathered up the paintings and the sketches and put them back in the portfolio. The room again seemed bare and unlived in, devoid of colour. She put the portfolio back in the top drawer and took out an orange pencil case with a smiley face. The act had the same effect on her as the unveiling of the paintings. She held the case in her hand, feeling the texture with her fingertips, lost in some private memory.

Footsteps pounded on the stairs. Charlotte came running into the room, with Bobby close behind. 'Nanny! Nanny! Can we go to the park and feed the ducks?'

Mrs Parker put the pencil case back and closed the drawer. She turned to Charlotte, without a trace of her previous emotion. 'Go downstairs please, Charlotte. I'll make you something to eat, and then perhaps we'll think about going to the park.'

The guided tour was over. The evidence of Natalie's talent remained hidden away in a musty bedroom. The experience had changed his understanding of both Natalie and her relationship with her mother, but the background detail was missing. Mrs Parker clearly didn't like to give too much away. Snippets of information alluding to a troubled past and a deep, inexpressible sadness at the way things had turned out, but no more.

She saw him to the front door.

He lingered for a moment, standing out on her gravel drive in the afternoon sun. Behind him, her neat front garden with its cascading willow and sculptured borders.

'Well, I hope Natalie feels better soon,' she said.

'I'm sure she will. I'll call in on the way back and cheer her up.'

She left him with mixed impressions. Like coming away from an illusionist wondering where you'd missed the sleight of hand. She clearly put a lot of work into appearances. Her house, the garden, even the refreshments. He admired her professionalism, how she entertained him as a prospective client, with carefully worded questions, the routine nod of her head and benign smile. And Natalie, the child – burdened by expectations, craving security instead of recognition and wondering what she had to do to earn it. He shared a similar burden. Fear of mediocrity – failure to live up to your own standards. The symbol of perfectionism, dangled in front of you but always out of reach.

He sat in the car and checked his phone. Two missed calls. One from the architect, the other from Bernie. A call from Bernie was unusual. The last time he had spoken to her, they had shared a table at Pat's sixtieth, watching the agile old veterans glide around the dance floor. That night, he had made a conscious effort to avoid any hostility between the two of them. But they rarely spoke.

He called her.

She ran through a breathless and garbled explanation of the last few hours. How she had tried to get hold of him earlier and had left two messages on his answerphone. He interrupted her stream of consciousness, unable to follow any of it. 'Bernie, slow down. What's up?'

'I told you, I had to leave Mum. I couldn't stay any longer. I had to pick Jasmine up from play group and I was already running late. Why didn't you get my message?'

'You had to leave Mum where?'

'At the hospital.'

'What for?'

She gave a cry of frustration. 'I thought Sarah would have got hold of you by now. Dad's been admitted. They think he's had a heart attack.'

The impending future turned small knots in his stomach. The conversation itself had a surreal edge. The novelty of talking to Bernie and preparing for tragedy in the same breath. The old man couldn't have chosen a worse time to fall ill. He had Natalie to think about, confined to her lonely bed with some nameless, psychological trauma.

'What ward's he on?' he said.

'He's in the Assessment Unit. And I'll warn you now, he's in a foul mood.'

He made his decision. The old man's needs were more urgent. Natalie would have to wait until later.

Thirty-two

The ward looked like a sanitised version of the twilight zone. Low lighting and a soft, peach veneer to hide the true nature of business. Curtains were drawn around two of the six beds. An attractive nurse in midnight blue gave him a cautious smile on her way out, a reminder that respect be shown the living and the dying.

The old man lay on a crumpled bed in the far corner. Bernie sat on a chair keeping watch. They both looked up as he made his way over. The balding and overweight man in the opposite bed pretended not to notice, beset with too many problems of his own.

Bernie stood up, businesslike in her beige suit and tied-back hair. She might have picked the outfit especially, a way of scoring points with the old man and the nursing staff without making too much effort. He tried to raise a smile for her but she didn't seem to warrant the effort.

'I came as soon as I could,' he said. The soothing bleep of a heart monitor pulsed in the background. 'Where's Mum?'

'Packing an overnight bag,' Bernie said. 'She'll be in later.'

The old man sat up and cleared his throat – an expression of contempt for his present surroundings. Bernie was there for him, offering words of comfort and plumping the pillows behind his back. Her nervous assistance had the reverse effect. The old man snapped at her to leave him alone. The canula in his bandaged wrist marked him as a patient, even if he refused to act like one.

Bernie stepped back from the bed and brushed a stray hair away from her cheek. He enjoyed her obvious discomfort for a moment before turning to the old man. 'So what happened?'

'I ate a cheese sandwich and ended up in this place!'

'Must have been some cheese.'

The old man ignored the comment and stared wilfully at the canula.

'He's had his blood pressure taken,' Bernie said. 'And they've done an ECG. The doctor wants a blood test but they can't do that until midnight.'

'Why not?'

'It has to be twelve hours after.'

'After what?'

She shrugged. 'The worst pain, I think.'

'Is he in pain now?'

They both looked at the old man. Bernie leant over the bed and said in a loud voice, 'You're not in pain at the moment, are you, Dad?'

'No, I'm not!'

The scene was absurd, actors forced to deliver their lines in a strange environment. The patient in the next bed turned over, rustling his bedclothes in protest at the invasion, the curtains partially drawn to hide his suffering.

Bernice moved to the end of the bed and picked up her handbag. 'I'm glad you're here now, Peter. I've got to get back.' She turned to the old man. 'You'll be alright won't you, Dad?'

'I'm not going anywhere, am I?'

He followed her out into the passage. Several nurses manned the busy reception area, industrious in their bland, colour-coded uniforms. Bernice stood back, clutching her handbag, waiting for him with a nervous frown.

'So, what's the score?' he said.

She shrugged. 'You know as much as I do.'

'Is it a heart attack or not?'

'I told you. They don't know yet.'

'They must know, they're Doctors for fuck's sake.'

She glanced awkwardly at the reception. 'Look – all I know is he had chest pains at lunch time and Mum brought him in. We'll just have to wait.'

A young nurse swept by carrying a tray of medical implements. He thought of the canula in the old man's hand, the indignity of lying around on a hospital bed after a lifetime's vigorous activity.

'What about the tests they've done so far?'

'His blood pressure's high, but then we already knew that. The ECG didn't show anything abnormal.'

He weighed up the evidence as a nurse with bad skin and a severe skullcap haircut breezed by. The waiting around was the worst. Natalie had understood when he'd called her, but now he felt bad about that. Deserting her to visit the old man on his temporary sick bed.

'Look, I've got to go,' Bernie said. 'I'll try to call in later if I can get away.'

Her nervousness caused him to pity her. She looked tired and worn down, as if she'd rushed out without her makeup. Even her top-up tan had faded. But pity was a wasted sentiment as far as she was concerned. He'd fallen for one of her hard luck stories once before and given her five hundred pounds to clear an overdraft. All she did was moan about the evils of credit companies and interest rates, without the slightest intention of paying the money back.

He tried to be reasonable. 'How's things with you? I haven't seen you for ages.'

'Fine,' she said quickly, avoiding his gaze. 'Things are, pretty good on the whole, I suppose.'

'Mum said you had some sort of infestation.'

She laughed. 'Some guy from the council came out. It turned out to be bees.' She went into a lengthy explanation about bees being vegetarians, and how they were attracted to the berries sprouting on the vine covered roof beneath her kitchen window. 'I felt really stupid, calling them out for nothing. But the guy was really good about it.' Her smile faded. She glanced at the exit. 'Sorry to hear about you and Claudia.'

He shrugged, unable to answer.

'Mum says you're not going to Spain with them.'

'Wouldn't be advisable under the circumstances, would it?'

She looked absently in the direction of the bay and bit her lip. She hadn't mentioned Natalie but she probably knew. His mother or Sarah would have told her. He couldn't expect her to take that much interest. She'd only met Claudia on a handful of occasions. The two of them had never really got on, sharing polite but strained conversation that skimmed the surface. Bernie had her own agenda and was only interested in herself.

She forced a smile. 'Oh well, better make a move. Can't keep Jasmine waiting too long.' She took a step backwards. 'Good luck with Dad. He's not in the best of moods, as you can see.'

He watched her go. The former model, shapely in her beige skirt and high heels, ponytail jigging behind her. Sarah always said Bernie had inherited her good looks from their mother's side. But that didn't explain where her harebrained personality came from. He supposed he should be more forgiving. She was family, after all. Faced with such a sudden crisis, they should all pull together and put petty squabbles behind them. Tragedy changed everything. It could have been her lying on the hospital bed and him in pieces, regretting all the awful things he'd said about her over the years.

He went back into the sombre ward. The patient in the first bay was sat up reading a magazine, her curtains drawn back. She looked up as he passed, no more than eighteen, her chubby face pinched with anxiety. The sonorous bleep of the heart monitor reminded him where they were and of the need for courtesy at all times.

The old man was sat up, watching the proceedings with a scowl. On the trolley table beside him – a newspaper, a bottle of Lucozade and a jug of water. He looked resigned, the brooding look of a man forcibly detained.

'Bernie gone?' the old man said.

'She's got to pick the kids up. Anything you want?'

'Bunch of grapes and a piss-pot at this rate.'

He stood by the bed, unable to resist a smile. 'Things could be a lot worse, I suppose. At least they put you on a mixed ward.'

'Where's the privacy in that?'

'Don't knock it. They'll move you in with the geriatrics if you play up too much.'

He took the chair that Bernice had left and breathed in the atmosphere. Hospital meals served on moulded plastic trays. Tubes and wires linking man and the latest technology. Mortality discussed in technical terms by Doctors who looked like school leavers. He thought back to his previous visit and hoped it would be his last. Even a fractured arm made you a victim, subject to the same indignities as the patients in a cancer ward.

'So how did it happen – you ending up in here?'

'I told you. I ate a cheese sandwich, then I got this pain, about here.' The old man indicated his chest with his finger. 'Your mother insisted I come in for a check-up.'

'Wise move.'

'Bollocks. I've been suffering indigestion for twenty fucking years, now all of a sudden I'm having a heart attack!'

The old man's outburst was broadcast throughout the bay. He glanced at the other beds in embarrassment. 'Well at least you're comfortable.'

'Comfortable? You must be joking. Any idea how long I've been waiting here?'

'I can guess.'

'Seven hours, that's how long. Seven hours waiting for some ignorant college boy to finish his game of squash and tell me what's wrong with me. I should have gone private years ago.'

The nurse in midnight blue came back and stood by the heart monitor. Mid-to late thirties, reasonably attractive, and almost serene in control. She looked down at the disgruntled patient and smiled. 'You must be a popular man, Jack. Plenty of visitors to keep you company.'

'Never mind them, when can I go home?'

She smiled disarmingly and unclipped an attachment from the machine. 'I've come to check your blood pressure again, I'm afraid. Either arm please, love.' The old man jerked an arm out. She wrapped a velcro cuff above the elbow and turned away. The cuff inflated like a swimming aid. 'Other hand please, Jack.' She attached a white clip to the old man's forefinger, which glowed a neon red.

She glanced up. 'Member of the family, are you?'

'I'm his son.'

She smiled, watching the red digits on the monitor.

'Is he likely to be kept in long?'

'I can't say exactly. We're still waiting for the medical Doctor to come on the ward. Been a bit hectic this afternoon.' She took the hand held device from the bed, and smiled at the patient. 'But I'm sure you're quite happy to stay with us a bit longer, aren't you, Jack?'

'Over the moon.'

She removed the finger clip and turned to the machine. 'Get plenty of exercise do you?'

The old man grunted in response.

'He plays a lot of golf.'

'Really? That's excellent. Plenty of fresh air. And they do say that walking is the best exercise of all.'

'Bar one,' he said, but she missed the innuendo, lost in the mechanics of her job.

She left with the same virtuous smile, an aura of workmanlike calm about her that nothing could threaten.

The Assessment Unit housed six patients, all awaiting results for various conditions. The balding and overweight man opposite lay staring at the ceiling, his name written in green marker pen, framed above his bed. The odd cough or groan from behind closed curtains lent a gravity to two of the cases, sectioned off to protect their modesty and shield the rest of the ward from contamination. The old man had no time for any of them, not even the young girl, who might have brought out his more paternal side.

'How d'you feel now?' he said.

'Pissed off with this place, that's for sure.'

'Any more pain?'

'No.'

'That's something to be grateful for then.'

'Is it?' the old man said flatly.

He picked up the small disc-shaped buzzer on the bed and smiled at the symbol. Press a button and a nurse would appear. He could think of worse scenarios. As if in answer, the overweight man in the opposite bed began to cough painfully. The heart monitor bleeped like a deep sea sonar and an uneasy silence resumed. He thought of Natalie, lying in bed, waiting for him to call.

'What happened with you and Claudia?' the old man said.

'We ended it.'

'What for?'

'Irreconcilable differences.'

The old man pondered this with a distant expression. 'I don't understand it. Neither does her Dad. I spoke to him yesterday.'

'He'll get used to it.'

The old man stared out at the view over the rooftops. 'Your business. I'm not interfering. Pass the Lucozade will you?'

He handed over the bottle, and glanced at the sport headline in the newspaper. Some eight million pound foreigner to brighten up the new Premiership season. Maybe the player would break a leg and end up on a similar ward, bemoaning the poor treatment and lack of privacy. The old man reserved his opinion on Claudia's sudden exit, concerned by his own predicament. Seven hours lying on an NHS bed, waiting for the Doctor to call.

The old man sipped his Lucozade from a plastic cup, deep in thought. After some time, he looked up and raised an eyebrow. 'Have you spoken to Barry?'

'What about?'

'I've offered him Henley Park.'
'So I heard.'
'You not happy about that?'
'I thought you might have run it by me first.'

The old man put the cup on the cabinet and settled back. He looked rested, almost comfortable now, a glint of fierce humour shining through. The dispute gave him what he needed, the chance to defend his position and attack what he saw as a weakness at the same time. The humour left him and he shook his head, overcome by a detached but wearying sadness. 'I've always gone out of my way to help you, Peter. I've offered you work. I've introduced you to people, and you've walked away.'

'I don't need the hassle.'
'Of what?'
'Owing favours to people I don't like.'

The old man nodded slowly. 'You could have taken on Henley Park for me. I'd have seen you alright.'

'What, like you did at Somerford?'
'That was a good earner for you.'
'And you. You made ten grand without lifting a finger.'
'I took a commission, that's all.'
'Is that what they call it?'

He wanted to avoid a debate about ethics. The old man had spent a lifetime cultivating people he didn't particularly like, or even respect, in order to get ahead. He had a saying for every occasion, to justify his actions in the light of any criticism. The most lucrative contracts and the choicest plots of land were always subjects of prime importance, like the stock market to a speculator. The old man's confirmed belief, that with the right contacts and financial backing, doors would open as a matter of course. But, lying on a hospital bed, the old man's options were limited. He looked tired, as if the long, hard campaign had finally caught up with him.

'You need to slow down,' he said quietly.

'Don't you start.' The old man glared at him, turning over a new line of thought. 'What happened at Priory Road?'

The incident had been forgotten, buried under a deluge of more pressing concerns. He fought the impulse to be evasive. 'I had a few problems.'

The old man said nothing.

'Look – I'm trying to run a business. Someone's unreliable, they've got to go. Isn't that what you always told me?'

'Fred was sick, for Christ's sake. He's got emphysema.'

'Tough. He can be off sick on someone else's job now, can't he?'

The old man shook his head, exasperated. 'I'm not getting in an argument with you, Peter. You did what you had to do and that's the end of it.'

'And that's why you gave Henley Park to Barry.'

The old man narrowed his eyes and took his time, speaking evenly. 'I offered it to Barry because *you* turned it down.'

He couldn't look the old man in the eye. It seemed absurd, arguing business politics around a hospital bed, threatening someone with a heart condition.

The old man watched him, nodding his head with a sly grin. 'It's the stubborn streak in you. You get it from your mother.'

'Is that right?'

'Maybe you should have carried on playing golf. Walter always said you were a natural.'

'I wasn't that good.'

'You were a damn sight better than me.' The old man chuckled at his own joke, such moments easier to recall. 'D'you want me to have a word with Barry?'

'What for?'

'Tell him you've changed your mind.'

'Who says I've changed my mind?'

The old man shrugged, the stalemate ending the conversation. Henley Park would go to Barry. The old man's future health depended on such decisions. His current well being depended on a medical Doctor drafted in from another ward.

He glanced at his watch. 'I'm going to have a word with the Nurse.'

'What for?'

'Find out if that Doctor's come off the squash court yet.'

He found her at the reception desk, passing a message to a colleague in functional grey. She noticed him and flashed her beguiling smile. 'Can I help?'

'I wanted to ask you a few questions.'

'Fire away. I'm all yours.'

'I'm sort of frustrated. No-one seems to know what's wrong with him. Is it a heart attack?'

'We can't be certain until the blood test is taken. And that won't be for another,' she glanced at her watch 'five hours or so.'

He said nothing, out of his depth. She stood by, understanding his fears, quietly reassuring. He enjoyed the subtle eye contact, the warmth of her company as respite from the sick bay. Here they swapped medical terms instead of telephone numbers, a harmless flirtation to take his mind off the immediate future.

She summed up the options for him in her firm but pleasant tone. 'If the blood test comes back negative, fine. We'll know he hasn't had a heart attack.'

'Then he can go?'

'Not necessarily. The Doctor might still ask for a treadmill test as a precaution.' She smiled at his reaction. 'It's just a test to see how the heart's working. All very safe, don't worry.'

'What if the blood test comes back positive?'

'It means he's had a heart attack. We'll keep him in for five days under observation, until the doctors decide the best course of action.'

He thanked her and went back to sit with the old man. The tedious process of waiting began again. Real time suspended, a gradual eroding of the senses with nothing to do but fill out the menus and annoy the nurses.

They talked about Leanne as a kind of filler. The old man was fine until he mentioned that Roy had bought her a laptop. 'What's she want one of them for?'

'I think they call it communication. All the kids have them these days.'

'What happened to a pen and a notepad?'

'Ask her yourself. I'll give her a call if you like. She can come up and visit her granddad on his sickbed.'

The old man looked up sharply. 'Don't bother. Soon as that shyster Doctor's been up here and given me the all clear, I'll be long gone.'

He stayed until the man in the curtained-off bay had a coughing fit. The outburst reminded him of the precarious nature of health, his own and everyone else's. The old man accepted his departure without complaint, already a hardened inmate, resigned to his fate.

'Is your phone on?' he said.

'Batteries low. Your Mother's bringing the charger in later.'

'I'll give you a call. See how the test went.'

The old man swore under his breath.

'Just look upon it as a rest.'

'Huh! Rest when I'm six feet under. Die of boredom in this place.'

He left the old man and joined a porter, pushing an empty wheelchair through the exit. The man had a deadpan humour that came as a relief after the stifling mood on the ward. They headed along the polished corridor, side by side. He commented on the strange lethargy that befalls patients once they are admitted to hospital.

'We see it all the time,' the porter said. 'One minute they're out mowing the lawn, then they come into hospital and can't lift a finger. Funny that, isn't it?'

'Must be something they put in the food.'

'Could well be,' the porter said, struck by the thought. 'Much more likely to be PIPS, though.'

'What's that?'

'Pyjama induced paralysis.'

He went out through the main entrance and onto the forecourt. A young couple stood hunched in the recess, smoking furtively. An ambulance stood with its back doors open, a bored looking paramedic in crisp white shirt and green trousers, lurking outside, waiting for custom.

The sharp smell of hand rub had gone. The sense of slow time remained; a moment needed to adjust to the traffic, the cool night air. He pictured the old man with his bandaged hand, waiting for a blood test, trying to run his empire from a hospital bed. Bernice would come back and visit later. Sarah would call in with her own brand of tireless support. The whole family tending to the old man's needs on a makeshift rota. The irresponsible son and heir would do nothing more productive than make an enquiring phone call and find more excuses to stay out of the picture.

He called Natalie. She sounded tired, off-key.

'Did I wake you up?' he said.

'No. I was just dozing in front of the telly.'

'Where's Charlotte?'

'In bed. How's your dad?'

He took a deep breath. 'I'll tell you some other time. Can I come round?'

'Er – not tonight. I'm tired. I really don't feel up to it.'

He made small talk with her, sensing her reluctance to answer. Pride stepped in and made him back off. The long pauses worried him more than ever, hinting at sudden changes of heart and awkward, drawn out endings. The inescapable fear that she would tire of him and find someone else.

'I'll call you tomorrow,' he said finally and hung up.

Strange how you could feel so lonely surrounded by people. He felt like crying, but the woman at the bus stop would see him and think he was unhinged. And real men didn't cry. At least, not in public.

He crossed the road and lost control. Silent tears on a deserted stretch of pavement, his shame exposed in passing headlights. He tried to stop but he couldn't. The tears were real, coming from a place he didn't know existed. He cried for James. For Claudia. The old man, lying on a hospital bed, stripped of his dignity. Most of all he cried for himself for failing to see it coming. Shards of broken glass trodden underfoot and all he could do was keep on walking.

Thirty-three

They strolled along the gravel track through the park. She kept her head down and ignored the scenery – the endless vista of tall firs and blue skies for the tourists to gawp at. Her black beret suited her mood, worn at just the right angle, part of the bohemian look she liked to create. He made a joke about the hat to raise her spirits, but she ignored him and quickened her pace.

They came to a crossroads, a colour-coded wooden stake set at the verge to further confuse travellers. She flashed him a weary look. 'Which way now?'

'Left I suppose.'

'I thought you said you knew where we were going?'

'I lied.'

The left hand path led them along a wider track. He slipped his arm through hers and felt her stiffen. After a few paces he let go, walking beside her in silence. The perceived gap between them increased. An uneasy balance, upset by the wrong word or some trivial action of his that she'd misread and taken the wrong way. He glanced at her with a mixture of desire and bemusement. The most difficult woman he'd ever known. Angry. Volatile. Quick to reject a gift as an insult and find a hidden meaning in everything. No matter what he did, he would never truly please her.

She strolled alongside him, her hands thrust in the front pockets of her jacket, absorbed in her private thoughts. For someone who claimed to despise exercise, she had a strong and energetic gait. Her moods made her unpredictable. He had a sudden vision of her kicking in the front of his car and bending back the windscreen wipers over some imagined slight.

'I had lunch with Marco yesterday,' she said.

'That was nice for you. How is he?'

'Worried about where he's going to live next, although he won't admit it.' She talked absently about Marco's final stay in the Ballroom and how blasé he was about the business of moving. He picked up on an undercurrent but said nothing. She'd been like it all morning. Withdrawn and unapproachable. Her comments about Marco opened up a new line of enquiry.

'So what else did you talk about?'

'Not much.'

'I find that hard to believe. Marco loves the sound of his own voice. You can't normally shut him up.'

She ignored the comment and kept walking. At the top of a long rise, she stopped and turned to him. 'How far to this café?'

'Not far.'

'I can't stay too long.'

'We'll go home now if you like.'

She looked away, disconcerted by the edge in his voice. They kept walking. To make conversation, he told her about the old man's recent brush with mortality. How he'd been discharged early Sunday morning with a clean bill of health.

'What was wrong with him?'

'Reflux.'

She repeated the word with a note of disbelief.

'It's an inflammation, like severe heartburn. Now he has to avoid things like coffee and spicy food. Apart from that he's alright. ' He explained about the blood test, the hours waiting around for a Doctor. The relief everyone felt when the results came back negative. He laughed at the incident, downplaying his own reaction. 'Only the old man could pull a stunt like that. Rushed into Casualty with a suspected heart attack and comes out with indigestion. He even passed the treadmill test with flying colours.'

'Are you close?'

'Not really.' His reply sounded hollow, a form of betrayal that didn't sit right. 'We clash too much, I suppose.'

'Is he like you?'

'In what way?'

'Argumentative.'

He looked at her, puzzled. 'I'm not argumentative, am I?'

She laughed for the first time that morning, a warm and sensual note that reassured him briefly. The moment didn't last long and she withdrew, focused only on her footfall and the winding track ahead. Her silence made him anxious. The lunch she'd had with Marco played on his mind. The thought they'd been discussing him, swapping notes on all his defects of character.

They came to a play area built into a clearing. A wooden teepee stood in the centre, from which squealing children spilled out onto a bed of wood-chippings. She stood at the railing to watch. He stood beside her, careful not to invade her personal space. A small freckle-faced boy waved from the top opening. The handful of adults at the railings waved back and cheered as the boy dropped from sight. He took a chance and slipped an arm around her waist. She accepted the gesture without a word, watching the children play. For one fleeting moment it felt like they were together.

'Do you think I'm selfish?' she said.

'In what way?'

'Just in general.'

He felt compelled to lie. 'No more than anyone else, why?'

'Never mind.'

He tried to gauge her mood, her sullen interest in the children tumbling into the woodchip. 'Seems like you're making a pretty good job of it to me.'

'A good job of what?'

'You know, raising Charlotte. Being a single mother and all that.'

She turned to him with a look of distaste. 'You don't have to patronise me.'

The freckle-faced boy emerged from the hole, his broad grin earning him a round of applause from the spectators at the ringside.

'Funny, isn't it?' he said. 'Other people's kids. It's like aversion therapy. You look at theirs and it puts you off having anymore yourself.'

She stared at him with indignation. 'Is that how you feel about Charlotte?'

'No. I like Charlotte. She's got a lot of good qualities.'

She shook her head, as if she didn't believe him. 'Can we go now please?'

He tuned-in to her marching footsteps, forging ahead on the gravel track, her black leather boots rimmed with dust. The avenue of trees narrowed, overhead branches obscuring the skyline. The sweet smell of pine and clean air enclosed them, the cries of excited children falling behind.

The restaurant area was teeming with children's buggies and raucous voices. The high vaulted ceiling gave an impression of space, a wide and softly-lit cathedral filled with noisy people. A long queue faced the twin serving hatches.

They found a table along the flagstones and made base-camp. Natalie slouched in the chair, chin tucked into her jacket. The black beret enhanced her solemn look, a public statement of her discontent.

He joined the long queue on the far side, and looked out over the seating area. Natalie sat alone at table number twenty-eight, the tortured artist in her skewed black beret. The queue moved forward. The couple in front were clearly inseparable, all linked arms and adoring glances. He envied their closeness, the ease of their conversation. Natalie was morose by comparison, slumped in the same position at the table, brooding over some intractable problem.

He divided the contents of the tray, coffee and custard creams for him, hot chocolate and a flapjack for her. She watched without comment. He took his seat and tried to be amenable. 'Cheer up, it might never happen.'

She gave him a flat and hooded look in response.

'Anything you want to talk about?'

'Not really.'

'You've been quiet all morning. I thought I might have done something to upset you.'

She gave a curt shrug and toyed with the flapjack wrapper.

'I've been thinking,' she said finally.

'What about?'

'My life.'

'Sounds ominous.'

She looked up sharply. 'I'm not in the mood for jokes, OK?'

She caught the eye of a besieged mother on the next table. The two of them shared a moments empathy before the woman's unruly children took over. He opened the custard creams and reassessed his position.

Stuck in a room full of noisy kids with a neurotic woman. She smiled less and less these days. The shortest honeymoon period in recorded history. Obviously, they weren't as compatible as her book on astrology suggested. But none of it mattered. He accepted, without question, the hold she had over him. What he couldn't accept was the prolonged silences, the intimation that he'd done something wrong.

'Still worried about your job?' he said.

'No, why?'

'You said the assessors were coming in.'

'That was last month.'

'Right,' he said unfazed. 'So you passed the test then?'

'It wasn't a test. It's all part of the procedure. Everyone has to go through it.'

The child at the next table shrieked and threw a plastic cup on the floor. The besieged mother leant over and lectured her in a furious whisper. He smiled to himself, the seeds of revolt being sown so early. Natalie sat unmoved, her gaze fixed balefully on him. He sensed her frustration and tried to feel sympathy, but his natural cynicism kicked in. If work was the problem, she could always find another job. The room at her mother's was a shrine to her talent. Years of dedication and sacrifice buried in a drawer where no-one could see it.

'I saw some of your work,' he said.

'What work?'

'The paintings at your mum's.'

She gazed at him, unsure. 'She showed you my portfolio?'

'Is that a problem?'

'No. I just thought …'

'We got quite pally, me and your mum. Did she mention me?'

'Yes, she did, actually.'

'What did she say?'

'She said you were charming.' He grinned stupidly. 'I don't think she meant it as a compliment.'

He chose not to respond. He'd enjoyed meeting her mother in such an impressive setting. The book lined study. The china cups. Even the faithful dog. The experience had given him insight into Natalie and her background. He felt that he knew her better, understood the conflict going on inside her with greater clarity. 'She's obviously really proud of you.'

'Huh,' she said, and looked away. 'She's got a funny way of showing it sometimes.'

He felt a sudden tenderness for her bruised and battered psyche, hidden away like the paintings in the upstairs room. Something her mother had said came to mind. 'You didn't tell me you'd sold some of your work in America.'

She looked at him in astonishment. 'What?'

'That's what your mum told me.'

'Er – I had three paintings in an exhibition in New York, years ago. Along with about seventy five other artists from all over the world. But actually, no – I didn't sell any of my work in America.'

'But you sold some of it here?'

'Yes. For a short period I did.'

'So what happened?'

'I became ill and couldn't work. That's something my mother could never understand. I can't just paint to order. I need a strong motivation.'

'How about money? That's the strongest one I can think of.'

She rolled her eyes. 'Money's not the be all and end all of everything. I know people who can't stand the work they do, but they can't change it because it gives them an income. I don't want to end up in that position.'

'So you carry on living in obscurity. What's the point in that?'

She glared at him, choosing her words carefully. 'Why would you hold an opinion on a subject you know absolutely nothing about?'

'I know what makes the world go round.'

She shook her head. 'Don't you think it's sad, that the only thing in life that means anything to you is money?'

The harassed mother bent across to wipe the boisterous child's face with a tissue. An older boy with tight curly hair and a snub nose sat quietly alongside, picking at a chocolate doughnut with his fingers. The noise level stayed consistent, like the brooding look on Natalie's face.

'Tell me about London,' he said deliberately.

'What about it?'

'You never really told me what happened. Why you swapped the bright lights for this place.'

'I got offered a better job. I told you that.'

She avoided his gaze. He settled back to study her reaction, the determined pout of her lips and hooded eyes.

'What about the guy you were seeing?'

'What guy?'

He shrugged. 'You mentioned him a while back. Some long term relationship you were in that didn't work out.'

She sat up and sniffed abruptly. 'I don't want to talk about that.'

'Why not?'

'I just don't, OK?'

The child opposite started making aeroplane noises, and dive-bombing the table with a finger of chocolate. Natalie ignored the distraction and gazed fixedly at the table. Her animosity roused his anger, the sheer futility of battling it out with her in a public place.

'How well did you know James?' he said.

She looked up. Her frown deepened. 'I didn't know him at all.'

'But you went to the wedding?'

'Marco invited me. I told you that before.'

He thought of the photograph propped on his mantelpiece. How good she looked in her pink jacket and navy hat. He wished he'd known her then. Maybe things would have been different.

'Why did he commit suicide?' she said.

The question surprised him. He stared back at her, unable to answer.

'Don't look at me like that,' she said quickly. 'You were the one who started the conversation.'

'He had mental problems.'

'I gathered that'

Her flippant tone roused a wave of anger in him. 'He jumped over a hundred feet from a multi-storey car park. Did Marco tell you that?' Her silence fuelled a deeper resentment. The past, like battle lines drawn up against him. 'You never get over it. It's with you all the time.'

'I can understand.'

'Can you?'

'I've been there before. In that same awful place.' She looked at him with cool hostility. 'If you haven't been there personally, you wouldn't understand.'

'So I don't qualify?'

'What do you mean by that?'

'I was the one who caused all the trouble in the first place. Maybe I haven't suffered enough.'

She drew a weary breath. 'Can we change the subject, please.'

'Why? Don't you want to hear all the sordid details?' He felt strangely jubilant, riding a wave of self destruction. Her blank stare willed him on. 'I've never really talked about it before. How I became the baddest man on the planet. Sleeping with my best mate's wife and ruining his life. But then I expect you already know.'

'I don't know what you're talking about.'

'Marco must have told you. That's what all this is about, isn't it?'

She gave a brief, humourless laugh. 'You're unbelievable.'

'Why?'

She smiled bitterly. The same vacuous look Sylvia used to give him. 'You just don't get it, do you? You're so wrapped up in your own problems, you haven't got a clue about anyone else's.'

'We must be well suited then.'

She reached for her bag. 'Take me home, please. Now.'

They drove back in silence. She hugged the passenger side and stared out through the window, the mood a virus, infecting them both. He tried hard to think of ways to retrieve the situation, but nothing he could do would change the outcome. He focused on the car ahead, alone with his thoughts and the hum of traffic. Marco's fat face loomed in his mind's eye, the instigator of the whole thing.

The school appeared over the brow of a hill. Wine-red uniforms fanned out over the pavement and onto the road. He found a space opposite the entrance and left the engine running. Natalie crossed the road to mingle with the mothers and pushchairs along the white lattice fence. Children's joyful voices drifted over, freed from the chains of lessons and rulebooks. Natalie stood alone among them, hunched over, arms folded. He tried to feel sorry for her, but the sense of betrayal persisted, that she had somehow forced a showdown for her own selfish reasons.

Charlotte raised his spirits briefly, leaping into the back of the car with a burst of energy. She sat up between the front seats, eyes bright with excitement.

'Hello, Peter!'

'Hello, Charlotte.'

'I've been to school.'

'Great. Did you learn much?'

'No!' she said with gusto, and they laughed at the heresy together.

'Put your seat belt on, please,' Natalie said.

'Can I go to Laura's house?'

'No, you can't.'

'Why not?'

Natalie whipped round to face her. 'Because I said so! Now put your seat belt on and shut up!'

Charlotte kept up an amusing monologue all the way back. Bouts of feverish humming mixed with quaint observations of people in the street. He tried to detach, but the journey became a requiem. With each passing landmark, the conviction grew that this would be the last time they would all be together.

He pulled in by the tower block. Charlotte leapt out and ran across the grass towards the entrance. Natalie sat resolute beside him, staring through the windscreen. He knew what was coming before she even opened her mouth.

'I can't do this any more,' she said.

He stared ahead. Charlotte danced a stylised ring-a-roses by the entrance.

'Did you hear what I said?'

He couldn't trust himself to speak.

She sighed and put her head back. 'Please don't make this any harder than it already is.'

His bitter laugh sounded distant and unreal in the confines of the car.

'What's so funny?' she said.

'You tell me it's over, and I'm supposed to make it easier for you. Isn't it supposed to be the other way round?' Her silence made it worse. One sickening possibility ran through his mind. 'Is there someone else? Is that what all this is about?'

She shifted uncomfortably.

'Just tell me the truth.'

Charlotte ran onto the grass and danced in wider circles. Her actions absorbed him for a moment. One small and vibrant piece of the scenery he would miss.

'So you just woke up this morning and decided it was over?'

She gazed at her lap, turning a ring on her finger. 'I told you. I can't cope with it anymore. I need to be on my own for a while. I'm just, worn out with it all.'

Charlotte tagged along with an older boy in absurdly baggy shorts. The boy threw a ball and a small terrier raced after it. Natalie's last comment stung him. The truth, ingrained in the silence. He had hoped that by keeping her talking she might change her mind. That hope faded.

'I'm sorry,' she said.

'Whatever.'

'Please don't be like that. You have no idea how difficult this is for me' She gazed ahead, her eyes rimmed with tears. Charlotte threw the ball for the dog. The boy with the baggy shorts looked on, swinging the lead in lazy circles.

'Is there someone else?' he said again.

She stared at him blankly. He felt stupid. Echoes of Claudia, confronting him in the café.

'There isn't anyone else.' She said and looked away. Her tone was flat, with no real conviction. He studied her face, as if for the last time. The curve of her mouth. The tip of her nose. Soon she would be gone and he couldn't stop her.

After a long pause, she opened the car door and put a foot outside. 'I'm sorry.'

'Natalie. You can't just – '

'Please, I've got to go.'

He watched her stroll across the grass towards the flats. She joined Charlotte, mother and daughter reunited. Then the two of them were gone. That part of his life erased as if it had never happened.

An elderly woman trudged by, pulling a shopping cart on wheels. She probably lived alone on the top floor and took the lift up every day with her sad haul of frozen vegetables. Everyone ended up alone. The security you felt was an illusion. Snatched away by the unseen hand when you least expected it.

Natalie was gone.

The sense of shock took hold. Like opening the front door to find your home ransacked and everything in it stolen. He should have seen it coming. The warning signs had been there all along. Instead, he'd been a fool, strolling along with his head in the clouds, blinded by sunshine.

Thirty-four

He sat at the bar, one hand around a clammy bottle of Beck's. The music and buzz of conversation was distracting, cold comfort from the trauma of thinking. The regular punters were oblivious to his dilemma, too engrossed in their own lives. He could have been a piece of furniture, an obstacle to be avoided on the way to the men's room. The petite bargirl shuffled by with a crate of beer, red-faced, blowing her peroxide fringe from her kohl-rimmed eyes. He thought of a clever comment to amuse her, to amuse himself, but the effort to make it was too great. Better to sit and say nothing, recalling the time he'd been a member of the human race.

He called Marco again and got no answer. The bargirl came back and hovered by the till. He noted her slim waist and the small peaks beneath her top without interest. Further along, a woman stood waiting, elegant in a light blue dress suit and copper tan. She looked up, catching his eye with a flicker of unease. He wanted to call out, tell her she'd misread the situation, but was rooted to the spot with a leaden inertia. The woman drifted away. A gang of lads took her place, bursting with frenetic energy and loud, childish laughter.

He checked his phone. One more bad habit he couldn't break. His in box was filled with trivia, pointless messages from people with nothing better to do. Racist jokes from Simon. A reminder from 3 that he had so many minutes remaining. He scrolled down and found an old text from Natalie. '*Still in class. Call you after x.*' The kiss must have been an afterthought, tacked on hastily at the end. He scrolled down again, aching, like finding letters from the deceased. '*I said I'd call you didn't I! x'* The exclamation mark was typical, a sort of jokey reprimand for calling her at work. Both messages were short and to the point. No poignant endearments or lovers innuendo.

Barry wandered in, smug as always, and nodded to the bargirl easing a twenty pound note from a fat leather wallet. The girl pulled Barry's pint of bitter while he leant on the bar and made himself comfortable. 'Fucking hot out there,' Barry said cheerfully. 'I just dropped Sean off. Felt and battened a roof in Southborne for me. Poor fucker nearly keeled over.' Barry supped his pint, watching the bargirl with a wicked glint. 'You need to get down that beach in this weather. All that talent laid out, covered in factor fifteen. Just what the Doctor ordered, eh love?'

The bargirl turned away unimpressed. Barry focused his attention on the bar and matters closer to hand. 'How's your dad? He looked a bit rough when I last saw him.'

He used the old man's health as a smoke screen. The hospital scare was a neutral subject they could both discuss safely. Barry made all the right noises, sympathising with the rest of the family for the worry it had caused. Henley Park crept up by stealth, unavoidable. He listened to Barry's hesitant confession in a kind of trance, lacking the strength to question it. 'I said I'd do it as a favour really, Peter. You know what he's like.'

'Sure.'

'That OK with you?'

'Fine, Barry.'

'I don't want you to think I muscled in on it, that's all.'

He pictured Sean, toiling away in the heat. Sean must have changed his mind about leaving. People stayed in dire jobs and failed marriages for the same reasons. Familiarity. Lack of imagination. He understood the attraction. His brief glimpse of a future with Natalie had similar overtones. War zones. Misunderstanding. The need to hang on when the ship was clearly sinking.

Barry waited patiently, his takeover bid needing a final endorsement. He summoned all his powers of diplomacy and forced a smile. 'Someone had to bail him out. Looks like you were the right man for the job.'

'Thanks, Peter. Means a lot to me to hear you say that.' Barry took a drink. 'Oh – sorry to hear about you and Claudia.'

They observed an awkward moment's silence while the cash register opened and slammed shut. He felt sick inside. His future prospects buried in one move. Barry talked about Martin, the more reasonable half of the Jarvis duo. Martin had bought a cottage in Exmoor and planned to move his family out in the next few weeks. The decision perplexed Barry in ways he couldn't explain. 'Why Exmoor, Peter? I mean, of all the places he could have gone. Stuck out in the middle of nowhere with a gale blowing and the phone lines down. He's not thinking straight.'

Martin's exodus into the wilds of Exmoor sounded inviting. Pack up and leave your troubles in storage. Find a place far from the likes of Barry and start again. The need to escape infected everyone.

Raul joined them. Barry took this as his cue to leave, draining his statutory pint and grabbing his car keys from the bar. Raul watched him go, frowning. 'What's his problem, man? Did I bring something in on my shoe?'

Barry's departure eased the tension. Raul turned his charms to the bargirl who served his bottled lager swiftly and drifted away. Raul took a drink and turned, frowning. 'You're quiet tonight, man. What's up – woman trouble?'

He forced a laugh. 'You could say that.'

'You wanna talk about it?'

'Some other time.'

He sat alone with the problem. It had to be this way. Sharing your misery only deepened the size of the hole. Raul would see this latest development with Natalie as a sign of weakness. Then would come the standard, male-oriented advice, full of clichés and wounded pride.

Tim's arrival caused him more anxiety. Now he had to look nonchalant, steel himself to any mention of Natalie. References to Claudia were easier to fend off. His reputation was less vulnerable in this respect. The wound Natalie had opened was still raw.

The bar filled with people, intent on their own enjoyment. He watched from his solitary bar stool – the observer, acutely aware of his own inadequacies. Laughter burst in corner pockets, a personal insult taken immediately to heart. He saw traits in everyone that he didn't like. Even Raul's voice became an irritant, calling out to people he hardly knew.

Tim caught him in a private moment. 'Heard anything from Claudia?'

'Not really.'

'So, that's it then?'

'Looks that way.'

Tim nodded solemnly. 'At least there were no kids involved. No mortgage to fight over. You got off lightly compared to some people.'

When the time was right, he would spill all the details. Tim would understand. The need to retreat and go into hiding. Protect yourself from senseless remarks that made it harder to deal with. He hadn't thought much about Claudia. Being with Natalie had lessened the impact. Now he faced the extent of both losses, a double blow he'd been unprepared for.

'Look out,' Tim said with a nod along the bar. 'Lord Brocket just turned up.'

Marco made his entrance, standing aloof at the bar. The bargirl leant over, straining to hear him above the noise. Marco barked his order at her upturned face and glanced over his audience. 'What's the matter? Did I miss something? Someone's round, maybe?'

Tim picked up the gauntlet. 'We were just standing round waiting for you, Marco. I knew there was something missing when I walked in, but I couldn't put my finger on it. Must've been your charisma.'

Marco gave no sign that he knew about Natalie. Their recent lunchtime rendezvous was the key, a hidden component in all that followed. Whatever Marco had said during the course of that lunch had poisoned her mind against him. Marco even had the arrogance to swan in and act as if nothing had happened. He had to sit back and bide his time, catch Marco with his guard down.

The chance came later, when Marco stepped up to order a drink. The full force of his loss hit him at once. The growing conviction that Marco was the prime cause.

Marco watched the harassed bargirls, oblivious. 'Piss poor service in this place. They should employ more staff. Ones that can speak English, preferably.' Marco was served and took a leisurely sup of his pint before settling at the bar. He looked relaxed and in good humour. 'Thought tonight would be a bit of a send off. I just got my marching orders. Looks like I'm being officially kicked out Thursday.'

The prospect changed his outlook. No more impromptu parties on a Friday night. The old Ballroom reduced to a pile of rubble. He fought against a strong feeling of regret. The house and Marco's brash persona would both be missed.

Sympathy for Marco could wait. He took a long drink and focused on the real issue. 'I hear you had lunch with Natalie the other day?'

'I did indeed. Why?'

'I wondered what you said to her.'

Marco's genial smile faded. 'What's this – a starter for ten?'

'I just want to know. For my own benefit.'

Marco took an evasive stance, inspecting his pint glass with a fixed smile. 'What always amazes me, is this need people have to dissect everything. As if that makes it easier to deal with. Why not leave it alone where it belongs?'

'Where *what* belongs?'

Marco glanced wearily around the bar, gauging his position. 'Look – I'm going to be honest with you now, OK? I spoke to Natalie last night. She told me what happened between you, so we don't have to go through this charade any more.' Marco let the disclosure sink in. 'Just accept it. It's not personal. It's just Natalie. You're better off without her, the way she is at the moment.'

'What d'you mean by that?'

Marco sighed heavily. 'Look, all I'm saying is, the writing was on the wall from the word go. It was never going to last. I told you that before but you wouldn't listen.'

The sickness took hold again. Natalie's rejection confirmed in such a clinical manner, from someone he classed as a friend. Only bitterness remained to fill the deep hole. 'Oh well. I suppose she could always go back to Brad.'

Marco stared at him in puzzlement. 'Go back to him? She never stopped seeing him in the first place.'

He tried to grasp the significance. Brad's smiling face. The candlelit table at Pascali's. It all fell into place. Her need to be alone. Her mantra – repeated so often – that she didn't want to get too involved. The truth struck him as a blinding light.

Marco looked genuinely contrite. 'I thought you knew. I thought she'd told you.'

He went outside, the cool night air a relief from the humid bar. He walked without direction, turning over the endless possibilities in his mind. All the things he would say to her. Her response to his accusations. Her pointless denial. He took out his phone and found her number. An odd fear surfaced. The call might expose him to more ridicule. Brad might even be with her, forcing a confrontation. The sense of betrayal spurred him on, the need to hear the truth from her mouth whatever the consequences.

The tones rang. He held his breath, waiting. The line went dead. He stared at the handset in disbelief, that she had the nerve to cut him off deliberately. The chance for recompense gone, snatched away at the last minute. He felt abandoned, utterly alone.

Tim came out and stood scowling in the pub doorway. 'What're you playing at? We've just booked a taxi and you're wandering about out here.'

He would have laughed any other time. Tim's rigid stance in the doorway as if *he* was the spurned lover.

The night was over, ruined by a treacherous woman. The only option left was to walk away.

Tim called after him. 'What the fuck's the matter with you?'

He crossed the road and kept walking, speechless with a cold and heartless rage.

Thirty-five

He parked in the road opposite the house. The spot gave him a clear view of the forecourt and the path that led up the side. From here he could watch the front entrance and the side door, noting any visitors or anyone leaving. The white brick building didn't look like a business premises. Apart from an indistinct sign above the window, it could have been bedsits, like the many old Victorian houses in the area. He knew he was in the right place. He'd dropped her off once before when she'd been stressed, blaming him for making her late. Monday afternoons, two to four-thirty. She took a life class for adults in a room on the first floor. Charlotte stayed with a friend. The fact that her car wasn't on the forecourt didn't bother him. She could have gone out. She could have come in with someone else and left her car at home.

He flicked through a newspaper, with one eye on the house. No-one would pay any attention to the beaten up pick-up, parked at the roadside. The Audi might have given him away, lost him the element of surprise. Here he could blend in with the scenery, biding his time.

By four-fifteen, no-one had arrived or come out. Cars passed at regular intervals. Foreign students strolled by with their backpacks and garbled chatter. He questioned his motives, the need to be sat out there at all, staking out the territory like a hired assassin. If she'd answered his phone calls, he wouldn't have needed to bother. They could have discussed the issue in a civilised manner. How she'd ruined his life and left him with nothing.

At four-twenty five a dark blue Honda pulled into the forecourt and parked in a bay by the front wall. The driver turned off the ignition but didn't get out. The relative quiet of the neighbourhood settled in.

His phone rang. The Estate Agent, asking for details of the house at Priory Road. He switched into business mode, detached, his interest lying solely in the building across the street. Talking to someone gave him a connection to the real world, however tenuous. He rang off and sat in the silence. Layers of worn-in dust clung to the interior, partially obscuring the dashboard panel. The sight reminded him of his priorities. He should have been looking at a landscaping job the architect had put his way. Instead he'd given in to the nagging voice insisting he confront her, see the thing through to the bitter end.

The front door opened across the road. Natalie came out and stood in the porch, talking to a woman inside. She had her hair tied up in a knot at the back and a canvas bag slung over her shoulder. He watched from his vantage point, his heart pounding. She hadn't seen him. They stopped talking and said an audible goodbye. The woman inside closed the door. Natalie turned and made her way across the forecourt. The nervousness left him, replaced with a clinical sense of purpose.

He was out of the pick-up and halfway across the road before she saw him. She stopped, clutching her bag at her side, watching his approach with a look of shocked disbelief. The element of surprise gave him the advantage, a sense of impending victory. He crossed the threshold and walked right up to her.

She took a step back in alarm. 'What the hell are you doing here?'

'Why have you been ignoring my phone calls?'

'What?'

'Every time I call you cut me off.'

'I don't want to talk to you! I've got absolutely nothing to say to you.'

Her belligerence made him falter. All the things he'd planned to say to her, lost in the moment. She looked at him with contempt but he also saw fear there, a scared animal trapped in the headlights.

'I don't like unfinished business,' he said.

'What're you talking about?'

'You know exactly what I'm talking about.'

A car door opened behind him and a familiar voice called, 'Natalie?'

He turned, and there beside the dark blue Honda, his tanned, surfer's face lined with concern, was Brad. 'What's the problem?' Brad said.

'Stay out of it. I'm talking to Natalie.'

Brad shut the car door and took a step towards them.

'I said stay out of it. I'm not saying it again.'

'What's the matter with you!' Natalie yelled at him, frozen with shock.

'Natalie,' Brad said with some authority. 'Ignore him and come over here.'

He pointed a warning finger in Brad's direction. 'Shut up and get back in your car.'

'Look, I don't know what – '

'Get back in your car *now* or I'll punch your fucking lights out!'

Natalie pushed past him and stood between them. 'How dare you! How dare you come here and threaten me like this. If you don't leave *right* now, I'm calling the police.'

He ignored her and gave a scornful nod at Brad. 'What about him? Does he know all the details? All the games you were playing with me while he was away?'

She stared at him transfixed, her eyes glazed with tears. 'Why are you doing this to me? Leave me alone!'

Her anguish brought him to his senses. He watched the scene unfold as an observer. Natalie's tear stained face. Brad standing at his car, no longer so confident. The neat tarmac forecourt, an open stage for their tense performance. Without a word, he turned and walked off, leaving the two of them to deal with the aftermath.

He sat in the dusty pick-up and turned on the ignition. His hands shook. His breath came in short bursts as if he'd been running hard. He noted them both, clinging together like earthquake survivors, watching his next move from the safety of the forecourt.

He felt nothing. The game was over. Now he had to face life without her.

Thirty-six

Priory Road stood like a monument to progress – a major work completed without him. The scaffolding had gone. The new windows shone a pure and virginal white. Even the tramline scars on the road had faded where the skip had been. Prospective buyers would see the finish – as advertised in the window at Hughes and Sons – a spacious, two bed property with fitted kitchen and full gas central heating. Ideally suited to a working couple or a small family with a shared income. Sasha would give them the usual spiel and a guided tour of the layout, pausing for the woman to check out the bathroom and the man to ponder the roof space.

He opened up and went inside. The smell of fresh paint and newly-fitted carpets clung to the interior. Mail had piled up on the mat; Indian take-away menus, a garden centre brochure, and various letters addressed to the previous tenant. He took the letters into the kitchen and leant against the worktop. The new double glazing made an airtight seal, only the remote hum of traffic to intrude. Even Sean's lingering influence had been removed. No more empty crisp bags to complain about. All the obscene artwork, pencilled on stud walls and door linings, plastered over. He could admire the finish with a critical eye, knowing that his input had been minimal. Pride in the job was a term applied to someone else. Hard-working tradesmen like Pat Clements. Forty years as a sub-contractor, hiring out his services to the highest bidder. But men like Pat were expendable. The only thing that mattered in the end was the profit margin.

He went upstairs and stood at the back window. The garden had also undergone a complete makeover. The brambles and the long grass had been replaced with a neat section of turf, bordered on one side by a shingle path. The dilapidated shed in the corner had been replaced, the new felt roof showered with cherry blossom. Barry certainly had an eye for detail. The heavy old roller sat beneath the tree at the bottom of the garden, its handle rusted into an upright position. A generous parting gift from the contractor to the new owners.

The old woman's garden had survived the upheaval. With the landscaping finished, the two adjacent plots now looked more in harmony. She could welcome her new neighbours with a sense of relief, and bore them with stories about the awful mess the builders had left behind. He gazed down at her private sanctuary without interest. The fusion of bright colours made no impression. Completion meant nothing beyond the cheque he would bank. Even the tabby cat perched on a wall shared his mood, staring out over the scenery with bored contempt.

He took out his phone. No new messages and no missed calls. The urge to call her came over him again. To hear the soothing tones of her answer machine as a minor consolation. *Hi, this is Natalie. I'm afraid I'm unable to take your call at the moment, but if you'd like to leave your name and number I'll get back to you ...* He saw her everywhere. Silhouette in a passing car. Woman getting off a bus in the pouring rain. The enigmatic face on a billboard, advertising lipstick with an airbrushed smile. The shock of losing her had turned into a hollow grief that haunted his waking moments. He had no appetite for food. No interest in work. All his relations were soured by the single, unbearable fact. She was gone and nothing he could do would bring her back.

He left the house and walked towards his car. A shrill voice called out behind him. He turned, caught out, and felt an immediate and overwhelming dismay. She was standing by her front gates in a shapeless cardigan and wine red carpet slippers – small and hawk-like, waiting for him. He took a few tentative steps towards her and forced a smile. 'Morning, Mrs Burton. How can I-' She ignored the pleasantries and ran through a list of complaints. The lorry that blocked her drive. Her damaged plants. The layer of dust in her conservatory. Soon it would be husband Frank, the central theme to her sad existence. The dust and the scaffold lorry would be forgotten, symptoms of a far deeper malaise.

He tried to be reasonable. 'I'm sorry you're not happy, Mrs Burton. You'll be glad to know that we've finished.'

Small, birdlike eyes registered suspicion, disbelief. 'Finished?'

'That's right. We're taking the roadshow somewhere else.'

The joke fell flat. He tried to empathise instead. Forty or fifty years putting up with the same person. The same disapproving looks at the breakfast table every morning. Most couples parted in less than half the time. But the search for the perfect partner had a universal appeal. Even the hardened cynics were out there, trawling the singles bars and the dating agencies, looking for happiness at the end of the rainbow. The old woman came from a lost generation. Marriage vows were sacrosanct. You fell in love with someone and expected to be with them for life. He came from a generation of malcontents, who never got further than the first hurdle.

He glanced at his watch. The old woman stood next to him. In the background, the For Sale sign to remind them of endings. 'Well, goodbye, Mrs Burton.'

'What about the gravel in my driveway?'

'I'll send the boy over later to sweep it up.'

'I'm really not happy, you know.'

'Sorry I can't help you with that one. Goodbye, Mrs Burton.'

He sat in the car and thought about Natalie. The process had a strange way of unfolding. He found it hard to recall her face, as though they had been separated years instead of days. And yet he could recall her body with the clarity of a photograph. The mole on her shoulder. The pale red birthmark at the nape of her neck. The slickness of her pale skin as she stepped out of the bath. Now she'd found someone else. Surfer boy Brad, with his crumpled chinos and easy smile. She must have planned the whole thing. Played one off against the other, until it all got too much.

He called in at Sarah's.

She felt morally obligated to rescue him from the swamp he'd fallen into. All he needed was an arm around the shoulder and a warm hug. Coffee and a friendly chat around the kitchen table. She tried to get him to talk about it but he clammed up, only able to give the basic details. She sat back defeated. 'I wish there was something I could say, Peter. I've never seen you so down before.'

'I'll get over it.'

'When was the last time you spoke to her?'

'Monday afternoon.'

'And that was it?'

'There wasn't much else to say after the performance I put in.'

Sarah pursed her lips and frowned, unsure how to react. Platitudes were the safest bet. The problem might go away of its own accord. 'Oh well – maybe it's for the best.'

He looked up, irritated. 'Best for who – her or me?'

'I meant, better that it happened sooner rather than later. At least you know where you stand. And if she's been seeing someone else, you're better off without her anyway.'

He shrugged, aware of the irony. Claudia must have heard similar sentiments from her friends.

'Maybe I was too much for her.'

'In what way?'

'Phoning her all the time. Putting pressure on her to see me.'

Sarah thought this over. 'Well, you said her job was stressful. And she had her daughter to look after. Maybe she just couldn't cope.'

He wanted to rationalise the situation. Find excuses and reasons why. But it all came down to one unavoidable conclusion. Natalie had ended their affair. The look on her face when he'd confronted her had said it all. He only had himself to blame. His obsession for her had stifled any feelings she might have had for him and turned her away.

'Like a butterfly,' he said absently.

'Sorry?'

'Hold it in your fist and you crush its wings. Let it go and it might come back to you. Some parable I heard from an old woman.'

Sarah smiled sadly. 'You will get over it, Peter.'

He wanted to believe her. The whole episode seemed pointless in retrospect, a waste of time and energy. The butterfly analogy made perfect sense. 'That's what I was doing all along. Chasing something that wasn't there.' The thought gained impetus. 'Maybe it's karma. Payback for all the stunts I pulled when I was younger.'

Sarah looked at him evenly. She knew the event he was referring to without either of them having to mention it. 'Please don't put yourself through all that again.'

'It's true. It's like a curse. I can't get rid of it.'

'That's just the way you see it now. It's not the reality.' She laid both hands flat on the table. 'Look – I know it's hard for you at the moment. But you will get over it. Trust me.' she smiled warmly and touched his arm. 'Fancy a piece of apple cake? …'

He spent the night alone in his flat. Television provided a temporary escape until a weathergirl with Natalie's slick black hair and lean, angular features came on. He switched off the set and stared at the walls instead. At least in private, you didn't have to put on an act. The benefits of isolation meant that you could sit for hours in the same morass without offending anyone. The advice columnists who suggested socialising and keeping busy hadn't done enough research. Wounded animals found a hiding place and stayed put until their wounds had healed. He had a far more effective solution and poured himself a large scotch from the single malt that Brendan had bought him the previous Christmas.

The phone rang as he lay on the bed. The longer the tones went on, the less inclined he felt to answer. Human contact in any form meant an intrusion. The single malt acted as a mild anaesthetic, dulling mind and body in equal measure.

He snatched up the phone. 'Yeah?'

'It's me.'

'I know it's you.'

'Can you talk?'
'I'm tired, Zoe. What do you want?'
'I just called to tell you I'm moving.'
'You told me that already.'
'Tomorrow.'
He laughed at this latest twist.
'I just thought I'd tell you. So you don't hear it from someone else.'
'Thanks, Zoe. That's really thoughtful of you.'
'What're you doing?'
'Lying here staring at the walls at the moment.'
'Why?'
'Forget it, Zoe. You wouldn't understand.' He searched for something else to say. Nothing came up but vacant lots. For Sale signs. Everyone moving on. 'Goodbye, Zoe. Hope it all works out for you.'

He lay back and reviewed his condition. Like falling down a ravine and inspecting yourself for broken bones. Zoe had brought him round from his self-induced coma but he felt nothing beyond a vague frustration. Her news had failed to move him. He almost felt pleased for her. Perhaps she'd found her soul mate in Ray, even if he did spend half his life in prison. Who was he to say they couldn't make it work, that she wouldn't find happiness changing nappies and serving Ray lukewarm dinners when he finally came home from the pub.

He had one voice call message from Leanne. *Hi – er, I was wondering. I know it's short notice, but erm, could you take me over to Gemma's tomorrow afternoon? Also I need to run something by you but, er, I suppose we can talk about it tomorrow. Can you get back to me and let me know. Thanks. Oh and, hope you're well. Bye.'* He tried to tap in to the unconditional love that was usually there beneath the surface, but all he found was inertia.

Tomorrow he would reschedule his afternoon and do his paternal duty. Love translating into action. One more form of penance along the way. Until then he would crawl into bed and try to sleep. Dreams inspired by the concept of loss and Brendan's single malt whisky.

Thirty-seven

He drove Leanne to her friend's, late in the afternoon. She talked about college and her current graphics project in an upbeat tone, unaware of his mood. The beauty of living in the moment. Yesterday's dramas forgotten and tomorrow's yet to be invented. When Leanne was happy the sun shone and nothing could cloud the horizon. Not even memories of their three hour trip to Bristol, arguing over road signs and her volatile grandmother.

She stopped, halfway through a scathing attack on a boy in her Art class, and turned to him quizzically. 'Is everything OK?'

'Fine.'

'You just seem – quiet.'

'I'm tired, that's all.'

'Maybe you need one of those early nights you keep telling me about.'

'Thanks, Leanne. I'll bear that in mind.'

The details of his failed romance stayed hidden. He could have taken a chance and shared his turmoil, but Leanne had already moved on. The victim this time was a college sports instructor who – in her words – thought he was God's gift to women. The monster had been spotted in the local pub, canoodling with a female head of year, and word had spread like a virus.

'Perhaps he is,' he said absently.

'Is what?'

'God's gift to women.'

'Er – I don't think so. He's a dick, full stop.' She lost interest in the conversation and pulled down the visor to inspect her face. Every time he saw her she had grown in some way. Not so much in the physical sense, but in subtle, indefinable ways. As an independent young woman, she expected to be treated with respect. She went to parties, drank too much and came home late, ignoring her curfew and worrying them all sick in the process. He tried not to make an issue out of her social habits, but it was hard. Sylvia liked to remind him of the most important factor – Leanne lived with her. He only had to put up with her bad habits on a part time basis.

Most of his memories involved loss of some form. Even pushing her on a swing in the park was tinged with sorrow, reminding him of the emptiness he felt whenever he dropped her home. The absent father. Granted occasional access to see his own daughter by some faceless court official. Even the most intolerable situations become bearable in time. He learned to adapt. She was his daughter and he loved her more than his own life. No court in the land could take that away from him.

One day he'd caught her smoking at a bus stop. She didn't try to deny it and he didn't push the point. She was sixteen and could do as she pleased. But the incident reminded him how much she had changed, and how much of her growth he had missed out on. The child who used to throw her arms around his neck and cling on to him, tearful at the thought of being parted, had grown up. Somewhere along the line he'd missed the transition. All the years he'd spent chasing money and women, and perfecting his swing on the golf course, had made him forget the things that really mattered. Then, when he finally realised how short-sighted he'd become, it was too late. The hardest lesson of all. You couldn't go back and change a single thing. The past was a scrapbook, the pages opened at random to remind you of all the things you'd said and done, the choices you'd made, and the areas you'd so wilfully neglected.

'Guess who I bumped into the other day?' she said.

'No idea.'

'Claudia.'

The page turned again. He tried to ignore the news, but Leanne insisted he remember, saying how good Claudia looked, and how well she was coping with the break-up. He wondered if it was possible to mourn two women at the same time. The regular, home loving partner and the tempestuous lover he'd left her for. He missed them both in different ways, but the loss of Claudia hadn't fully registered. The pain of one seemed to cancel out the pain of the other.

'Would you get back with her?'

'What?'

'Claudia. Would you get back with her if you had the chance?'

'Leanne, I don't want to talk about it right now, OK?'

He slowed at a pelican crossing. A group of morose-looking pedestrians shuffled across in single file. Leanne's observations on his private life sealed any further means of escape. He was stuck with the thinking, the endless permutations that amounted to the same thing.

Leanne clearly enjoyed the intrigue and wouldn't give up. 'I don't know why you split up in the first place. No-one said anything to me about it. Was it meant to be some sort of secret?'

'Leanne.'

She flashed him an impish grin. 'Got anyone else yet?'

'D'you want to walk to Gemma's?'

He stopped outside a café. She checked her face in the mirror, sighing deeply at some terrible flaw that only she could see. She pushed back the visor in disgust and began rooting through her bag.

'Have you got everything?' he said.

'Yes.'

'You sure?'

'I'm only staying at Gemma's.'

She sat back, clutching her bag on her lap, and stared through the windscreen. He remembered her answer phone message. The vague hint that she was planning some new deception. 'You said there was something you wanted to ask me.'

She wriggled herself into an upright position and fiddled with her bag. 'I don't want you to say no without even thinking about it.'

'What is it?'

'I know I've already had things this year, and I went camping and everything,

'but – '

'Leanne.'

She fixed her gaze firmly ahead. 'I want to go to Paris.'

The request seemed reasonable enough on the surface. She'd been to Barcelona with her college class. Numerous day trips to London, Brighton. But always under supervision, always under the watchful eye of a responsible adult.

'Who with?'

'Gemma and Hayley.'

'Just the three of you?'

'No!' she said, her laughter a burst of relief. 'Gemma's mum and her new boyfriend.'

The amended picture was less acceptable. The new boyfriend upset the balance, created an element of doubt about the security arrangements. Gemma's dad wasn't even in the picture. This was the reality. An epidemic of single parents, forced to raise kids on their own, drafting in extra help in emergencies.

She sensed his resistance and turned to face him. 'I've already asked Mum. She said it was fine. As long as I didn't use the money from my savings account.'

'And that's where I come in.'

'Well, yeah – sort of. But I'm not like, asking you for all of it.'

'Just some of it.'

She laughed nervously, her face flushed with embarrassment.

'How long are you planning on going for?'

'Three days.'

He pictured her at the mercy of some smooth talking French lover boy, running his oily fingers through her long blonde hair, telling her she had the most beautiful eyes he'd ever seen. In a city like Paris, she would be beyond his control. She could do exactly as she liked without so much as a phone call home and he would be hundreds of miles away, unable to intervene if anything happened.

He thought it over, with her seated beside him anxiously awaiting the verdict. The answer came naturally, without prompting, and without the need for any arduous soul searching.

'Why not?'

She turned slowly, wide-eyed and open mouthed. 'You mean I can go?' She stared at him in wonder, biting down on a huge smile in case he changed his mind. 'Oh thanks! This means so much to me.'

She leaned over and gave him a hesitant kiss on the cheek, one hand on the door, poised for a sudden getaway.

'I'll call you,' she said, beaming at him from the pavement. She crossed the road, clutching her shoulder bag, and gave a cursory wave from the other side. After pausing briefly at a shop window to check her reflection, she joined the throng of shoppers and was soon out of sight. His precious butterfly, released from captivity.

He wandered out onto the High Street among the afternoon shoppers. A basket of second hand books sat outside a charity shop. He sifted through them with scant interest, vaguely hoping to find a book on separation. All he found were glossy paperbacks and a worn copy of *The Brotherhood*, which he thought of buying for the old man as a joke.

He crossed the street. A hair stylist with an immaculate bob of white hair caught his eye through a salon window. He recognised the look right away. Suspicion based on previous experience. The legacy of unreliable boyfriends to cloud all future relations. He got the same look from a gum-chewing girl, pushing a toddler in a buggy and quickly moved out of her way. Young mothers, condemned to an endless round of school runs and children's parties, picking dirty clothes up off the bathroom floor and wishing they could find a reliable babysitter.

He was struck by a profound thought. In the last few hours, he hadn't once thought of checking his phone. Progress – on a small scale. Something had shifted inside him. In some perverse way, he'd been set free.

He took out his phone and went into contacts. Her name came up at the touch of a button. He went into options and scrolled down. The selection presented him with a question. *Delete all details?* He thought about how much she'd meant to him. His desire for her that had eclipsed everything.

He pressed Yes.

Natalie vanished from his contacts.

He stopped at a travel agent's window. Colour brochures and scenic blow-ups advertised tempting holidays at bargain prices. Turkey. Greece. Amsterdam. Even Paris for three days, including flight and hotel.

He walked on down the High Street. British summertime. James had a birthday in July, but he couldn't recall the date. Somehow it didn't matter anymore. The memory had lost its hold. The pain of losing something precious had left a hollow. But out of that place had come a strange awakening. The light shining in the darkest corner.

Clarity. Understanding. Acceptance.

About the Author

Adam Dickson has been writing on and off since he left school and was a student of the late Bill Stanton's Writer's Tutorial. He has three more novels completed in first draft form and many short stories. In addition, he has co-authored *Triathlon – Serious About Your Sport* for New Holland Publishers which was published in May 2012, with two more titles on Swimming and Cycling for Beginners which will be published in February 2013.

His second novel *Drowning By Numbers* will be available in Summer 2013. He is currently working on his third novel.

Lightning Source UK Ltd.
Milton Keynes UK
UKOW040946150313

207691UK00001B/1/P